A Dream of Mansions

 DREAM
OF MANSIONS

by Norris Lloyd

 Random House, New York

c.1

To Bill

So much of adolescence is an ill-defined dying,
An intolerable waiting,
A longing for another place and time,
Another condition.

THEODORE ROETHKE

A Dream of Mansions

How Hallie Jones came from a dreamy girlhood to maturity in a small town in Georgia where she discovered that the South didn't represent old mansions and romantic cavaliers but was often a grim place.

1

Greenwood would have green vistas, white columns behind curving driveways, spires and monuments, stores with plate-glass windows, fountains and waterfalls, light and air and grace and order. She could move through the town as if she had lived in it in another childhood, dreamily, its landmarks expected, yet come upon with a sweet shock of surprise as she rounded a corner. Greenwood existed, had taken shape on a map in her mind; a map drawn up to her own specifications. And now, in early June, 1920, she, Hallie Jones, was approaching the real Greenwood from the north, riding on the Macon, Dublin and Savannah Railway. As the train backed out of Macon across the Ocmulgee River, she drew in a river on her map. Water was an embellishment to any scene; if she could not have the ocean a river would have to do.

Benny and Virginia, sitting behind her, made snorting noises about the railroad. "M. D. and S.," said Benny, "must stand for Mighty Damn Slow," his voice sinking on *damn* so Mama would not hear. Virginia laughed until she choked when he added a few minutes later, "No, must be Murder, Death and Starvation." Hallie listened, heard them from far away because she was watching the passing towns for signs, for clues, to Greenwood. Smithville was an old army cantonment, abandoned now; its broken-down barracks gave back a blank stare. Ripple Creek, Wheaton and Verdery had nothing, not even depots; only a cindered path at each one with a sign bearing the name of the stop; a store or two across the highway, forlorn wooden structures plastered with advertisements of Cardui the Woman's Tonic and Smoke Prince Albert. She began to worry about Greenwood, feared Greenwood would be like them, felt she must hold on tighter to the map in her mind. Greenwood was the county seat; it would have a courthouse at least, and a real depot. It had to have a real depot because Papa had gone there to work in it.

Mama had been talking to Mr. Daughtry, the conductor, as if the coach were her own sitting room and Mr. Daughtry her honored guest. Mr. Daughtry's nostrils had the black shading of a chimney from the engine smoke. Mama had introduced herself and Hallie, motioned to Benny and Virginia in the seat behind her the first time Mr. Daughtry came through, said in a loud carrying voice that she was Mrs. Jones, wife of Mr. Jonathan Jones, the new agent down at Greenwood. She had presented her pass and said, jokingly but proudly, as if she and Mr. Daughtry belonged to some secret society, some honorable fraternity of railroad people, "Got four new deadheads." Now everyone on the train would know they rode free. Mr. Daughtry brought back the flagman on one of his trips through and introduced him to Mama, and Benny said in a high, put-on voice, "Where're the fireman and engineer? Aren't they coming to tea too?" But Mama was having too good a time to hear. She was inquiring about the conductor's and flagman's families, whether they lived at Macon or Vidalia. (Though the line was called Macon, Dublin and Savannah, it stopped short at Vidalia.) Mama told them all about her family, two daughters back in South Carolina, one son in the cemetery there, these three here; she ran on about Clover back in South Carolina whence they came.

After Verdery Mr. Daughtry said, "Greenwood. Your stop's next," and, suddenly sensitive for such a common-looking man, he said to Hallie, "Town's on the other side." Hallie moved past him to a seat across the aisle. She had to concentrate on her map of Greenwood, had to will it into being; it must have a white Southern mansion which she would name Montpelier, Montpelier, Montpelier; she said it over and over in time with the wheels, letting the word chime through her mind. Mr. Daughtry stood up, jammed his hard blue cap down to the sweaty red line on his forehead, said in a loud, station-calling voice, "Greenwood, all off for Greenwood." The train whistled for a crossing, a few Negro houses came up, a cotton gin, another crossing and there was the Courthouse, a red brick building with a gaunt tower above trees too small for it, shaped like all courthouses with a tower and a clock stopped at 8:10, a courthouse of the reddest brick she had ever seen, red as the red clay from the gullies on the way down from Macon.

Mama said, "Hallie, got everything?" and Hallie drew away from the window, afraid to glance out the other side, afraid to look further, picked up her suitcase, and with her heart sinking slowly and heavily to rock-bottom went to the door.

Mr. Daughtry said, "Here you are, young lady," and swung her gallantly onto the stool and then to the cindered walk. She raised her head and looked now. There was a row of stores across the street; a row, but hardly better than the slatternly stores at the other stops, still a row, with tin awnings deep as sunbonnets over the sidewalk. Oh, Lord, she said, oh, Lord, she should have known, and there was Papa coming toward them, rubbing his mouth in preparation for kissing, seeming distracted as if his mind were on God or the train. He kissed them hastily, looked up the cindered walk which passed for a platform to watch a

5

colored man swinging some crates off the baggage car, said, "Hold on here a minute until the train passes and I'll be with you," and hurried back into the station.

"I like a little town," said Mama as they surveyed the street. "You can get to know everybody." This remark of Mama's positively made Hallie want to cry. Was Mama merely trying to look on the bright side, or was it, as Hallie felt more and more lately, a sign of her insensitivity to finer things? More and more Mama simply did not come up to her idea of what a cultured woman of the South should be. She had gone to the Seminary for Young Ladies over in Seneca, in South Carolina, a good enough start, but all that remained from that period was the dining-room picture, an oil painting of a dead fish with staring eyes on a plate in front of Issaqueena Falls, and on the topmost rock of the Falls an Indian maiden stood, with hands pointed in front of her, ready to leap (from unrequited love). When Mama was pressed to tell more of the curriculum of the seminary, she said, her blue eyes vague behind her glasses, music. But all that she could play now with her clumsy, big-knuckled fingers was a song called "The Music Lesson," dramatically rendered upon request, in which the girl "sang so loud that her voice broke down and she drove the neighbors out of town," and ended with Mama sending her voice up to a high squeak, then collapsing on the stool. Hallie could recall the days when she was delighted with this song, called for it repeatedly herself, and collapsed with laughter as Mama collapsed. But now, oh, Lord, older, twelve and a half, wiser, she saw it in its true light, a vulgar exhibition.

The train whistled and pulled out, Mr. Daughtry waved and called good-by to Mama, and, ever hopeful, Hallie turned to look in the other direction. An asphalt highway paralleled the tracks, and behind a fence a field of purple-green vetch stood a foot high. Guinea hens, unsettled by the departure of the train, settled back on the fence with a few last maniac cries. Beyond the field behind the trees stood a row of houses. In the Greenwood of her dreams, white Southern mansions might sit there across this field behind these splendid trees, but, as she feared, these houses were brown and ugly, completely lacking in style and taste, only one of any size looming up behind the trees with fretwork and scrolls, gimcracky trimmings of rust color on faded sand. A large *F*, fancy as the initial on an embroidered pillowcase, adorned the side of the house below an attic window. Near the highway, in a weedy setting next a filling station stood a monument. She sighed; at least a monument, though on her map of Greenwood it stood amid trees and grass on the courthouse square. Nevertheless, a monument. A soldier of white marble, gun at rest before him, mounted on a tall shaft, glittered in the afternoon sun. A monument to Southern heroes, one symbol to rescue Greenwood from utter drabness and nothingness.

Papa came back to them now and the Negro man followed him carrying a limp mail bag slung across his shoulder. "This is Adam," said Papa, "Adam Lincoln. He helps me around the station."

Adam smiled and made a bow. He was very tall and black and the bow he made was jerky because of his height. "Mighty glad to see you all down here," he said.

"Adam's just going to step across the street there with the mail, and soon's he gets back to watch the depot I can walk you up to the house." Then Papa said to Mama as they waited, "A fine Christian man. A hard worker. I don't know how I'd get along without him."

An old man stopped Adam in the middle of the street, looked toward them, then came on across with a kind of crawfish gait. Obviously he had asked Adam who they were, then came on and leaned up against a baggage cart and stared at them roguishly. Hallie thought, he's like the town, run-down, worn-out, uninteresting and—turning away from his roguish, curious eyes—repulsive. Benny murmured to Virginia, "You think he's the village idiot sent out to give us a welcome?"

"Hallie," Mama said, "have you fallen asleep? Adam's back now and your father can come with us."

7

After the look at the town Hallie guessed what their house would be like, knew it and yet hoped all the way up the sandy sidewalk, past the Methodist Church and around the corner past the Baptist Church, knew it in her bones and hoped she would be wrong. But she was not. The house was a hit-or-miss old barn of a place with a wide porch trimmed with fancy banisters and gingerbread work across the front. Rooms had grown to the back in a haphazard, unplanned fashion. A long dark hall ran through the center of the front of the house and ended in another hall that was half porch and half room. It must have been porch before the wing of bedrooms was added. Now it was cool and dark, and Mama said, as if she would have built it that way herself, "Isn't this a wonderful cool room? We'll eat out here when it's hot."

She began pushing the furniture, delivered yesterday, into place even before she had taken off her hat. Mama's enthusiasm, contrasted with Benny's and Virginia's gloomy looks, would have made Hallie sorry for her if she had not felt so gloomy herself. Mama actually had not wanted to come to Greenwood, at least not at first. She had not wanted to leave Clover, or to leave South Carolina with Sis married and Helen at Winthrop and—here Mama's chin had trembled when she said it, as if she were accounting for each one of her children—with Jonny alone in the Clover Cemetery. She talked this way during the first days when Papa seemed dazed and uncertain at losing his job with the P. and N. He had worked hard, even overtime, day after day during the war; Hallie had been so proud of him and his patriotic work, moving troop trains, getting the boys across; then the war was won, the boys came home (more overtime) and suddenly there was no more work. At least none for Papa. He started dyeing his hair with Kolorbak though Hallie had never seen it anything but white; and when Mama complained of the peculiar color and the funny smell, he said he was tired of being spoken of as Old Man Jones. Even with the dyed hair he could not find a job, not in South Carolina, and when finally he heard about the job on the M. D. and S. in Georgia, Mama seemed glad to go, seemed to like the idea of a new town, a fresh start.

Benny had not wanted to come either. He had stopped school when Papa was out of a job, and delivered telegrams for Western Union. When he heard that Greenwood was too small for a Western Union, that Papa had gotten the station-agent job because he was a telegrapher, he had not wanted to come. Mama moaned and said she had done wrong to let him stop school, though it had seemed a good idea at the time. But she and Papa both said Benny had to come and here he was acting sarcastic about everything in Greenwood, and influencing Virginia to be sarcastic too.

When she and Virginia looked over their bedroom, the one furthest back in the row of rooms like a caboose on a freight train, Virginia said, "Well, thank goodness it's big enough so you won't be all over me," as if Hallie were a fractious child. There was only two years' difference in their ages. But Virginia had already had her fifteenth birthday and for a while that made her closer to Benny.

Mama called out, "Who's that?" and Hallie went up through the dark back hall to the kitchen where Mama was opening the door and inviting a Negro woman in.

"Mrs. Jones, I'm Aunt Relly," said the woman. "Adam Lincoln sont word up to me I better get on up here and help you get settled."

"Adam Lincoln must've read my mind," said Mama. "I was standing here thinking I should've asked Mr. Jones to ask Adam if he knew of someone who could help me for a few days. Of course I have the children." She glanced toward Hallie, who slunk away toward the door. "But for a day or two to get settled, I would really appreciate some help."

Aunt Relly pulled a large white apron out of a bag and tied it around her waist. She waited with her hands across her stomach which poked out a little, making a handy place for hands to rest. As she stood there, her lower lip stuck out, probably from a wad

9

of snuff, she reminded Hallie of Mama—another sign of Mama's commonness. There was an air about them, as if each knew what needed to be done. Mama's lower lip sometimes stuck out when she was thinking hard. They were both bony around the shoulders and their chests flat; Mama's breasts, Hallie knew, hung as slack and wrinkled as deflated balloons beneath her dark-blue traveling dress. Aunt Relly's bosom had the same flatness, as if the breasts were finished and done with. Aunt Relly knew her place though; she inquired now in a helpful voice, "Where you want me to start, Mrs. Jones? The kitchen?" And she fetched a deep breath from down in her insides, drew it up with such gustiness that her head shook.

"I'll change my dress," said Mama, and Hallie slid away to explore the yard.

Two ladies called on Mama before she had time to change. Going out the front door, Hallie met Miss Lill coming from the big white house across the street. She loped across the street like a schoolgirl; but she was followed by three small children who called her Mama. Miss Lill reminded Mama that she had already issued an invitation for all of them to come to supper at her house their first night. Then Miss Beulah came, from an unpainted house catty-cornered to them. She seemed to drop in mainly to look them over, rolling her milky protruding eyes around at the furniture, at them, telling Mama what the occupants of the house before her had done; how she was glad to see them leave as they had obstreperous boys.

Were they the ones who built the tree house in a shaggy water oak leaning over the swing end of the front porch? It was the only redeeming feature of an otherwise bleak and undistinguished house. Hallie climbed the trunk, scruffy with dried tree fern, to the tree house. She took refuge there while Aunt Relly and Mama labored to bring order into the house below. She felt restless, restless as a bird wanting to light but unable to find the proper branch. She lay on the bare gray boards of the tree house, a knothole in exactly the right place for her nose when she lay on her stomach. She thought nostalgically of Clover over in South Carolina. It gleamed white and pure as a Greek city full of aristocratic intellectuals. Clover's downtown architecture was modern and gracious. The Dempsey Hotel, six stories high, stood grandly above the town square of stylish brick stores with large plate-glass windows. (She could not bear to think of that slattern row of Greenwood stores with windows lidded by sunbonnet awnings.) Their own house back in Clover, a brown bungalow, was not a Southern mansion, it was true, but it was a house designed and built under Mama's direction and not just grown of itself like this Greenwood house. And Montpelier, Montpelier, the mansion that gave point and purpose to Clover; with its six round columns, its fan light, its ironwork balcony looking out on the spacious porch from the second-floor hall, its curving driveway, where on happy occasions passing to and from school or riding sedately by in the carriage to church, she saw Theodosia, the only child of the owner, Mr. Ely Barton, galloping down the driveway on a Shetland pony, her red curls bouncing. Hallie had never been inside Montpelier, could only imagine its spacious hall and high-ceilinged parlor, but brooding on it now in the tree house, in the first days after coming to Greenwood, feeling the meagerness and meanness of Greenwood, she almost began to think of herself as *from* Montpelier. In comparison to Georgia the whole state of South Carolina took on an aura of grace and contentment. South Carolina had been settled by English lords and ladies, or thin-nosed patrician French Huguenots. But Georgia . . . everyone knew Georgia had been settled by riffraff from the jails of England. She could not bring herself even to examine Greenwood further; here village idiots met trains, dull neighbors gossiped to Mama; nothing good could ever happen here.

When Mama called "Hallie-e-e," and Virginia took up the cry she would descend to be drawn briefly into the settling of the house. She leaned over the crates of books and rescued her own, pouncing on them as if they were ship bottles bearing some potent message from the other shore of Clover. She stacked her books in a pile, and when Mama was away in another part of the house she carried them to the tree house, began to read them again, hungrily. Or, holding them tenderly, staring first into the leaf-green light overhead, she drew pictures on the flyleaves: a flag emblazoned with a palmetto in the upper left-hand corner. Under the flag she wrote a little verse, "Oh, South Carolina, the palmetto state, I'd like to leave this state I hate." Or simply, "South Carolina, I love you." Virginia, investigating the tree house for herself, came upon the books and gleefully told Benny about the pictures and verses. Benny, rolling his eyes at Hallie and snickering so the hot blood flew up her neck to her face, said, "She ought to change her name to Caroline."

2

On the other side of the street, opposite their vegetable garden, the Baptist Church stood, domed and solid as a statehouse against a background of tombstones and cedars. Papa had already been made a deacon. He said proudly at one of their first suppers that he had offered to keep the communion service at their house; it was so close to the church. Virginia moaned and said afterward she wondered who would wash all those little glasses, and Benny said, "Lord, I reckon every time the church doors open we'll have to be on hand."

The first Sunday came. Hallie longed for it and dreaded it; longed for it, hoping it would reveal some hitherto hidden virtue of the town, and dreaded it because she would be singled out, sized up. Eyes like Miss Beulah's would be turned upon her, curious, speculative. Papa called to them to be ready on time as he left for the depot to let the train pass up the line; afterward he came back and got his Bible and walked over with them to the church. Hallie held herself straight and withdrawn in her starched dotted Swiss. She came from a finer state with higher standards and must bear herself accordingly. Miss Lizzie Wallace, who ran the boarding house where Papa had stayed during the months before they came, was waiting on the front steps of the church; she actually seemed to be standing there watching for them, and exhaling a great breath like sour milk, she drew Hallie smotheringly into her big soft blue voile bosom, exclaiming, "I declare, I'm so glad to meet Brother Jones' little girls. You know, child, your father's a *saint*." Papa's face, always a little red under his brown-dyed hair, turned even redder with pleasure.

Up in the Sunday School room off the balcony, a sign on the door saying "Intermediate Girls," Miss Emmy Belton, wearing a high-piled pompadour and with a voice as molasses sweet as Miss Lizzie Wallace's, said, "Aren't we *fortunate* to have one of Brother Jones' daughters in our class?" and looked around at the class for agreement. A prissy-looking girl pulled her organdy skirt over for Hallie to sit down and said, giggling, "Are you a Jones? I thought for a minute you were a Ducket," and giggled again. Miss Emmy said, "Meet Laura Fitzgerald." After the giggling Hallie held herself with even more dignity—and a good thing too, because the girl who sat in front of her, a girl with a neck so thick it pressed upon her ears, turned out to be named Essie Jones. (There always had to be another Jones, Hallie was inured to that, but why did it have to be one like Essie?) The girl turned her little pig eyes around toward Hallie when Miss Emmy introduced her and later when Miss Emmy called on her for a memory verse she sat still, looked at the ceiling long and wonderingly; Miss Emmy said, "Be ye kind . . ." and Essie finally finished with "one to another."

13

Next to Essie sat a girl with fat reddish Mary Pickford curls. Margaret Craig. Her broad face and green eyes were always expressing something. When she was called on for a memory verse she said the whole thirteenth chapter of First Corinthians. Her voice ranged from loud to soft, and she paused dramatically in the right places. At first Hallie felt embarrassed; Margaret must be showing off to say such a long memory verse, and her voice could carry down into the church where the Barathea Class was meeting, but when she dropped her voice to a whisper on "When I was a child, I spake as a child, I understood as a child . . ." Hallie found herself being caught up and carried away, and when Margaret said the final verse, " 'And now abideth faith, hope, charity, these three; but the greatest of these is charity,' " in a low, firm, attained voice, Hallie felt released too, and thereafter respectful of Margaret's talent.

On the way out of class she asked Margaret where she lived. Margaret turned down the corners of her mouth and said with a sob in her voice, "I live in the jail. They only let me out on Sundays."

Then, seeing she had mystified Hallie, she resumed her normal voice with a giggle and said, "Aw, I'm just teasing. But I *do* live in jail. Papa's sheriff."

In preaching service afterward, thinking over the Sunday School class, Hallie thought Laura Fitzgerald was hateful and Essie Jones a Mongolian idiot or nearly one, with her thick fingers, her short body and her neck thick as her head. There was not an interesting girl in the class—with the possible exception of Margaret Craig.

During the next week Hallie lay in the tree house hopeful that Margaret Craig might come and call to her and give her a reason for coming down out of the tree. But Margaret did not come and when Miss Emmy called the roll next Sunday Margaret Craig was missing and Miss Emmy said she imagined she was off visiting in the country. There was nothing to do but stay in the tree house and read.

That next week even reading began to pall. Hallie climbed

down and ventured out into the town, scuffing down on the sandy sidewalk to the depot; the ugly depot, painted the color of all railroad buildings, a railroad color, horrid orange or horrid mustard.

Back in Clover, when Papa worked for the P. and N. (the Peeing Inn, Benny had called it), Hallie had only paid occasional visits to his office because several men worked there besides him. Here in Greenwood Papa ran everything with the help of Adam Lincoln. Papa was always there in the depot, his coat off, wearing elastics on his sleeves. The office was crowded with furniture and always hot. There was a strong heady odor of tobacco juice, Papa's hair dye, indelible pencils, carbon paper, and occasional whiffs of cottonseed meal or fertilizer from the warehouse. In the afternoons Papa stood by the telegraph table placed across a bow window and looked out and up the road to watch for the first plume of smoke to show for the 4:34. The sun beat in through the fly-specked windows onto the telegraph table. Papa stood there at attention, listening as the telegraph rapped out some message. Hearing its staccato click of danger, its rattlesnake rattle, Hallie would imagine some crisis news, a trestle burned out over a raging torrent; help, help, stop all trains, stop all trains . . . She would watch Papa to see if he blanched, but he would only listen more intently, send a trajectory of spit into a spittoon near the typing table, wipe his mouth on his brown-stained handkerchief, and look mildly out the window. She would relax then and whirl in the chair in front of the typing table, turn to the desk to study the mound of dog-eared rate books, the scrambled pads of Macon, Dublin and Savannah Railway forms, and a large book with the mysterious single word DEMURRAGE written across its front (a word that crept into her head at night before she went to sleep, carrying some portent, some dread). Now Papa seemed to be pulling himself together for something, to be preparing for some action there at the window, leaning forward to look, spitting hastily and forgetting to wipe his mouth, then suddenly stretching an arm out the window and pulling the rope signal. In a minute the engine slid into view, bell ringing, steam sizzling, the engineer framed in the cab window, at ease, ready to call greetings, everyone momentarily at rest except Adam Lincoln catching mail and express thrown by unseen hands inside the baggage car.

The depot was not really interesting. She went there out of sheer desperation, but once she started visiting it there seemed to be some small reason to go back each day. For a while she resolved to learn the Morse code so that she would be the first besides Papa to know the secret news arriving in Greenwood— accidents and deaths that befell Greenwood citizens away from home, the rare good news of births and weddings, the felicitations on birthdays and graduations. She saw herself knowing before anyone else, but going around town with her mouth tight shut, observing an ethical code of silence like a doctor, but nevertheless knowing, knowing.

Every day Papa wrote a memory verse at the head of his Daily Orders. He could not forget about religion for long at a time. This close intermingling of religion with everyday life—answers were given in memory verses, Biblical phrases interlarded his everyday talk—caused a kind of estrangement between him and the rest of the family. Papa wanted everyone to be as religious as he was. Hallie was sure he did, though he never actually said so. He did not talk much at all at home; close-mouthed, Mama said. On Sundays, however, when Brother Jamieson, the preacher, finished his sermon and asked the congregation if anyone present were moved by the spirit to speak, Papa was always moved. He stood, his tongue became unloosed and he poured forth his admonitions, predictions and prophecies in a river of words that began in the Old Testament, ran softly through the Psalms, and ended in a cataract of Verilys, Wherefores, Whatsoevers and Woes, all accompanied by a stiff outthrust arm waving back and forth over Mama's head at the congregation. These Sunday sermons, differing from Brother Jamieson's only in length, gave the family, or at any rate Hallie, the idea that he expected them to

16

live up to some high standard religiously. She felt that he watched, like God, for some failure in their devotion.

One day when she came to the depot and did not find Papa in the office she walked out to the warehouse, sniffing the sharp smell of guano, cow feed and dust. Sparrows rustled to the rafters as she peered in and over in one corner in the dimness Papa rose from his knees. Adam Lincoln was with him. Adam dusted his knees as he stood by a sack of cottonseed meal. His black face was noble and uplifted as he came into the light and he kept looking toward the rafters as if still caught up in prayer. He towered a foot above Papa, who was small-boned and stooped, with a red, tortured, thin-lipped Scotch face. Papa called Adam "Brother Adam" occasionally these days; "Freight's going to be late, Brother Adam," he would call toward the warehouse door. But, "Mr. Bailey wants his cow feed, Adam," he would say. Sometimes one, sometimes the other.

Papa never said she should not come to the depot, and he always greeted her as if he were surprised and not unpleased. But then he never showed enthusiasm like Mama. His answers were always soft whether he was turning away wrath or not. Mama's voice was often too loud; she spoke too enthusiastically and Hallie was ashamed of her exuberance. Still, you could always tell how Mama felt. Her answers would be soft sometimes and loud and hard sometimes. Papa often seemed like a man who was standing out on the street and looking at a lighted Christmas tree inside a house, and she felt sad about this and guilty, remembering how he had rocked her in his arms on the slow warm evenings back in Clover. She had climbed into his arms as he sat rocking on the porch. He would do nothing but rock and occasionally lean forward to spit in the vines and she had lain in his arms, lulled by the rocking, her hands on his, and his on the arm of the chair. When he leaned forward, gripping the chair arms, the veins in his hands forked toward his fingers like ropes. Yet now she felt glad when he went to the depot and the talk could flow light-heartedly without him.

Still she continued to seek him out at the depot since there was nothing else to do, admiring at times his courtly air that reminded her of the Old South. He would rise from his chair at the typing table when Miss Lizzie Wallace came in. "Just going by," Miss Lizzie would say in her silly high voice. He would bow and say, "Lovely day, Miss Lizzie. How are all my friends down your way?" And Miss Lizzie would simper and pat her frizzy yellow hair and say, "Oh, Brother Jones, I declare we miss you so. I tell you I think the world and all of Mrs. Jones, but I do wish she'd a let us keep you a little longer." Papa's man-of-the-world air with Miss Lizzie made Hallie wonder if he had been different when he was boarding.

Sadly, however, Papa's courtly bow was about the only characteristic he had of the Southern gentleman. Of course he could have been one had it not been for the War. Papa's father had been killed in the First Battle of Manassas. Hallie kept a picture of her grandfather, her hero, in his clean gray uniform, framed in her bedroom. Papa remembered his father being brought back from the War and buried out in Varennes churchyard near Clover, but that was all he remembered of him. Hallie was proud that Papa's grandfather had been a slave owner with a large plantation and had lived in a beautiful old Southern mansion. Everything had changed after the War for the whole South and for Papa. Instead of growing up to be a gentleman and going to the University down in Columbia, learning to read Latin and Greek, becoming a doctor or a lawyer or a planter, Papa never went beyond the fifth grade in school. When he was nearly grown he scraped together a little money and went off and learned telegraphy and here he was, common and ordinary in this common, ordinary office, chewing tobacco like a mill hand.

"Papa, have you been chewing a long time?" Hallie asked him one afternoon, hoping the habit might not be too deeply ingrained.

"Ever since I was about eight years old, I reckon," he said, and leaned to spit. "Ever since one time I was crying with the tooth-

18

ache, and a old colored woman, Sarah was her name, give me a bite off her plug and said for me to hold it over the tooth that ached. It helped, and I been chewing ever since," he said. "Really don't care to add up how many years or how many pounds," he added apologetically. He must know as well as she that true gentlemen of the South did not chew, that if they used tobacco in any form they smoked either cigars or a pipe.

On the other hand, thought Hallie, weighing, sizing up, sifting, searching out items to put in Papa's column in her mind labeled "Southern Gentleman," there was Papa's coat of arms. The Jones family coat of arms. For this they must thank Aunt Rose, Papa's older sister from Charleston, who had shown it to them when she visited in Clover just before they moved away. Aunt Rose wore a high collar of net, the boning standing stiff as a piece of chain mail around her skinny throat. She had a businesslike shirt-waist bosom, festooned with watch and fob, a D.A.R. pin and bars. She had been born and brought up around Clover like Papa and the rest of her family but now she spoke with a Charleston accent hard to understand; Mama said it sounded as if Aunt Rose had a mouthful of hot potatoes. On this last visit she had spent her days in the Clover Cemetery copying inscriptions off grave-stones or visiting country churchyards in a hired hack. "But why?" Virginia had asked. "Why?" "What's it aboot you mean?" said Benny, slitting his eyes and giving a thick imitation of Aunt Rose's Charleston brogue. "Why, she raily rawbs gra-ives."

Then Aunt Rose showed them the Jones coat of arms and even Benny was impressed. She said she had recently located it in the archives of the Historical Society in Charleston where it had been lost for years. It was beautiful; the tiny figures carefully drawn and water colored, the Latin lettering gilded. Hallie spent several days making a copy under Aunt Rose's direction. She drew in the three beaked eagles (buzzards, said Benny, lapsing again), the Knight's casque with flowing shaded plume, and the inscrip-tion, *Ubique Reminisci Patriam*, in yellow paint, a poor substi-tute for the gold of the original.

19

"What does it mean?" she had asked Aunt Rose.

Aunt Rose thought a while and said, "It means that wherever we are, we must remember our heritage." Then, as if she thought heritage was too big a word for Hallie, she said, "For example, wherever we are, we must remember the Old South." It was not so much the meaning, as the fact that it was written in Latin that impressed Hallie. In the old days her ancestors had known Latin so well that they even wrote it on their coat of arms. The Jones family and Papa should have more respect.

But Papa gave no indication that he remembered the Old South, or that he was a man with a fine coat of arms and ancestors who spoke Latin. For all the citizens of Greenwood could tell he descended from the lowliest poor white ancestors up in Clover. When Mr. Barksdale, the owner of the planing mill, came in to see about flatcars for his lumber, Papa could have been a little more withdrawn and dignified to show that he was not accustomed to working in an ugly smelly office in a small town like Greenwood. But, rising from his typing table or turning from the telegraph keys, he would greet Mr. Barksdale with an air of deference, a kowtowing, almost a servile bowing and scraping, a "What can I do for you today, sir?" and he continued to call him Mr. Barksdale though Mr. Barksdale called him Brother Jones in the fraternal spirit of a fellow Baptist. Mr. Barksdale was no taller than her father, but he looked more solid. He had thick straight black hair parted on the side, light gray eyes which never wandered from the business at hand to flicker recognition in her direction. He had the air of a man with money. When he spoke, mostly about flatcars for his lumber, he spoke with an accent different from the crude speech of the natives of Greenwood; it had another kind of crudity, and when Hallie heard he was from North Carolina she realized it was a Tarheel crudity and wondered why Papa should show him such deference.

Then there was Mr. Jess Bailey, tall, godlike and pure as Galahad. He came into the depot office holding a bill of lading in his hand and saying, "Brother Jones, hasn't my lard come yet?" or cow feed, or some other commodity that he dispensed from his dark, dusty store on the corner across from the depot. He would throw her a "hey" as to a child, dimpling briefly. Though he had amazing good looks, his speech and his mundane preoccupations did not warrant Papa's hurry to the warehouse to check up on his freight, his quick offer to trace his goods.

Or when Papa talked on the telephone to the kaolin mill up the line, meeting with a placating tone their complaints about a freight car that came too late or came too soon, oh, it seemed a miserable attitude and unbecoming to a Jones who had a plumed helmet and a Latin inscription on his coat of arms.

When Papa had nothing else to do he worried with the Bible or read the Macon *Daily Telegraph*. One day in the slack season before the watermelons ripened she found him studying a new book, a thick book with fine print, and when she looked over his shoulder and asked, "What's that, Papa?", he said, "Out of this book"—holding it off so he could see it better—"I could fix you up a ticket to go anywheres in the United States. Canada, too, maybe, though I never sold a ticket to Canada. You remember Mr. Ely Barton, over in Clover?" He paused to spit and wipe his mouth.

Remember Mr. Ely Barton? No more of him than fierce black eyebrows above a red face in his pew in the Baptist Church back in Clover, but she remembered his house, Montpelier. Or *her* house, Montpelier, the model for the Southern mansion of her dreams, gleaming in that beloved fair white country of South Carolina. . . .

Papa went on, fingering the pages of the big book, "Well, now like the time Mr. Ely Barton wanted to make a trip to San Francisco he came to me and said, 'Brother Jones, I want you to figure me out a schedule,' and I figured him out one, going out one way, up by Chicago, Yellowstone Park, and back another, the southern route, seeing the Grand Canyon. He took a drawing room. That was just after he bought another cotton mill, and it was the second drawing room I ever sold all the time I was at the P. and

N. The first time was when they took that Adams girl up to Asheville when she was dying of t.b. Well, when Mr. Barton came back from his trip he brought me that silver spoon; you've seen it, has written on it, 'Greetings from San Francisco.' He says he never missed a connection and he had a mighty nice time."

Why Mr. Ely Barton should want to leave his beautiful home Montpelier even to take a trip was more than she could understand. But there was every reason for leaving this ugly town of Greenwood, go anywhere, anywhere away from here.

For a few days, then, she went back to the depot to plan trips with Papa. She went to San Diego, California; to Portland, Oregon; and to Niagara Falls, sometimes riding in the Pullman, sometimes sitting up. Every afternoon until the watermelon season came on she and Papa figured out a trip together. But after the watermelons ripened Papa was too busy to play with the schedule book. Freight cars had to be ordered and shunted onto the side tracks for the watermelons. He held barked conversations with someone on the phone, someone she imagined standing in an ice house in Macon; Papa talked as if the person on the other end of the line were far away and cold. The red-necked, red-faced farmers came in and complained about the weather or the market, or the tardiness of the freight cars, or how fast the ice melted. The little office became crowded and even hotter and she wandered out where the Negroes were packing the watermelons, hoping that one would crack and be laid to one side, its great red dewy heart exposed for her to grab quickly. There was always the feeling that there might be some largess connected with these trips to the depot, although there rarely was anything but Papa's nickels for ice-cream cones. She was constantly on the lookout for a box of chocolates crushed en route, Nabisco wafers open to the birds and to her, watermelons left standing free and unattended. The Negroes threw the swollen green globes from black hand to black hand, cradling them momentarily, then packed them away in the cool dark cave of the freight car.

It was on a hot afternoon in early July in the middle of the watermelon season that she saw Mr. Jess Bailey on his horse for the first time and fell in love and thought Greenwood, even without Montpelier, might become bearable. She had seen Mr. Jess Bailey over at the depot, and on Sundays sitting in the choir at church. Papa had chosen a pew three rows from the pulpit on the left side of the church and directly under the choir. A tenor voice floated out over her head that first Sunday, its source unmistakable even in the Doxology, and later confirmed when he sang a duet "In the Garden" with his sister, Miss Annie Laurie Jones. But Hallie had never seen him riding a horse until this particular afternoon.

She stood near the watermelon trucks in the sultry heat, the sun glittering on the dust of the street, and finally feeling overpowered she decided to watch the loading from a shaded bench in front of Mr. Jess Bailey's store on the corner. The bench had been placed in some hopeful relationship to a stunted chinaberry tree making half an umbrella slanted toward the street. Hallie knelt on the bench; it faced in, and she wanted to look out at the siding. She knelt there with her face in her hands and her elbows on the back rest, lulled by the rhythm of the watermelon packers, a rhythm punctuated by a grunt forced from their stomachs rather than their throats, as though the watermelon swung toward them struck them in the pit of the stomach. Then another rhythmical sound came into the piece, like the right hand doing a run over a sober chording left hand; hoofbeats, as far away as the Courthouse, and first she said some Negro on a mule, but the pacing was different from the forced march of a mule, quicker, more delicate. Then she saw that the hoofbeats were made by a horse, a brown horse with a white blaze on its forehead and white socks on its thin elegant legs that seemed to spurn the dust it stirred up as it came. Caught in the haze of dust by the afternoon sun, the dust turned golden, and encircling them in a little cloud, horse and rider seemed to come gold-tinged from a myth or fairy tale. She sat leaning raptly on her hands to watch this knight riding out of the mists and disappearing again, when suddenly they turned toward her, came cantering directly toward her and her heart almost stopped, thinking she was to be chosen, she was the princess. The rider said, "Whoa, Lady," and she saw it was Mr. Jess Bailey and this golden horse was Lady. Mr. Jess Bailey jumped down in front of her; mischief played in his blue eyes and his dimples twinkled as he bent toward her and said, "Honey, what you praying for?" He was tall and handsome in his tan army pants and puttees, taller and handsomer and purer than she had ever seen him, and Hallie was dazzled, felt magic still in the air, and was tongue-tied. She knew that some light badinage was in order, and she strained for the right answer. Mr. Jess Bailey threw the reins over the horse's head and drew her up to the chinaberry. Hallie leaned over, playing for time, traced the blaze on Lady's forehead and said, "I was praying for a horse just like yours." Mr. Jess crinkled his blue eyes and his dimples showed again and he seemed to look at her, look at her as if seeing her for the first time, really look, as if he were examining her for something. He turned to the horse and said, "Lady's a right pretty horse." Then, his blue gaze on her again, piercing her, he took hold of one of her plaits and lifted it gently from her shoulder, held it for a second but did not pull it, just picked it up, held it for a heartbeat, and laid it down again on her shoulder. "Honey, stick around and I'll take you for a ride sometime," he said, and went on toward the store.

Hallie sat down weakly on the bench, facing in this time, facing in toward the door where Mr. Jess Bailey turned to smile and give half a wink before he entered. She sat staring at the door, feathered wings stirring inside her, fountains playing. Then she turned on the bench to look at Lady. She stood to pat her, to plait her mane, feeling some promised ownership, wondered when Mr. Jess Bailey would keep his promise. When it happened—tomorrow or next week—would she mount Lady alone, ride solemnly down the street, holding herself with the innate grace that belongs to all gentlewomen on horses, the rough crowd in front of the cotton office looking up to see her pass and saying, "Great

God in the morning, look at that there girl ride." "Who's she?" "Why, she's that Jones girl, Miss Hallie Jones, just come to town." "A natural-born rider if ever I've seen one." Or (and here her imagination took such a turn that she got up off the bench and started for home, feeling the need of privacy for her thoughts) would she prefer to be taken up on the horse in front of Mr. Jess Bailey (sidesaddle like Guinevere or astride)? Astride, in front of Mr. Jess Bailey, his arms could encircle her and hold the reins, his breath blow on her neck, and when she turned to smile at him, to thank him, his lips might accidentally touch her cheek. She had arrived home by this time, and she climbed to the tree house to savor this dream. Now turning to thank him, she turned so far around her lips met his. She saw herself on the horse riding in front of Mr. Jess Bailey, the figure her own, of course, but a changed one, one she had longed for and feared would never come. Her button breasts had sprouted and she was a ravishing creature who despite her youth strangely captivated Mr. Jess Bailey.

The dream hung over her all day and she thought of Mr. Jess Bailey and his promise again before she went to bed, thought, "Oh, Greenwood, Greenwood," almost lovingly, touched her breasts to see, curled herself into a satisfied ball, thought of Mr. Jess Bailey riding her on his horse up a long curving driveway between great trees to a Southern mansion called Montpelier.

3

For a while then the days assumed a character, a shape. Rather than presenting time, undifferentiated time, the days became segmented and properly ordered. When she wakened in the morning she could look forward to the hour when she would go to town and wait for Mr. Jess Bailey to take her for a ride on his horse. And awaiting that day and hour, she went through a routine of preparation, actually hoping the event could be postponed so that she could get herself ready. She did deep-breathing exercises in her room each morning after Virginia was well out of the way; if she was never going to grow breasts she could at least develop her chest. She tried doing her hair different ways; once she went to town with it flowing around her neck, but it became moist and sticky and she plaited it up again. He had touched one of the plaits before; he might do so again.

She sat so long on the bench in front of Mr. Jess Bailey's store that Virginia remarked her skirt looked like a washboard. She even cultivated the dough-faced Essie Jones, whose mother, Miss Annie Laurie Jones, was Mr. Jess's sister, married to Mr. Add Jones, the rural mail carrier. She helped Mr. Jess run the store. Hallie inquired of Essie who came and sat with her on the bench sucking an all-day sucker—the juice dribbling repulsively down her chin so that Hallie could not look at her—if Mr. Jess Bailey, Senior, was away somewhere on a visit. Written on the front of the store was "Jess Bailey & Son." But it turned out that the elder Jess Bailey was dead, and when Hallie later visited the Bailey lot in the cemetery behind the Baptist Church she found that he had been dead since 1912. A large stone with "Father" on one side and "Mother" on the other was filled in with the facts of life and death for Mr. Jess Bailey, Sr., and a blank space awaited Mr. Jess Bailey's mother, with whom he lived.

Hallie, offhand and subtle, not looking at Essie, inquired where her uncle kept himself these days, and Essie replied, "Oh, Uncle Jess, he's always out huntin for kaolin." Kaolin, Papa said, was nothing but white clay. It was mined at High Point, a flag stop on the M. D. & S. and Papa had to provide freight cars to carry it away. Being sought for by Mr. Jess Bailey, kaolin now took on mysterious properties, attributes of the Holy Grail or a bright plumaged bird. How did one hunt for kaolin? Did Mr. Jess Bailey ride on his beautiful horse over hill and dale, holding a divining rod like a spear before him? Or did he walk, lonesome through the woods and fields, his horse reins loose over one arm while he stopped and turned the red crust with the toe of his shoe seeking for the white clay beneath?

Mr. Jess did not come to the store all week, at least not while she sat on the bench waiting for him. She had to wait until Sunday when he appeared as usual at church, bringing his mother in his Hudson Super Six, handing her out gallantly as though she were frail. She was not frail; she was dumpy and had a mole with two hairs in it near her nose. She wore a lavender hat and lavender gloves to match and when she prayed, as she sometimes did aloud, she pointed her lavender-gloved hands together like a child saying his prayers by the side of the bed at night. She prayed aloud in a voice sometimes near to tears. Hallie, regarding her closely and turning her eyes on Mr. Jess in the choir, decided he must resemble his dead father.

All the next week he was off somewhere, hunting kaolin still, she supposed. His Hudson was parked in front of the store on Saturday afternoon. Peering into the dimness on the pretext of searching for Essie she saw him in the back at a rolltop desk, holding long discourse with Negro customers. It was the first of the month; Papa felt the first of the month too, and spent longer hours totaling his accounts, collecting what was owed.

Benny said at supper one night, "What's Hallie always doing down in front of Mr. Jess Bailey's store, mooning around?" and she felt herself reddening as if Benny had pried into one of her nightly visions.

She did not give up the visions but she did give up going to town and sitting on the bench in front of the store. Mr. Jess seemed intent on the pursuit of kaolin. There was no point in sitting there waiting and waiting. Oh, she would wait; there was nothing else to do but wait, but she must pretend not to. She walked over to see his house; unprepossessing, with peeling tan banisters, steps leading onto the sidewalk and dusty cannas growing from a washtub in the side yard. It was a common house on a street of common houses in a common town. She became dissatisfied again with Greenwood.

The weather got hotter; the dog days had come. Clouds stacked up in the afternoon, up and up into the high hot heavens. Sometimes a yellowish unearthly glow would appear, expectancy would be abroad in the sky. Was this the end of the world? Lightning forked over the cemetery cedars, thunder tumbled out of the thunderheads, at last a torrential rain fell, and the earth steamed afterward. (Clover had cooling showers in the afternoon, sweet, cool Clover, beautiful as its name.) She gave up going to town altogether and lay, between showers, in the tree house, listening to the rustle of leaves, the distant rise-and-fall drone of the cotton gin, the small movement of birds. Sometimes she was drawn to watch the McGhee house across the street.

From its big porch came the voices of the little McGhees, sweet and constant as the chitter of sparrows, broken occasionally by the loud schoolgirl voice of their mother, Miss Lill McGhee. At noon Doc McGhee would drive up in his car for dinner and soon that old man, Lucius Ledbetter, the repulsive tramp who had stared at them as they arrived in town, would come walking up the street with a strange sidewise motion, like a crawfish, or a dog going forward by going a little to one side. His head seemed permanently drawn to his right and the arm and leg on that side did not seem to work properly. Miss Lill always fixed him a plate after the others finished eating, and Hallie would see him sitting at a table on the screened porch near the kitchen, a cut above the help but a little lower than the family.

She wondered about Lucius, wondered why the McGhees allowed him around. Sometimes he slept in the McGhee's garden house, an octagonal structure beyond the fig trees filled with tools, old fertilizer sacks, an occasional setting hen, and a cot which presumably had been placed there for him. But Doc McGhee would roust him out from time to time, saying that the place smelled, that he would have to wash if he stayed there. But Lucius would not wash just for a place to sleep. He would move away for a while and sleep somewhere else. Where? Hallie wondered. (When she asked Mama she said, "Oh, I suppose somebody hangs him up on a hook somewhere.") Miss Lill seemed to be the only one who could get Lucius to wash. After eating he would sit on the porch in a rocking chair with one or more of the little McGhees in his lap. All through the drowsy hours after dinner, when the world was still and hot and Hallie lay drugged in the tree house dozing over *St. Elmo* or *Maori and Settler*, he would sit and rock the babies while the older children played near him. A gentle hum of talk came across the road to the tree, the little McGhees saying tenderly, "Lucius, Lucius," asking him something, and Lucius murmuring an answer, apparently a satisfying answer. She drowsed along with them, hearing the slight creak of the rocking chair, hearing Lucius occasionally clearing his throat, hearing his tobacco landing with the snap of hail on Miss Lill's japonica bushes. The little McGhees lay there quiescent under the hum of talk that must be as mean-

29

ingless as the chitter of sparrows in the water oak. Suddenly the children, and Hallie too, would be jerked to attention by Miss Lill, stamping out like an angry schoolgirl after her nap.

"You, Lucius," she would say, "put those children down this instant. Haven't I told you not to come up here smelling like an old goat. Get down, Seymour, get down, Baby." Baby put her arm around Lucius' neck and kissed him (why did Miss Lill let her?) before she slid down to the floor and put her thumb in her mouth. Lucius stood up and without a word stalked off, stiff-legged. Miss Lill shrilled after him, "Look at him, walks like a goat and smells like a goat," laughing as she said this and turning toward the children to receive their laughter. But they did not laugh. They sat solemnly on the floor with their thumbs in their mouths, and when Lucius appeared next day, apparently washed and acceptable, they climbed back up into his lap when he had finished his dinner. The creaking and humming would go on as before.

Or she would half listen to Miss Beulah visiting with Mama down on the porch under the tree. Miss Beulah was gradually acquainting Mama with the town. Hallie would rouse up, rest her head on one hand and hold her breath the better to hear when Miss Beulah got on the subject of love and sex. In all of Miss Beulah's stories babies were started by a process of the "girl gettin into trouble" which either terminated in a "shotgun weddin" or a "life of shame" for the girl. Miss Beulah claimed to possess the peculiar talent of being able to tell when a girl was pregnant long before the girl knew it herself; she said she could do it just by looking into the girl's eyes. All deliveries were excruciating, whether the child was conceived in sin or in holy wedlock. No matter, they were all born in anguish, and Miss Beulah rather specialized in stories of agonizing deliveries. Hallie listened one day to her telling the story of the birth of Sanford Joiner, who had just passed by the house on his way to Royal Ambassadors.

"Speakin of people cuttin up"—though Hallie had not heard

her mother so speak—"you should have been here when Emma Joiner had Sanford. She carried on worse than any woman I ever heard in all my life. He was her first, last, and only one. Seems she got her legs crossed, kept saying she wouldn have this baby, just wouldn. Old Doc Evans he got so mad at her he said her husband ought to take her out and horsewhip her. Anyhow, she carried on so you could hear her plum down to my house. I tell you the whole town was in an uproar. You could hear her carryin on, sayin over and over, 'I won't have it, I won't . . .' We were all worn out. Finely Doc Evans just had to use the forceps and pull Sanford out."

Miss Beulah sat back after this and the swing creaked a little and Hallie sat in the tree waiting for more. Then Miss Beulah giggled and said, "Bubber says it was just like gettin a watermelon through a keyhole." Bubber was Miss Beulah's brother, Mr. Willy Featherstone, and he often summed up a story for her.

She watched Mr. Willy Featherstone too on his regular goings out and comings in, as Papa would say Biblically. But he and Miss Beulah, the McGhees and Lucius Ledbetter were really of no more interest than the birds; they were something that went on, like sun rising and setting, thunder rumbling, rain falling, cotton gin droning. She was still waiting for Mr. Jess Bailey and while she waited her thoughts went back to South Carolina and she sought consolation in her books; she reread *St. Elmo* by Augusta Evans Wilson, *In Ole Virginia* by Thomas Nelson Page, *Romeo and Juliet* by William Shakespeare.

Then Elberta came to them and for a few days she forgot about Mr. Jess and his promise to take her for a ride.

One Saturday afternoon in early August Aunt Relly came to the house with two brush brooms to sweep the yard. Hallie heard her out on the back porch mumbling, which was not unusual. But today the mumbling seemed louder than usual, the explosive sighs that racked her body a little deeper, her "Lord a mercy on us" delivered with more intensity. Hallie went out to see if she could make some sense out of these mutterings and found her sitting on the edge of the porch working over the brush brooms, pulling the tender young branches tighter together, weaving the thongs that held them with her limber brown hands. Mama too came out on the porch.

"Mrs. Jones," said Aunt Relly, "you goin to want a cook when school gits started, ain't you?"

"I thought you had the job down at school," said Mama.

"It ain't for me," said Aunt Relly. "It's for . . ." Here she bent over the brush broom closely worrying a piece into position. "It's for a kind of niece of mine. She's come up from the country to stay with me."

"Just come?" asked Mama. After all, Aunt Relly had been at the house only yesterday to scrub the kitchen and she had not mentioned a niece.

"Yes'm, she just come up this mornin. She was settin on the doorstep when I come back from the woods with the brooms."

"Didn't you know she was coming?" asked Mama. She sat on the edge of the milk table, automatically straightening the white cloth covering the churn and quart cup and bucket, and shooing away the flies. Hallie sat on the steps with Aunt Relly.

"No'm. I didn count on her comin up right now. I reckon she didn either. She come kind of sudden." Aunt Relly heaved a sigh from somewhere down in her insides that set her head to shaking again.

"I usually do the cooking," said Mama vaguely, as if she were thinking over her household arrangements; the milk things, the bread things, the stove . . . they were the most important. Mama often said she wished some of her girls would learn to clean, because she never got around to it. Sometimes she talked about someone helping with the cooking but she always seemed to know how to do it better and while showing how it should be done she ended up by doing it herself. "Of course," she said, "I'd have to teach her my way."

"Oh, I don't mean she's a trained cook," said Aunt Relly, looking now at Mama hopefully. Her eyes were the same cocoa-brown color as her face, the whites muddy. "I wouldn say any more than that she's a real plain cook. But she's young and you could train her. What I want most, what I really am lookin for, is a place where she could get some good trainin."

"My idea has been to train my daughters." And Mama looked at her only daughter present with disappointment in her gray eyes. Hallie thought perhaps she should disappear right now before Mama suddenly decided on a new routine. But Mama went back to the business at hand. "What's your niece's name?" she asked.

"Elberta," said Aunt Relly. Hallie wanted to laugh. Only a Negro would name a child Elberta. "The Great Elberta Peach" was written on the framed picture of a large golden peach with the two green leaves hanging in the hall.

"Elberta's going to live with you then?" said Mama.

"Well'm, I imagine so. It do look as though she would." Aunt Relly seemed distracted again and jerked at the twigs as if she must make them obey her.

Mama came and stood at the edge of the porch and leaned against a post where she could see Aunt Relly's face better. "Seems to me you're not telling me everything about this girl," she said.

Aunt Relly seemed to be relieved at that, and she fetched a deep breath and said, "She had to come, Mrs. Jones. Her pa run her away from home."

"Oh," said Mama.

Aunt Relly leaned over and carefully spit into the corner between the steps and the porch. Her lower lip was still pendulous, though she had spit out the snuff. "Well, he's not really her pa, he's her step-pa," she said.

"Then it's her mother who is your sister then?" said Mama.

"No'm, it ain't exactly that way. It's her step-pa who's my brother. So she ain't rightly my niece, not by blood anyhow." Aunt Relly had finished the two brooms and now she sat there holding them.

"And you think your brother did wrong to run her away from home?" asked Mama.

Aunt Relly reached deep for one of her sighs and brought it up with, "Lord, Lord, I really cain't say he done wrong. The fact is she just hain't got anywheres else to go." She swept a little space in front of her with one of the brooms as if she were trying it out, then said, "She ought to be right good help after you get her trained, say until February or March, long in there."

"Wouldn't the man marry her?" asked Mama with more interest in her voice. Mama's lower lip hung out a little like Aunt Relly's, but not from snuff. Besides the hanging lower lip there was something else alike about their faces, the same eagerness to know.

"She won't tell who he is," said Aunt Relly. "You cain't pry her mouth open and make her. That's why her pa run her away from home, 'cause she won't tell."

"Did she tell you?"

"No'm, she won't tell nobody. She just gits stubborn and shets her mouth real tight and sets there just like this with her mouth tight shet." And Aunt Relly poked out her lips into an exaggerated pout, and her head shook from side to side. "You cain't do nothin with her."

Hallie knew as soon as she guessed that Elberta was going to have a baby what Mama's decision would be. Mama could not resist anyone who was going to have a baby; it was part of her vulgarity. Or was it just her curiosity—she always wanted to know everything—or was it her love of offering advice? Hallie had been mortified many a time when Mama would meet utter strangers wheeling a baby carriage along the street; within two minutes she would be giving them advice on toilet training.

"I brought up ten myself," Mama would begin, which always made Hallie squirm, as if they belonged to a family of rabbits. "Six of mine and four stepchildren, not counting the ones I've looked after as if they were my own." This was a mortifying reference to the time just before they left Clover when Papa had no job and Mama had "pitched in" by taking care of motherless children in her home. "I always hold their little behinds up to a warm fire," Mama would continue with her advice to young mothers casually encountered on the street. "That usually brings things on." At that moment Hallie always wished the ground would open in front of her feet and swallow her.

Aunt Relly brought Elberta around on Monday morning. Papa had left for the depot and Benny and Virginia had not appeared. Hallie sat at the big kitchen table where they ate breakfast. She had just finished her coffee when there was a rap on the porch and Aunt Relly called, "Mrs. Jones, we here."

Behind Aunt Relly there was a tall thin white girl who stood in the door hesitantly. Hallie thought at once, Oh, there's some mistake, this is a white girl.

"Here's Elberta," Aunt Relly stepped in and motioned toward the girl who still stood half in and half out of the door, looking as if she might turn and run any minute.

"Come on in, Elberta," said Mama. "You'd better close the screen door before the flies come in." Elberta jumped in suddenly and the screen door shut with a bang. She stood there with her arms crossed awkwardly, hugging herself as if she were cold. Her hair was very black, black as a crow's wing, but it was not kinky. It was blacker than any white person's hair in Greenwood, where there was a range of color from white to dark brown. Back in Clover there was a Greek family who ran a café near the depot; Elberta had hair as black and eyes as brown and nose as straight as Mrs. Pouloplos'.

Elberta tried to fold herself into a small space near the door, and then Hallie could see that she was a Negro girl all right: her faded shapeless dress, her run-over shoes with holes cut out for the toes to spread, and a face of a color that Hallie often thought about and tried to describe to herself in the weeks afterward. It was not a whiteness like her own which Mama often referred to as "sallow," or like Virginia's which was fair with quite a lot of pink in the cheeks. Elberta's face was the color of rich cream that rose to the top of the flat milk pans overnight. Suddenly Hallie felt she understood the meaning of the word "bright." Elberta looked "bright." Her black hair was arranged like the other Negroes' who came in from the country, plaited in little plaits all over her head. She drew the ends of these into a knot on the back of her head.

Aunt Relly said, "You train her, Mrs. Jones. She's just a ignorant country girl and you'll have to train her good." She turned to Elberta. "Where's that apron I told you to bring?" she asked gruffly.

Elberta clutched a paper sack under her arm and now she pulled out a faded apron and tied it over her dress. Hallie studied her as she picked up the breakfast dishes and carried them over to the kitchen table. Elberta's elbows were as skinny as her own, and the apron strings were tied around a waist as skinny as hers. There was no poking out beneath the apron strings. How could Elberta be so sure she was going to have a baby? Or her father be so sure that he took a horsewhip and drove her away from home? Hallie could imagine Elberta cowering in a corner of the cabin as she had cowered inside the screen door here, sobbing that she would not tell her lover's name, and her stepfather standing over her with a horsewhip, flicking it over her head, saying, "Unless you tell me who your lover is, never darken my door again," and Elberta clutching her mother and going out the door sobbing, "I'll never tell, never, never." Hallie wondered how Elberta could have been strong enough to stand up to her stepfather; she looked so beaten now.

Elberta called her "Miss Hallie" although Mama laughed and said at once, "That's not necessary, Elberta, she's too young for that." But she persisted and now as Hallie finished her coffee she said, "You through, Miss Hallie?" and Hallie said, "Yes, thank you, Elberta," and liked that touch of the servant-mistress relationship of the Old South.

Miss Beulah came by to visit before the breakfast dishes were cleared the first day Elberta came. Mama said, "This is Elberta, come to cook for us."

Miss Beulah acted surprised to see her there, though Hallie felt sure that she had arrived so early because she had seen Elberta come with Aunt Relly, or that her brother, Mr. Willy, acting as lookout from his swing in the breezeway, had alerted her. Miss Beulah said, "Are you Samanthy Tribble's daughter, lives down in the Dewy Rose Community?"

Elberta said, "Yes'm."

"But your name's not Tribble, is it?" Miss Beulah persisted. And Elberta hung her head down and her long black lashes lay along her golden cheeks and she said, "No'm, no'm, my name's Smith."

"Oh, yes, I remember now," said Miss Beulah. "Elberta Smith."

When she moved toward the front door to leave Miss Beulah said, shaking her head and clicking her tongue, "Uh, uh, just like her ma. She tell you who the man is?"

How could Miss Beulah possibly tell Elberta was going to have a baby? Could she really tell by looking into the girl's eyes?

"I haven't asked her," said Mama. "She just came."

"Well, if she's like her ma, she won't tell, though everybody in the county knows now who Elberta's father is. She looks just like his daughters. And Elberta's mother is a mulatto. Ain't it terrible the temptation they always put before our young boys? Even the best families has this kind of thing happen in it. You would be downright surprised to know who Elberta's father is."

Strangely enough, Mama did not ask. She merely said, as she opened the screen door and held it for Miss Beulah, actually seeming to hurry her along, "Well . . ."

"If I were you I'd ask," said Miss Beulah. "Just come right out and ask her."

Mama said, "She's just come. Maybe it's none of our business. What's done is done now, I reckon. Maybe she wouldn't want to marry the man even if she could."

Miss Beulah gave one of her exaggerated half sniffs, half snorts. "More'n likely he won't have anything to do with her, even if he's a nigger. But I imagine you'll find she takes after her ma and he's a white man. I just have a feelin."

And since Miss Beulah's seventh sight had worked in predicting a baby, Hallie wondered if she could pierce the walls of Elberta's stomach where the little thing lay hidden and could see, tiny as it was, whether it were white or black. She hoped Miss Beulah would settle down on the porch but she seemed to have something on her mind. "I've got to get on down to see Lizzie Wallace," Miss Beulah said, and took off, hurrying.

The next few days Hallie spent watching Mama train Elberta. "Scald the milk things with really boiling water, Elberta," Mama said. Elberta stood over the black tea kettle with a look of concentration and when it belched steam she carried it to the table to pour over the strainer and bucket and quart cup.

"Don't dry them, Elberta," Mama said, "let them dry themselves."

"Well'm," said Elberta patiently.

"Some things you do dry with a nice clean dish towel, but the milk things are special. They really shouldn't be touched by human hands any more than you have to. They'll get germs on them."

Elberta picked up the strainer by an edge and held it out from her. "Well'm," she said again.

Mama was able to go off to Macon now that she had Elberta, riding on her pass on the up train and down again in the afternoon, lugging home a string bag full of groceries from the Piggly-Wiggly. Hallie would go out to the kitchen to keep Elberta company. She did not look like the kind of girl who would put herself in the way of a man, tempting him, as Miss Beulah suggested. She did not roll her eyes or swing her hips, or act in any way like a girl who tempted men.

Hallie corrected Elberta's English, pretending that she was "Meh Lady" teaching the Negro children on her Virginia plantation. "Do you have brothers and sisters, Elberta?" she asked once. Elberta was trying to rub the black off the bottom of the frying pan. When Mama was cooking in a hurry she would often jerk the lid off the stove and put the pan right next to the fire.

"Yes'm," said Elberta, "several of 'em." She kept busy rubbing the bottom of the pan with Dutch cleanser.

"Of them," corrected Hallie. "Are you the oldest?"

"Yes'm."

"How many brothers and sisters?" persisted Hallie. Elberta certainly did not offer anything; she seemed only interested in scrubbing the pan.

"Six."

"Six of each or three of each?"

Elberta looked as if she were bothered by mosquitoes. "Four brothers, two sisters," she said. She picked up the dishpan full of water and went out to throw it under the sweet-shrub bush. She stood by the bush for a minute and touched the brown bloom; she stroked the bloom on the bush, then crumpled a petal and held it to her face. Suddenly Hallie had a glimpse of a tall girl, princess pale and princess proud: the Princess Giselle out of a fairy tale, a put-upon princess waiting for a glass slipper or for a word, a magic word that would transform her from her low estate to her rightful one. Then Elberta came back to the kitchen and wiped out the pan, and Hallie had to remind herself again that she was only a Negro girl.

She remembered words spoken by Miss Beulah, words that had floated up to her in the tree house, words half heard and not really taken seriously, laughed at by Mama, but now they came floating back. Miss Beulah said that you could always tell Negro blood no matter how white the skin because even a drop of Negro blood produced blue fingernails and a stripe running down the spine. Sometimes Elberta's fingernails did look a little blue, but at other times they did not, and Hallie could see no black stripe appearing above her dress in back. But there were other signs that showed she was a regular Negro girl. She could pick

39

up a hot coal in her hand, as she did once when she was burning trash outside and wanted a light. She picked up a coal quickly from the range, threw it in the coal scuttle and went out with it. Hallie had never seen a white person pick up a live coal. And every day Elberta acted as if the kitchen door were the door to a Negro cabin and she swept the yard around the back porch, leveling out the scratchings where the chickens had fought for the watermelon seeds spit there by Hallie and Virginia and Benny.

And her talk. It was the lowliest kind of Negro. She used *h's* in front of words like *it* and *ain't,* dragged out her *No'm* and *Yes'm* beyond anything Hallie had ever heard. She said *we'uns* and *you'uns, chunk* for *throw,* and talked about *lighterd* for the fire. When Mama asked her if she had been to school for long she said, "No'm, I hain't had too much chancet to go to school. Seems like we'uns had to lay by the cotton or chop the cotton or I had to stay home and work whilst the others were layin by or choppin. But I can read and write," she said proudly, and raised her eyes and smiled and looked pretty. It was hard to remember that Elberta was a Negro girl.

Elberta gradually became more at home, laughed with Mama in the kitchen, and stopped calling Hallie "Miss." But she never became talkative, and Hallie lost interest. Furthermore she really did not look as if she were going to have a baby and despite Miss Beulah's confirmation Hallie thought there might be some mistake. Elberta's coming, however, freed Hallie even more from household duties, and she returned for long hours to the gray boards of the tree house during those early days of August, returned to waiting for Mr. Jess Bailey. She took a pad of the M. D. and S. paper Papa had given her one day when rain blew in and stained it, and thought of writing a story with a tall fair-haired horseman as the hero, who like herself came from a humble home but was undoubtedly destined for greater things—destined to find a nymphlike girl in a water oak, and finding her, sweet, gentle, intellectual, he had taken her up on his horse and they cantered away to a beautiful Southern mansion where they lived happily ever after.

She descended to the orchard for a bucket of peaches and brought them up to the tree house, puckering her lips as she bit through the fuzzy skin, sucking at the soft pink flesh, the juice running down onto the boards and through the knothole made for it. The peach pits followed and she squinted through the knothole at the little pile she was making on the ground below. But the peaches made her hands sticky and when she picked up the pencil to write the story she did not like the feel. She lay back resting her head on a pile of books and stared into the leaf-green light above. Oh, this long drawn-out waiting for something to happen.

Greenwood, Greenwood, she thought with disappointment and disgust. Her intellect was her only hope. She must rise above her drab surroundings and become, if not blue-blooded, then a bluestockinged daughter of the Old South. She thought of all the books she would read, the titles of the Harvard Classics which Mama had gotten Papa to buy at a railroad warehouse sale over in Clover, their red covers marred by rain. She would read them all, learn whole sections and astound everyone with her learning as Edna Earl had done in *St. Elmo*. She would begin at once, she thought, pillowing her head on the pile of books, she would begin improving her mind as well as her body. But she lay there, feeling a weight in her limbs, a drowsiness she could not resist, a boredom that was not entirely unpleasant. A catbird rose on its toes to call her name, peaches ripened below in the sun, and at midday their rich ripe scent floated up to her, almost palpable on her tongue. And when she lay still and thought of Mr. Jess, feathered wings moved gently inside her.

4

Sundays in Greenwood. Sundays were a week long. They were the doldrums, the Sargasso Sea where time was caught and held by down-pulling weeds, hot days that sullenly refused to move on. After the tiresome hot Sunday School class with Miss Emmy droning on, after the sermon with its one bright spot that she could feast her eyes on—Mr. Jess Bailey . . . then Sunday dinner; Elberta went home, her tin plate piled high, then nothing . . .

One Sunday after dinner Hallie went back to the caboose bedroom and lay on her bed, lay there sweltering in her slip, mindlessly reading the feature section of the Atlanta *Constitution*.

Virginia lay in the other bed asleep under the funny papers, Mutt and Jeff over her face, the Katzenjammer Kids over her feet. There were a few stray flies around that no one had the energy to swat. How could Virginia sleep in such heat? Hallie thought of the tree house; the gray boards might be cooler than the bed. Virginia's breathing and the rise and fall of Mutt and Jeff over her chest seemed almost too even; there was a rigidity about her hands half under the funny paper. The front door slammed; Papa going down to meet the 4:34.

The funny papers moved, and Virginia peered out. She went through an elaborate sequence of yawns and stretches and little moans and mutterings about nothing to do; then throwing the funny papers aside, she jumped out of bed, ran to the closet and pulled out her best summer dress. Hallie watched her from behind the *Constitution*. Virginia ratted up her hair and pulled it into enormous puffs on each side of her face. She held two little strands in her mouth, chewing on them as she pinned up the puffs, then brought the damp strands back to bisect the puffs, neat as geometry.

"Mama'd wring your neck if she saw you ratting up your hair like that."

"You hush," said Virginia, digging into the top drawer.

"Where're you going?" Hallie asked, putting down the paper and sitting on the side of the bed.

"Oh, nowhere." Virginia stuck a pencil in her mouth, wet it and worked on her eyebrows, then rummaged again in the top drawer and brought out a shiny thing which she dropped down her front.

"If Papa sees you with lipstick on he'll have a fit," said Hallie. She stood up now and started putting on her skirt.

Virginia pulled a white chiffon handkerchief out of the drawer and poured perfume on it.

"Good Lord," said Hallie, and hurried with her dressing.

She was still tucking in her blouse as she followed Virginia out to the front porch. Mama sat there in a rocking chair surrounded by the Macon *Daily Telegraph*. She was reading the weddings and engagements page and did not look up.

Virginia sat down gently in the swing, almost as softly and gently as Hallie herself when she wanted neither to be seen nor heard.

Mama murmured "Taylor-Blake . . ."

"Do we know them?" asked Virginia.

"Oh, Blake. Says here on his mother's side he comes from a fine old Southern family from Dahlonega, and on his father's side from one of the early settlers of Georgia, Thomas Blake, first settled around Savannah."

"Thomas Blake must've been a jailbird," said Hallie. "Georgia was settled by jailbirds."

Mama went on with her reading. Then she said, "Must be she's that little girl works in Penney's in Macon. She waited on me the other day, said she was getting married."

Virginia froze to attention and held the swing steady as a big black Buick came around the corner. No one was visible behind the wheel. The car slowed down in front of the house and at first all that Hallie could see was an elbow stuck out of the window. Then a head with puffs of brown hair identical to Virginia's rose from behind the wheel, then a face with round high-colored cheeks. A hand languidly waved. This was May Belle Ballard, one of Virginia's new friends. Her father had licked the boll weevil the year before and bought the new car. May Belle showed complete disdain for it, spoke of "our old Buick" although it was bright shiny new, and slung it carelessly around corners to show her contempt.

"Mama, may I go riding with May Belle?" asked Virginia, rising to her feet without creaking the swing and moving quietly to the steps.

Mama looked up now and saw Virginia for the first time. "Goodness, Virginia, for a minute I didn't know you. Well, I guess you've got to go somewhere. Now where is it you want to go with May Belle?"

"Just riding. You know, riding around town. Not far." Virginia was halfway down the steps.

Mama flapped the *Telegraph* and said, "I can't see why a short ride on Sunday afternoon should doom you to Hell's fire," and then, as if she wished she had not said exactly that, added, "You better be back at 4:55."

"Mama," complained Virginia, standing at the gate which she had reached in one jump. She stood there looking at Hallie, who had followed her down the steps.

"Aw, let her come," said May Belle generously. "She can sit in back with Dan." Dan was a large spotted hound dog, who leaned out the back seat, his long tongue hanging and dripping, gazing lovingly toward them all.

Hallie dived into the back seat and tried to force Dan over to the other window. Proud as she was, knowing secretly that she was a daughter of the Old South who had come from a state more aristocratic than Georgia, that poor as they were in the possessions of this world and that Mama and Papa fell far short of being truly shining examples of the Old South, still they were far ahead of the poor white trash in Greenwood even if they did not own a car. When he first arrived in Greenwood Benny had used his Western Union money to buy a stripped-down Ford that would not run. Mama had given him permission because it gave him something to work on, but you could not call it a family car; it would only seat two, and the passenger had to hold on precariously around curves. Now that he had made it run, he was always off fishing.

May Belle slung the car around the corner and Dan slid over and put his head in Hallie's lap and did not want to move. They headed toward Main Street, passed the county jail where Margaret Craig lived, passed the line of stores with no one in view except Lucius Ledbetter sitting on the bench in front of Doc McGhee's store, a lonely figure. As they came toward the depot Hallie and Virginia slunk down out of sight. Papa's frown deepened on Sundays. He had never said they could not go out driving on Sunday, never said it to them directly, but in his Sunday speeches in church he referred to sinners "carousing around in cars" on Sunday, "frolicking around breaking the Sabbath," and laying themselves open to temptations which he did not name directly but which Hallie supposed must be drinking, gambling, dancing and fornication. Better not to let him see them taking the first step, "carousing around in cars." But she rose up again hopefully as they passed Mr. Jess Bailey's store, her dream of him ever present, hopefully looking for him, knowing he would not be there.

A Ford full of boys had fallen in behind them and from it came toots and hoots and yowls. The car would speed up and bump them gently, then pass them in a cloud of dust. May Belle drove expertly, though with many startings and stoppings down the long street of houses, past a field of ripening corn, up a little rise to the schoolhouse. They turned in here, and the Ford ran circles around them, honking and hooting while May Belle swung the car in a turn, then back the same way, past their own house with Mama still reading on the porch and not even looking up.

When they came to the schoolhouse again and May Belle was slinging the car around, Hallie leaned forward. "Where does the road go?" she asked. She motioned to the road which led past the schoolhouse, through fields of yellowing corn, and then vanished in the woods.

"There's really nothing down there," said May Belle. "That's the old back road down to the Big Sandy and on over to Wakefield County. There's really nothing down there unless you count the old Featherstone place, Magnolia Hall. You know Mr. Willy Featherstone, lives with his sister, Miss Beulah, catty-cornered to you folks? That's his old home place."

The town was full of Featherstones; all the houses across the tracks including the one with the fancy F, were occupied by Featherstones. "Is it an old Southern house?" asked Hallie, hope surging in her bosom, and the picture of Greenwood, the vistas, the white columns, the special light that played down from an arching sky, came into her mind again. Montpelier, Montpelier.

"It's a right pretty old place," said May Belle, "kind of a pretty old Southern house. Mr. Barksdale, he's the one who owns the planing mill, he moved here from North Carolina, he bought it and painted it up, fixed up the lawn and everything. Looks real nice now."

The boys had made their circuit in the Ford and started slowly back toward town. "Couldn't we go see the old Featherstone place?" asked Hallie.

"Usually on Sundays we just ride around," said May Belle, as she turned the car toward town. She looked at the Ford that now paused up the road, waiting for them. It moved on again

46

slowly. Then she said, giggling and swinging the wheel, "Maybe it might be fun for us to take a little turn down there."

They drove past the fields of corn, descended a red hill into the woods, crossed a wooden bridge with the hollow slapping sound of rough timber—oh, the immemorial excitement of crossing water—and breathed the damp scent-laden air of the creek bottom. Hallie and Virginia sniffed and oh'd in ecstasy.

"Sweet bay," said May Belle, and Hallie felt suddenly, *sweet bay, sweet bay*; if her picture of Greenwood could be endowed with qualities to please the other senses, sweet bay would be the proper and pervading scent.

When they came up the hill and passed the orchard they saw the house, saw its whiteness, its columns. The huge magnolia trees were in bloom. Two white gateposts marked the driveway and May Belle turned in between them so they could look up the vista of trees and see the house standing there, pure and white as a Greek temple, with square columns instead of the round fluted ones at Montpelier, the balcony of wood rather than ironwork.

"Montpelier," Hallie said.

"No, Magnolia Hall," said May Belle.

Of course . . . Magnolia Hall, and rightly so because of the trees. The trees were more than she had asked for, though she should have known from the name.

"I'll just go in a little way so you can see better. Mr. Barksdale won't care. He's a very nice man," said May Belle, inching the car along the driveway. "He'd just moved in here and got this place all fixed up when his wife died."

Was this where Mr. Barksdale with the crude North Carolina accent lived? Hallie had never suspected it, though she remembered her father had once said that Mr. Barksdale reminded him of Mr. Ely Barton back in Clover, the one who owned the cotton mills and took the trip to California. Mr. Barksdale was the one who had given the stained-glass window to the church, the Good

Samaritan window back of the choir. Under the picture it said, "In Loving Memory, Adelaide Wingate Barksdale, Friend to the Friendless."

"Does Mr. Barksdale live in this big old house all by himself?" asked Virginia.

"He has a daughter, Miss Corrine Barksdale. She's real pretty. You ought to see her. Just finished GSCW. I think Mr. Barksdale wants her to come back here and keep house for him. He almost gave up this place, he felt so terrible when Mrs. Barksdale died. His daughter's always off visiting up there in North Carolina where they come from."

May Belle moved the car slowly up the driveway, stalling in the sand and racing the motor to start again. Back of the shrubs that edged the roadway there was a sweep of lawn up to the magnolias, and just in front of the magnolias there was a little white house. White birds flew straight up from it, then veered and swerved as May Belle backed and stalled.

As the car quieted, the birds settled down again on the house, spread their tails, and marched nervously in and out of the square holes.

"How darling," said Hallie. "What a darling little house."

"That's a dovecote," said May Belle. "I reckon there's lots of old houses like this, but this is the only one I know has a dovecote."

"Did Mr. Barksdale bring it from North Carolina?" asked Hallie, then thought it unlikely that North Carolina, "Yankee Carolina," as they called it over in Clover, could produce anything so fine.

"No, that's a real old dovecote," said May Belle. "It was here when Mr. Willy Featherstone was a boy, I hear, maybe even when his father was a boy. They say the dovecote's old as the house."

"I don't see why Mr. Willy Featherstone would want to leave a place like this," said Hallie, immediately picturing it as it must have been in the old days, with gracious gentlemen and ladies walking among the magnolias, chatting to each other on intellectual subjects, often breaking into Greek and Latin, sitting on the porch listening while someone played the rosewood piano inside the long windows, old-time darkies bringing refreshments at the proper moment and being thanked graciously by the ladies and gentlemen, ever thoughtful, ever kind. In the mornings one of the young women, the one with the sweetest face, would go off to the Negro cabins and teach the little black children their lessons, just as Meh Lady did in Thomas Nelson Page's story.

"Pa says Mr. Willy really hated to give it up. His family built it long years ago," May Belle said.

As if the beauty of the place made her more vulnerable, tears sprang to Hallie's eyes at the thought of Mr. Willy Featherstone bidding the old place farewell.

"Mr. Willy Featherstone used to keep white horses too," said May Belle, and Hallie took the white horses and fitted them immediately into her dream; they pranced in the clover field there beyond the magnolias, their pink nostrils flaring, their hoofs gleaming as black and shiny as her patent leather shoes just after being rubbed with a biscuit.

"Maybe we ought to go on back now," said Virginia. "I didn't hear the train whistle but it must be past time."

"I reckon the boys think we been swallowed up," giggled May Belle, as she backed out of the driveway.

They turned toward town, and Hallie tried to ignore Dan's hot body next to hers as she leaned out the window in the hollow taking great gulps of the bay-laden air to last her on the drive back. Then she settled against the seat, thinking of Magnolia Hall, the magnolias, the dovecote, and the white horses. She thought sadly again of Mr. Willy Featherstone who lived now in that common house near hers. To think that she had watched him as he came and went and then dismissed him as of no interest whatsoever.

May Belle slowed the car to a crawl and together she and Virginia said, "M-m-mm?" A young man was getting out of a car in front of Miss Lizzie Wallace's boarding house. Someone handed a suitcase out to him, and as they passed slowly they could see him swing the suitcase rakishly over his shoulder as he leaned to talk to the people inside the car, a flash of a brown face, crisp curly hair.

May Belle had come to a sitting-up position behind the wheel; she drew in her breath as they passed by.

"I guess Miss Lizzie's getting a new boarder," said Virginia.

"I saw him first," said May Belle.

But Hallie dismissed him for all his rakish good looks in favor of Mr. Jess Bailey whose noble figure was enthroned in her heart. Then, because she was discouraged with Mr. Jess and his preoccupation with kaolin and was tired of waiting for him, she put him to one side and thought of Mr. Willy Featherstone, born and brought up in Magnolia Hall, the only Southern mansion in Greenwood, a Southern mansion with a dovecote and magnolia trees. Poor Mr. Willy Featherstone had been dislodged by an interloper, Mr. Barksdale from North Carolina, who lived there with his cold and haughty daughter, Miss Corrine. Ah, we are alike, Mr. Willy Featherstone and I; both dislodged from our rightful homes; I from Montpelier, years back, by the War, and he, more recently, by some skulduggery on the part of Mr. Barksdale. Mr. Barksdale had money; he could buy Magnolia Hall and a stained-glass window for his wife, but that did not mean he *belonged* in Magnolia Hall. Oh, Mr. Willy Featherstone, she thought, taking him to her bosom. Why should he have been turned out of Montpelier and Paradise?

5

Mr. Willy Featherstone was a small man with a red face that made his blue eyes seem very blue. Compared to his sister, Miss Beulah, he seemed frail; his pants hung slack on his hips; his chest was a little caved in under his tie; his Adam's apple was like a swallowed pear. He wore a tie today, as if he were going somewhere or had just been, and a shiny black alpaca coat, although the day was hot. Hallie made these observations next morning when she went to call on him, pretending she had come to inquire about Miss Beulah, who had passed their house a half-hour before.

Mr. Featherstone was in the swing in the breezeway, and Hallie realized as she stood on the top step that, poor as the house was, this porch was not a bad spot to be in hot weather. The planks were weathered a cool silver gray, and green light sifted through the magnolia (one magnolia to remind him of Magnolia Hall). If any breeze came at all Mr. Featherstone would catch it there in the swing; he did not look as if he ever swung vigorously enough to stir up a breeze of his own.

"Miss Beulah?" he said, leaning forward with a kind of bow and motioning Hallie onto the porch, into a chair or the other swing, his generous arm sweep including all. "Now, you know Miss Beulah. Why she flew out of here whilst ago, said she was going down the street to see Miss Lizzie Wallace; you know

Miss Lizzie where your Papa had board and room when he first come. Miss Lizzie's got some new boarders now. Then whilst she's down there, I imagine Miss Beulah will have some other business to take care of . . ."

He laughed a little, and a brown stain appeared at one corner of his mouth. Hallie waited, expecting him to stop and spit, but he only swallowed hard.

"Thank you, sir," said Hallie, feeling with one bare foot for a lower step. She was sorry to see that he chewed, but if he chewed he ought to spit. It was dangerous to swallow tobacco. "Mama just wondered if Miss Beulah were at home. Reckon we may see her later."

She cut across the yard under the magnolia and into the road where the dry dust gushed like mud between her toes and left her feet red. Sitting there in his swing, Mr. Featherstone did not look like a man born and raised in a Southern mansion with a dovecote, a man whose family had specialized in white horses. She stood there puddling her feet in the dust and thinking, seeing the white horses switching their tails beyond the fence in the clover field next to Magnolia Hall. She could see Mr. Featherstone as a boy, fair of hair and bright of eye, standing in front of the dovecote, the doves throbbing their four notes of well being, like small satisfied kittens purring. She had said last night, after Papa left the table, that she had seen white doves fly up from the dovecote down at Mr. Willy Featherstone's old home place.

"There's no such thing as a white dove," said Benny. "They must be pigeons."

"Why do they call it dovecote then?" she had asked, and thought at once that pigeoncote did not sound as good. Dovecote, dovecote, a word like the call of the dove far away in the woods on a spring morning.

"You couldn't get doves to live in a dovecote," said Benny. "They're wild birds." Benny ought to know. Back in Clover every once in a while he would go hunting and bring home a few limp

52

gray birds, their feathers ruffled, little feet frozen into claws. She always turned them down when they appeared on the table. Even the gravy seemed to be full of bird shot.

All right then, they were not doves, they were pigeons. But doves in a dovecote sounded better and went better with Magnolia Hall.

One day Mr. Featherstone had been a man of an uninteresting age and unexceptionable demeanor who lived across the street. Now he had a light shining on him, like the shaft of light breaking through a cloud in a Bible picture, on Jacob about to climb the ladder, or on David going forth to meet Goliath. The light was a reflection of that brilliant white Southern mansion, Magnolia Hall, as good or better than Montpelier, and it shone on the man who had been born and bred there. Seeing him in that bright light, suddenly everyone seemed to be talking about him. There was Miss Lill McGhee, waiting, as Hallie returned, by the sweet shrub, just waiting as if she knew what was in Hallie's mind. Did Mr. Featherstone descend his steps at that moment, pulling on a flat straw hat purposefully like a man set to go about the business of the day, and did Miss Lill happen to glimpse him out of the corner of one eye? Or did she simply see him there on his porch, idly swinging?

As Hallie paused near her and Mama to pick a sweet shrub, bruising its brown petals and smelling it, Miss Lill said, "You never would think, now would you, Mrs. Jones, that old Mr. Willy Featherstone—lives over yonder with Miss Beulah—you never would think, would you, that that old man useter be one of the fanciest horse riders around here. Seeing him now, I mean, would you ever imagine him and his family owned a whole stable full of horses and that Mr. Willy was able to tame 'em and ride 'em, no matter how obstreperous? He even went into horse races and won prizes. You oughter hear old Gus carry on about him." She waved across the street where an old Negro man was poking around among the japonicas on her lawn. "Old Gus said, oh, they were really high-spirited horses they had in those days, and white, why they were white as milk ever' one of 'em. Old Gus, though I guess he was young Gus then, he said Mr. Willy'd take fifty cents from his pocket and throw it at him when he'd open the gate for him and if he missed it, Mr. Willy'd reach in his pocket and grab another and throw that at him as he went out the gate and down the road lickety-split. And fifty cents in those days! Why, that was a lot of money . . ." Miss Lill stopped to draw breath.

This scene fitted perfectly into the landscape Hallie had dreamed for Magnolia Hall in the glory of its past. Against the background of the house itself, the dovecote and doves, the magnolias, the white horses prancing in the clover field, young Willy Featherstone on his milk-white horse rode as gallantly as Marse Phil on his horse Paladin in Thomas Nelson Page's story "Meh Lady."

She climbed the tree house after Miss Lill had gone back across the street, took the stained M. D. and S. paper out of a tin bread box she used to protect it from showers. At the top of the page she wrote in capitals, MAGNOLIA HALL. Under it she drew a straight line dividing the page in half. On one side she wrote "Mr. F." (Benny and Virginia were without honor when they found writing obviously not intended for their eyes.) Under "Mr. F." she wrote "born in Southern mansion," "dovecote and doves," "white horses," "incident of horse and fifty cents" (showing that he was free with money, perhaps generous to a fault). And on the other side of the line she wrote "Mr. B." for Barksdale and underneath his name "rich." She chewed her pencil and wrote "has daughter Miss C.," and then a question mark, for although she could very well imagine the haughty Miss Corrine, she had not seen her and until she had, in all honesty she had to put a question mark. But that reminded her that Mr. Willy Featherstone had a sister, a peasant sister, Miss Beulah, who gave not the slightest indication that she had been born in a Southern mansion. She wrote in the "Mr. F." column in small letters, "Miss B."

Where did Mr. F. go every morning? He left his house,

purposefully pulling on his straw hat, and went down the sidewalk beyond the orchard toward town. The train had gone up to Macon, whistling good-by as it passed the Negro schoolhouse. The next day Hallie descended the tree and followed Mr. F. at a discreet distance, kicking the sand on the sidewalk with her bare feet, killing time by pausing to study the massed wires going into Mr. Victor Ambrose's house where he ran the telephone company in his dining room.

Mr. F. passed out of sight around the corner by McGhee's Drug Store and Hallie moved on faster and when she too turned the corner a minute later she drew up short because there was Mr. F. sitting on a wooden bench in front of the drug store. On the window was written in golden script, "J. S. McGhee, Gen'l Merchandise, From the Cradle to the Grave." Having seen him walk to town so purposefully, she did not expect to see him sitting on the bench; she expected to see him, well . . . perhaps doing some business at the cotton warehouse, or buying stamps for an important letter. She halted for a minute scratching her bare toes into the rough brick sidewalk, and Mr. F. waved his arm with the same hospitable gesture he had used on his porch. "Set," he said. Hallie sat. "Hot," he said, though he did not mop his brow, and his red face was no redder than usual. Hallie murmured the appropriate answer and sat, her bare feet folded under the bench, toes seeking out the curved grooves in the bricks of the sidewalk. The tin awnings built over the wide sidewalk gave her a feeling of sitting back in a cool cave and looking out at the sizzling street. Across the street, across the tracks and the paved road leading from Macon to Dublin, the Confederate monument glinted in the bright sun.

"That's my pa," said Mr. F., looking in the same direction.

"Sure enough," Hallie said quietly, trying not to show the flutter of excitement she felt. This fitted into the picture exactly. Oh, he did belong in Magnolia Hall. Now she was sure. Mr. F.'s father had been one of that brave band of Southern heroes who had gone off to fight against dreadful odds, their ladies in the doorways of the white Southern mansions, fluttering their hand-

55

kerchiefs in farewell, waiting to use them for crying after the heroes had safely ridden away.

A truck loaded with logs roared by in the direction of the planing mill, Mr. Barksdale's truck, Mr. Barksdale's logs, and the guinea hens in the vetch patch across the highway flew screaming into the air.

And as if he encompassed the town by his wealth, by his power, Mr. Barksdale himself came by, said, "Good morning, Mr. Featherstone," and continued on his way toward the Courthouse. Mr. F. grunted a good morning, not the usual courtly "Good morning, good morning" with which he favored others. "Ah, hah!" Hallie felt like saying. She framed a question with some care so that he could not consider her prying. "I saw Mr. Barksdale's house, Magnolia Hall, last Sunday," she said. "Sure is a pretty old place."

"Uh huh."

"It's the prettiest house around here," she added, thinking he would feel this to be a compliment. (After all it *had* been his house, was built by his ancestors.)

"Guess if you got the money you can have pretty much what you want in this world," he said. "You can come down in here, buy anything you want, whether folks like it or not. Lord, if you got the money . . ."

He did not finish his sentence, but drew his handkerchief out of his pocket. He seemed to be working on himself for an appearance at an important interview. He wiped his mouth carefully and blew his nose, waved his handkerchief in the air, and then folded it into a neat square. "Well," he said standing, "guess I better get on about my business." She stood, too, murmuring something about seeing Papa at the depot, trying to give some reason for being there at all. Should she continue down the street? He might think she was trying to trail along like a child, hoping for a handout of some kind, a candy bar or Cracker Jack. Down the street Miss Toulou Vass came out of the cotton warehouse, passed the group of men who always hung around its door and moved with her little dancing steps toward the post office. Then Benny turned Mr. Jess Bailey's corner in his stripped-down Ford, backfiring and stirring up dust, and pulled in next the bench in front of the post office. She did not want Benny to see her and ask why she was mooning around downtown with Mr. Willy Featherstone.

"Thank you," she said again, and walked out into the bright street, across the tracks and highway to the monument. This was not her first visit; she had paid her respects soon after they had arrived, but now that she knew the soldier carved in stone on the pedestal, knew he was Mr. F.'s gallant father, he had a new light shining on him too. She pushed through the dusty brown weeds at the foot of the monument. The inscription on the marble, read once before and forgotten, struck now with the force of a poem. "Featherstone Fusileers . . . In memoriam, heroes of Plum Branch County, Fourth Regiment, First Company, Featherstone Fusileers, Captain W. B. Featherstone." Beneath, carved in noble script:

PATRIOTS

Who, Animated by the same Faith and Actuated by the same Love of Country, Beset with the same Trials and Dangers, Endured with the same Fortitude, and fought as Heroically to Maintain Local Self-Government as the Colonial Fathers to Attain the Same and with them Immortalized in the same Halo of Glory.

At the words "Halo of Glory" tears came to Hallie's eyes. She read on, tears veiling the words, her nose running.

> But their memories shall remain for us
> Their names bright names without stain for us
> The glory they won shall not wane for us
> In legend or lay
> Our heroes in gray
> Shall forever live over again for us.

She looked around to see if anyone in front of the filling station was watching, then wiped her nose on the hem of her dress. "Heroes in gray—" Heroes of the same breed as Paul Revere, the Minute Men, Launcelot, Galahad, Charlemagne, David fighting against Goliath—and among these heroes in gray was the father of Mr. Willy Featherstone. And Mr. F. who should have succeeded to that "halo of glory" and all its perquisites was now disbarred from Magnolia Hall, his rightful home. He lived in an unpainted house with his peasant sister, his place at Magnolia Hall usurped by a rich man from North Carolina, Mr. Barksdale. It was not fair, and her tears flowed, and quickly she blew her nose again.

She did not follow Mr. F. on through town that morning. She turned and went home the way she had come, climbed into the tree house and wrote in her notes under "Mr. F."—in the left-hand column—"father, captain of Featherstone Fusileers." She chewed her pencil and shaded in "Featherstone Fusileers," did a stick figure of a soldier with a musket, and after a while saw Mr. F. return up the sidewalk and disappear into the house carrying a newspaper under his arm. His dinner must be ready. Then she heard Mama calling her to come.

6

Miss Beulah. What could be said for Miss Beulah? She was Mr. F.'s sister, and therefore Captain William Featherstone's daughter, therefore of noble blood. She too had been born and bred in Magnolia Hall. Of course she left it many years ago, for although she was always referred to as Miss Beulah, Hallie knew that she was really Mrs. Vance, and that she had several grown sons and daughters with children of their own scattered about the county. Miss Beulah had been a regular visitor at their house since the afternoon they arrived, except for periods when she went off to visit one of her sons or daughters.

Next morning, when Miss Beulah called at the front door, "Anybody home?" and came on down the hall to the kitchen, Hallie looked at her with fresh eyes, trying to see the white mansion and hero father reflected in her too. Miss Beulah was short and almost square, built a little like a bulldog, her head outthrust on her short neck, her round face showing some crisis of complexion long past, some crisis that had left its impress of pockmarks and crevices. (Mama said pellagra.) Even imagining her younger and slimmer, she still did not seem like the kind of girl whose brother, Marse William, cut such a handsome figure on his horse Paladin.

Elberta was busy in the bedrooms, and Mama stood at the end of the kitchen table kneading bread, pushing the dough away and then bringing it back to her, slapping it against the bread board.

"Nice to see you, Miss Beulah," Mama said, as if Miss Beulah's visit were a rare and unusual occasion. "Can't you stop and sit a while?"

"Can't stay more than minute, anyhow," said Miss Beulah, settling down in a rocker near the table. "I'm on my way down to Lizzie Wallace's to see how she is this mornin. I told her she shouldn't . . . I said, Lizzie, if Royal Wallace could see you he'd turn over in his grave, but she went ahead . . . you can't give Lizzie Wallace advice, though she's always askin for it. She went ahead and took two. There she is down there, alone in her house with two *of* them. I declare, Bubber and I just can't see how she can do it. Some mornin she's goin to wake up and find out she's . . ." Miss Beulah looked at Hallie and went on guardedly, "she's goin to wake up and find out she's shown mighty poor judgment."

Hallie stayed to listen now. She had heard without listening many conversations between Mama and Miss Beulah, from the tree house, or in the kitchen. When she was present Miss Beulah would look at her questioningly, then look at Mama, and then go on talking in a curious shorthand apparently intended to deceive.

"Two what?" asked Mama, sticking her hand in a bucket of Snowdrift and greasing the brown bowl. She brushed some stray hairs back from her face with the back of her hand, holding her hand as if it were a bird claw, a claw that had stepped in dough. "I don't know what you're talking about, Miss Beulah." Hallie considered Miss Beulah's usual fears: snakes, Negroes. It seemed unlikely that Miss Lizzie Wallace would have two of either in her house spending the night.

"Highway men," exhaled Miss Beulah. "Two of them fellows workin on that new stretch of road up there near Verdery." She rolled her eyes toward Hallie who leaned against the porch door, as much as to say, well, really, I don't think I should go on. Mama gave the bread another punch, laid it in the brown bowl, covered it with a dishtowel, and put it on the range reservoir.

"I'm all through here for a little while," she said. "Let's go out to the porch. It's cooler."

"I really can't stay," said Miss Beulah on the porch, but she sat down in a rocking chair, and Mama sat down near her. Hallie crept over to the swing and sat down, carefully, carefully, putting her toes down to keep the swing from moving and creaking. She sat there making herself small and insignificant.

"Now," said Mama, "what was that about the highway men?"

"Why, Lizzie Wallace took in two of them," said Miss Beulah, as if it really were snakes. Now Hallie remembered the young man getting out of a car on Sunday when they were out riding with May Belle Ballard, and May Belle had said she saw him first. "She's furnishin room and board. They got the same room

60

Mr. Jones had when he roomed down there. And I just heard yestiddy that one of them is the brother of that highway man ran off with Mary Emily Cartledge."

"Cartledge?" said Mama. "Kin to Mr. Shadrack Cartledge down at the cotton warehouse?"

Yes, Mr. Shadrack Cartledge leaned against the big door of the cotton warehouse in the middle of the block of stores. He looked unhappy and dissatisfied, nevertheless tall and darkly handsome as St. Elmo in Augusta Evans Wilson's book. Miss Toulou Vass who played the piano in church worked there too, acting as a kind of office girl to him.

"That's him," said Miss Beulah. "It was his wife, Mary Emily, ran off with the highway man. She's sister to Miss Toulou Vass. She was Mary Emily Vass before she was married to Shadrack, brought up just as nice . . . I declare . . ." Miss Beulah shook her head. "Well, I told Lizzie Wallace, I said, Lizzie, you don't know what may happen to you some night, you alone in there with those two highway men."

She rolled her popped gray eyes toward Hallie, and Hallie guessed that she meant Miss Lizzie Wallace might lose her virtue although she was uncertain that that was the right term to use about a lady as old as Miss Lizzie Wallace, who had had two husbands and a son who had absconded with funds from the cotton gin and gone to the dogs in Macon. (Miss Beulah's very words.)

"I didn't know Mr. Shadrack Cartledge was married," said Mama. Mama always had to get everything perfectly straight.

"Oh, yes, he *was* married, but I reckon he's divorced now," said Miss Beulah. "Let's see now, it happened two, three summers ago, long before you folks come. Shadrack Cartledge went off fishin down to the Big Sandy. He went off down there, with two three other fellows; you know that crowd, do more drinkin than fishin . . . Jess Bailey" (Mr. Jess drinking?) "S. C. Vermillion, Sam Johnson. He said he was goin to be gone several days. And he would a been, I reckon, but a accident occurred. S. C. Vermillion, you must've seen him around town, dynamited a creek down there, guess he just threw the dynamite in the creek like a firecracker and he didn throw fast enough, and he blew off part of his arm. So then the fishin trip was over, sooner than they expected, and they come flyin up through here on their way to Macon, S.C. bleedin like a stuck pig. He near about bled to death before they got him to Macon, he's just got a stump now. He got elected to the Legislature right afterwards; one of the best we ever had up there in Atlanta."

Miss Beulah had run down. She paused now to breathe. Hallie wanted to say, "Go on about Miss Lizzie," but Miss Beulah had gotten completely away from Miss Lizzie and the highway men.

Mama brought her back. "You were telling about Mr. Shadrack Cartledge . . ."

"Oh, yes, well, he come drivin up here with the fishermen, but he figgered he didn need to go to Macon too, so he got out down yonder at the crossroads and walked out to his house, he was covered with blood where S.C. had bled all over him and everybody else . . . Anyhow he walked out to his house and come in the front door and saw a man's hat, so he picked up his shotgun off the hat rack and walked on out to the bedroom and there was a man just jumped out of bed . . ." Here Miss Beulah leaned toward Mama and whispered, "Buck naked," and rolled her eyes, her popped gray eyes, milky as marbles. "He was reachin for his pants and when he saw Mr. Shadrack he just flew out the back door like a shot out of a cannon holdin onto his pants. Mary Emily, she jumped up out of bed, tried to grab aholt of the gun, and they had a little tussle there and then Shadrack pulled away from her and went on out the back door and let fly at that highway man just takin off across the cotton patch, wearin nothin in the world but his birthday suit." Here Miss Beulah looked slyly at Hallie as if she were spelling a word to confuse a small child. "Well, Shadrack just let fly with that shotgun and filled that highway man full of bird shot. Lord, I bet he's pickin bird shot out of his backside yet."

She stopped for breath and fanned herself with her straw hat as if the telling had warmed her up.

"I declare, Miss Beulah," Mama said, laughing, leaning back and laughing hard, but more as if she enjoyed Miss Beulah's telling than as if she condoned the story. If she were asked, Mama would be sure to say that she thought such carryings-on were low and vulgar, beneath the standards of the Jones family certainly, and yet she seemed to enjoy hearing Miss Beulah talk. Mama was a little vulgar too, you could see. Now she stopped laughing and said, sobering up, "Did Mr. Shadrack do anything to his wife?"

"Nieuw, Mary Emily was so mad at him for comin back like that . . . She kept sayin to him, or so I hear, 'What you mean sneakin back out here before you said you was comin? I hate a man don't stay away when he says he's goin to.' She left him too. Left that beautiful old house . . ."

"Went off with the fellow got the bird shot?" asked Mama.

"Nieuw"—Miss Beulah pronounced no as if she had learned it from a cat—"oh, nieuw, she went off with *another* highway man, man named McClure, brother to this one I been tellin you about, stayin down at Lizzie's. Frank, I think his name was. The one down at Lizzie's is Boyce—Boyce McClure."

"It seems kind of hard on the highway man, to get shot like a bird when after all Miss Mary Emily was half to blame," said Mama, trying to be fair.

"Yes, some folks say Shadrack shot the wrong bird, but Bubber says—you really ought to hear Bubber on the subject—he says, 'A Southern gentleman must protect his honor.' "

A phrase reverberated, tingled, in Hallie's mind . . . *left that beautiful old house.* In her excitement she took her foot from the floor and the swing creaked and Miss Beulah and Mama stared at her as if she had just flown in.

"Where does Mr. Shadrack live?" she asked. She might as well ask now they recognized she was here.

"He lives out on the Abbeville Road . . . Cartledge Old Home Place."

"Is it like Magnolia Hall?" asked Hallie, holding her breath, holding the swing still to receive the answer.

"Just like Magnolia Hall. An old ante-bellum mansion," said Miss Beulah. "But Shadrack just let it go to rack and ruin. He kind of camps out in it now, since Mary Emily left. He don't even keep a cook. He goes with Ada Pratt, but . . ."

As she had listened to the story told by Miss Beulah she had pictured the drama taking place in an ordinary house. Now, with an old Southern house for its setting, it seemed to be a different drama. Mr. Shadrack seemed even more like St. Elmo, a handsome devil of a man, coming home covered with the blood of his friend, finding his wife unfaithful. In the ballads the unfaithful wife would die and a red rose grow from her grave.

Miss Beulah went back to the subject of Miss Lizzie and the highway men. "They ast me about takin in some of them," she said. "Two of them even came round and looked at our spare room. Bubber told me later he wouldn have such riffraff on the place."

Elberta came to the door and said to Mama, "You through with the bread board, Mrs. Jones?"

"That's right, Elberta. You can wash it now."

Miss Beulah said to Mama in a low voice, "You ast her yet?"

"No."

"She's from the Dewy Rose Community just like those two highway men." Miss Beulah jumped to her feet as if a rattlesnake had slithered from beneath her rocking chair. "Boyce McClure! Why Boyce McClure is brother of Frank and naturally that means he's a son of Wake McClure. You know Wake McClure; he owns more land than anybody else in Middle Georgia. He practically owns the Dewy Rose part of Plum Branch County."

Miss Beulah had a look of horror on her face that did not seem to go with the simple accounting of acres and wealth. She fanned herself rapidly with her straw hat, then absent-mindedly jammed it down on her head. "Wouldn it be terrible . . . You know I never did tell you who Elberta's father is . . . but wouldn it be terrible if one of his own sons . . ." She became even redder in the face and moved toward the steps. She stopped and looked hard at Mama again. "You sure you didn't ask her?"

"I figured it was none of my business," said Mama.

"Oh," said Miss Beulah, "I really must hurry. To think that one of Wake McClure's own sons might be the one . . ." She positively moaned with horror (or pleasure). Hallie realized now that Miss Beulah thought Boyce McClure might have been tempted by Elberta to fornication. Yet neither party looked the part assigned to them by Miss Beulah; Elberta seemed too shy to tempt anyone, and Boyce McClure looked more as if he would do the tempting.

"Hallie honey, do me a favor. Go tell Mr. Willy I won't be home for dinner." Miss Beulah stopped briefly at the gate, then turned in the direction of Miss Lizzie Wallace's.

Mama laughed as they stood watching the solid figure stumping down to the corner. Mama said, "There's someone she reminds me of."

"Aunt Rose?" asked Hallie, though she could not tell why.

"Yes," Mama said and whispered, "but don't tell your father I said so. Your Aunt Rose and Miss Beulah really are birds of a feather."

Aunt Rose had more dignity. She knew about the Old South and its heritage. She had located the Jones' coat of arms. Aunt Rose put on at times, with her crazy Charleston accent and her talk of Huguenot ancestors. Mama had always laughed at her. But on the other hand Aunt Rose did not think much of Mama either. She seemed to hold it against Mama that her family had never owned slaves, seemed to give the impression that Papa had married beneath him.

What about Miss Beulah, then? Hallie climbed to the tree house to try to fit her into Magnolia Hall. Miss Beulah certainly held her brother in great respect, though calling him "Bubber" was not dignified. But she quoted him often; he pointed the moral, if any, to her stories.

65

"A Southern gentleman always protects his honor" might have come right out of Thomas Nelson Page. Hallie wrote it down in the left-hand column under "Mr. F." "Just like gettin a watermelon through a keyhole" was another of Mr. F.'s summaries. Hallie winced at that one and did not write it down.

Miss Beulah did not act at all as if she had come from Magnolia Hall. She was not a Southern lady. Mama liked to hear her talk, but Mama thought she was silly. She was not even as much of a Southern lady as Mama. "Could not have been born in Magnolia Hall," she wrote in the column under "Miss Beulah." "Perhaps adopted?"

Magnolia Hall, Magnolia Hall. The words made almost as sweet a chime now as Montpelier, Montpelier. The bells swaying gently in her mind made her think of something pleasant. *That beautiful old house like Magnolia Hall.* She turned to a fresh page of M. D. and S. paper and wrote down CARTLEDGE OLD HOME PLACE.

7

Hallie was disappointed in Mr. Willy Featherstone. As she walked back across the street after giving him the message from Miss Beulah she wished he did not talk the way he did. He had giggled and called his sister a "cutter." It did not fit in with

Magnolia Hall. His manners were beautiful; his way of bowing and saying "Good morning, good morning" might come straight out of Thomas Nelson Page. But he was not robust or tall, not physically accomplished like those Virginia planters of the Old South who rode, dueled, fought, practiced law and ran a plantation, all skillfully and with equal ease. Mr. F. did not fit that picture. He did have a glorious past, however—i. e., Magnolia Hall and his horse Paladin. Perhaps she was at fault some way. She did not inspire him conversationally; he felt he must stoop to talk to her, felt she would not understand classical allusions or Latin and Greek quotations. Perhaps he had looked her family over and decided they were not worth the effort. Oh, if only she were like Edna Earl in *St. Elmo*, able to turn the conversation immediately to learned discourse.

The next morning, resolved to improve her mind, she went to the tree house early with *Greek Drama* from the Harvard Classics. Through the tunnel of leaves she could observe Mr. F. in his swing. She still did not know how he spent his days. There was a possibility that he managed his affairs at a time when she had not yet observed him. When she saw him start for town she descended too, leaving *Greek Drama* hanging on a limb. She found her sandals and started for town in the opposite direction. She would have to be careful. Last night at supper she had giggled when Mama got after Benny for saying "Shut up," and he had said in retaliation, "Mama, what's Hallie always hanging around downtown for? Every time I go down she's either mooning on that bench in front of Mr. Jess Bailey's store or hanging around with Mr. Willy Featherstone." That was unfair; he only could have seen her with Mr. F. that one time, and she had not stopped in front of Mr. Jess Bailey's store for more than a week now.

Virginia, given encouragement or reminded, said, "Mama, don't you think Hallie should wear dresses that cover her knees? They're so *bony*."

67

"She's just a child," said Mama in her offhand voice, not wanting to encourage anybody.

"She's going to have feet big as a nigger field hand's if she doesn't wear shoes," said Virginia.

"Hush," said Mama. "Haven't I taught you not to talk like that?"

Hallie now had time to look at her feet in the sandals as she meandered along, trying to imagine Mr. F.'s gait and speed on the other side of the block. Her feet were not excessively big, but they were broad. Virginia's feet were long and narrow, and Virginia said narrowness was what counted. None of them had feet as small as Mama's. She wore a size three and a half and could buy bargains of sample shoes. Mama's feet were really Southern; they really could be described as " 'bout as big as two little white ears of popcorn," like Meh Lady in the Thomas Nelson Page story. But there Mama's resemblance to a Southern aristocrat stopped. Moving upward from her feet, there was no doubt that she was bowlegged. Her legs were well-shaped but she walked bowlegged as a cowboy. "Too many children," Mama said; "lost all my calcium." Her light brown hair was sloppily arranged, little tendrils constantly escaping from her loose knot down her neck, tendrils that once, Hallie remembered, she had loved to wind about her finger and arrange in little curls. Now the escaping locks irritated her and she would often have to say, "Mama, your hair needs pinning up." If she had remained quiet, had not called attention to herself, Hallie could have accepted her looks. But she talked in a loud, eager voice—too loud. Oh, sometimes, Hallie thought, cringing inside at Mama's exuberance, sometimes she was sure that she, Hallie, was the only member of the family who knew or cared anything about the Old South, the only one who remained faithful to Clover, the only one who really suffered here.

Miss Ada Pratt sailed into view on Schoolhouse Street and Hallie slowed her pace to let her get to the intersection first and turn toward town. Miss Ada Pratt, the paramour of darkly hand-some Shadrack Cartledge who was the owner of "that beauti-ful old house" abandoned by the impetuous Miss Mary Emily. Miss Ada Pratt appeared downtown every morning just after the train went up to Macon, about 10:22 to be exact, on her way to work in Mr. George Bullard's store. She was a tall woman, a big woman, and now she moved slowly and sedately toward town, her bosom riding high and shelflike in front, the rest of her body below stiff and straight. Her hair was the color that green walnut hulls make on the hands, hennaed, Hallie was sure; still it looked as if Miss Ada achieved the effect herself with a year-round stock of green walnut hulls. She wore her hair pompadoured high in front and carried back to a great coil held in place with tortoise-shell hairpins, almost the same color as her hair. She walked in the measured pace of a woman who carried a load on top of her head; perhaps she had to walk that way to keep from shaking down the edifice of hair. The only time Mama had ever told Hallie sharply to go play or go read was when Miss Beulah had started in on Miss Ada Pratt. Wondering, Hallie decided that Mama did not like it that Miss Ada Pratt did not have babies. She never sent Hallie away when Miss Beulah was telling a story about a girl who had lost her virtue and then had a baby.

Miss Ada lived down toward the end of Schoolhouse Street with her father, an old man who was bedridden and blind and lay in a back room yodeling all day. He had gone away, had left Miss Ada and her mother long years ago when Miss Ada was a little girl, had gone out West and worked, learned to play the guitar and yodel. Then when he got sick and almost went blind he came back to Greenwood and said, "Here I am, honey, here's your papa."

"She didn even know him," said Miss Beulah. "He could of been lyin as far as she was concerned. But course we all recognized him. He was Selby Pratt and no mistakin him, even though he was a mighty sick man and changed. You got to hand it to Ada;

with all her faults she took him in, and now she has to go down there to Bullard's store and work to pay for Clara, that nigger woman who takes care of him."

"Why doesn't Miss Ada marry Mr. Shadrack?" Mama asked once. "Haven't I seen them keeping company?"

"Ada don't want to *marry* anybody. She could of married before. Lord, there's always been men around Ada Pratt, too many men. She . . ." And that was when Mama had sent Hallie from the room. If Mr. Shadrack married her, Hallie thought now, he would take her to live in his Southern mansion, wherever it was.

Miss Ada disappeared around the corner at Bailey's store and a moment later when Hallie rounded the corner she saw Mr. Jess Bailey's horse tied to the chinaberry tree. Her knees went soft; a curdling took place in her stomach. Could this be the day? She wanted to collapse from sheer weakness on the bench but she did not dare. She walked slowly, very slowly, stopped and patted Lady, murmured to her, "Someday, someday," then moved on as slowly as she could and still move, hoping any minute to hear the screen door open and a voice say, "Why there's Hallie! Hey, Hallie, today's the day . . ." But there was not a sound from the store. They might all be sleeping inside. The only sound was from up the street, the sudden loud laughter of Mr. Buck Ducket squatting with the group in front of the cotton warehouse. She moved on toward the post office and sat down on the bench in front of it. From there she could survey the street in both directions.

Mr. Buck Ducket's laughter roared out again, laughter that seemed to go with his great red bull neck and his red hair. The Duckets were newcomers to Greenwood too, though earlier than Hallie's family; they had come with Mr. Barksdale. Everybody else had always been here. Ever since that first Sunday in church when Laura Fitzgerald had said, "Oh, I thought you were a Ducket," Hallie had kept an eye on the Duckets to see how they compared. The more she knew of the Duckets the less she liked Laura Fitzgerald. There was a great tribe of them. Miss Beulah said that Bubber said that ten years from now there wouldn't be anybody in this town but Duckets. Seeing Mr. Buck Ducket, big and red and full of loud laughter, it seemed possible. Benny loved to tell about Mr. Buck. He had bitten off the tip of a man's nose in a fight up in North Carolina, and he told Virginia that Mr. Buck had said down in front of the cotton warehouse about someone he did not like, "Why, if he don't act right I'll just put his head between my legs and f-a-r-t it right off." Benny had spelled the word out to Virginia. Hallie did not know the rest of them except as tobacco-spitting men or snuff-dipping women. They traded in town on Saturdays and went to the Methodist Church on Sundays.

Miss Toulou Vass emerged suddenly from the door of the cotton warehouse and came toward the post office. Oh, Miss Toulou Vass was a golden girl with Rapunzel hair, thick and heavy and shining; it hung halfway down her back so her hump could not be seen easily. She always wore full middy blouses and pleated skirts (on Sundays they were of silk), and from the front and from a distance she looked like a girl in school. Close up, however, her face, though it was beautiful with its golden skin and downy golden hairs and long golden lashes, was not young. She walked to the post office now, moving to a tune she was humming, her full-pleated skirt swaying a little above her patent leather one-strap shoes. Did Miss Mary Emily Cartledge look like her? No wonder the highway men and Mr. Shadrack had loved her. How strange that Miss Toulou continued to work for Mr. Shadrack. Her sister had run away from him, even divorced him and married another man, yet every day Miss Toulou was there in the shade of the cotton warehouse, sitting like a small child, her feet on the rungs of a cane-bottomed chair, watching the warehouse for him, and knitting.

"Hey, Hallie," said Miss Toulou as she went into the post office. She walked as light and airy as if she were dancing to the "Japanese Sandman," one of her favorite tunes. She played it as a marching song sometimes for the Sunday School. Once she had worked "Ja-da" into the offertory—in a very slow and solemn way, of course, but it was unmistakably "Ja-da." Mama said she thought it was a disgrace the way Miss Toulou played; her time was unreliable, and sometimes if she did not like a hymn she would stop after the first verse, leaving everyone in the congregation ready to plunge on into the second. Mama said she thought Brother Jamieson ought to get Miss Naomi Featherstone to play, she would be more dependable, but Miss Naomi could not take on the job as long as she had to hold a baby. Hallie liked the way Miss Toulou played and hoped that Miss Naomi would not take over. She liked the extra *oom-pahs* Miss Toulou sometimes put in the bass, and the way she played the second verse high up in the treble to vary the effect.

"Howdy, Lucius," Miss Toulou said now to Lucius Ledbetter, who was approaching the post office with his crawfish walk. He looked in at the post office door and seemed to wonder for a minute whether or not he should go in. Then he decided against it and came over and sat down by Hallie on the bench. Lucius Ledbetter—Loony Lucius, Benny called him—was no stranger to her, although she had never talked to him; she had only watched him from the tree as he rocked the McGhee children. She had wondered why they loved him so; he was a dirty, disreputable old man. Two or three times she had seen him talking with Adam Lincoln out in the depot warehouse. Once she saw Adam take something from his pocket and hand it to him. A white person taking money from a Negro—that showed how low he had fallen.

Now, sitting next to him on the bench in front of the post office, she turned to look at him. He was looking at her too and he smiled. He had Santa Claus eyes, twinkling and merry, but bloodshot brown. He gave her such deep, deep attention that she turned away embarrassed. She glanced up the street to see if Mr. F. had made any progress (after all, it was he she had come to watch), hoping that he had so she could inch away from Lucius Ledbetter's burning gaze. But Mr. F. still sat quietly in front of the drug store, probably contemplating his hero father on the statue. Then as she watched, thank goodness, he stood and came down the street, said, "Good morning, good morning," in his courtly way to the group in front of the cotton warehouse. Buck Ducket was telling a story and no one seemed to hear his salutation. He bowed again toward the door—that would be to Miss Toulou Vass who must be sitting just inside—then came on down to the post office and said, "Good morning, good morning," to her and to Lucius Ledbetter, enfolding them in the same bow. Then he went purposefully into the post office as if he expected an important letter. Miss Sallie Mae Cartledge, the Postmistress, leafed through the letters and shook her head. Mr. F. bowed to her and turned away with a shrug that said, oh, well, if not today then tomorrow, and returning, repeated his same salutation and went back to the group near the cotton warehouse.

Everything moved slowly here on the street. If it were a play it would be a very slow play. Everything in Greenwood was slow. Now, again motion; Mr. F. walked into George Bullard's store. Business with George Bullard? A partnership? Except for asking for his mail why had Mr. F. bothered to come down? She left Lucius Ledbetter on the bench and followed Mr. F. into the store. But he was simply buying a sack of licorice from Miss Ada Pratt and making a joke which only he laughed at. Miss Ada Pratt stared at her standing there looking, so Hallie fished in her pocket for a penny and pointed to the banana-flavored caramels. "Two, please," she said.

Mr. F. leaned over the group of squatting men who talked and laughed on the sidewalk, and Hallie walked past in a hurry, watching her chance when someone was not aiming a stream of tobacco juice toward the edge of the sidewalk. Mr. F. was in the group, but not of it, she could see at once. His tie, for one thing, and his neat black shoes and the coat made him look fragile and aristocratic compared to the red necks, the exposed hairy chests, and big brown brogans of the farmers and sawmill workers.

A new face now joined the group; the highway man Boyce McClure squatted in the circle, immediately a part of it. In his work clothes, with his healthy tanned face, his vigorous way of scratching a match on his overalled behind, Hallie could feel that a weak girl might become weaker with him around. Could Elberta have been the weak one? Her interest moved on; it still seemed unlikely Elberta would have a baby.

Lucius Ledbetter waited quietly on the bench, making a cat's cradle with a piece of string. The right hand was not much help, she could see, except to hold the loop. The left hand did all the work. She sat down and took out a piece of candy, unwrapped it, and was about to put it into her mouth when she realized that Lucius was looking at her. She held out the other piece. "Have a piece of candy," she said.

Lucius smiled and shook his head, opened his mouth and pointed, exposing a few scattered, tobacco-stained teeth.

"Cain't afford to lose no more," he said. "Already have to just about gum everythin I eat." The caramel *was* chewy. He put the string away into a tattered pocket and looked at her as if she had said something and not finished it.

"Hot, isn't it?" said Hallie.

"Uh huh," said Lucius, disappointed.

Hallie cast up and down the street for a topic—toward the tracks, toward the depot, then in the other direction . . . the Confederate monument.

"Mr. Willy Featherstone told me that was his father," she said.

Lucius Ledbetter laughed—hunched, choked laughter that seemed squeezed out of him. "Said hit were his father, did he?" he said, choking between laughs. "Oh, said hit were his father. The old suck-egg dog."

"Who?" asked Hallie. Who could be a suck-egg dog? Certainly not Mr. Willy Featherstone and certainly not Mr. Willy Feather-stone's heroic father.

"Him," said Lucius Ledbetter, pointing at Mr. F. who at this moment leaned back and laughed his high laugh and slapped his thin flanks at some joke made by Mr. Shadrack Cartledge.

74

"He's just a old scoundrel," Lucius said, "and, for that matter, so were his pa. Did you climb up and see were there a toe missin on the soldier? Cain't be Cap'n Featherstone ef'n there ain't a toe missin." He started his hunched giggling again.

"Was Captain Featherstone's toe shot off in the War?" asked Hallie. A toe might not be as serious as an arm or leg but it would be a great inconvenience.

"He says hit were shot off by a cannon ball in the First Battle of Manassas . . . he says."

The First Battle of Manassas, the same battle in which Papa's father had gone down and left his children fatherless so that Papa had never gone past the fifth grade and had not grown up to be a planter and a Southern gentleman. It was really that battle that caused her to be where she was today—in the dreary town of Greenwood.

"Was it shot clear off?" asked Hallie, coming back to the other hero of that battle, trying to see the cannon ball bounding toward the foot and wondering how it could pick off a big toe like picking a grape off a bunch, without disturbing the other toes.

"He says hit were shot off clean . . . leastways that's what he says when he got home."

Hallie bridled at the tone. A toe was not much, but it would be disabling and there was no use making fun of it. It would have been a great handicap to lead his men after that. She spoke up. "It must've been mighty hard going all through the War, marching and everything, with his toe missing."

"Who says he went all thu the War?" Lucius Ledbetter laughed again. "He just barely got up there where they was holdin the War, just barely got there when he *says* along come this here cannon ball and taken off his big toe."

"Why do you keep saying he *says?*" asked Hallie. When Lucius first sat down beside her and looked at her as if he knew her, as if he might have been waiting for a chance to talk with her, she had liked him, though she was surprised to find herself liking him. He was a tramp and obviously not respectable. But now she felt his talk was silly. "He *says* . . . " she repeated disapprovingly.

"Well'm, everybody knows or should," said Lucius. "Anyhow they knew when them as was left got back home. *They* said Cap'n Featherstone cut off his toe when he was choppin up some green lighterd; his hatchet slipped and first thing he knew he was holdin up his toe. They weren't even in the War yit . . . just near enough to hear them big guns goin off on a hill up ahead. He cain't go fightin with his toe missin, so he taken out for home."

"Didn't he go back again?" asked Hallie. "Didn't he go back to lead his men?"

"No'm, too fur. Besides he were right busy down here."

"Well, why does it say 'Captain of the Featherstone Fusileers'?" asked Hallie, motioning toward the monument.

"Well'm, he left here Cap'n with his men, and he come back wounded and naturally was called Cap'n ever since, till he up and died, 'twant too many years ago. I remember even after I come up here to town I useter see him, a right ol man then, limpin around town. He were still limpin on account of losin his toe in the War." He laughed again and his eyes squinted up and almost disappeared in the folds around them.

"What did his Company do?" asked Hallie. "Who led them?"

"My pa," said Lucius, "Lieutenant Lucius Ledbetter, later on Cap'n Ledbetter."

"Well, then," said Hallie, feeling she had him trapped now, "why didn't they write Ledbetter Fusileers on the Monument?"

"I guess them as pays for a monument kin write on it what they's a mind to," said Lucius. "Them Daughters of the Confederacy, or whoever, is just full of Featherstones. Hit don't matter. Pa just about killed anybody called him Cap'n after the War was over. Says he just never wanted to hear War again."

"I guess your father wasn't wounded," said Hallie, feeling angry at Lucius and more angry with his father.

"No'm, he weren't wounded but he said the War sure made him sick. He useter say when I was a boy hit made him sick unto death."

Hallie felt her face turn red and her eyes grow wet, not from the sadness she had felt at the monument, but from anger. She could see now why Lucius Ledbetter's father never got his name on the monument, a man who did not even think enough of the War and what he was fighting for to want to be called Captain afterward. "I don't believe you," she said, standing up. "I don't believe they'd put Captain Featherstone's name up there, above the writing and that poem, unless he really were a hero." She never wanted to talk to Lucius again. For all his twinkling blood-shot eyes and his gentleness with the McGhee children, he was a jealous old man trying to get some glory for his father. She said sternly, "I don't think it's true and I think you're just jealous." Then, not quite daring to leave with those the last words she said, "I've got to go now. It's about dinnertime."

"Not yit," said Lucius, looking up the street, "you kin always depend on Doc McGhee startin out right on the dot of twelve. Then I know hits time for dinner."

"Well, I have to go," said Hallie. She turned and walked back the way she had come. The sandals felt hot on her feet, and when she was around the corner she unbuckled them and carried them in one hand. Looking at her bare feet on the hot sandy sidewalk she thought it would be hard for a cannon ball to pick off just one toe. But she found it impossible to believe Lucius Ledbetter. After all he was called Loony Lucius, at least by Benny. He must have come from some place down in the back-woods by his talk. He did not amount to anything. As far as she could see he did not work, held no proper job. There was no reason to believe a man like that when it was his word against Mr. Willy Featherstone who had come from Magnolia Hall, who had said himself that his father had led the heroic company from the county.

Later, in the tree she took out her notes on Magnolia Hall

and wrote, "Mr. F. must have interests out of town." Then she thought of Lucius Ledbetter's hateful remarks about Mr. F.'s father. They sidled into her mind, made her feel uncomfortable. She would not write them down. She would not believe them and she would forget them at once.

8

The next Sunday Margaret Craig appeared again at Sunday School after having been away for weeks. She and Hallie walked out together from the Sunday School room.

"Are you going to be in eighth grade?" Hallie asked Margaret. A silly thing to say. All Intermediate girls were going to be in eighth grade, even that nitwit Essie Jones.

"Uh huh." Miss Toulou had begun a marching piece in the main part of the church. "You going to take expression?" Margaret went on.

"I don't know. Are you?"

"I always take expression," said Margaret.

"Who do you take from?" asked Hallie.

"I take from Cousin Bootsie Craig," said Margaret, "but she only takes one or two pupils. The school always has a teacher. I hear maybe Miss Corrine Barksdale's going to teach, although Cousin Bootsie says she's very young and inexperienced. She just graduated from GSCW, and Mr. Barksdale has asked the school board to hire her so she can be here with him."

Miss Corrine Barksdale, that haughty creature who preferred

North Carolina, would live in Magnolia Hall, in Mr. Willy Featherstone's old home place, and though Hallie had never seen her she knew she would not like her. She would be tall and cold, her breath would smell and her voice would squeak. It was quite unlikely that anyone would want to take expression from her.

Miss Toulou's marching piece suddenly turned into a dancing piece as they came down the stairs and into the vestibule with doors leading to the church, the choir and the outside. Margaret Craig swayed her hips from side to side in time to the music.

"You going to take music lessons?" Hallie asked.

"Lord, I reckon so. Papa says Miss Naomi Featherstone will starve if we don't. I hate it though, all those scales, and Miss Naomi always holding a baby with its nose running or its diaper needing to be changed."

"How about Miss Toulou Vass?" asked Hallie, listening to her do a tricky run that did not interfere with the lilt of the piece. "Wouldn't she teach?"

"She never has but she sure knows how to play," Margaret said, standing at the foot of the steps doing a little jig. She started toward the outside.

"Aren't you going to stay for preaching?"

"I'm off to the races, dear." Margaret raised an imaginary lorgnette and looked down her nose. Then in her normal voice she added, "Papa has to go up toward Verdery. There are some dangerous criminals loose up there. He's going to drop us off to have Sunday dinner with Aunt Lucy Willis on the way up. I reckon we'll come back later in the afternoon."

During the next few days Hallie lay in the tree house waiting, waiting for school to start, waiting as usual for Mr. Jess Bailey to take her for a ride on his horse, waiting, waiting. She lay on her stomach in the tree house, her pad of M. D. and S. paper in front of her. She doodled and chewed her pencil, crossed out "M. D. and S." and wrote in more romantic names such as Moscow, Dardanelles and Samarkand, or boys' names such as Marmaduke, David and St. Elmo, or, reverting to the dreariness of Greenwood, Murder, Death and Starvation.

Mr. F. was disappointing; he never *did* anything. He was a Southern aristocrat and he had a hero father; but he went downtown, walked back, sat in his swing, went back downtown. There was nothing much there to watch. Then what about the Cartledge Old Home Place, she thought, turning her pad to the page where she had written in the name. She had not even seen it, did not even know where it was. Margaret Craig would know. She decided to walk toward the jail and see if Margaret Craig had come home.

Margaret was sitting in the porch swing with her mother. Mrs. Craig did not look like the mother of a potential actress. She seemed tired for so early in the morning. "You girls can finish these peas," she said. "We need a lot, Margaret. Your father's bringin in two prisoners."

Hallie took her place in the swing, and Mrs. Craig let a lapful of black-eyed peas slide from her apron into Hallie's lap. The pan sat between Hallie and Margaret and they dropped the peas into it.

"What you been up to?" asked Margaret Craig.

"Nothing much." In one way she felt she had been busy and then again when she looked back on the days since she had come to Greenwood she could not think of much that she had done. The first days were actually a blur now. And she had not read a single new book, only old ones. She had not done much she could talk about, at least not yet to Margaret Craig. "Did you have a good time out in the country, where was it, with your aunt?"

"Aunt Lucy Willis." Margaret took a row of peas and tried throwing them into the air and catching them with her mouth. The swing swayed with her exertions. "It's kind of boring down in the country. Not much to do. But Mama always wants us to visit around in the summers."

The peas pinged into the pan for a minute, then Hallie looked across the road at the monument and said tentatively, "You know Mr. Willy Featherstone?"

"'Course I know Cousin Willy Featherstone," said Margaret. "He's kin to us, I reckon. Some kind of kin. Mama's Aunt Hennie Lou Willis was sister to Cousin Willy Featherstone's mother, or something like that."

"May Belle Ballard took us down to see his old home place one Sunday."

"Right pretty old place," said Margaret. "They used to keep white horses down there. Fancy white horses, nothing but white horses. That's what Papa says. I don't really remember seeing them. It was Cousin Willy Featherstone's father raised the horses."

"He's the one over there on the monument," said Hallie, motioning across the street where the monument shone white against the vetch.

"Yeah, Cap'n Featherstone," said Margaret. "Isn't that a place for a monument, though, over there in front of that vetch patch. It ought to be here on the Courthouse Square."

"Why didn't they put it here?" asked Hallie. The monument in Clover stood in front of the Courthouse; other monuments she had seen were in courthouse yards.

"Featherstones said it ought to be there, right where Featherstones could see it," said Margaret. "Papa says even though we're a little kin the rest of the town ought to've risen up on their hind legs and said they couldn't. But they didn't, so that's where it is."

How could the occupants of such undistinguished houses wield such power? The houses looked as miserable today as they had that first day she had spotted them across the tracks and the field of vetch. The fancy *F* stood for Featherstone—some lowly relative to Mr. F. Lucius Ledbetter said the Daughters of the Confederacy was full of Featherstones. "Mr. Willy Featherstone's old home place is much prettier than these," she said, indicating the row of houses.

"I just love Magnolia Hall," said Margaret, "now that Mr. Barksdale has fixed it up. I remember how it looked before. Of course all those big magnolia trees were there already and the house itself, but he painted it up and fixed the lawn and now it seems like a different place."

"Prettier than Mr. Shadrack Cartledge's?"

"They *are* alike," said Margaret, "the houses are. But Magnolia Hall has been fixed up nicer. It's the best one of the three now. That old run-down Ledbetter place on the Big Sandy, down near Tranquil Church, it's the spookiest one. It stands up on a little hill looking down on the river. It's the most ha'nted-looking place I ever saw." And Margaret gave a shiver that set the swing moving again.

"Which Ledbetter is that?" Hallie asked carefully and slowly. "You don't mean Lucius Ledbetter you always see hanging around town?" She felt overwhelmed at the thought of a *third* house when she had not even seen the second.

"Uh huh, Loony Lucius. He came from down in there. But there's Duckets in it now, sort of roosting in it Papa says. The house is about to fall in on top of them, I reckon. But that's where old Lucius was born, and his brothers."

"Brothers?"

"Mr. River Ledbetter. He lives out with the Fitzgeralds—you know Laura Fitzgerald. Well, Mr. River Ledbetter stays out there and helps Mr. Fitzgerald some way. And then there's Mr. Byrd Ledbetter. I don't really know him. He lives up in Atlanta, and Papa says he's doing right well. Papa says he's got more git-up-and-go than the other Ledbetter boys."

This news about the Ledbetter house was unpleasant. The house might be old and run-down and even haunted but if it were an old Southern mansion, then Lucius Ledbetter and his ideas would have to be given more respect, and Hallie remembered her irritation with him. She remembered that she had accused him of envy and even worse . . . she had accused him of lying.

Margaret had the Ledbetter Old Home Place on her mind. "Oh, it's really ha'nted, honey," she said, rolling her eyes and making her hands shake, demonstrating extreme fright. "One time Papa took us on a trip down there with him. Every once in a while there's some kind of fracas in the Tranquil neighborhood and Papa has to go down and straighten things out. We stopped off and went in wading in the Big Sandy. I'll get him to take us sometime when he has to go down." Margaret began to slide the hulls from her lap into the sack. "Mr. Shadrack Cartledge's house is in the other direction, on the Abbeville Road not too far from town."

"Could we take a walk out there sometime?" asked Hallie. This was why she had searched out Margaret this morning.

"Not by ourselves," said Margaret, "not without a man."

"We could walk out on the big road," said Hallie. "Nothing would hurt us."

"There's snakes," said Margaret, giving one of her best shivers. "Snakes. Or there might be a drunk nigger. Papa wouldn't let me. Anyhow, it'd be more fun if we could get a man to go along and we could walk through the woods. I know the way."

"Couldn't we take that walk today out to Mr. Shadrack Cartledge's?" Hallie asked the next Sunday as they came down the steps from the Sunday School room.

"We have to get a man to go along," said Margaret. Her curls had been freshly done and she had a barrette in her hair with diamonds in it. "How about Benny?"

When Hallie asked Benny after church if he would like to take a walk in the woods he said, "Sure, why not," agreeably, and Virginia said she would like to come too. Hallie did not say anything about wanting to visit Mr. Shadrack Cartledge's old home place. Benny and Virginia were too quick to catch on to some interest of hers and then talk about it until she could hardly bear to think of it herself. Benny kept reminding her, even now when she was thirteen, that she had been a terrible show-off at four or five, long ago before she could remember; she had caused him intense suffering by putting her fingers up over her eyes for horns and running at visitors with a "Yah, yah, yah," to attract attention. Even now, to show his slightest disapproval he put his fingers up over his eyes and said, "Yah, yah, yah," causing her to blush and hate her stupid past. She could imagine that if she said she wanted to go visit an old Southern house Benny would say, "Thinking of moving out, Hallie?" and then, his fingers making horns, "Yah, yah, yah." Or when all the family were sitting at the table he would announce, "Say, did you hear that Hallie is looking over real estate around here? She's thinking of buying Mr. Shadrack Cartledge's place."

Margaret Craig showed up as they finished eating their Sunday floating island. Hallie hoped she would not bring up the real reason for the excursion. She worried too that Papa might decide this was an unsuitable expedition for Sunday, but Mama said right away when Margaret Craig walked in, "I think a nice walk in the woods is a good thing for you children to do on a Sunday afternoon. Be back in time to get something to eat before B.Y.P.U."

At that Benny looked sour and muttered as they left that he did not care if he ever got back for B.Y.P.U. When they had moved to Greenwood and he and Virginia went over to B.Y.P.U.— Hallie still went to Sunbeams on Saturdays—they found that Papa was already a regular member. "It's Baptist *Young* People's Union," said Benny. But Papa had heard they needed more members and he had begun attending. "Next thing you know he'll be going to Sunbeams," Benny said to Hallie.

Margaret Craig led off through the Baptist churchyard and cemetery, then under a barbed-wire fence. They stepped on wreaths and rusty flower cans discarded from the graves, then through a weed-grown field and into the woods. A slick brown-needled path ran between pines, and the long green needles overhead caught the sun and burned bright as silver darning needles. A good hot Sunday; if they were not here in this pine-needled place, Hallie thought, she would be lying back on her bed sweating in her underwear, reading the Sunday papers and feeling as hot and wrinkled as the bed.

Everyone was happy to be in the woods. Benny, sulky when they started, now put his hand over his mouth and gave an Indian war whoop. Margaret Craig clutched her red curls and took off down the path screaming, "Save me! Save me! They're trying to scalp me!"

Benny chased her and grabbed one of her fat curls which hung moist against her sweaty neck. "Which do you want, girls?" he hollered, holding up the curl.

When they came down the hill into a little valley where the grass grew thick around a stream, Margaret Craig drew back squealing, "I can't go on, I can't. Oh, this place is too snaky." Her voice shook with such real fear that Hallie expected to see her blanch and sway, but she stayed red and sweaty, the freckles standing out across her red nose.

"Come on, I'll protect you," said Benny. "Walk right in back of me and I'll let that old water moccasin take a chunk out of me first." Oh, Benny could be so nice and good-looking when he tried, but Hallie was surprised to see how forward Margaret Craig could be. She walked very close behind Benny and put her arms around his waist.

She continued to squeal, "I'm scared," and she went on stepping gingerly on the grass, shying away from snake holes and holding tight to Benny. Hallie jumped every time she squealed; every crackle of a twig was a snake's hiss and she shied as nervously as Margaret.

On the other side of the valley the woods thinned and they walked through a neglected field overgrown with sumac, past a Negro house where two children played with a swing made of an old tire on a rope. Soon they stood on the edge of a deep gully, a great red fierce gash in the earth with little standing islands where small trees clung, their roots exposed in the clay below.

"Wow, Grand Canyon of the Colorado," yelled Benny and plunged down the steep red side.

"We can follow this gully up to Mr. Shadrack Cartledge's place," whispered Margaret, dropping back to Hallie. Thank goodness Margaret had sense enough not to speak so that Benny and Virginia could hear.

They walked up the sandy bottom of the gully, spoiling the neat patterned sand that bore the convolutions and rhythms of the last stream that had swept through. Rounding an island they came to a wider place where another gully ran into the first and made a little amphitheater. As Hallie paused and looked up the second gully which seemed to disappear in shadow, Margaret Craig gave one of her best shivers and said, "Don't go up there. That place gives me the creeps."

"Snakes?"

"No, that's where Mr. Shadrack Cartledge threw a nigger he killed. At least that's what the niggers say. They won't go near the place."

"Did your father find him?" asked Hallie.

"That was before Papa was sheriff, right after Mr. Shadrack Cartledge came back from the Big War. He'd been a sergeant or something in a colored regiment. Papa says he don't think there's much truth in the story. But he did say that Mr. Shadrack Cartledge caused more niggers to go to Dee-troit and New York than the boll weevil. He can't get one to work for him out here now."

"A mean-looking man," said Virginia. The gully became shallower and they came out of it into an open field where a poor stand of corn grew down to its edge.

"We're on Mr. Shadrack Cartledge's place now," said Margaret. "See the back of his house yonder."

A big square house at one time painted white loomed up beyond a few scattered buildings. They walked through the scraggly corn and over a broken-down rail fence into a pasture. But no animals grazed here. After Miss Mary Emily left him and went off with the highway man Mr. Shadrack must have lost heart.

"I wonder if we ought to go snooping around Mr. Shadrack Cartledge's house," said Margaret. "You know he's a fast man with the buckshot," and she turned toward Benny and went *zing, zing, zing*, pointing a gun.

"What're we going up here for anyhow?" said Benny. "Why don't we go back to the gully and play follow the leader or something?"

Hallie said, "Oh, don't go back now. Let's just go up a little farther so we can see the front of the house." She led the way past a row of empty chicken coops, past a gray detached kitchen. Everything about the place showed neglect.

Virginia stopped and held back. "We oughtn't go poking around anybody's house like this," she said. "We hardly know Mr. Shadrack Cartledge."

"I know him," said Margaret, "and that's why I think maybe we oughtn't poke around."

But Hallie continued to move forward, stepping on the sickly sweet, sloppy ripe chinaberries fallen to the ground, then in back of some shrubs where they could see the front yard. Mr. Shadrack Cartledge's Chevrolet stood in the driveway. Margaret placed her fingers over her lips and pointed to the car and they leaned down behind the shrubs. Hallie inched her way along until she could see the front of the house. It was like Magnolia Hall, exactly: the little balcony off the second floor hall, the fan-shaped light over the double front door, even the same square columns. Magnolia Hall glistened white, and paint peeled here; this house was gray rather than white, but it was the same house, the same old Southern mansion. And as they leaned on their knees back of the shrubs looking onto the porch as if they were watching a play take place on a stage, watching it from the wings rather than from the front, the door opened, and Miss Ada Pratt came out, patting her edifice of hair. She paused at the door and pulled down her corset under her dress, gave it a hitch that seemed to make her stand even straighter, then walked with her slow and stately walk over to a rocking chair and sat down, pulled out a package of cigarettes, struck a match under the arm of the chair, lit the cigarette and sat there, straight in the rocker, blowing smoke through her nose. Mr. Shadrack slouched out after her, yawning a little, and curled himself up in a rocker near hers.

Benny, kneeling next to Hallie, had turned away once as if to go, then had come back; now he sat staring, too. Virginia whispered to Margaret Craig, "First woman I ever saw smoke," and Benny scowled at her, and then Virginia motioned with her head that they should leave. But Hallie did not go. She had to stay; the play had not been acted out. Miss Ada Pratt rocked in the chair, but she did not talk. There was no sound from the porch except the faint creak of the rockers. Miss Ada Pratt took big angry puffs from her cigarette and blew out clouds of smoke through her nose.

Suddenly Mr. Shadrack hurled himself out of his chair and began jumping up and down on the porch, doing a wild dance (the play had taken an unexpected turn for the better), stamping on something. The four behind the shrubs moved a little, uncertain. Should they cut and run? But he did not come toward them. He danced up and down on the porch and squeezed out curses as he danced.

"What in the world ails you, Shadrack?" asked Miss Ada. But she did not seem to be too interested; she hardly looked his way when she talked. "What're you doing that for?"

Mr. Shadrack kicked something off the porch into the dried-up kudzu leaves from the vine growing over the porch. "Just killin a lizard, honey," he said. "You wouldn't want a nasty little old lizard runnin up your leg, would you?" He leaned over and ran his hand up her leg playfully, which she brushed off by jerking her chair around.

"You're a mean buzzard, Shadrack," said Miss Ada Pratt. "Honestly . . ."

Mr. Shadrack still stood over her. He laughed until his face seemed all screwed up. "All right, honey," he said. "Next lizard comes along I'm going to let it run right up under your corset. Then you'll come yelling to old Shadrack, begging him to undo you." He laughed and moved over behind her chair, then slid his hand down over her neck as if to tickle her. But he did not tickle her; he let his hand slide down inside her blouse and stay there.

Miss Ada did not look happy but she did not push his hand away. "Sometimes I think I'd rather have a lizard on me," she said.

This remark excruciated Shadrack. "Ada, you're a cutter," he said, laughing his squeezed-out laugh. But he did not remove his hand from her bosom. Rather he slid his other hand down on the other side, and strangely enough Miss Ada with a look of disgust on her face reached up and undid her top button.

Benny whispered, "We'd better go."

They ran leaning over toward the back of the house, squatting down behind chicken coops as if they expected to be pursued. Benny's face was red and going back to the gully he did not seem as gay as before. When they came to the wide amphitheater he pulled out a package of cigarettes.

"You girls want to try one?" Benny said, his voice suddenly deeper.

"Papa'd really wring your neck if he could see you," said Virginia.

"Well, don't care if I do," said Margaret Craig. She picked out a cigarette and sat down on a hummock, crossing her legs and holding herself up very stiff and straight like Miss Ada Pratt.

"Where'd you get them, Benny?" asked Virginia. "I'd try one, but, Lord, suppose they smelled it on me at B.Y.P.U.?"

"You can chew sassafras on the way home, or sweet gum," said Benny, lighting the girls' cigarettes and his own. "You want one, Hallie?"

"I don't think so," she said, but she did not know why. A

cloud seemed to have passed over the bright sky, though when she looked up through the trees the sky was as blue as ever.

"You tell and I'll fix you," said Benny, and he raised his two fingers and made horns and said, "Yah, yah, yah."

"You're a mean old buzzard, Benny," said Margaret Craig, in Miss Ada's husky voice. "Leave her be, leave her be."

"I wouldn't tell," said Hallie. "I don't want to smoke, that's all." She felt sad and vaguely uneasy, sad to be out of favor with Benny, and she tried to shake it off. "Miss Ada Pratt must have back trouble," she said. "She's always sitting up so straight."

"Back trouble, nothing," said Margaret Craig. "Come here." Hallie leaned over her and she said in a loud, exaggerated stage whisper guaranteed to carry to Benny, "Corsets. Miss Ada Pratt falls to pieces, they say, when she takes off her corset." And to demonstrate Margaret collapsed and fell right off the hummock.

Benny jumped up and threw away his cigarette and started tickling her. "Where's that lizard?" he said. "Gotta find that lizard." And he tickled Margaret Craig while she panted and writhed and screamed for mercy and help. Virginia dropped her cigarette and grabbed Benny's back. Hallie suddenly felt excited and grabbed Margaret's arm to help pull her to her feet. Benny jumped back and pushed Virginia over, fell himself, and Margaret Craig jumped on top of him yelling, "The lizard's on you now, Benny," and began tickling him.

When they finally stopped, sweaty and sandy, they had re-captured some of their earlier gaiety. On the way home they picked sassafras toothbrushes in the field. Hallie thought of the scene illuminated on the stage of the porch of the Cartledge Old Home Place. It was a scene unbecoming to a beautiful Southern house. She could never imagine a scene like that taking place at Montpelier. She was glad Miss Ada Pratt was not really mistress there.

And Mr. Shadrack? Was he really a Southern gentleman? There was a quality to his squeezed laughter that she did not like, but in looks he did resemble St. Elmo, a man torn by the forces of good and evil who was finally tamed and redeemed by the love of a good woman, Edna Earl.

Virginia leaned toward her as they went through the cemetery and blew in her face. "Can you smell it on me?" she asked.

9

Sunday was Sabbath now only in the memory verse that began with R—Remember the Sabbath day to keep it holy. Here in Greenwood she did not feel holy on Sundays; she only awakened to the thought that today is Sunday and one ought to feel holy. Papa's prayers were louder on Sunday. He had taken a long drawn-out bath behind the kitchen range the night before and combed hair dye into his hair. Today he would put on his best blue suit before going to the depot, and kneeling in the blue suit, pure and clean (cleanliness is next to godliness), his prayers would have a special rhythm and power. Papa remembered the Sabbath day to keep it holy, but Hallie had not felt completely and deeply holy since she was eight and had been converted in a great upheaval that had lasted for two weeks. The day she had been saved, when holiness had descended, she had gone stumbling past her mother's feet, sorry for God, felt her father's hand on her back, felt a crying out inside and a seeking, felt tears wetting her cheeks, felt herself a black lamb about to be washed whiter than snow, and, longing, longing to be saved, she had gone to the front row where Dr. Langston had put his hand gently on her head and drawn her to him. Afterward the whole family stared at her and dropped their voices in her presence for being so precociously holy. She had walked around as light as an angel, feeling saved. Then toward the end of the second week the angel wings of holiness had become heavy; she had wanted to argue her right *not* to be holy too.

Oh, she had moments now when she felt the same crying out, the same longing for conversion, the same resolution that from this day forward life would not be the same. One day back in Clover, a blaze-blue summer day, she had sat on a rose-covered stump, exactly in the middle of the world (a world shaped like a bowl with her in the center). She sat there on the stump looking off at the light shimmering on the green alfalfa across the road and felt as open, as trembling, as pure as the day she had darted up the aisle in the First Baptist Church in Clover. She saw a great light washed over the earth, bright as Halley's Comet, but all she had done as she sat on the stump was to lean one arm out toward heaven and say, "Here am I, here am I."

She lay in bed now, on this first Sunday in September. It was still summer and her first thought was that here was the same old Sunday, a Sunday which could peter out into boredom and into wishing for something different, into waiting, waiting. Suddenly she remembered that this Sunday was different; that instead of being like the seventh day, this was more like a first day, a day when decisions would be made, a day when the future, at least the next nine months of it, could be glimpsed even though through a glass darkly. Margaret Craig had said to her to be sure to go to church on Sunday; all the new teachers would be there (at least all that were Baptist, and most of them would be). Lying straight under her sheet, Hallie thought of tomorrow when she would go into the eighth grade. High school. Her new teachers would be in church today and they would see her and perhaps they would say as they went home, "Did you see that dark-eyed child in the dark blue taffeta? She looks so *bright*." So she put on the taffeta when she dressed, though Virginia looked askance and said, "It's still too hot to wear that. You're going to sweat on it."

Later, after Sunday School, Hallie and Margaret Craig and Laura Fitzgerald, even thick-necked Essie Jones, swished down the steps together to church, feeling already a clubbiness from tomorrow when they would all be eighth graders together. Papa walked past them to the outside door and gave a cough and a throat clearing that went *cl-a-a-rk*; the wad of tobacco landed under a prickly shrub near the door, a shrub obviously nourished on tobacco. Margaret Craig joined her mother and her milk-faced brothers and sisters in a back pew, and Laura Fitzgerald sat by her mother, a tiny old woman so frail that she looked as if she could not last through a sermon. Papa came now and swept Hallie before him to their pew where she pushed past Mama's feet. Virginia tucked in her dotted swiss and made room for her. Papa wanted Benny to sit in the family pew too, but these days Benny lingered outside with two or three other boys. He would slide in later when the first hymn was being sung and sit in a back row with his friends.

Mr. Jess Bailey took his place in the choir, and his sister, Miss Annie Laurie Jones, Essie's mother, sat next to him. She sometimes sang a solo in a rich, throaty contralto. A stout stranger came into the choir as if he were at home there. Mr. Jess Bailey smiled and shook hands and Hallie guessed that he was Mr. Holden, the school principal. He would teach her algebra (tomorrow, farewell to arithmetic). Two young women came in the other door looking dressed-up and hot in wine-colored fall suits, wearing wine-colored gloves. Teachers. The younger children in front turned around and stared, eyes big with wonder at what tomorrow would bring.

Miss Toulou Vass was playing a little wandering piece that she seemed to be making up as she went along. Now she brought it to an end with several crashing chords, swung around on the piano stool and sat there waiting. Her long golden hair caught golden light sifting through the Good Samaritan in the window

93

back of her. She sat there waiting with a little smile of expectancy on her face as if she too was waiting, waiting, like Hallie, who was always waiting. Hallie loved to look at Miss Toulou Vass; she would ask Mama if she could take piano lessons from her.

Now Miss Toulou swung around again and began to look in the hymn book. Brother Jamieson came out from the little door at one side of the baptistry. He always entered very solemnly and unsmilingly, as if he had been sequestered with God back there behind the pulpit and was still frowning from the sight. As he sat down in one of the carved chairs a young woman appeared in the doorway across the church. Behind her was Mr. Barksdale. Mr. Barksdale stepped in front and led the way up the aisle, then stepped to one side to allow her to enter the pew ahead of him. Mr. Barksdale acted like a proud father, but could this be his daughter, Miss Corrine Barksdale, that haughty, cold princess? Oh, but she was pretty. And tiny. She hardly came to her father's shoulder, and she seemed young and shy. Hallie could not help staring at her. Miss Corrine Barksdale's curly brown hair escaped in little tendrils that framed her face. Her brown fall hat left a knot of hair exposed and from it hung three perfect little curls. Hallie had never seen anyone wear her hair like that and she fingered her own tight braids and wondered.

Brother Jamieson walked to the pulpit as Miss Toulou Vass crashed out some chords and then the Doxology. May Belle Ballard's mother always sang too loud. When Brother Jamieson announced the first hymn, "Stand Up, Stand Up for Jesus," Mrs. Ballard's voice soared out high and nasally above all the other voices. May Belle sang with tight lips and her red cheeks became even redder. Hallie's family pew was in front of the choir and she could hear the voice of Mr. Holden booming out, and Mr. Jess Bailey's tenor climbing high and sweet. She always felt happy to be sitting underneath Mr. Jess Bailey's voice; she could look up and admire him as he sang, and sometimes when he saw her watching him his sky-blue gaze crinkled into a smile and his dimples appeared briefly.

94

Mr. Jess Bailey made her think of the Song of Solomon which she sometimes read at bedtime. Seeing him smile she would think, "His eyes are as the eyes of doves by the rivers of waters, washed with milk, and fitly set." And, "Thy lips, O my spouse, drop as the honeycomb: honey and milk are under thy tongue . . ." Standing there now singing about being a soldier of the Cross, his blond hair curled crisply across his forehead, he was even more like Galahad ready to search out the Grail.

> My strength is as the strength of ten
> Because my heart is pure.

Hallie tried this out to the tune of "Stand Up, Stand Up for Jesus." Thinking of Mr. Jess Bailey being like Galahad, pure and distant and intent on his holy mission, she thought she would have to stop her dreams of him before going to sleep, her wanton dream of riding on the horse in front of him, his arms encircling her to hold her on the horse, his breath blowing the hairs gently on the back of her neck. She was riding through some green place, beside a stream, he had just murmured in her ear, "My dearest, most precious little angel girl . . ." and she was just turning her lips to him when the song was finished and she had to climb down from the horse and sit ashamed in the pew.

As they sat down Mr. Shadrack Cartledge came in, rather sloped in, as if he knew he was late, as if he had struggled to keep from coming at all but the force pulling him in had won out at last and here he was, a devil of a man, as good-looking in his way as Mr. Jess Bailey—though Mr. Jess looked like an angel and Mr. Shadrack like a devil. Mr. Jess Bailey always looked calm and good; if evil had ever struggled there it had been quickly overthrown.

Or perhaps Mr. Shadrack was late (thinking now of the scene on his porch) because he was struggling to get Miss Ada Pratt to come with him. Miss Ada was a Baptist and her mother must have taken her to the Baptist Church when she was young, but nowadays, Miss Beulah said, she never set foot inside a church. "Says she works too hard all week," said Miss Beulah, accenting the word *work* and lifting her eyebrows all at the same time. "Says Sunday's a day of rest." Brother Jamieson had tried to get Miss Ada to come to church. He had prayed over her during the revival. He had said, as if his heart would break, that there were those whose names were written on the book, but their hearts had been hardened against God and they were stiff-necked with pride; Hallie thought that he referred to Miss Ada.

Brother Jamieson began reading the Bible message for the day, beginning in the Psalms. He would shut the Bible with a bang and stand back and draw a deep breath before he plunged into his sermon. Since the revival in late July he had been calm in his sermons, probably feeling that everybody who would join, had. Hallie had seen Brother Jamieson talking to Lucius Ledbetter about coming to revival but apparently Lucius never set foot inside a church either. Brother Jamieson had even asked Miss Lill McGhee if she could get Lucius cleaned up and send him to church, but Miss Lill had laughed and said, "Don't you know all those Ledbetters are heathens?" Then she asked, "Do you think it would give Lucius more *ambition* if he got saved?" and Brother Jamieson said he thought it would. But then Miss Lill had said, "Aw, he don't do anybody any harm. Except that he never does a lick of work and don't wash, he acts real Christian."

Mr. F. did not come to church either, and Hallie did not even know if he were Methodist or Baptist. He said that he could hear every word the preacher said sitting right there on his own porch. Mama said she believed he exaggerated. It was true, however, that on the Sundays when the Methodist Church had services the two preachers seemed to vie with each other to see whose voice could ring loudest in the other's church. Hallie had often heard Mr. Buck Ducket "heisting" the tune over at the Methodist Church. " 'Blessed assurance,' " he roared in a voice as loud as his laughter, " 'Jesus is mine.' "

"Let us pray," said Brother Jamieson, closing the Bible and

holding his arm out over the congregation. Hallie ducked her head and closed her eyes, but she had found that during prayer was a good time to feast her eyes on Mr. Jess Bailey. As she looked up now she saw that Mr. Jess Bailey did not have his eyes closed at all. He was sitting there as if *he* were the one feasting *his* eyes, looking at the top of Miss Corrine Barksdale's bowed head. He looked and looked so intently that when the prayer was over and Miss Corrine straightened up Hallie expected her to look full into Mr. Jess Bailey's face. . . . Oh, *she* would have felt that burning blue gaze upon her, had felt it one time, blue-burning as a desert sky, and she would have turned to him and given him a loving smile. But Miss Corrine did not even look at him. Hallie did not want Mr. Jess Bailey to fall in love with Miss Corrine Barksdale, but then who was Miss Corrine Barksdale (interloper, usurper, outlander) that she should spurn Mr. Jess Bailey?

Mr. Holden poked Mr. Jess Bailey with the hymn book for the next song, "One Sweetly Solemn Thought." They sang, and while they were singing Miss Corrine Barksdale glanced once toward Mr. Jess Bailey, just once and fleetingly, as if she heard a tenor voice and looked to see whence it came and that was all.

Brother Jamieson settled down now to preaching. The progress and intent of the sermon could be told by the rhythm without listening to the individual words. It was a preaching kind of rhythm that followed a certain pattern, as if the flow of words were a river into which each word was dropped and lost like drops of water. The river passed slowly through quiet lowlands, gathered strength and force in a great lake, and when enough power was built up it burst the confines of the dam and cascaded down in a flood carrying all before it.

As the waters gathered into the lake, building up and up so that Hallie knew the dam could not long hold them back, she looked at Papa hoping as she did at this time every Sunday (but this Sunday more than ever, thinking of the new teachers present, and Mr. Holden there looking down on them, and Miss Corrine Barksdale across the aisle), hoped against hope that this one Sunday Papa would allow the sermon to go by without adding to what had been said. Papa could never keep silent when Brother Jamieson asked after the Sunday sermon if anyone had a few words to add. He had several phrases he was particularly attached to. "Whited se*pul*chre" he would say. " 'Woe unto you, scribes and Pharisees, hypocrites! for ye are like unto whited se*pul*chres, which indeed appear beautiful outward, but are within full of dead men's bones, and of all uncleanness.' " Each member of the family had reminded him time and time again that the accent was on the first syllable, not the second, but in his excitement he would always say "whited se*pul*chre" and they would blush as they listened. Or he would say *"foward"* instead of *"forward,"* rhyming it with Howard or coward. It was one of his favorite words and he would use it over and over in one short speech. . . . "Let us go *foward* together," he would say, jabbing his arm into the future, or, "Foward, foward, into the fray," his arm even more emphatic, or "Let *foward* be our motto."

Hallie ceased thinking of Papa because just then Brother Jamieson let the dam break, the waters that had been so carefully stored up began cataracting over, and he could be heard, Hallie was sure, at the Methodist Church—empty today because they were meeting in the country—or over at Mr. F.'s house, or even downtown at the stores. When Brother Jamieson, red-faced, stepped back to draw breath, Papa leaned forward and said, "Amen!" in a loud voice, so that everyone turned to look at him (the rest of his family hanging their heads in their pew beside him), and then Brother Jamieson hollered even louder as if the Amen had given him encouragement. Mama started twisting her wedding ring and Hallie kept her head down, burning with shame, thinking that Papa had sounded like someone at a protracted meeting or a Negro revival.

Brother Jamieson dropped his voice to a whisper; he was near the end of his sermon. The end always came in this low, whispered, dulcet rhythm, the water ran through green pastures again, white birds flew up, God's love poured down like April sun o'er everything, and then when the last, last whisper had been squeezed from him as if he had been wrung dry, Brother Jamieson dropped his head forward on his breast and said, "Will Brother Jones lead us in prayer?"

Papa kneeled in his pew, and again Hallie wanted to hide under the pew for shame. Virginia was right. She *was* sweating in her blue taffeta dress. Ordinarily when Papa was called on to pray he stood like anyone else and addressed God standing, but here at the end of the sermon when Brother Jamieson had given everything including his last breath, Papa obviously thought the moment called for some special gesture. The prayer went on and on, took on a river form like Brother Jamieson's sermon, used the same pacing and climaxes while Mama turned her wedding ring round and round on her swollen knuckle.

As Papa's voice rose and fell beside her, Hallie became accustomed to her shame and finally raised her head and opened her eyes. Mr. Jess Bailey was looking that same look at Miss Corrine Barksdale, and as Hallie followed his gaze she saw Miss Corrine suddenly lower her lashes as if she were determined to be more reverent. Hallie closed her eyes. She was not going to like Miss Corrine Barksdale. It was not fair. Miss Corrine had everything. She was far prettier than any of the other teachers who had come in before her. She wore prettier clothes. No one had curls like hers, or such a sweet air. And she had Magnolia Hall, the finest Southern house anywhere around.

After threatening to do so for several minutes Papa concluded his prayer and rose from his knees looking as worn as if he had really been wrestling with God. Brother Jamieson said, stretching out his arms to the congregation, "Let us sing 'Just As I Am,' " and he walked slowly down from the pulpit and stood in the aisle holding out his arms. Miss Toulou Vass played softly and the choir sang in hushed tender voices, the music melting Hallie as the sermon had not done, as the prayers had not done, turning her mind inward to look at herself and her own shortcomings. The worst one was that she hardly thought about God from one day to the next; sometimes even as she knelt in prayer she thought of Mr. Jess Bailey, not God. She began to feel sorry for Brother Jamieson standing there with pleading in his arms and no one answering. Her eyes moistened with tears; perhaps the song was for her, perhaps she was intended to come without one plea. She trembled, feeling pulled up the aisle, held herself back through the second verse and the third, and weak as water, was almost ready to give in and go after the fourth. But thank Heaven, Brother Jamieson dropped his welcoming arms sadly to his side, then raised them again and in a discouraged voice said the benediction.

10

The whole school fell in love with Miss Corrine Barksdale. Mr. Holden introduced her at morning assembly and she stood by him, tiny despite her high-heeled shoes, wearing a brown suit with a pink rosebud at the neck. She gave a demonstration of her work, some lines from Shakespeare, which she said very simply without waving her arms at all. How wonderfully her voice carried when Hamlet was thinking to himself, "O! that this too too solid flesh . . ." She clipped out the words in "Speak the speech" and her voice rose to a high organ pitch when she spoke of the world being a stage. Then she gave a little talk about how much expression was needed in everyday life. "I teach expression," she said, "not elocution."

As they filed back to their rooms after assembly the girls could talk of no one else but Miss Corrine Barksdale—how sweet, how pretty, how wonderful she was. Margaret Craig kept pointing out that Cousin Bootsie Craig said she was inexperienced, but no one paid any attention to her at all.

Virginia mentioned Miss Corrine immediately at supper and said she would like to take expression, and Papa said, "Mr. Barksdale says he hopes Miss Corrine will have a good class, this being her first year of teaching and all. He's afraid she'll want to go back up there to North Carolina if she doesn't have a good class."

"Then I think they should both take," said Mama. Mama would often talk about how they were all on the verge of bankruptcy, but when it came time to take lessons she seemed to forget it.

"I'd rather take music lessons," said Hallie. She could not explain that she did not approve of Mr. Barksdale or his daughter occupying a house that rightfully belonged to poor old Mr. Willy Featherstone. She was not so easily impressed as the other girls; she would not let herself be carried away by Miss Corrine's sweet manner and her pretty curls.

"I'm not going to take music," said Virginia. "Not this year. I'm going to put all my time in on expression."

"Mr. Barksdale's mighty nice to me down at the depot," said Papa. "He went to the trouble to write the superintendent up in Macon that he'd got a lot better service since I'd been down here watching things. I appreciated that." You could see that Papa felt almost as pleased by this as he had by the silver spoon Mr. Ely Barton over in Clover had brought him from San Francisco.

"Then why can't Hallie take both music and expression?" asked Mama. "She's got all the time in the world. It seems to me if a child's ambitious to learn music she ought to be encouraged."

"I'd kind of like to take music from Miss Toulou Vass," said Hallie, striking while the iron was hot. Even though Miss Toulou was the Baptist pianist she would have to overcome Mama's opposition. Mama had something to say nearly every Sunday at dinner about Miss Toulou's playing. "She's a law unto herself," was the last remark. "Apparently Miss Toulou knows more about writing hymns than Moody and Sankey."

Now Mama looked uncomfortable. "Don't you think you ought to learn more of the *fundamentals?*" she said. "I don't really believe Miss Toulou knows how to *count.*"

Benny laughed. "Sure she knows how to count. But sometimes she counts fast and sometimes she counts slow. I think she makes the hymns more interesting."

This admission on the part of Benny that anything connected with church was interesting seemed to establish a victory for Hallie. The next day she made a trip to the cotton warehouse, to keep an eye on affairs and to ask Miss Toulou if she would teach her music. Miss Toulou sat on her chair inside the door, her feet tucked up on a rung as usual. When Hallie asked her if she would teach her piano she seemed so pleased that little drops of perspiration sprang out around her nose.

"Why, honey," she said, "I'm real proud you asked me. But wouldn't you rather learn guitar or uke? I'm taking a course up in Macon and I could teach you everything I learned."

Hallie stood in the doorway and considered. She rubbed her toes on the worn brick sidewalk. For once there was no crowd of Duckets or farmers clustered around the opening. Mr. Shadrack was in the back talking to some Negroes moving cotton bales. She thought about the guitar and ukelele, tried to see herself playing one of them. They could not erase the picture of herself playing a rosewood piano with candles lighting her face. It was a mysterious picture with shadows in the background (set in the vaguely imagined parlor of Montpelier) and in the shadows a man listened raptly with his eyes feasting on her face. Sometimes he was moved to sing along with her in a tenor voice.

"I've always liked the piano best," she said. So Miss Toulou agreed to come to her house and teach her every Tuesday.

At her first expression lesson she was cool and distant with Miss Corrine. Virginia had gone to her first lesson the day before and she and May Belle spent the whole lunch hour practicing breathing exercises; holding their hands on each other's stomachs they recited, "An Austrian army awfully arrayed / Boldly by battle besieged Belgrade." When Hallie went to her lesson she held herself stiff, said in a precise, cold, not-caring voice, "Good morning, Miss Corrine," and explained she had come for her lesson. Miss Corrine came up to her as if she had been waiting all day for her, waiting while all those other mediocre pupils took up her time.

"Hallie honey, I'm so glad you decided to study with me. Why that first Sunday I saw you in church I said to myself, who is that child with the lovely sensitive face? And I said then I hope I have a chance to teach her. And here you are," and Miss Corrine stood poised on her high heels, her brown eyes warm with welcome, her mouth a little large for her face, giving her a humorous look, and Hallie's stiff posture, her determination to show her that someone in this town had standards, that someone was not so easily taken in by her airs, that she, Hallie . . . why, suddenly it all melted away and she stood there loving Miss Corrine, feeling silly of course that she was melting so easily, but knowing immediately that Miss Corrine was the most understanding, the sweetest, loveliest person in the world. And though she held herself back from the general acclaim of Miss Corrine—feeling already the relationship was not a general one at all, but was different, and therefore must be clutched privately to the heart—she thought of her in bed that night before she went to sleep, thought of her at the time usually reserved for thinking of Mr. Jess Bailey, sleepily thought of both of them at the same time, thought, they are meeting in my thoughts, they are meeting but their gaze is on me, not on each other. After that the days of her lessons, Monday and Thursday, assumed a luster the other days lacked.

Laura Fitzgerald sat in front of Hallie in eighth grade. Though Hallie still was not sure she liked her they had become more friendly. Hallie could not forget or forgive that first meeting when Laura had pulled in her organdy skirts and said she thought

Hallie was a Ducket. The remark had been pure malice; all Duckets went to the Methodist Church. Laura was prissy; there was no doubt of that. She carried her head tilted to one side on her long neck, and this made her long nose go up in the air. There was often a redness around her nose and she sniffed a lot in class or sighed, particularly in algebra class, and this and her long neck made her seem fragile and a little delicate. She would sit looking off into space feeling her hair, training it to curl up at the ends, and when Mr. Holden asked her to go to the board she would walk up like a sleepwalker and stand there arranging her hair until Mr. Holden would say, "Laura, are you with us?" She often turned to whisper to Hallie or she sent her little notes like, "Is Benny back in school?" when Benny had hardly been absent more than a day with a sore throat and Hallie was surprised Laura even knew.

One day in September Laura turned around during Latin class and said, "Do you like scuppernongs?" Miss Gannett looked toward them just then so that all Hallie could do was roll her eyes and smack her lips. Oh, scuppernongs. Oh, to stretch out like one of the Romans pictured in Caesar, not on a couch before a table laden with dainties but up on an arbor in scuppernong season. Later Laura said, "Ask your Mama if you can come spend the night Friday night and we'll eat scuppernongs."

They sat on the front seat of the bus Friday afternoon as it took the road out toward Antreville (Antreville Short Route, it said on the highway), the same road May Belle Ballard lived on. Maynard Johnson, who was in the eleventh grade with Benny, drove the bus; he took it fast around the red clay curves and hollered at the children in back who kept up a racket. In between times he carried on a conversation with Hallie and Laura. Hallie kept looking ahead, wondering if she would know Laura's house before she came to it; Laura's prissy airs might indicate a background above the ordinary. She did not live in a true Southern mansion, of course, but Margaret Craig said it had been fixed up to look like one. Claude Ballard, May Belle Ballard's younger brother who was in the fourth grade, leaned over from the seat in back breathing down their necks. As if he had read Hallie's thoughts right through the back of her head, he leaned over further and said, "That's where Laura lives," and pointed to an abandoned barn falling down near a pecan orchard. Seeing Hallie's startled look he screamed, "Look where Hallie's going to spend the night with old Laura Fitzgerald," and this time pointed to a Negro house leaning crazily over the red gully next to the road.

"You hush," said Laura, and whacked him over the head with her *Algebra*, then turned to resume her conversation with Maynard. In a moment they stopped in front of a modest white farmhouse and Claude carefully stepped on Laura's feet as he went by. Maynard leaned sidewards from the driver's seat and spanked him on the behind. "Stop that cuttin up or you'll walk," he said.

So that was where May Belle and her big Buick lived. She had stayed in town to visit with Virginia and she might even spend the night now that Hallie was away, and sleep in Hallie's bed.

A minute later the bus pulled over to the side of the road before a square warehousy kind of store. "Here we are," said Laura. Over the porch steps of the store was a sign that said "Fitzgerald and Sons."

"There's Daddy now," said Laura, "on the porch." (Part of her prissiness was calling her father "Daddy" instead of Papa like everybody else.) They went on past the store toward a square house with a big porch across the front. The porch was held up by four round unfluted columns, but there was no fanlight over the door or little balcony as at Magnolia Hall or the Cartledge Old Home Place. The columns had been tacked on as an afterthought; nothing else went with them. The house was painted a dazzling white; it might have been finished yesterday.

They entered a fenced-in yard and a wizened little man waved to them from a rocking chair. A long lanky figure was stretched out on the steps, a Daniel Boone kind of man, thought Hallie. The little old man rose from the rocking chair, side-stepped a vinegar jug in his path and wiped his mouth in preparation for kissing. Laura greeted him as if she were returning from a trip away, not just from school. Then he leaned his wrinkled face with small tobacco-brown eyes toward Hallie. He expected to kiss her too. He aimed for her lips but she turned her face and he kissed her on the cheek and said, "Mighty proud to meet you," then made a courtly bow which waved an aroma of fruit cake and chewing tobacco toward her.

"Two Southern belles," he whinnied. "River, ain't often you git a chancet to have two Southern beauties like this to squire around." This must be River Ledbetter, born in a Southern mansion, the Ledbetter Old Home Place. River did not rise from his lolling position on the steps nor even look in their direction. "Sho ain't," he said agreeably.

They entered a bare unpainted hall with a stairway in back and Mrs. Fitzgerald came out of a bedroom and stood hesitantly at the door. "Mama," said Laura, throwing her books down on the table. "Come on, let's go eat scuppernongs." Hallie ducked a little bow toward Mrs. Fitzgerald and followed Laura on through the rich atmosphere of the house compounded of roasting ham, pears packed away in bureau drawers, spiced peaches, and that fruit-cake smell, heavy and rich, the smell richer than the house looked, she thought. Then she came out onto the back porch, and there in a side yard was the scuppernong arbor, a magnificent generous arbor, old and tangled with vines as thick as arms growing up the posts and spreading out over the chicken wire top.

Underneath the arbor chickens were scrabbling in the dust for fallen scuppernongs, and Hallie looked up into the vines and saw the yellow-gold globes of ripe scuppernongs among the leaves. Her mouth watered greedily just looking at them. She sometimes thought she had never had enough fruit. Mama said the red birthmark on her chest near the rib line was an apple. (Mama said she had never had enough fruit either, particularly apples, and she talked about Walhalla where she had lived as a child. There the mountain men brought red mountain apples down in covered wagons. Hearing Mama talk about the crisp red apples tumbled into the covered wagons made Hallie's mouth water too.) Later, in the peach season, Hallie studied the birthmark and thought perhaps she was marked with a peach or, in Clover on a rare trip to the Greek market, an apricot. And now, smelling the intoxicating richness of sun-soaked scuppernongs, she thought perhaps she was marked with a scuppernong, pink, overripe and winy.

"Climb up here," called Laura. "Stop looking and eat."

She followed Laura up the vine on one of the supporting posts and worked her way out on a crosspiece, cradling her feet in vines and lying along the beam as if at a Roman feast. She popped the scuppernongs in her mouth and spit the skins through an open place in the vines to the chickens below. All afternoon they lay there, the sun slanting down on them as the afternoon wore on, the windmill creaking gently from time to time as a breeze blew up over the pasture from the woods, only moving a foot or two to find a more easily reached supply of scuppernongs.

"Maynard Johnson is right cute, I think," said Laura, breaking the silence of sustained eating. "I think he could go for me if I'd let him. But . . ."

Laura's voice trailed off either from lack of interest or a resurgence of appetite. That was another reservation Hallie had about Laura; she seemed to want to talk about boys all the time, which was not too bad, but it seemed obvious that she would never be a success with them because of her prissy airs. "Stuckup," Benny said.

"Did Benny take any girls out over in Clover?" asked Laura as if she had thought of Benny at the same time.

"Not that I know of," said Hallie. Back in Clover she had not thought whether he had or not.

"I think Benny's awfully cute," said Laura. "He always looks as if he's going to bite somebody's head off. And when you say, 'Hey, Benny,' he sounds so rough . . . really it just gives me the shivers when he turns and looks at me and says, 'Hey,' the way he does."

This kind of talk coming from Laura made Hallie feel painfully embarrassed for her. After all Laura was a child—to be sure, she was a year older than Hallie, but still a child—an eighth grader, and Benny was a man, or almost a man. Laura must be as boy crazy as Virginia said she was. She could not tell Laura that at supper the night before when she said she was going to spend the night with Laura Fitzgerald, Benny had said, "With that old stuck-up Laura Fitzgerald? What on earth do you see in her?"

"She's got a big scuppernong arbor," said Virginia.

"Don't talk like that, Virginia," said Mama. "Laura Fitzgerald seems like a real nice girl."

"I should've washed my hair and let it dry out here in the sun," said Laura, leaning back on the vines and not eating. "I wonder if Benny has a girl around here?"

Hallie did not answer. Laura did not seem really to expect one.

A window was raised in the kitchen and a colored woman stuck her head out the window. "You chillun get down. We gonta eat." Even then Hallie could not resist taking a few last scuppernongs.

The dining room was small, the chairs bumping into the sideboard when they were pulled out from the table, and the sideboard crowded with jars of pickled peaches, a bowl of dusty imitation fruit, candlesticks with no candles, and flypaper. Mrs. Fitzgerald sat on the edge of her chair at one end of the table, nervously twitching a fish pole with shredded paper to shoo away the flies. The colored woman appeared with a large plate of fried chicken, paused while she looked Hallie over, then slammed the dish down in front of Mr. Fitzgerald. "Ef hits cold hit ain't my fault," she grumbled.

The table was already loaded with food, sliced ham, sweet potatoes running with sugary, buttery juice, a mound of rice, black-eyed peas with pot liquor, and pickled peaches. River came in, scraped his chair and settled his long legs under the table.

"Guess somebody better say grace," said Mr. Fitzgerald, "or Hallie'll tell her pa on us." Hallie wished Papa's saintliness did not follow her everywhere. Mr. Fitzgerald turned to River. "Brother Jones is a mighty fine man," he said, "mighty pious."

Mrs. Fitzgerald tucked her head down and said a short grace in an unassuming voice.

"Sugar, what you want, a pully bone?" asked Mr. Fitzgerald, forking over the crisp brown pieces of chicken. When he leaned toward her the fruit-cake smell enveloped her.

"Yes, sir, a pully bone, thank you," said Hallie, hoping it was a very small fryer and trying to avert her eyes from all the food on the table. Her belly filled with scuppernongs pressed against her skirt belt, and scuppernongs seemed to be stacked up all the way through her chest and into her throat.

Aunt Lootie came with hot biscuits and then with hot corn bread. "Ain't no use cookin less'n you eat," she growled when she saw the biscuits had hardly been touched.

"These little gals don't eat enough to keep a bird alive," worried Mr. Fitzgerald, trying to force another piece of chicken on Hallie. "River, you ever see such gals?"

River made no audible reply, but perhaps the deep swallow of buttermilk he took at that moment signified his agreement. Hallie wished he would talk; if she were not so full, if she did not have to concentrate on waving away the food offered by Mr. Fitzgerald she would have liked to start a conversation about the Ledbetter Old Home Place.

"We're not much hungry, Daddy," said Laura. "We just ate us a bait of scuppernongs."

"Scuppernongs ain't nothing," said Mr. Fitzgerald, "just juice. Miss Martha Nelle," he said, addressing his wife for the first time, "git some hot biscuits and jelly for these little gals."

The rich smell of fruit cake still hung over the room but when dessert finally came it was not fruit cake but ambrosia. Perhaps the fruit cakes were stored in the dark old sideboard and the smell crept out to hang over the house. Hallie's head felt dizzy from the smell, and when Mr. Fitzgerald leaned toward her to try to force on her a hot biscuit with jelly in addition to the ambrosia her head felt not her own; for a minute she thought she might be sick. But just then River's long legs under the table moved, kicked her a little, there was a scraping of chairs, Mr. Fitzgerald found a toothpick on the sideboard and they moved out into the open airiness of the hall.

Mr. Fitzgerald led the way to his bedroom and stretched his meager frame out on the bed covered with a crazy quilt. River slunk off like an Indian disappearing into the forest. Mrs. Fitzgerald lit a fire in the grate. It was not really cold but Laura and Hallie sat in front of the fire dutifully, too lazy and full to move. Mr. Fitzgerald tossed restlessly, belched and complained, "Ain't anybody goin to read?"

Mrs. Fitzgerald's wrinkled lids hung down over her eyes, giving her a hooded, watchful expression. She looked too old and dried up to have Laura, but Miss Beulah had explained to Mama, "Laura was a sure enough change-of-life baby. Her Mama thought she had indigestion and then she thought she had a tumor, and then one day she had Laura. Lord, I don't know how old the oldest Fitzgerald boy is, the one's up in Atlanta. He's done right well, I hear."

Mr. Fitzgerald tossed on the bed and said again, "Ain't anybody goin to read?" Mrs. Fitzgerald looked at Laura, but Laura stood up and said to Hallie, "Let's go out and talk to River."

River was lolling on the steps again. Dogs lay arranged around him. Now it was dusk, the sky was filled with apple-green light, and there were shadows under the trees. At any minute she would see the first star. Laura said, "Shoo," and the dogs moved, but only closer to River, and the girls sat down on the steps. River said nothing in welcome, but he did not look interrupted. There was a faint suspicion of chill in the air; a new season was being hinted at. The dogs moved restlessly around River, changing their positions.

"River, can't you tell me and Hallie a story?" asked Laura.

" 'Fraid I don't know a story," said River, moving a dog to scratch himself.

"A love story," said Laura. "Tell us a love story," she said, and jabbed Hallie in the ribs so that she could enjoy the teasing.

"Tell us about when you lived in your house down on the Big Sandy," said Hallie, trying to divert Laura.

"Tell us a love story from down on the river." Laura had a one-track mind and would not be diverted.

"Did your mother ever tell you stories, River?" asked Hallie helpfully.

"Mama was a great hand for storytellin," he said. "Oh, she used to tell us stories when we were little fellers; walkin along through the woods she'd tell us about Indians. Settin before the fire at night she'd plead with Pa to tell us stories, to tell us about when he was up North."

"But love stories, River," said Laura, "didn't she ever tell any love stories?"

River turned and twisted on the steps like one of his dogs bothered by fleas. When he spoke his voice seemed rusty from lack of use. The words came slowly and he would stop and dig his hands deep in his pockets as if he expected to bring out the right word from down in there.

"Well'm, hit weren't exactly a love story Mama used to tell or get Pa to tell. Hit were about her and Pa. She used to say to Pa, 'Lucius, tell the boys about when you first seen me.' That was the way hit'd begin."

"Well . . ." said Laura, leaving the word hanging in the air for River to catch on to. Hallie held her breath, waiting.

"Oh, she'd have to keep after Pa. He weren't a great one for talkin, like Mama. She'd have to keep on after him and keep on after him, and finely he'd start in." River's father did not sound like the brave Captain of the Featherstone Fusileers. Lucius Ledbetter, who had told her his father was Captain of the Featherstone Fusileers, was an old rogue, trying to make his father out as brave.

"Did the story begin with the War?" asked Hallie, thinking River might be like his father and need encouragement.

"Pa never did like to talk about the War. Up to the time he died when I was oh, fourteen-fifteen years old he still got mad ever' time he thought about hit. Anyways, this were when the War were over." River squirmed and changed his legs, his left pulled up and the right one down. "He rid the train and walked down to South Ca'lina from up there, up North, then he taken a little branch line up toward the mountains. Hit were a tunnel been started up there for the railroad to go thu the mountains and then the War comes on and they didn't finish it. He were comin back from the War and saying to hisself he don't need to hurry home, his mama were dead, his pa had died whilst he was away, he seen his brother killed up there in the War, ain't nothin callin for him to come home. He says he just might's well look at the mountains. He taken the train to the end of the line, some little old place over there in South Ca'lina, I forget hits name, then he taken out walkin. He had his gun from the War and a knapsack and he kind of camped out up there in the mountains. Sometimes he'd stop and stay two-three days at some little cabin, stop and talk to the folks up there. He says he hit one or two never even hearn tell of a War, just roosting up there on them knobs mindin their own business. He come all the way up to the top of the mountains and started down again and he reckoned maybe he were back in Georgia when one day he passed a chile sittin on the side of the road cryin. That's what he always said when he told us this story—'I passed this chile on the road with her apron over her face, cryin her heart out.' He ast her what were the trouble and she kept on cryin and cryin and finely she says her pa done fell down and hurt hisself and he's too big for her to lift back in the cabin. Pa ast her how long her pa been layin there and she says she thinks hit were the day before yestiddy. Anyways Pa made her lead him back to her pa and hit were true, he were dead, layin there where the tree caught him. He were clearin off a little piece of land more uphill than any other ways. And he were a right big man. Pa just dug him a grave right there and laid him in it. Then he ast this chile where were her mama and her other relations. Her mama had died two-three years before. Seems her pa kept sayin he were going to take her back to her mama's family, lived somewhere's down in there in South Ca'lina, round Pendleton, I think he said, but he heared tell they were a War goin on and he says he'd just wait twel hit had run over. Pa says he don't know where Pendleton is, and if hits South Ca'lina hits the other side of the mountains now, so he says to her she just better come on home with him. And he always said when he told us this, 'Lord, I kep wonderin who were going to look after this chile, Mama bein dead and all,' but then he thinks maybe Adam, he were a nigger they had had before the War, he thinks maybe Adam and his wife Hattie if they're still around might look after this chile for him. So he puts her up on her mule, she were still cryin, her face all swelled up from cryin, he says he ain't rightly had a good look at her because of her cryin. He put her up on the mule—that was all that was left alive in that place except for the chickens—and at the last minute this chile jumped down and ran and got a rooster and said he were her pet and she were goin to take him too."

River stopped and laughed, his laughter too sounding rusty and uncertain. "I vow hit must have been a sight, that little chile with her face all red and swelled up from cryin sittin on a mule and carryin a rooster. They started walkin down the mountain, Pa leadin the mule, and he says comin down the mountain the dogwood had come out and lay like snow in the woods, and the redbud were showin. The weather got warmer in the daytime; hit were still a little cool at night. And walkin down the mountain Pa says he begun to feel maybe he had a reason to come home, he were bringin somethin back besides his mean old thoughts. And that little chile he were talkin about, why by the time she reached Macon she were singin. Just ridin along on that mule and holdin the rooster and singin."

Here River stopped his story as if in contemplation of the picture.

"How old *was* she?" asked Laura.

"She weren't no child," River laughed as if he had managed to fool them. "Hit's a fact she were little, a skinny girl, I reckon, but she were about seventeen. When Pa would get to the part about her sittin on the mule and singin, Mama would always say, 'Tell the boys about you singin too, Lucius,' and Pa would kind of grin and he always said, 'I outdone the rooster and the mule.'"

"Did they get married," asked Laura, determinedly, "and live happily ever after?"

"Pa says they might's well get married in Macon. Then he wouldn't have to worry no more about who were goin to look after her."

Laura seemed to want to hear him say the words. "Did they live happily ever after, River?" she asked again.

"Well'm, now, I reckon you might say so. Pa were quair, he were right quair after the War. He didn want to see people. He just wanted to stay down in there at Tranquil and mind his business and sometimes he wouldn't even talk much to us. But Mama were always happy. She says once she had just about everythin she wanted. So I reckon you'd say she lived happily ever after."

All the stars had come out now and hung low in the sky. There was no moon and darkness was thick under the trees. The heavens were deep and full of sad faraway worlds. The dogs moved restlessly; one whined and tried to run in its sleep. Hallie thought of the Ledbetter Old Home Place down near Tranquil Church, the third old Southern house, not yet seen, full of ha'nts, Margaret Craig said, and wondered if the ha'nts were the "little chile" who came down from the mountains and her soldier husband. The story moved her as she was sometimes moved by a ballad or a hymn; dampness sprang to her eyes for no reason at all.

She said now, feeling the silence too sad to keep, "Do any of your family live down in there now, River?" She knew the answer herself but wanted to hear River say.

"No'm, they ain't any Ledbetters down there now except them

in Tranquil churchyard. House is full of Duckets," he said, and spit into the bushes along the steps.

"Did you sell out to the Duckets?" asked Hallie. Laura had heard her love story and was lying back satisfied.

"Well'm, I didn't exactly sell out to the Duckets. After Mama died and the place were so run-down, the sheriff come down in there and says he's going to take hit for taxes. I says take hit, go ahead take hit, I don't care. He kept sayin that for years, comin down in there sayin he were goin to have to take hit. Finely I says go ahead and I moved on up here with the Fitzgeralds. They'd been after me to come on up here."

"Did the Duckets buy it?" persisted Hallie.

"No'm, them Duckets don't own no land. They was just brought down in here by Mr. Barksdale, runnin around the country cuttin down all the trees. I hear they'd a starved to death if Mr. Barksdale hadn't brought them down here. Now the county's as full of Duckets as a dog is fleas. No'm, hit happened when the sheriff finely put hit up for sale there weren't anybody fallin over hisself to buy hit. Finely Adam Lincoln, works down at the depot, he come in and put down the money. He owns hit now."

"Adam?" said Hallie.

"Yes'm, and then Mr. Barksdale rented hit for the Duckets. I were down there the other day, huntin. I went in and ast for a drink of water, like I never been 'round the place before. Mama would turn over in her grave if she could see what they done to her kitchen. Hits papered with funny papers like a nigger house."

Mrs. Fitzgerald appeared at the door and said, "River, Mr. Fitzgerald is ready for his medicine."

River raised up from the steps and the dogs got up too and whined at him as he picked up the vinegar jug and went toward the door. "Later," he said, "wait now."

Laura and Hallie followed River in and while he was pouring something from the jug at the washstand Laura leaned over and kissed her father good night. Hallie stood by the door, hoping that she would not have to kiss Mr. Fitzgerald good night. He lay restless now under the flickering light bulb; the crazy quilt was over him and he had fought it out of shape. She could imagine Benny if he heard about her kissing Mr. Fitzgerald saying, "Did you kiss Mrs. Fitzgerald? And did you and Laura kiss each other good night?" She would never hear the last of it.

They went upstairs and Laura felt for the light cord in her room. It was a big bare room and at first Hallie thought Laura had not settled down in it permanently, that she was awaiting some future improvement, like painting the walls or building a closet. A wire was strung across one corner for clothes, the washstand with its bowl and pitcher were across another corner, and the big dark bed sailed in a sea of slippery, sliding grass matting.

When they were in bed Hallie said, "Is River a relative of yours?"

"Maybe a little bit, second cousin once removed or something like that. Not close. But all the Ledbetters are kin to everybody in the county."

"His brother is Lucius Ledbetter up in town?" She knew it but did not want to believe it. Now that she had heard River's story and about the Ledbetter Old Home Place, she could not refer to him as Loony Lucius. She had twinges of conscience for accusing him of being jealous.

"Uh huh, and Byrd Ledbetter, his brother, lives up in Atlanta. He's doing right well, Daddy says, does something or other for the roads up there."

The moon had come up and Hallie could see out the window, past the store, across the fields to the dark woods.

"Every night before I go to sleep I can't help but think about Benny," said Laura. "I think all kinds of things," she said, and waited. Hallie thought perhaps as a proper guest she should question Laura further, but if Laura gave her confidences then she would expect some in return. She could not tell her about Mr. Jess Bailey.

Laura turned toward her and took her hand and tickled it slowly across the palm, giggling a little at the same time. "Did a boy ever do that to you?" she asked.

"Not exactly," said Hallie, not wanting to give herself away.

"You don't even know what it means?" asked Laura, shock in her voice.

"Well," said Hallie, plunging, "maybe it means he likes you."

Laura shook the bed with her laughter. "Sure it means he likes you." Then calming down, "Honey, hasn't anybody ever told you *any*thing? If a boy does that to you it means he wants you to do something . . . you know . . ."

"Oh," said Hallie. In her dreams Mr. Jess Bailey had done many things but he had not tickled her hand first.

"That little old Claude Ballard came up to me the other day right in front of the other boys and tickled my hand like that," said Laura.

"What did you do to him?"

"He was just showing off in front of the other boys," said Laura. "I told him I'd tell his Mama if he didn't watch out."

Dogs began barking over toward the woods and their bays went over the hills and measured the distance to town. The smell of the grass matting came up to her and she seemed to be riding in a boat toward a strange foreign land far, far away from home. The dogs barked again, and their bays went down the red clay road, past the Ballards, past the McGhees' pond, past the deep silent woods and, waking dogs along the way, carried back into Greenwood where Mama and Papa lay sleeping high on their pillows in the silent house without her. For a minute she wished she were home; they might be missing her.

A huge clamor of dogs rose close by, as if all the hounds in the neighborhood had been turned loose, all the rangy hounds from Fitzgerald's, May Belle's Dan, all the hounds that lay sleeping all day, moving only to scratch or fight flies, had wakened and were gathering at some rendezvous.

"What's that?" asked Hallie, rising on one elbow.

"What's what?" said Laura, sleepily.

"All that dog barking."

"That must be the men out possum hunting. I guess River went."

Hallie wished she could be out there in the woods with River and the dogs, or at home—any place but this strange bed.

"Who all went?"

"Oh, just River and the niggers, I guess," said Laura, and turned the other way as if the topic did not interest her.

"Will they bring a possum home?" asked Hallie, thinking if she stayed until morning she could go down early to see it.

"Aw, they don't hardly ever catch a possum. They just go out huntin them," said Laura. "Daddy wouldn't let us eat a possum. Every once in a while the niggers get one and cook it and eat it, but River just goes along with the dogs."

Hallie thought again how River looked like Daniel Boone— brown, lanky, with a face that carried secrets of the dark woods and animals. River was not the kind of man she expected to find coming from an old Southern mansion, but she liked him, she could not help but like him. At least he was a great improvement over his brother Lucius.

11

Miss Corrine invited Hallie and Virginia to tea at Magnolia Hall. "Come home with me after school," she said, "and I can run you back later." May Belle Ballard said she was mad at Miss

Corrine for not inviting her. "Why couldn't she have invited Virginia and me together? We're older," she said, and looked askance at Hallie. But Hallie knew that Miss Corrine had invited her because she felt a special way about her.

It was a good thing that Miss Corrine only asked them a day ahead. Hallie pushed Mr. Jess completely out of her mind that night before she went to sleep. Her thoughts were entirely with Miss Corrine and how lovely she was. How warmly she would meet Hallie as she came into her classroom; she would put her arms around her shoulders and look deep into her eyes. Sometimes she would say, taking hold of one of Hallie's plaits (this was almost as breathtaking as having Mr. Jess touch them), "Hallie, I wish I knew what went on in that head of yours. You're a mystery to me."

Both Hallie and Virginia dressed more particularly the next day. They were going to tea at Magnolia Hall. They waited outside school for Miss Corrine and walked with her to the parking lot where she kept her Ford. As the road ran downhill toward the bridge over the creek Miss Corrine said, "Have you ever smelled anything as delicious as that damp smell of bay?" and Hallie and Virginia sniffed too, speechless. The white pigeons flew up from the dovecote as they turned into the driveway. "Don't you love that old dovecote?" Miss Corrine said. "Father was about to have it taken away when we bought the place; it was falling to pieces and filthy inside. No one had cleaned it out for years. It *smelled*. But Mother thought it would be beautiful with white pigeons in it to match the house. She got it fixed up and then Father ordered the pigeons. She hardly lived long enough to see them. Now Father wouldn't take anything for that dovecote. He says the sight of those pigeons flying up is the most beautiful sight in the world to him." Then, as if taking them truly to heart, she said, "You know, for a long time I could hardly bear to drive up this driveway and see them. So I just stayed away up in North Carolina, visiting my aunts. Now I really am in love with this old place."

Could the change have come because she was "in love"? She never mentioned Mr. Jess Bailey, but it was perfectly obvious that they were going together. He had prevailed upon Miss Corrine to sit in the choir though she giggled and said she could hardly carry a tune. But they sat there side by side each Sunday now, sharing the same songbook, Miss Corrine's lips moving in a semblance of singing even if she could not carry a tune.

Miss Corrine stopped the car in front of the steps and they walked up onto the big white porch behind the columns (a fountain of delight in Hallie's chest), stood momentarily beneath the little balcony and looked out—oh the expansiveness of space seen from the big front porch—then entered the wide dark hall. A round silver dish on a console near the door made a pool of light like an eye, one calling card swimming in it. A stairway curved away at the end, waiting for a bride with a train to descend. They turned into the living room (in Magnolia Hall it would be called the parlor) and Miss Corrine disappeared to talk to the cook in the kitchen. Soon the cook came, wearing a big white apron, her head wrapped in a white turban, bearing a silver tea set and tiny flowered cups. Miss Corrine pulled a chair up to the table and sat there like a small girl having a tea party. Hallie was not used to hot tea. The cups were fragile, and her fingers felt suddenly as swollen and stubby as the fingers of Essie Jones. She sipped hastily and put the cup down quickly for fear it would crash from her hands. Miss Corrine offered them tea cakes from a cut-glass dish, and the cook appeared from time to time asking if Miss Corrine wanted hot water or more tea or tea cakes. Hallie sat suspended dreamlike in the hour, the high ceiling, the dark furniture, the red figured rug on the floor all sinking, slowly sinking into her, or she into them. "Oh, Miss Corrine," said Virginia, finding her voice, "this is the prettiest room."

"It is a beautiful room," said Miss Corrine. "Mother was awfully good at fixing up houses. I didn't see it before it was painted, but I hear the house was almost as bad as the dovecote.

I was still in school up in North Carolina. Then Father thought I should go over to GSCW since we were going to live in Georgia."

"GSCW is a very fine school," said Virginia. It was nice that at least one of them had a voice. Hallie simply could not do anything but look and feel.

"Oh, it is," said Miss Corrine, "but I wanted to go on. Two years . . . why you hardly have time to get started."

Hallie tried a sip of tea to prepare to enter the conversation.

Miss Corrine said, "Don't tell Mr. Holden, but sometimes I think I'm only one jump ahead of you girls."

"Would you keep on studying expression?" asked Virginia.

"They call it speech at Columbia. I even sent off for a Columbia University catalogue." She made a little face, as if to say it was a silly thing to do. "But I'd settle for the University of North Carolina. I still would like to go *somewhere*. There's so much still to learn." And this time she made a gesture with her hands, opening them out toward the world, laughing at herself at the same time.

Then perhaps she was not in love with Mr. Jess Bailey. Perhaps she just went with him this year for company and next year she would go away. Hallie wanted her to go and to stay.

"Father was so lonely I felt I just had to stay with him this year."

Mr. Barksdale with his eyes on the business at hand never struck her as the kind of person who would be lonely. She would have said "lonesome"; "lonely" was a prettier word.

"Let's talk about you for a change." Miss Corrine smiled into their bemused eyes. "I've been meaning to tell you girls how well you're doing. I want you both to try out for the contest at the end of school."

"Have you met Miss Bootsie Craig?" asked Virginia.

"No," Miss Corrine smiled. "I haven't met her. I hear she was quite good in her day."

"I don't like her method of teaching as well as yours," said Virginia. Her sister was wonderful; she might have been going out to tea every day.

"From what I've heard," said Miss Corrine, "she seems to teach elocution, not expression—and certainly not speech." She smiled again.

Miss Corrine seemed to be so much at home, as if all this lovely furniture, the silver tea service, the red rug, the cook in a white turban, the silver card tray—all the splendid setting of Magnolia Hall—were her accustomed environment. Yet she wanted to go away to study. She might become as learned as Edna Earl in *St. Elmo*. She belonged in Magnolia Hall, Hallie thought painfully, painfully because she had thought the opposite so hard.

As they went back through the hall, Hallie looked at the silver card tray and longed for an engraved visiting card to leave. (Southern ladies always used real engraving which you could tell by running your fingers over it; printing was considered tacky.) On the porch they stood for a moment underneath the balcony, and if it had not been the first visit and a rather formal occasion Hallie would have liked to ask Miss Corrine if she might run upstairs through the hall and step out and survey the world from it. Did Miss Corrine sometimes stand there like Juliet when Mr. Jess Bailey came riding up on his beautiful horse? Miss Corrine must have read her thoughts or felt them because she said suddenly, "Perhaps next spring some of us can come down and do some scenes from Shakespeare. When you have your breathing right." She looked at Hallie warmly when she said this. And Hallie was sure, absolutely sure, that at that moment Miss Corrine thought of her reading the part of Juliet.

That night the dainty tea cakes, tasting like so much paper at the time, exploded on her taste buds in all their vanillaed and rose-watered delicacy, in all their buttery crispness, and Hallie winced as she remembered that she had eaten six—six, like a gluttonous child. She blushed in bed. Would Miss Corrine remember too?

Later, of course, Miss Corrine invited the other members of the class to tea. Two at a time. May Belle Ballard was angry again because she was invited with Laura Fitzgerald. "Just because we live out on the same road and Miss Corrine will have to drive us home together," she said. But Hallie and Virginia were the first and Hallie knew that Miss Corrine had talked to them in a way she had not talked to the others.

12

Now that she had visited Magnolia Hall she wanted more than ever to see the old Ledbetter place. River and his love story floated in and out of her mind like a ballad. She still felt sad about Lucius (sad to hear that he came from a fine old house or sad that he was practically a tramp?); she must go to see it. She reminded Margaret Craig of her promise to get her father to drive them down but Margaret always said, "Papa's too busy just to drive us down. Someday when there's trouble down in there he'll take us."

But Tranquil stayed as tranquil as its name. Hallie considered asking Benny to take her in the stripped-down Ford. She would have to admit that she wanted to go down in the country to see an old house and then Benny would likely say at the supper table, "Have you heard? Hallie is looking over real estate. She's thinking of buying the old Ledbetter place."

In any case, Benny now had a job working at McGhee's Drug Store after school and on Saturdays. One Saturday afternoon

Laura Fitzgerald bought four dishes of ice cream. Hallie accompanied her for the first one and they sat at a little table in front of the case full of Nunnally's chocolates. Laura had not paid the slightest attention to anything Hallie said but kept her eyes on Benny the whole time, watching him dish out ice cream and dopes and make milk shakes. When he sprinkled in nutmeg on top of a vanilla milk shake Laura seemed to be in a kind of ecstasy. Hallie thought how really sad Laura's case was; she definitely was not the type to attract men, with her long nose always a little red on the end, her mousy hair that needed washing.

November came and still Hallie had not had a chance to visit the Ledbetter place. The mornings were cooler and the pecans were dropping in the back yard. Margaret Craig might lose interest now since it was too cold to go swimming in the Big Sandy. One Saturday morning it seemed unusually cold and when Hallie came shivering into the kitchen to dress, Mama said, "First frost last night. Good hog-killing weather," and Elberta, who was washing dishes, her stomach a little poked out (she *was* going to have a baby, after all), said, "Yes'm, this is the day for it. Down home, I reckon they's already at it."

Hallie was still sitting at the table in the warm kitchen when Margaret Craig called in the back door. Margaret panted out as if she had run every step of the way, "Papa has to go down to Tranquil today. Says he'll carry us if we'll hurry. We got to be right ready and waiting when he comes back."

They sat bundled up in the swing on the jail porch, waiting for Mr. Craig to come back. Floyd, one of Margaret's younger brothers, a scrawny little boy with a milky transparent face that showed his blue veins, strained over a broken-down bicycle near the front steps.

"He's going to try to go too," said Margaret, talking out of one side of her mouth like a ventriloquist. "Pretend it's no fun."

"You gonta look for persimmons?" he said, watching them steadily.

Margaret puckered her mouth and made a face. "Who would

want any of those old things?" she said. "Papa's out looking for criminals, not persimmons. We probably won't even get out of the car."

"What's Hallie going for?" he asked suspiciously.

"I wish Papa didn't want us to go," said Margaret Craig. "I'd much druther stay home on Saturday morning," she said, stretching and yawning as if faced by the most boring prospect. "Having to sit still in the car, seeing nothing but a old run-down ha'nted house . . ." Margaret was carried away with her part.

"I'm going too," said Floyd.

When Mr. Craig drove up Floyd ran and jumped into the back seat and refused to be dislodged. Hallie and Margaret sat in front.

"Papa, I declare," said Margaret, "the only way you can get shet of Floyd is lock him up in one of the cells."

"Reckon we don't have a empty one his size right now," said Mr. Craig, "but if he ain't nice I'll find one for him when I get back. You going to act nice?" he said in a threatening voice, turning his big red whiskery face to look at Floyd.

"I will, Papa," said Floyd, meek as an angel.

They drove past the stores and down Schoolhouse Street, past the schoolhouse with its Saturday-morning loneliness, past corn stalks standing in the field, and dipped down toward the branch before Magnolia Hall.

"Bang, bang, bang, bang," yelled Floyd behind them, leaning out the back seat and pointing an imaginary gun at the pigeons flying up from the dovecote as they went by.

"Papa, make Floyd stop."

Mr. Craig gave Floyd a fierce look but said nothing.

In the pasture beyond the house where white horses used to prance in the heyday of Magnolia Hall five or six black and white cows were grazing now.

"I should think Mr. Barksdale would keep horses instead of cows," said Hallie, feeling that cows were inappropriate to Magnolia Hall.

"He's starting him up a herd of dairy cattle," said Mr. Craig. "They's goin to be big money in dairyin, I hear. Lord, I hope they's somethin folks can raise and make a little money. Boll weevil's done ruined cotton."

"Horses are prettier than cows, I think," said Margaret.

"Hell, honey, they don't raise cows for looks and that's a fact. When they used to raise horses down here it was because they could *sell* horses. They ain't any money in horses nowadays. Mules, maybe, but not horses."

Mr. Jess Bailey, of course, appreciated horses and knew how to ride them. If he persuaded Miss Corrine to give up going to the University he might bring horses back to Magnolia Hall. Yet Hallie wanted Mr. Jess to look at *her* with love. Sometimes at night she thought she could not bear it that he would never take her on his horse, never brush her cheek with his lips. But with him raising white horses Magnolia Hall would fare well—and Miss Corrine, she had to admit, was born and bred for Magnolia Hall. She fitted it perfectly, and though he came from a shabby, common house in Greenwood, Mr. Jess would fit there too.

"Where'd all the horses go they used to keep down at Magnolia Hall?" asked Margaret. "Did they all get sold?"

"Lord, that was all so long ago," Mr. Craig said, "though I guess they used to keep some nice saddle horses down there even when I was a boy. Everybody kept a horse or two to ride on or pull the carriage to church. But they ain't been any real horse-raisin down here on a big scale since the War. That's what I used to hear anyways. It was in the time of Mr. Willy Featherstone's father, he was Willy too, Cap'n Willy Featherstone; he went up to the War and come right home. Seems he got some little injury up there." Mr. Craig grinned as he said this. "He got some little injury up there and he come on home and pretty soon he was hobblin round the country buying up horses. All the fellows that could had gone off to War and the niggers cut loose and they wasn't anybody much left to plow. Most ladies couldn't plow or make feed and the horses got bony and they was right glad to sell them off to Cap'n Willy Featherstone cheap. Then Cap'n Willy would take them in a big string up there to North Georgia and sell them to the army. He kept some of the best ones, the prettiest ones, for breeding and when the fellows come home from the War, them that did, and they didn have a horse, why they had to go to Cap'n Willy to buy one. Nobody else had horses."

Floyd leaned over the back seat and breathed down their necks trying to hear. They were riding through flat country now on a rough sandy road, through fields of stiff cotton plants holding wisps of cotton and corn fields with the yellowed stalks standing.

"I reckon the South was glad they could get horses somewhere," said Hallie, seeking to find excuses for Captain Featherstone. She could not give up the hero on the statue easily. This was the same kind of talk that Lucius Ledbetter had given her back last summer on the bench in front of the post office.

"That's exactly what old Cap'n Willy used to say. He ain't been dead too many years. I remember him sittin around downtown. When the fellows come back from the War and some of them found their horses down there in Cap'n Featherstone's stables actin as brood mares for his horse-raisin business, they didn like it. But as Cap'n Featherstone said, he just did his duty furnishin the South with horses."

Mr. Craig could make excuses for old Cap'n Featherstone, or repeat the excuses that Cap'n Featherstone had made for himself; even Hallie could make them for him, but she had a feeling of guilt at the same time. Mr. Craig was saying the same thing Lucius had said, except that Lucius had not told her the whole story. And because Lucius was poor and old and had no standing she had not believed him, she had told him that she thought he did not tell the truth, told him that he was jealous. Since then when she saw him on the street, though he looked at her expectantly with his bright Santa Claus eyes, she had looked away and pretended not to see him at all.

They had reached the dark woods now and the red road tilted down. Palmetto fans grew beyond the ditches and vine ropes hung from the trees. Floyd had his head out the window and his tongue out like May Belle's Dan scenting the breeze. He leaned even farther out as they clattered across the boards of Big Sandy Bridge and tried to spit in the slow red water underneath. Up the hill on the other side, a Negro house sat alone in a cotton field. Oh, the loneliness of Negro cabins in their far fields, the smoke a signal to the world of . . . what? This morning the smoke stood straight up in the still, chill air.

"I imagine they's hog-killin," said Mr. Craig, turning off into the rutted road that ran through the cotton field to the Negro cabin. He parked under an oak near a small runabout Ford.

In the back yard Adam Lincoln from the depot was shaving the pink carcass of a hog stretched between two posts. He had his coat off and an apron tied around his waist and he looked like the most dignified black barber that ever shaved a pig. Several children were piling wood under the big pot and the steamy vapor from the pot and the smell from the burning wood hung in the chill air. Adam laid down his knife and came over to the car.

"How you, Mr. Craig, how you all?" he said, including the children, then stooping from his height he peered into the car and added, "There's Hallie in there too. How you today?"

Mr. Craig said, "Fine, fine. Everything all right down in here, Adam? All these your children?" he said, gesturing toward the children, who had stopped feeding the fire and stood now staring at the car, standing as if caught in a game of statues.

"No, sir, Mr. Craig, you know these ain't my children. These my grandchildren. They keep Mary company whilst I'm up in Greenwood at the depot. Their papa's gone to Dee-troit."

"Looks like a pretty good hog you got there," said Mr. Craig.

"He's a pretty nice hog. Mr. Jones give me the day off so's I wouldn't have to do my hog-killin on Sunday. First good day we had for it."

"Sure is nice and plump," said Mr. Craig. "They's nothing like a nice fat pig when the weather cools off."

"Yessir, he's nice and plump. Guess I ought to get a couple good hams off him. Mary really knows how to raise pigs."

"They's just nothing like it," said Mr. Craig, "a little fresh pork or sausage for breakfast. Or hog liver," he added.

"If'n I had something to put it in I could give you a piece of the liver," said Adam, looking toward the table.

Mr. Craig leaned over to the back seat and felt around on the floor of the car among the guns and handcuffs and chains and rusty wrenches and came up with a tin pan.

"Just lay it in there," he said.

Adam went away and came back with the pan covered with a piece of newspaper.

"Son, put this back there on the seat with you," said Mr. Craig, starting up his motor again. "Well, just stopped by to see how you all were gettin on down in here," he said to Adam. "Got to get on down in the country on some business."

A woman appeared in the door of the cabin and watched them drive away. Adam went back to shaving the pig and the children's tableau moved again.

"I always thought Adam lived up in town," said Hallie.

"He does all week," said Mr. Craig, "but this is his home place. He leaves his wife down in here runnin the farm and he works up there in town durin the week and preaches on Sunday. Nobody can say Adam is lazy."

"Did they used to work for the Ledbetters?" asked Hallie. She was remembering that when Lieutenant Ledbetter came home from the War with his bride he hoped that Adam would still be there.

"Yeah, they're Ledbetter darkies. His pa was named Adam Lincoln before him; he was freed by old Mr. Ledbetter when he come home from the War. He freed him and give him fifty acres. Well, the family's done right well. Nobody knows how many acres they got now."

"Does Adam own more than fifty acres?" asked Hallie.

"Honey, Adam Lincoln is gettin on to be one of the richest men, black or white, in Plum Branch County. I can't say it was exactly hard work, though both this Adam and his pa before him were right hard workers. It was more like luck. When the old Ledbetter place was up for taxes, ain't more than a few years back, nobody would consider buyin it. What was cleared was old wore-out land, wore out by cotton; nobody ever put a sack of fertilizer in it. Then there was I don't know how many acres of old swamp land runnin along the river, swampy, full of mosquitoes. The house was fallin down; you'll see. In some places the land had just been let go so long little pines had sprung up in it again, what hadn't been gullied out, so's anybody who wanted to plant cotton would have to clear the land again. Well, it just set down there, nobody come up to buy it, and finely Adam walked up and he plunked down around seven hundred dollars in cash—that's what they were askin. Everybody said he was just a land-hungry old nigger. He says to Mr. Sawyer, he was the sheriff before me, he says he didn care about the house. But Mr. Sawyer says it's the same price, house or no house, all part and parcel. So Adam says he reckoned he'd take the whole thing. Lord"—here Mr. Craig leaned back and laughed —"Lord, he hadn no more'n bought it than here come Mr. Barksdale from up there in North Carolina. Come down here and built a planing mill and all them Duckets come along to run the sawmills and what with those swampy woods near the river and that new growth of pine that old nigger's really been rakin it in. I wisht I had his bank account."

They had turned into a road that ran through the woods as Mr. Craig talked and Margaret Craig said, "Here's the road down to the old Ledbetter place. Even the road down here is spooky." She shivered as they moved deeper into the shade of the deep woods. Soon light shone up ahead and they came out into a clearing behind a house. A barn tipped crazily toward the woods as if it longed to lean over and join the trees. Pig pens and smoke house stood up straighter but they too were in need of props. As they came into the yard they could see that hog-killing was going on here too.

"Well, if hit ain't the sherf," said a hearty voice, a voice like Mr. Buck Ducket's but somewhat smaller in scale. The figure that went with it was smaller too. "How ya, sherf? All these your chillun?"

"All but this'n," said Mr. Craig, motioning toward Hallie and climbing out from under the wheel. "See you're hog-killin, or maybe I should say pig-killin," he said, sizing up the runty small pink carcasses hanging between the posts.

"They's kind of measly," said Mr. Ducket. This was Mr. Ray Ducket, brother of Mr. Buck Ducket. "Kinda measly little old pigs, but my wife says she's cravin some fresh pork. You cain't turn down a woman when she gets to cravin somethin that way," he said, smiling weakly and winking at Mr. Craig. "Here's my wife now," he said. "Sugar, this here's the Sherf and his chillun, all except this'n."

"Proud to meet you," said Mrs. Ray Ducket, spitting expertly over the banisters. Her lower lip was poked out with snuff and her stomach was poked out with a baby. Maybe that was why Mr. Ray Ducket did not dare say no when she said she wanted pork, afraid she would mark the baby with a pig. "Won't you all come in and set by the far?" she asked. The Ducket talk had a special quality all its own. "Far" for fire, "sherf" for sheriff. There seemed to be a curdling and thickening of words that sounded strange in Greenwood; common as the Greenwood talk was, the Ducket talk was of a lower order.

The back porch Mrs. Ray Ducket stood on sagged toward one end. The boards of the house were silver gray; if they had ever had paint it had been so long ago that not a trace remained. Piles of rotting brick and lumber suggested that part of the structure, perhaps the detached kitchen, like the one at Mr. Shadrack Cartledge's place, had fallen down completely.

"No'm," said Mr. Craig, "we can't stay long. Just come by to talk to your old man a little and see how you folks gettin on down here in the country. You children go play" (a camouflage for the serious business of tracking down a dangerous criminal?).

The little Duckets, who had been standing there on bare blue feet staring at the newcomers, shuffled uneasily as if something might be expected of them.

"Go git some of your play-pretties," said Mr. Ray Ducket to the oldest child, a little girl with stringy brown hair who seemed to be wearing her mother's sweater. "This here's Darleen and this here's Ray Junior, we just call him Junior, and Delta, Paul and Woodruff. Junior, go git that bladder ball I made for you."

Ray Junior went over to the woodpile and picked up a repulsive swollen white object with stringy bloody gristle attached to it, and kicked it toward them. "Ketch," he said.

Hallie jumped to one side to avoid the ball, distaste rising in her throat. She walked toward the front of the house. After all, she had come to see the house, not the Duckets. An old Southern house now owned by a Negro and lived in by riffraff, poor white trash. Darleen trailed along with her.

They stepped over broken fences, tin cans and rusting equipment. As they passed the crumbling chimney and came up to the front of the house Hallie could see a clearing between house and river, not a lawn exactly—it could not be called a lawn—but a clearing between the dark woods on either side. As she stood there looking at the red river flowing at the foot of the hill a big black bird, perhaps a crow, lazily flapped its way from one wood to another. The open space was like a theater for birds. She walked on across the hard-packed dirt yard and looked back at the house.

"What you starin at?" asked Darleen.

"I'm just looking at your house," said Hallie, feeling as if she had driven out of the sun and into a dark shaded place. The house was exactly like Magnolia Hall—same six square columns, same balcony over the door, same wide expanse of veranda—and yet not the same, as in a horrible before-and-after picture. A board from the near pillar had sprung and made a little cubbyhole; Darleen ran to it now, extracted an old envelope and a folded newspaper, examined them and put them back.

"That's where I gets my mail," she said.

The fan light over the door had cardboard in two panes and a pillow in another one; the veranda steps sagged dangerously, and Hallie felt sure that Juliet would fall, balcony and all, into the arms of Romeo if she attempted an appearance here. How sad, how sad to see an old house falling into decay. Looking at it from the front, the whole house seemed to lean a little like the barn.

River, Lucius, and Byrd, the one off in Atlanta, had lived here with their mother and father, and though from River's story they did not sound like traditional ladies and gentlemen of the Old South the story River had told about his mother and father had been as sweet and sad as a ballad; she could not help liking him. But before them there had been other Ledbetters. The one who had built this house must have been gracious and cultured; he must have had a special love of watching the river and the birds. Magnolia Hall with all its great trees did not have as fine a position at the top of a hill. Oh, if this were mine, she thought, I would name it Montpelier.

"Didn't they ever have a name for this house?" she asked Margaret Craig who had come up and stood by her.

"Ledbetter's Old Home Place is all I ever heard," said Margaret. "Look at that old red river. If it wasn't so cold I'd sure like to get in it. You all go in washing much down here?" she asked Darleen.

"No'm," said Darleen. "They's snakes down there."

Over to one side the children had a tire swing hanging from a water oak. River must have sat under that tree in summer surrounded by his dogs. Lucius with his crawfish walk had gone up and down those steps, sat rocking on that porch. Now he looked the way the house looked. It sagged and he sagged. But someone might still save it; oh, it could be saved, she thought, straightening the house, painting it, cutting the clearing between house and river to make a sweep of lawn, perhaps installing a dovecote. What about Byrd who had done so well off there in

Atlanta? Wouldn't he come back and save the house if he only knew?

Floyd came up to them now with another nasty blown-up bladder. "Mr. Ducket made me one too," he said. "Ketch—" And he threw it toward Hallie, who screamed.

"Floyd, you stop that or I'll tell Papa to lock you up," said Margaret.

"You children come on now. We got to be gettin on home," called Mr. Craig.

"Papa, you're not going to let Floyd take that nasty old bladder in the car, are you?" asked Margaret.

"They ain't nothin wrong with a bladder ball, Sister, just pig like any of the rest of it. Come on up to see us when you come to town," Mr. Craig said to Mr. Ray Ducket.

"I'll bring you up some sausage when my old lady gets hit made." Mr. Ray Ducket stood by the car with one foot on the running board, loathe to let them go.

Mr. Craig said, "You better fix up that back porch. Jack it up a little before your wife or one of the children fall off it and get hurt."

"Sometimes I think hit'd be a blessin if the place just burned down. Hit's fallin apart faster'n we can fix it up. I never really liked movin into a house owned by a nigger anyhow, but Mr. Barksdale rented it before we come. But I ain't going to put in a lot of work fixin it up."

"I'd hate to see it fall down," said Mr. Craig. "You got a growin family. Maybe you ought to buy it."

Hallie cried out to herself, no, no, the Duckets are not the right kind of people to own Montpelier.

"Lord, I ain't gonta buy this old run-down place," said Mr. Ray Ducket. "We cain't use some of the bedrooms, the roof leaks so."

"We'll pray it don't rain then," Mr. Craig said with a laugh and stepped on the starter.

As they went back down the dark road through the woods

Hallie thought suddenly of the reason for their trip. She spoke to Margaret quietly, not wanting Mr. Craig to think she was butting in. "Did he find out about the criminal?"

"Pa," said Margaret Craig, "did you find out about that nigger?"

"What nigger, Sister?"

"I thought there was a nigger in a fight down in here and you came down to try and find him."

"Oh, *him*," said Mr. Craig. "That's right. I spoke to Mr. Ray Ducket about him. He thinks he's lit out for Macon." Mr. Craig drove along silently for a while, then said, "And, Sister, I got to git out around the county a little you know. 'Lection's comin up and all them Duckets could swing a lot of votes." They drove in silence for a while. "Besides, it was a good day for hog-killin," he said.

13

Benny said that Virginia and May Belle Ballard were "Boyce" crazy. "Seen any nice Boyce lately?" he would say as they sat down to supper, and Virginia would turn red and say, "You hush!"

It had taken May Belle and Virginia awhile to find out about the young man they had seen moving into Miss Lizzie Wallace's on that Sunday afternoon. Then after they learned his name they did not know much more about him than Miss Beulah had to tell: that he was a highway man, that he was a brother of Sam

McClure, the highway man who had been caught (naked) in bed with Miss Mary Emily Cartledge, and the son of Wake McClure, who was the representative up in Atlanta.

Elberta was from the Dewy Rose Community too, and now that she obviously was going to have a baby—she had begun to look like a pear in shape as well as in color—Hallie wondered again who could be the father of the unborn baby. If Miss Beulah had discovered anything about Boyce McClure and Elberta, for once she had failed to pass on the news.

One day when Mama had gone down the street on an errand Hallie asked Elberta if she knew Boyce McClure from the Dewy Rose Community. She watched Elberta closely as she asked the question, waiting for some telltale blush to sweep up from her neck. Elberta was ironing; she stopped and stood very still, lashes lowered on her cheeks, her hand on the iron. "McClure? I hearn tell of McClures down in there. There's lots of McClures." She looked embarrassed, though Hallie could see no blush. "What did you say his name was?"

"Boyce," said Hallie.

"Well'm, I ain't right sure," said Elberta, putting her finger in her mouth and letting it sizzle against the iron. She looked uncomfortable, but there did not seem to be any more questions to ask. Hallie was glad that Mama had not been around to hear her. She would have said something like, "Well, good morning, Miss Beulah, I didn't hear you come in." Mama could not stand prying, even though she might like to know herself.

May Belle and Virginia talked about Boyce McClure constantly. They rarely mentioned his name but Hallie had figured out their code; they spoke of him with words that related to electricity. May Belle Ballard would say, shivering with delight, "I was *shocked* to death down the street just now," and Virginia would begin quivering and shivering in sympathy; or Virginia would say, "Something is wrong with my magneto," and May Belle's full red lips would turn down at the corners and Hallie would know then that Boyce McClure's "magnetic" personality had disappointed Virginia in some way.

Virginia and May Belle seemed to share their crush equally. Boyce McClure's schedule made him as distant and unattainable to one as to the other. He left Miss Lizzie's house on a highway truck early in the morning and came back late in the afternoon. On Saturdays he was available for admiration down in front of the stores, or on rare and soul-stirring occasions in the drug store, having a dope at the counter when May Belle and Virginia came in to buy ice cream. Once Hallie was with them. May Belle and Virginia made each spoonful of ice cream last about ten minutes; May Belle barely touched the tip of her tongue to the spoon. Hallie had long since finished hers and was thinking of leaving when Boyce McClure came in, wrapped his long legs around one of the stools at the counter and said, "Dope, please," to Benny. He really was very handsome, with crisp curly brown hair, brown face and blue, blue eyes. The blue blaze of his eyes which he turned on them momentarily reminded Hallie of Mr. Jess Bailey in all his unattainable charm. As Boyce turned back to his dope May Belle had a choking fit from having swallowed all the ice cream on her spoon at one time.

After he finished his drink Boyce disappeared from the drug store and from town. That was the usual Saturday pattern; he would find neighbors up from Dewy Rose doing their weekly trading and would catch a ride with them back to his home. This Saturday-night disappearance was of great concern to Virginia and May Belle. "Somebody turned the light off," they would say dismally as they saw him climbing into a crowded Ford car, Dewy Rose bound. Did he disappear each Saturday to go home to see his mother, or did some Dewy Rose siren lure him back?

In December Miss Lizzie Wallace's chickens stopped laying and May Belle Ballard was called upon to deliver a dozen eggs to her house every Saturday morning. After one of these deliveries, May Belle came by to see Virginia, her color even higher, her air triumphant; Miss Lizzie Wallace had introduced her to Boyce McClure. Virginia pouted after hearing the news and said she was "mad" at May Belle, though she did not explain why to Hallie. But when May Belle appeared later in the day they went off downtown together as usual. Of course, now Boyce knew May Belle's name. When they passed downtown as they sometimes did fifteen times on a Saturday afternoon, she would say, "Hey, Boyce," and he would say, "Hey, May Belle," but not, "Hey, Virginia."

At about this time Virginia began a new piece in expression, "The Highwayman" by Alfred Noyes. For a long time she insisted on calling it "The Highway Man," but Miss Corrine was very firm about accenting words. Miss Corrine gave Hallie "The Midnight Ride of Paul Revere," a fine piece with some exciting moments, but Hallie secretly envied Virginia "The Highwayman."

" 'The wind was a torrent of darkness among the gusty trees, The moon was a ghostly galleon tossed upon cloudy seas,' " intoned Virginia, looking at herself in the mirror and enunciating the *d* in wind and the *n* in galleon as Miss Corrine had taught her to do. When she came to the part "Bess, the landlord's daughter, Plaiting a dark red love knot into her long black hair," Virginia would forget her directions and, carried away, her voice would rise to a high nasal pitch. Or often she would stop reciting and stand brooding, looking at herself in the mirror. Virginia did not resemble the landlord's daughter in any way. Her hair was light brown and she had prevailed upon Mama and Papa to allow her to bob it only a few months before.

"Why don't you ask Boyce McClure to come to B.Y.P.U.?" asked Hallie one day when she caught Virginia practicing her piece in front of the mirror.

" 'Watch for me by moonlight, I'll come to thee by moonlight, though hell should bar the way,' " said Virginia in a deep, passionate voice. She seemed not to have heard Hallie.

138

"Didn't Miss Lizzie Wallace say he went to the Baptist Church when he's down at Dewy Rose?" asked Hallie.

"Uh huh," said Virginia.

"Then it's really your duty to invite him to come to B.Y.P.U. He's a stranger in our midst."

"Maybe May Belle and I . . ."

"No," said Hallie firmly. "You should just ask him yourself. He's a stranger in a strange land and if he doesn't come you could still count it as community service."

"Oh," said Virginia. She leaned against the bureau looking at herself thoughtfully. "I don't think I could go all by myself," she said finally.

"I could go along just to keep you company," said Hallie.

Boyce McClure's movements were well known by now to Virginia and May Belle and even to Hallie. Usually he came back to Greenwood late on Sunday afternoon, in time for supper at Miss Lizzie's—just cold fried chicken and biscuits, Miss Lizzie said. That very Sunday afternoon Virginia put on her black and white ratiné skirt and her red sweater. She and May Belle had made the skirts one Saturday afternoon from a pattern that described them as "very gamine, very Parisienne"; all the time they were sewing they sang the "Marseillaise" in French, which they were just learning in school.

Hallie watched Virginia's preparations now and said, "You want me to come with you?"

"You can come if you want to," said Virginia, not looking at her and seeming not to care whether she did or not. She continued to rummage in her top drawer for something, then added, "Please wear something besides that filthy skirt if you're coming."

Miss Lizzie Wallace's house had a small family graveyard next to it. A sagging iron gate had the name "Tarver" written on it; inside the rusty iron fence, cedars crowded over the graves casting a permanent green pall on the gravestones. Virginia stood behind one of the cedars next to a large stone that said "James Worthy

Gallant and Elizabeth Tarver Gallant." Elizabeth Tarver Gallant had a birth date but the date of her death had not been filled in. Miss Lizzie must plan to lie by her first husband.

"You're standing on Miss Lizzie's grave," said Hallie, and Virginia jumped off so quickly she dropped her lipstick.

"Is it on straight?" asked Virginia, sitting down on Miss Lizzie's half of the tombstone and pinching her cheeks.

"It looks all right," said Hallie. "Come on."

"Is he on the porch?" asked Virginia in a weak voice, hanging back.

"It's too cold," said Hallie. "He'll be sitting inside by the fire." Then, seeing Virginia lagging, "If you don't ask him to come to B.Y.P.U., May Belle will."

Miss Lizzie Wallace came to the door smiling her brave smile. Her favorite Bible verse was "Though he slay me, yet will I trust in him," and she quoted it often in church with a sweet smile when she rose to testify to the Lord's power and glory. Sometimes she talked about the starving millions in China, smiling bravely all the time, or how she had endured the loss of two husbands and a son who had gone to the dogs, and yet she smiled, smiled all the time. Now when she came to the door she looked surprised but then smiled and said, "Come right in, girls. Aren't you good girls to come call on an old lady."

"Yes'm," said Virginia. That was not what Hallie expected her to say and she looked to Virginia to set Miss Lizzie straight. But Virginia just stood there with her lipsticked mouth a little open, her whole face suffused with pink. Finally Hallie said, "Well, Miss Lizzie, Virginia and I have a message from the B.Y.P.U. for Boyce McClure."

"Oh, I should of known girls with a papa like yours would be about the Lord's business," said Miss Lizzie. "Come on in and I'll call him."

Miss Lizzie pointed to the door of the living room. There was no fire in the grate; the boarders must be sitting in their bedrooms. Hallie and Virginia tiptoed in to the room where the half-drawn shades and heavy curtains gave a Sunday feeling and sat down on a shiny tickly sofa whose insides were threatening to come out. It was a horsehair sofa made out of real horse hairs, as Hallie could see when she pulled at the one tickling her particularly under her left knee.

Virginia made sick-at-the-stomach noises. She was pointing to a portrait over the mantel, a gruesome picture of a man with his brains exposed. Apparently he was an ancestor of Miss Lizzie's who had been scalped by the Indians, not only scalped but trepanned by a vicious savage, and the artist had realistically drawn in every convolution and cell of the exposed brain. Virginia had her upper lip elevated in disgust, her nose wrinkled when Miss Lizzie came in and said, "He'll be here in a minute. He was taking a little nap."

"Oh," said Virginia, standing up as if she would dive through the door.

Miss Lizzie waved her back. "He won't be a minute," she said. Then she sat down and looked at the portrait over the mantel with the girls.

"Did he suffer much?" asked Hallie nodding at the picture.

"Well, if you aren't the sweetest little girl I ever did see to ask," said Miss Lizzie, shaking her head in contemplation of such sweetness. "He did have a rather lingering illness, consumption, I guess it was. He was bedridden for seven or eight years," she said, smiling sweetly. "Still, his wife and children all died before he did, and Mama, he was her uncle, had to look after him on his deathbed."

"He died of consumption?" asked Hallie.

"Yes, just the old-fashioned slow kind of consumption. Not the galloping kind they have nowadays."

Surely if Miss Lizzie's uncle had been scalped she would mention it.

Miss Lizzie continued, "I declare, I felt so bad about his picture I decided I was just going to do something about it. We had a fire just after I was married to my first husband, that was

Mr. Gallant, and we lived for a while out on his farm in the country, and I had my things out there, and when we had this fire, somebody, I just don't know whether it was Mr. Gallant or me, one or the other of us in our excitement threw Uncle Walter's portrait out the window and it landed on top of a tea-kettle spout—I reckon one or the other of us had thrown the tea kettle out too—and it poked a hole right through Uncle Walter's head."

Hallie let out her breath which she had been holding ever since she had decided it was Indians.

"Well, afterwards, I felt so sick about that portrait I just thought I would cry," Miss Lizzie said, smiling. "I decided I'd fix it myself, and I did, kind of like mending a hole in a dress. You know, you take a little piece of cloth and sew under the hole of the dress and that's what I did. Got a little piece of canvas and pasted it on and then I painted in the hair just like it was, black and kind of curly. Oh, it looked just fine and I was so proud. But somehow or other the paint I used kind of faded and I think it needs touching up again. One of these days I'm going to fix him up again."

The convolutions which looked like brains actually were curls. Hallie tried half closing her eyes and looking at the picture as if they were curls, but it did not help.

Miss Lizzie said, "Here's Boyce now. Come on in, Boycie. These girls are out doing the Lord's work."

"Yes'm?" he said.

Boyce looked as if he had been sleeping, his hair pushed up in back, his nose a little red, but there was an interested awake look in his blue eyes as he stood there waiting and gently scratching himself.

"This is Virginia, and this is Hallie, and they're the daughters of Brother Jones—you know, down at the depot. He's one of the saintliest men I've just about ever known."

"Yes'm. Pleased to meet you," said Boyce obligingly, and sat down in a rocker near the door. He was very tall and he sat down with the grace of a man who also might ride a horse very well. With his blue eyes, his crisp hair, and his shirt open at the neck, he had the air of a *highwayman*—not *highway man*—who might come riding, riding, riding in the moonlight. Then she thought about Elberta and how Elberta might have "tempted" him as Miss Beulah suggested. He still looked as if he might have done the "tempting."

Hallie waited for Virginia to begin. Virginia should take the lead; she was corresponding secretary of the B.Y.P.U., she was older, and she had the poem.

Miss Lizzie seemed to find the silence abhorrent. She looked from one to the other, smiling.

"How old *are* you girls nowadays? My, I never saw anybody grow like you. Just like weeds."

Virginia sat studying the picture of Great-uncle Walter as if she had come only for that. "Virginia's fifteen and I'm thirteen now," said Hallie.

"I declare," said Miss Lizzie.

Boyce McClure put one foot up on his knee and scratched it a little as he waited. He had a hole in his sock. Hallie thought that if Boyce McClure responded to Virginia's invitation there was no reason why she herself should not *visit* B.Y.P.U. even if she were still supposed to go to Sunbeams on Saturday. If he should come, this very evening might begin an adventure that could culminate in Boyce McClure knocking, knocking, knocking on her moonlit door. He might fall passionately in love with her; every Sunday night they would walk home from church together (too bad she lived so close) and they would sit on the doorstep holding hands, the road a ribbon of moonlight, and he would look deeply, deeply into her eyes and say . . .

"How *is* Brother Jones?" asked Miss Lizzie, unhappy about the silence.

"All right, I guess," said Hallie. Miss Lizzie had seen Papa in church that morning. He had given a long vague discourse punctuated with "Let us go *foward, foward*," making a sharp jab at the future over the top of Mama's bowed head. "Reckon he'll be coming home from the depot soon."

Virginia leaped to her feet and started for the door. "We better go," she said.

Boyce McClure looked from one to the other. He stopped scratching his feet and started scratching his head.

"Virginia honey," said Miss Lizzie, "didn't you have some message for Boycie here?" She smiled encouragingly at Virginia.

But Virginia didn't wait. She said from the door, "No'm, Papa says sometimes when we're in this neighborhood we ought to come see you."

"Give my love to your father," Miss Lizzie said to Hallie. Virginia was already out the front door. "You girls were so sweet to come. Weren't they, Boycie?"

Virginia was standing in Miss Lizzie's graveyard spitting on a handkerchief and rubbing off her lipstick when Hallie caught up with her.

"I don't think you can count it," said Hallie.

"Can't count what?" said Virginia. She stared dreamily at herself in her compact mirror, as dreamily as when she stood in front of her mirror at home reciting "The Highwayman."

"I don't think you can count a visit to Miss Lizzie under Community Service."

"Well, at least he knows my name now," said Virginia.

"That's not what I was talking about," said Hallie. "I mean you can't count a visit to Miss Lizzie as a good deed. After all, Miss Lizzie is not sick. She's not a shut-in, her hair is too yellow for her to be aged, you didn't read the Bible to her, and you didn't take her any hot nourishing soup to help in her convalescence."

"Why should I take Miss Lizzie any soup?" said Virginia irritably, speaking from another world. She put the handkerchief away in her pocket and went back through the sagging gate marked "Tarver" and down the street like a sleep walker.

"His eyes are so blue," she said, sighing.

14

Now that Hallie had seen it, the old Ledbetter place haunted her like a sad gray ghost; its silvery boards shone under the lemon-yellow winter sun on the banks of the Big Sandy; a bird flapped its way across the bird theater. The more she thought about it—dismissing the Duckets for what they were, poor white trash, buckras, interlopers of a lower order than Mr. Barksdale and Miss Corrine—the more she sought the proper inhabitants for the old place. Then the figure of Lucius Ledbetter, broken and ramshackle as the house, came to her. Thinking of Lucius caused her some disquiet; she had a small tight ball of guilt inside when she remembered that she had thought of him as an old tramp and had accused him of lying and being envious.

The last time she had seen him was on Thanksgiving Day over at the McGhees': a warm Thanksgiving Day and Lucius sat on the porch with the children after eating and Hallie had heard Miss Lill say in her loud schoolgirl voice, "Lucius, you goin to give those children your cold if you don't stop coughin on them. Don't come up here any more now until you get shet of that cold."

One day after Christmas Miss Lill brought a basket of Schleys over to Mama. "Seems to me I haven't seen Lucius Ledbetter over at your place in a long time," Hallie said as she cracked two of the pecans in her hand and looked away from Miss Lill as if she were not really interested in the answer.

"Why," said Miss Lill, "I was just telling Doc he ought to see about Lucius. Why, that old coot didn't even come up for his Christmas dinner. And he just never misses bringing some little trash for the children on Christmas."

"Maybe he went up to Atlanta to see his brother?" said Hallie.

"Honestly, Mrs. Jones," said Miss Lill, turning her eager, curious eyes on Hallie, "Hallie talks like she's been living down here all her life. Now tell me how she knows all about Mr. Byrd Ledbetter."

Hallie did not meet Miss Lill's eyes. She pretended to be interested in picking out the nuts. Mama did not say anything and after a pause Miss Lill went on, "You can be mighty sure that old Lucius isn't visitin up in Atlanta. Mr. Byrd's too high-toned. Probably don't even let on he's got two old tramps for brothers down here in the sticks."

Next day at supper Papa said that Doc McGhee had found Lucius down in Adam Lincoln's shanty next the tracks. Doc had come in to talk to Adam about it and Papa had heard them. "Wouldn't you'd a thought Adam would've *mentioned* Lucius was down there?" asked Papa. But no one answered that no one ever told Papa anything. Mama was confided in by utter strangers, but no one ever told Papa anything unless he asked.

"Reckon he takes after his boss, being close-mouthed," said Mama. She always had to ask Papa who went up to Macon and who came down.

"Is he bad off?" asked Hallie.

"Doc McGhee brought him up to his house. Says he's a sick man. He told Adam he better burn that bed old Lucius been sleeping in."

"Where did Adam sleep?" asked Mama.

"I says to him, 'Adam, where you been sleeping all the time Lucius was down there with you?' He says he's been sleeping on a pallet on the floor."

"I hope Adam doesn't catch it, whatever it is," said Mama.

"Doc McGhee says he should've known something was up because Adam came in every day or two to buy a bottle of cherry bark cough syrup. He asked Adam once if he was drinking it instead of water and even then Adam never said a word about Lucius being down there."

"I declare," said Mama, "he really does believe in minding his own business."

"Adam is a real Christian," said Papa, sounding a little disappointed that Adam had not confided in him as one Christian to another. "I remember now he was always praying for the sick in our midst; every day he would particularly pray for the sick. I just thought he meant anybody who was sick."

Miss Lill put Lucius to bed in a little room beyond the dining room detached from the rest of the house; you could enter it either from the dining room or the big porch that ran around the house. Aunt Relly came by after school and bathed him and cleaned up his room, and Dellie, the McGhee cook, took his meals in to him.

"Maybe I could take Lucius some rusk," said Hallie when she came in from school and found Mama taking it out of the oven. She had decided to get rid of that nagging ball of guilt; she would do just one little thing for Lucius, one thing that might show she had not really meant he was lying and envious, or that would show at least that she no longer meant it. If Mama asked her why she wanted to take something to Lucius she would say that she could count it as a good deed at Sunbeams next Saturday.

But Mama did not ask why. "That's a nice idea," she said. "Take a half of one of these and wrap it in a napkin. Tell him to eat it while it's hot."

Miss Lill was down at the store and Dellie told Hallie to go on in when she said she had something for Lucius. As she knocked on the door Lucius was coughing, a loose resonant cough that seemed to come from deep inside him. She waited for the sound of throat clearing to stop before she looked in.

He was propped up high on the pillows, and his small brown bloodshot eyes turned on her with the same interest that she remembered. The face around the eyes had suffered some kind of change, however; the cheeks had sunken and the neck flesh sagged. But his eyes seemed brighter.

"Hey, Hallie," he said. "Come on in."

"Mama thought you might like some rusk. She just baked it," said Hallie, taking it up to his bed and removing the napkin.

"Smells good," he said, holding it and sniffing it to show his appreciation. "Now just lay it down there." He gestured to a table by the bed on which pink paper flowers, stiffly waxed, sat in a blue vase. "The chillun brought me those," he said. "Won't you set awhile?"

"I mustn't stay," said Hallie, taking the chair by the bed. She folded her hands in her lap, and Lucius put his head back against the pillows and turned his bright brown gaze on her expectantly. By his look he always seemed to be awaiting the answer to an important question.

"I was down to your old home place not long ago," said Hallie.

" 'Tain't my old home place any more," said Lucius. "It ain't any Ledbetter's old home place. Belongs to Adam."

Hallie was sorry she had started the conversation that way. He would be embarrassed that his old home place was owned by a Negro. She tried to think of something to say.

He went on, "Hit ain't fell down yet?"

"Well, no," said Hallie, "but Mr. Ray Ducket says it won't be long."

"Hit was standing a long time before them Duckets, reckon it may even outlast *them*." *Them* was said in the same tone of voice that she felt about the Duckets.

"It's like Magnolia Hall," said Hallie, "except . . ." She could not express the difference. The Ledbetter place—Montpelier, she had named it—was like the bleached bones of an old skeleton wracked by the sea and finally tossed on a beach, whereas Magnolia Hall was the living, moving man in bright shining garments.

"Built by the same carpenter," said Lucius. "He come up here long years ago. My great-grandpa was still livin in a log house.

But he'd got together a slave or two, made him two or three good crops of cotton, and when the feller came thu from somewheres down near Savannah and says he knew how to build nice houses, why the folks here got him to build three of them: Magnolia Hall, my old home place, and that old Cartledge house where Shadrack lives now. Wood was all cut down on the place and the houses built one right after another."

"Don't you and River and . . . your brother up in Atlanta . . ."

"Byrd?"

"Don't you and River and Mr. Byrd want to go back down there and fix up your old home place? I don't think the Duckets are looking after it very well."

"Reckon we didn't look after hit very well, either," said Lucius, and laughed a little, which made him cough. He coughed so hard and so deep that when he finished he had to lie back and close his eyes before he had strength to spit into the child's chamber lying on the bed beside him.

Then he opened his eyes again and he said, "Mama always said hit were a shame not to keep a pretty place like that up any better'n we did. She come from a little cabin up there in the mountains (oh, I know, thought Hallie) and she says she just never drempt she were going to live in a pretty old place like Pa's, and she wished . . . many's the time I heared her wish, that she could buy some paint."

"Couldn't you buy the paint?" asked Hallie, thinking again that Lucius' mother was the right kind of woman.

"No'm, reckon not. Pa wouldn't hardly come up to town to buy vittles, much less paint."

"Why don't you write your brother up there in Atlanta, Mr. Byrd, and see if he doesn't want to fix it up?"

"Lord, Byrd don't keer about that old place," said Lucius. "He's got himself a fine place up there in Atlanta, got himself a wife and some boys. Why, I imagine that Byrd's even got to see the ocean."

"Got to see the ocean?" murmured Hallie. But it was not

really a question; more an expression of her own longing. She longed with all the passion of a child born inland to see the ocean; tried to imagine its untellable vastness, its dark and swirling depths, its monstrous waves. "Did he get to see the ocean?" she murmured again.

Lucius must not have heard her question because he did not answer it. He said, "Mama used to say she had 'bout everything she wanted except she wanted to see the ocean. Mama really loved water. She made Papa cut down ever last tree betwixt the house and the river so's she could always see hit runnin by. She even liked little tiny branches runnin thu the woods. Lord, she'd set by one and watch the way hit made the sand so clean and sometimes different colors, and the way the ferns dipped over in the damp places and those swamp lilies grew close by, and the way hit all smelled." Lucius rested his head back against the pillows and talked slowly, dreamily. "And waterfalls! Why, Mama used to go right crazy over waterfalls. Ever year in the spring she'd take us boys down to Sanford's Mill to see the water-fall. Hit were a right long piece and we'd go walkin thu the woods even when Byrd were too little to walk all the way. Me and Adam would have to take turns totin him when he pestered us. But Mama said she'd walk twice that far to see a waterfall. Oh, Mama really loved water."

"Is that why she named Mr. River River?"

"Yes'm, after she named me Lucius after Pa, she says she was goin to name her chillun for the purtiest things she knew. So she named River River and Byrd Bird."

"Oh, B-i-r-d," said Hallie.

"Bird, like a bird that flies," said Lucius, flapping his hands a little. "They tell me Bird's done changed the spellin on his name. When he run for Commissioner I seen he spelt hit B-y-r-d."

"I like B-i-r-d better," said Hallie.

"Me and River used to say to Mama, 'Mama, if you'd a had girls would you a named them Honeysuckle and Magnolia?'" He panted and coughed again and lay back against the pillow. For a while he kept his eyes shut and his fingers picked at the feather-stitching on the quilt. When he opened his eyes he looked at the room and at Hallie with surprise, as if he had been away for a while in another room, then his eyes focused and brightened and he said, "Mama said one of you boys just got to see the ocean. She used to say to Pa, 'Lucius, tell the boys about the ocean.' He seen hit when he were up there to the War. But he says he seen too much blood at the same time, he don't keer to talk about hit. He were up there all thu the War and he says he seen too much blood, from the First Battle of Manassas right on."

"Oh, the First Battle of Manassas," said Hallie. "That's where my grandfather, Papa's father, fought. He was killed there too," she said, feeling proud.

"Pa did say when anybody ast him about the War, he says, ever mornin he was there he ast hisself why. Says he kept tellin hisself over and over what the preacher said up here in the Baptist Church—that were the old wooden buildin they had before this new one, and that's where he got recruited. Says ever mornin he ast hisself why he was there and ever mornin he couldn find the answer. Says . . ."

"Didn't *you* want to see the ocean?" asked Hallie, knowing she was interrupting. The attitude of his father toward the War, a war hallowed in the memories of all true Southerners, had caused the trouble between them before. She would distract him.

"Yes'm, I'd a liked right well to a seen hit. But we decided, guess that was after Pa died, that Bird had more chancet. I was the po'liest one, and River liked the woods and he didn want to go, so Mama sent Bird up to one of Papa's uncles in Atlanta, and me and River stayed on and worked the farm. But finely, when Mama died, we thought one of us ought to come on up here to town and work, and that were me."

"Maybe if Mr. Bird knew about the house he'd want to save it," Hallie said. Suddenly she saw Lucius, his cheeks firm, his eyes bright—but not as bright as today—sitting on the porch at Montpelier, looking at the Big Sandy red and slow at the foot of the hill, birds flying back and forth across the bird theater, and River lounging on the steps with his dogs.

"Oh, Bird's got other fish to fry," said Lucius. He slumped a little in the bed now and closed his eyes.

"Mama says I shouldn't stay long," said Hallie, standing.

He opened his eyes again. "Come on back and set anytime," he said smiling, even twinkling at her. "I'm a goin to be gettin up and about one of these days soon, but twel I do I just soon have company."

As she walked across the street swinging the napkin Hallie remembered that he had not really eaten the rusk, had only smelled it. Thinking back over their conversation she wondered if she had done and said the right thing. She still had an uneasy feeling about him. Calling on him with the rusk was something any girl, any member of the Sunbeams, might do and write down on Saturday when the good deeds for the week were solemnly collected by Miss Eugenia Featherstone. Of course she had sympathized with him over the loss of his old home place, had even suggested how he might get it back, and to do him credit for all his countrified talk and his lack of refinement (he was as little like Marse Chan as anyone she knew) she had envisioned him living back down there in the Southern tradition. But of course Lucius had no way of seeing into her mind; perhaps he still remembered that she had once accused him of lying and of being envious.

If he just wanted to sniff at things, she thought next day, she would take him flowers. She poked among the rosebushes to find two pale blooms with brown edges, borrowed a brighter rose from the begonia in the living room, then she called over to where two of the little McGhees were playing in the ditch and asked if their Mama was home.

"She's gone down to the store," they sang back, and Hallie went over. She could not bear the idea that Miss Lill with her wide-eyed curiosity might say in front of someone, "How come you're so interested in that old tramp Lucius, Hallie?"

Lucius already had a caller. When Hallie entered Adam rose from the rocker beside his bed. She seemed to see him for the first time as a man who sat in a room in a chair like other men— rather than pushing the hand cart in the warehouse, or carrying the mail or shoving a keg. Compared to Lucius, flushed on his pillows, Adam's frame was the frame of health. He seemed stronger and blacker than she had ever seen him.

"Hallie, I'm mighty glad you come," Lucius said, with the snicker that reminded her of the first time she had talked to him on the bench in front of the post office. "Hallie, this old black preacher ain't going to stop until he converts me. Been workin on me, workin on me, how many years now, Adam?"

Adam laughed and said, "Guess me'n you about the same age, least we were when we were boys." He turned to Hallie. "Mr. Lucius and me grew up together down in the Tranquil section." It was the first time she had ever heard anyone call Lucius Mister, but of course it was only right and fitting that Adam should.

"Set down, Hallie," said Lucius, gesturing toward the rocker. "Adam, git the chair out of the corner there. Hallie's goin to visit a little, ain't you, Hallie?"

"Thank you," said Hallie, clutching the flowers and wanting to be sure that when she gave them he would understand why.

"Her pa is the most Christian man I ever met," said Adam. "That man is sure goin to Heaven when he dies, goin to have a special place alongside the Almighty."

"Lord a mercy," said Lucius, "he sounds too good to live. But course Adam here ought to know, he's a goin to sit up there real close too, ain't you, Adam? He's even goin to try to save a place for me."

"You shouldn't make fun of such things, Lucius," said Adam. Then Hallie realized that Adam expected that *she* should call Lucius Mister.

"Adam here comes from a real bull-headed family," said Lucius. "When Pa come back from the War he found Adam's pa settin down there waitin for him, him and Hattie. They'd hid the horses when that old buzzard, Cap'n Featherstone, was a roundin them up. Pa give Old Adam fifty acres and told him to pick out a name. Old Adam, he says he wants to be named Adam Lincoln. Pa didn't like that and he says Adam and Hattie ought to let Mama pick out a name. She was right good at namin things. Mama says he ought to be called Adam Free*man*, but old Adam, he was just as bull-headed as Adam here, oncet he made up his mind he won't swerve. He says he'll be named Adam Free*man* Lincoln, then. Pa didn't like that Lincoln part but he says he guess Adam has a right to pick out his own name."

"Mr. Lincoln were a great man," said Adam.

"Pa said he don't know what were so great about Mr. Lincoln. Said his Pa woulda let his slaves go free. Said he didn't think the niggers were worth all that killin."

Hallie gave Adam a quick sidewise look to see if he were mad at Lucius, calling him a nigger and saying they weren't worth the War.

"Reckon if your pa had been mine he'd a felt different," said Adam, laughing a little as he said it, but a dignified laugh, not a silly laugh. He did not seem to mind the way Lucius talked; he seemed *friendly* to Lucius. He was the master of Montpelier now but surely he would be willing to give it back to its rightful owners.

"Guess Mama would say if one of us boys couldn't hold on to the old home place she'd as soon see Adam Free*man* Lincoln have it," said Lucius. Could he read her mind?

Adam said soothingly, "Git well now, Lucius, and you can have it back any time you want it. We'll get Mr. Barksdale to throw the Duckets out." Could Adam read her mind?

"Pa always said they were all just as stubborn as mules, ever one of them." Lucius snickered and coughed, then went on, "Pa told Old Adam, this Adam's pa, he ought to get hisself a graven image from Africa or make hisself one out of corn shucks, stid a goin up to the Baptist Church and singin 'Wash me and I shall be whiter than snow.' But Adam here he keeps on doin the same thing."

"I respect your papa," said Adam, "but he hadn't been saved; I reckon he didn know what the Lord could do for him."

"Oh, Pa was really down on the church," said Lucius. "Said he found out about hit when that old Baptist preacher recruited him for the army. He and Mama used to argue. Mama said folks just went to church because they wuz lonely, said he shouldn be too hard on them. Pa said they went because they were scared, scared to die all by theirselves. He says he ain't scared."

"He could a done with a Friend like the rest of us," said Adam.

"Naw, he helt out, helt out to the end. Said he's never gonta set foot inside a church and he never did, and when he died Mama wouldn even let 'em take the coffin inside the church. Just had him laid in Tranquil churchyard 'longside his folks."

Lucius talked fast like a top spinning, then wobbled to a stop when he needed to cough. While the cough racked him, Adam leaned over and put his big black, pink-palmed hand under Lucius' head and then held the small chamber for him to spit into.

"Where's your syrup?" Adam asked.

" 'Tain't no good," Lucius gasped. "Doc says hit ain't no good."

"How come he sells it then?" said Adam. "I'll get you a bottle so's you can have it in the night."

Lucius lay back against the pillows with his eyes closed. His cheekbones glistened and with his eyes closed his face had a stretched, lifeless look. But suddenly he opened his eyes and said, "See, see what I told you? Ain't he bull-headed? Aimin to go down there and tell Doc what's good for me." He snickered as if he would like to be there to see it happen.

"Hush," said Adam, "hush, you better not talk so much."

"I think I ought to go now," said Hallie, but then she saw that she was still holding the bouquet. She should have put it in water instead of standing there clutching it. Now she held it out to Lucius, thinking hard because she could not say it, hoping that

Lucius could feel her apology coming down through her arm and out into the feeble blossoms: oh, Lucius, you were right and I was wrong and I am sorry.

He took the bouquet as he had taken the rusk and sniffed it, smiled one of his Santa Claus smiles and said, "Smells almost as good as a magnolia."

"I'll bring you a magnolia later," Hallie said, feeling released, feeling understood. She would beg or borrow or steal a magnolia from Miss Beulah's across the street when the season came.

"I'll be waitin for it," he said.

"Maybe you ought to put those in water," said Hallie at the door, lingering there to look at his face, to see more of his smiling eyes so that she would not have to think how his face looked when they were closed, waiting perhaps to say something further (but what?) and feeling suddenly terribly sad and choked so that she could not have said it even if she knew what to say.

Adam stood up and reached for the bouquet. "I'll fix 'em," he said. He took the puny bunch of flowers in his big hand and Hallie could see that the feeling that had run down her arm into the flowers had now passed to him. He said, looking at her solemnly and knowingly, "They're pretty, Hallie."

Hallie waved a hand to say good-by and went out into the dusk of the big porch. Miss Lill was just coming back from the store and she called and said, "Honey, how's old Lucius doing? You sure are real sweet to come over and see him." She did not wait for an answer. Her arms were full of groceries and she headed for the kitchen.

The sky and air were green and chill as pond water; a sad time of day. Often Hallie had contemplated the vastness and sadness of the world as the sun set, but this was a different sadness. She lingered in the street between the two houses; she did not want to go into the warm open brightness of the kitchen where her face and feelings would be exposed. The water oak was green-black and cold but she crawled up and sat on the boards of the tree house, then lay on her stomach and felt cold and sad. She wanted to make it all different. She wanted the world to be different for Lucius. Bird (or Byrd) should return like a knight in shining armor and restore the old house to its rightful owners, prop it up, paint it, establish Lucius in a reclining chair on the sunny porch behind the columns, and hire Adam to fetch and carry in the old Southern way (knowing his place, not telling *her* whom to call Mister). Then she pondered on Adam's black hand tenderly raising Lucius up to spit, remembered how gently he held the flowers and said, "They're pretty, Hallie," and thought, he's waiting on Lucius because he wants to, not because he has to. And the look that Lucius turned on him was that of a brother. Adam seemed to act more like a brother than either River or Mr. Bird. She began to weep, to weep for all the gray bones of Ledbetters in Tranquil graveyard, to weep for River, to weep for Lucius, to weep that Lucius had never seen the ocean and never would see it now.

15

Hallie was finishing her coffee in the kitchen, watching Elberta as she worked at the zinc-covered table. She moved carefully around the sharp corners; her stomach poked out now beneath her apron. Then Miss Beulah called at the front door and came in, obviously the joyful bearer of bad tidings, her step light, her mouth turned down at the corners. "Miss Lill says Lucius is sure a sick man. Doc says he won't last another day." And Elberta said, "Yas'm, Aunt Relly says she spent all yestiddy afternoon puttin flatirons at his feets." Miss Beulah shook her head at that and said, "It can't be long."

Therefore Hallie was prepared when she heard the next day that Lucius had died. Prepared and yet made weak by the news. "Adam was with him when he died," Mama said.

"I'm glad Adam was with him," said Hallie, and this made her want to cry even more, but she refused to give way. Virginia had come in from school with her and she would never understand how Hallie, the silly fool, could burst into tears for an old tramp like Lucius Ledbetter. Mama would think it strange too, and the last thing in the world she wanted to do was to explain. She simply would not explain.

What would she explain? That she loved Lucius; that she loved his mother, that little mountain girl who rode a mule through the springtime, holding a rooster; that she disapproved of his father yet pitied him too? Nothing was clear; she loved where she disapproved. Her throat tightened and tears came to her eyes and she wanted to run to the tree house and stretch out on the gray boards and sob.

"Doc was planning to go ahead with the funeral tomorrow; he'd already picked out one of his own coffins for him but then he thought he ought to wire Mr. Bird Ledbetter, that's Lucius' brother, lives up in Atlanta. He says to wait and have the funeral Saturday and he'll come," Mama went on.

So Lucius had to be sent to Macon to the undertaker to be embalmed—which involved buying a more expensive coffin from the undertaker, more expensive than the plain wooden boxes Doc kept as part of his "cradle-to-grave" supply. Of course Doc fully expected Mr. Bird to pay for it. "Seems as if he's gettin thoughtful about his brother kind of late," said Miss Beulah, who was passing on this information. "But I guess he feels he wants to do the right thing by his loved one," she said piously. "A little measly coffin sure reflects on the livin."

Actually Miss Lill was the one who decided the funeral should be held in the Baptist Church. She said that since Lucius had died in her house and she and Doc were both Baptists she reckoned she could choose a church for him. "After all, Brother Jamieson's been after me for years to get him to church," she said, laughing. Miss Beulah repeated this remark, shaking her head and clicking her lips to show it was in poor taste.

Hallie thought that Adam should have been the one to choose the church. He was the only one who seemed to love Lucius and respect him. Doc and Miss Lill had taken him in and cared for him, it was true, but they had never seemed to respect him. Perhaps Lucius should be buried down in the Tranquil cemetery next to his father and mother. But Doc said no, it was too far to take him and too far for anybody to go to the funeral.

Miss Beulah said that she had been asked to sing. Miss Toulou Vass was going to play, and Miss Beulah and Mr. Jess Bailey and Mr. Holden and Miss Annie Laurie Jones were going to sing a quartette. "Just what we been singing at funerals all along," said Miss Beulah, "but I think we ought to get together and run over a few songs now that Mr. Bird is comin. And his wife I imagine. They probably go to one of those big churches up there in Atlanta."

Hallie waited on the porch on Saturday, even after Mama and Virginia had gone on over to the church. Benny worked at the drug store while Doc attended the funeral, and Papa could not leave the depot because Adam had to go. She waited to see Mr. Bird arrive, thinking she would get some idea from his face what the future of Montpelier might be. Because from now on, the only hope of saving Montpelier would lie with Mr. Bird. Lucius was dead, and anyone could see that River lacked get up and go. Then Mr. Bird would have to be her knight riding down to Tranquil on his white horse, turning out those Duckets with his flaming sword, painting the house white, mending that broken column where the little Ducket girl had her post office. Lucius would not rest on the porch watching the bird theater—she almost cried again when she gave up this dream—but the house was still there, sitting above the river, begging to be saved.

A small group of men waited in front of the church. A car drove up with River and Mr. Fitzgerald in it and they joined the group.

The hearse arrived, followed by a black car almost as long as the hearse. It must be at least a Pierce Arrow, Hallie thought, and hope quickened in her bosom. This must be Mr. Bird. A man was driving and a pretty woman with a blue hat trimmed with varicolored feathers sat beside him. Mr. Bird got out of the car and in a courtly manner came around and opened the front door for her to descend. She put her arm through his and they stood waiting, heads bowed slightly, while the coffin was taken from the hearse and Doc and Shadrack Cartledge and four other men took hold of it. Adam stood off to one side, his wife Mary beside him, watching to see if the men were handling the coffin right. He looked so big and strong standing there it seemed as if he might have carried the coffin alone, and would too if they did not do it properly. Mr. Bird and his wife fell in line behind the coffin and Adam and Mary came behind them. Hallie watched all this as she moved slowly from the porch to the walk in front of the church. Then she ran quickly around to the side door, down the side aisle and into her seat in time to see the coffin come in at the front door, followed by Mr. Bird and his wife. Adam and Mary went up and sat in the balcony, and Adam leaned forward and rested his arms on the railing.

River sat in the front pew with Mr. Fitzgerald. Mr. Fitzgerald was some kind of cousin, of course, but probably not close enough to sit in front; perhaps River just would not go up there without him. River looked solemn, as usual, and not at ease. In a dark-blue serge suit, much too short in the sleeves, he seemed like a wild animal suddenly caged. His long skinny hands and bony wrists seemed to be as long as the rest of his arm and he was having trouble deciding where to put them. His legs caused him trouble too as the pallbearers crowded together getting the coffin in place on the table in front of the pulpit. When he pulled his feet up out of the way his knees seemed to come up too far and he threw his long hands around his knees trying to anchor both. Mr. Bird and his wife stood in the aisle as the pallbearers placed the coffin, then very politely he stood to one side while his wife sat down. As Mr. Bird sat down he leaned over to shake hands with River. River seemed surprised to see him and offered his hand, when he found it, timidly and awkwardly, while Mr. Bird shook hands as if he did it often.

Brother Jamieson had walked to the pulpit and now he began to read in his ordinary voice selections from the Psalms and the Old Testament suitable to the occasion. " 'There is a time for . . .' " he read. " 'For now we see through a glass, darkly; but then face to face,' " he intoned quietly, moving into the New Testament, saving himself for his sermon.

Hallie contemplated the back of Mr. Bird's head, a round head shaped like another head she knew that had been carried tucked over one shoulder, thinking of the other head as it was in life, not as it must lie now at this moment in the coffin two feet in front of Mr. Bird. Mr. Bird's head sat squarely on his shoulders, and Hallie could tell from her glimpse of him that his face did not sag and that his eyes were clear, not bloodshot brown. When he shook hands with River he seemed suddenly to give the whole matter the same deep attention that Lucius used to give to her. Perhaps Mr. Bird was a real Southern gentleman (for all his strange fascination Lucius certainly had not been). Perhaps Mr. Bird even knew the classics; perhaps he had seen the ocean as his mother hoped, and perhaps he would come back and take Montpelier from Adam. Though loyal and kind to Lucius, Adam of course had no right to the Ledbetter Old Home Place; at one time he had said he did not want it, even said right out he would give it back to Lucius. Perhaps if Mr. Bird did not hurry away after the funeral she would have time to ask—subtly and indirectly, of course—if he would come take back Montpelier.

Brother Jamieson's voice dropped to a period and he sat down, and the quartette stood and sang "In the Sweet Bye and Bye," with Miss Beulah's alto ringing out clear and strong and true.

In the chorus she came in alone with "in the sweet" and "bye and bye," singing without looking at the notes, her two feet placed solidly on the floor, her short square body swaying a little, her eyes half closed. There was something about Miss Beulah's alto that seemed to make alto the most beautiful voice in the world, and yet Hallie knew it was hard to sing. She and Virginia had both tried but they always ended up singing the melody. She had once sighed to Virginia after a funeral that if she died young she hoped Miss Beulah would sing at her funeral, and Virginia had said in a businesslike voice, "What are your favorite songs?"

When she did not think of the coffin and that Lucius was inside it she could almost enjoy this funeral. Papa was not there to add a few words as he always did on Sundays. Mama seemed relaxed too; she was not twisting her wedding ring. In the balcony Adam leaned forward and rested his elbows on the railing. Mary sat back, comfortable and dignified. Perhaps Adam was getting ideas for his own sermons; he could not have many opportunities to hear a white preacher like Brother Jamieson.

Brother Jamieson prayed. "Lord," he said, "we are gathered together to perform the last rites for this our brother, made of clay like the rest of us, cut down suddenly in his manhood. Was he ready, Lord? Our days are numbered even as are the sands of the sea, and Thou knowest the day on which we shall be called before Thy throne to answer for our sins of omission and commission. Lord, wilt Thou say to us, 'Well done, good and faithful servant, enter thou into the joy of thy Lord,' or shall we be cast into outer darkness where there shall be weeping and wailing and gnashing of teeth? Lord, each and every one of us must face up to that question. Oh, that this our brother hast made the right decision. Amen."

Brother Jamieson kept his head hanging and his eyes closed for a second or two as if he were thinking. Hallie too was thinking. Would Lucius be cast into outer darkness, where there was weeping and wailing and gnashing of teeth? Not only had he never set foot inside a church, but his father before him had not been there for years, and had even recommended a graven image for Adam's father to worship. Where was Lucius now, thought Hallie, trembling, as Brother Jamieson began his sermon. Brother Jamieson obviously could not allow the Lord to be flouted so openly without pointing out the consequences, and yet it was not polite to the family to suggest that he was now roasting in Hell. Brother Jamieson never said that he was, but he pointed out what would happen to those who flouted God and were stiff-necked and proud and laughed at the church. Working up to his climax, he called upon all men present to search their hearts and ask themselves where they would stand on Judgment Day. River and Mr. Bird sat with heads bowed. Did River quake inside? He always went walking with the dogs on Sundays. Even in the winter, Laura Fitzgerald said, River took the dogs for a walk every Sunday. And Mr. Bird? He looked unworried; probably he attended church regularly, and his wife looked as if she might teach Sunday School.

Brother Jamieson had risen to the dam-bursting stage (describing the torments of Hell) and then had reached the calm-pond stage (describing the joys of Heaven). Now he stepped back, rested a moment, wiped his face with his handkerchief, and said, "Is there any desire on the part of the relatives for one last view of the deceased before he is committed to the grave?"

When Mr. J. H. Gardiner died, his widow had asked for one last view and then had hysterics as they screwed on the top of the coffin. Mr. Bird shook his head and when Mr. Fitzgerald nudged River he shook his head too.

"Is there anyone here present who wishes to be heard before we transfer the ceremonies to the graveside?" Brother Jamieson's glance flicked toward the place where Papa usually sat and Hallie sighed with relief. Even though Papa had not known Lucius well he would have thought of some remarks to make in general. River did not show any sign that he had even heard the question and Mr. Bird again shook his head slightly. Perhaps he felt that he had been away from his brother too long to say anything. In a way he hardly knew Lucius; he had hardly seen him since they were grown up except when their mother died. Perhaps Doc McGhee, a kind of cousin and old friend, or Miss Lill, who sat now in the second row behind River and Mr. Bird, might have some testimony to offer. Doc could testify to his sweetness with his children, or Miss Lill might apologize for calling him an old goat. Or should she herself rise and publicly say that she had been mistaken in Lucius. She had thought he was an old tramp and had called him a liar, but now she would testify that she loved him; yes, and the thought of her love brought tears to her eyes and she sniffed and wiped her nose and Virginia raised an eyebrow in her direction.

In the quiet of waiting a deep voice suddenly boomed out, boomed out over the heads of the congregation, and there was a rustling in the pews as they all turned to look upward. "Brother Jamieson," the voice said, "I'd like to offer a prayer." Adam stood tall in the balcony and stretched his arms out over the congregation, closed his eyes and prayed: "Lord, Thou lookest upon the heart. Thou knowest that this man was gentle as a lamb, as innocent as a dove. Lord, if there is no place saved for him on Thy right hand, let him sit upon Thy footstool. He's on his way there now, Lord, mountin up there straight to Thy throne on strong and powerful wings. He's thrashin thu the air with a noise like the wind in the trees, and when he comes, Lord, take him by the hand and say, Lucius, you may a talked one way down there, but I seen you and I knows you. Enter thou into the joy of thy Lord. For Jesus' sake, Amen."

Hallie's closed eyes were flooded with tears. It was beautiful to think of Lucius flying powerfully through the air, heading straight for the throne, when in life he had crawfished along. She blinked her eyes to hide her tears and saw Miss Lill blowing her nose and Doc scratching his bald head and moving his hand down toward his eyes. Brother Jamieson said nothing, not even

164

"Amen." He must feel sheepish. Everyone must feel now that Lucius would sit on God's footstool, not out in the dark.

The quartette sang, " 'Rock of Ages, cleft for me,' " as the pallbearers lifted the coffin and carried it out toward the cemetery. And when the coffin was poised over the hole the quartette stepped forward and sang, " 'Abide with me, fast falls the eventide.' " River looked dazed and out of place. Mr. Bird stood close by Brother Jamieson at the graveside and Hallie could see that he was very sad. Standing there watching the proceedings so attentively and sadly, he looked even more like his brother Lucius. He might be just as easy to talk to as his brother Lucius. (Lucius would never waste time in small talk; he always talked about what was important.) Brother Jamieson dropped a clod of dirt on the coffin as they lowered it into the grave and said, "Dust thou art, to dust returnest," and Hallie moved quietly over toward Mr. Bird. After Brother Jamieson pronounced his prayer of benediction Mr. Bird raised his face and smiled a little smile to all around him, as if to say he was home again.

The crowd meandered slowly toward the parked cars. Mr. Wake McClure, the representative up in Atlanta, came up to shake hands with Mr. Bird, and so did Mr. Craig and Doc McGhee and Mr. Fitzgerald. Mr. Jess Bailey shook hands and hurried back to the store. River stood there, one arm cradling the other. He was carried along with the crowd as they walked toward Mr. Bird's car. Suddenly Mr. Bird seemed no longer sad; he talked in a happy way as if being there greeting his friends was what he had been longing to do. Mrs. Bird went around and got into the Pierce Arrow by herself and Mr. Bird stood by the car facing the little group who had followed him, talking now to the whole group in a voice like Lucius', with talk almost like Lucius', but as if he had unlearned it and then learned it again.

"Friends," he said, "I been away too long. You're my neighbors, my kinfolks, some of you kissin cousins—amongst the ladies, that is. I aim to get down in here oftener, get to know you better. It's a sad day for me, a sad thing that brings me here, but friends, praise God, it's made me think. Yessir-ree, all during this funeral I been thinkin, been a thinkin that the old Latin fellow was right when he said, '*Ubique reminisci patriam*,' which to me, friends, means you cain't go back on your raisin." (Hallie jumped with surprise when she heard Mr. Bird speak Latin, and felt a warm surging hopefulness when he picked out the words on the Jones coat of arms. But she had always thought the words meant that one must remember the Old South.) "Yessir, *ubique reminisci patriam*—you cain't go back on your raisin."

"Listen to Bird put on," snickered Mr. Fitzgerald to River, jabbing him a little in the arm and yet seeming proud of Mr. Bird too.

"I want to get to know my neighbors," Mr. Bird went on, "yes, and my own relations." He looked at River, but River did not meet his eyes; he was staring at the ground. "You know me, friends, you know who I am, I come from down in here; I was just as po as gully dirt, and I know your problems. Oh, it ain't easy nowadays. I know what you got to put up with. Land's all wore out in some places, the boll weevils sent to try our patience worse'n boils worried Job, you cain't get help when you need it, niggers ain't worth killin. Many's the time I've heard my pa say, 'A nigger just ain't worth killin' . . .'"

That wasn't what his father said, thought Hallie. His father said they weren't worth *all that* killing. There was a difference.

"Maybe some of you here present remember my old father down in the Tranquil section, praise God, a man who gladly went out and fought for the South in the War Between the States, was lieutenant in the Featherstone Fusileers under Captain Featherstone, a man who went out to serve God and the South."

He paused and turned toward the car and Hallie feared that he was going to say good-by and then she would never know . . . never know. How should she ask it? Was he coming back to save Montpelier? She could not ask that right out. And suddenly she was asking a question that she did not even know she was thinking about.

"Mr. Bird, did you ever see the ocean?" As soon as she said it she felt a fool. If Benny or Virginia ever got wind of it she would never hear the last of it.

Mr. Bird turned and looked at her with his bright brown interested eyes that said, like Lucius', "What you say to me is the most interesting thing that can be said."

"Honey," Mr. Bird said, "you've asked me a good question." He turned to the group around him. "Friends, this little girl wants to know if I've ever seen the ocean. I want you to know that I not only have seen the ocean, but I've seen what's on the other side of the ocean. I had the opportunity, friends, to serve my country in the last war, in that great war for freedom and democracy. When I was called in 1916, I went like my father to serve my country. Let me say right here that we licked the Kaiser but now we got a bunch of uppity niggers on our hands. But I saw the ocean and, friends, I want you to know that the ocean off the shores of Georgia is the prettiest ocean you've seen anywhere. From Rabun Gap to Tybee Light we have one of the most beautiful states anywhere in any country of the world. I'm glad this little child has asked me this question because I want to say to her, and say to you, praise God, that I'm proud of my state and none of it's as pretty as Plum Branch County. I've made a resolve, friends, just while I've been here. I'm comin back. I'm comin back to my old home place. I've neglected my family and my friends and the house of my fathers long enough. I'm comin back. We goin to plant us a crop of watermelons down there in that river bottom—how about it, River?—and when you all drop in we goin to cut you one of the biggest juiciest watermelons ever grown in the whole state of Georgia. And I mean I've seen some big'uns."

Hallie had been disappointed at first that he had used the ocean only to get somewhere and to come back. That wasn't what his mother had meant. But her heart had risen when he said he was coming back to his old home place. She had asked the right question after all. She had the answer now. Mr. Bird would come back and take care of Montpelier. Hallie wished that Lucius could hear him (in the coffin now almost covered, or up there on God's footstool). A man with a Pierce Arrow would fix up his old home place; he would not come and camp in it like the Duckets.

Mr. Bird got in behind the wheel. Looking at Mr. Fitzgerald, he said, "Look for me down this way soon now—I'll get in touch with you," and started backing out.

Mr. Fitzgerald poked River again. "Sounds pretty nice, don't it, River? You gonna go back down in there and git your old home place back."

River showed no signs of joy. "Maybe he don't know he's gonna have to buy hit back from Adam."

"Adam don't want it," said Mr. Fitzgerald. "What would a nigger do with a house like that?"

"If Adam hears how Bird talked about niggers he may not let go so easy. He's stubborn, that nigger is," said River.

"He sho outdone Brother Jamieson," said Mr. Fitzgerald, slapping his flank and laughing a high, squeezed, horse whinny. "He sho weren't going to let him thow Lucius out in the dark."

"I don't think Adam would want that old run-down place," said Mr. Craig. "You oughter see it. 'Bout to fall apart. I can't really see what Mr. Bird wants with it, either."

"He's fixin up to run for somethin," said Mr. Wake McClure. "I thought he was hardly goin to get away from the graveside before he started 'lectioneerin."

"Couldn't be Governor," said Mr. Craig, "not yet. Maybe Lieutenant Governor?"

Mr. Fitzgerald slapped River on the back again. "What you think about having a brother in the Governor's seat, River?"

Hallie looked around. Now that Mr. Bird had left with Mrs. Bird she was the only girl or woman around. She walked across

168

the street but instead of going inside she climbed the tree and sat there for a while. She could still hear the rise and fall of Mr. Bird's voice, a rich rise and fall that reminded her of a similar voice she had heard when they lived over in Clover, back in South Carolina. Once they had all gone to hear Coley L. Blease, Mama taking them, shamefacedly because Coley L. Blease was for the lintheads in the cotton mills, not for people like themselves, not to be taken seriously for some reason that Hallie did not understand. He was a sight to be admired as one would go to hear a Redpath Chautauqua singer or Kryl's band when it came to town, a sight to be looked at and applauded. But Coley L. Blease was beneath the Jones family, and the lint-heads who whooped and hollered when he spoke in the same tones as Mr. Bird, and nudged each other and shook their heads wisely, were cheap. Papa never voted for him, and Mama couldn't vote then. She said she might have been tempted because he put on such a good show.

But Mr. Bird seemed to love his old home place. He planned to come back and save it. He would take it from Adam, which would be all right; Adam said he did not want it. Mr. Bird knew Latin and had seen the ocean. He had the same eyes as Lucius and almost the same voice.

Yet she was not entirely happy as she sat there, though she kept telling herself she should be.

16

Mama told Elberta she could stay home starting about the middle of February, but Elberta said she would rather work. Miss Beulah came by and after leaving the kitchen said, "Tch, tch," shaking her head. She added, "If you don't watch out you're going to have a nigger baby in one of your beds."

But that did not happen. One day Elberta came as usual. She was there in the kitchen when Hallie came in for breakfast. Mama was doing the milking because Elberta had trouble now squatting down to do it, but she still came to work early. There was a kind of brown stain under her eyes, and Hallie heard her panting when she leaned over to get a stick of firewood for the range. And when Hallie just happened to come home that day for lunch, wondering, Elberta was still there doing the same things she did every day.

Next morning, however, Aunt Relly came as Hallie was entering the kitchen, knocked on the back porch and called, "Mrs. Jones." Mama seemed to know just why she had come.

"Did Elberta have her baby?" Mama asked.

"Yes'm, she had hit last night. Started in gettin her pains about sundown and long about daylight she had hit." She shook her head. "Lawd, Lawd."

"Is she all right?" asked Mama. Aunt Relly had such a morose air as she looked down at the floor that Hallie was sure that the delivery must have been like those in Miss Beulah's worst (or best?) stories. But then Aunt Relly often shook her head and said, "Lawd, Lawd," for nothing much.

"Yes'm, she's all right, I reckon. They was both sleepin when I left."

"Then the baby's fine too," said Mama. "Boy or girl?"

"Hit's a boy," said Aunt Relly. "Thank the Lawd she done have a boy." But even as she said this Aunt Relly did not look particularly happy; she merely rolled her eyes toward the ceiling as if having a girl would have been the worst thing that could have happened.

"I'll come down after a while," said Mama, "but I'm glad to hear everything went off all right."

"Yes'm, reckon so, guess hit went off all right," said Aunt Relly, shaking her head dolefully. "Well'm, Elberta says I ought to come on up here and tell you she wouldn't be here today. She thought you mought be lookin for her."

"Tell Elberta I haven't been looking for her for the past two weeks. Tell her just to get a good rest and I'm coming down to see that baby." Despite Aunt Relly's dark looks, Mama acted as if Elberta's baby was as good as any other baby.

"Mama, can I go too?" asked Hallie. "I never saw a real little newborn baby. Let me go, Mama."

"Honey, you've got to go to school. You can go down some time in the afternoon in the next few days. It's going to be little for several days."

That afternoon when she came home from school Hallie asked about the baby. "Is he cute, Mama?" she asked, thinking of a little brown baby.

"He's a real nice-looking baby," said Mama.

"Does he look like Elberta?"

"Well, it's too early to tell, I guess," said Mama. "Not much right now," she added.

Hallie went to Aunt Relly's a few days later to visit the baby. The room was dark and warm and smelled like a baby. Elberta was sitting up in front of the fire and Aunt Relly was doing her hair. She had already plaited one side into tight little plaits but the other side still hung to her shoulders and carried the sharp ripples and waves from the plaits in the straight black hair. Elberta looked very pretty sitting there in front of the fire wearing a pink Japanese kimono Mama had given her. The baby was in a wash basket on the floor near the fireplace, a tiny baby, sleeping with his eyes screwed up tight, his face red.

"Ain't he pretty?" said Elberta, proudly. "He's just a pretty little man." And she leaned forward away from Aunt Relly's fingers plaiting her hair and picked up the baby and held him for Hallie to see. When she pulled him up close to her breast and nestled him there the firelight on the baby's head showed a fine fuzz, a gold fuzz that caught the firelight when it flickered.

"You better not wake that baby up," said Aunt Relly, and she pulled Elberta's hair crossly.

Elberta did not seem to mind. She said, "I want Hallie to see him with his eyes open," and she unwrapped the faded blanket around him and tickled his feet a little. "Say hey, Miss Hallie," she said. The baby curled his red toes up and moved his arms a little as if he were going to stretch. The eyes with their fine gold lashes unsquinched and the baby opened first one eye and then the other. They were a deep clear blue.

"See him, Hallie, ain't he a pretty little baby?" said Elberta, rocking him against her. Aunt Relly gave up trying to do Elberta's hair and muttered to herself and shook her head before coming around and taking a chair by the fire.

"He's darling," said Hallie, "oh, he's darling. Oh, I wish I could hold him."

The baby stretched and rolled his head and made motions with his mouth, closed his eyes and turned his head nuzzling against Elberta.

"Oh, he's lookin for his titty," said Elberta, and opened her kimono and tumbled out a breast to him. She worked the dark nipple into his mouth and then sat back, holding him tight to her. "He's always hongry," she said happily.

Aunt Relly poked the fire, broke a coal that was flaking up, worked her snuff around in her mouth, carefully aimed a stream of spit to sizzle into the hot coals and sat back. She did not seem to be in the mood for conversation.

Hallie watched the baby, his eyes closed again, he and Elberta lost in some happy trance together. The only sounds were the sputtering of the coals, the baby's sucking and his satisfied swallowing. There was something about a Negro cabin that Hallie liked. Everything was here. Everything was in one room except for a kitchen stove in a lean-to out back, but even that was not necessary; a black kettle sat to one side of the hearth and a black spider hung on the wall. In round frames touched with peeling gold a dark man and woman surveyed the scene from above the mantel; there was a jar of paper spills under the woman's chin. It was surprising to see Negro portraits; to think that they had grandmothers and grandfathers, established lines of ancestors like white people. There was a washstand with a flowered bowl and pitcher and the big bed where Elberta and Aunt Relly slept, the headboard of some dark wood, carved and curlicued and towering almost to the ceiling, decked out with high pillows in embroidered pillowcases. And near the fire, of course, the baby's wash basket. Everything that was needed.

Elberta seemed to swim up out of her trance. She smiled at Hallie.

"Mama said I shouldn't stay long," said Hallie. The baby had let go the breast, fallen back into sleep with his mouth wet and his nose red. "I'll come by sometime when I can hold him."

"Come any time, Hallie," said Elberta, "but I'm comin back to work next week. Your Mama says I can bring the baby while Aunt Relly's workin."

When Elberta came back to work Mama fixed up a wash basket for the baby next to the kitchen range. Papa leaned over the basket and poked the baby and clucked at him. The baby opened his eyes and Papa picked him up and held him. "You named him yet, Elberta?" he asked. He rocked the baby in his arms.

"Naw, sir, still just callin him Baby," said Elberta.

"You can't go on like that forever," said Mama. "He's got to have a name. A nice boy like that ought to have a nice name."

"Why don't you name him for Papa?" said Hallie, seeing Papa hold the baby and remembering how it was to be rocked by Papa long ago on the porch at Clover, remembering all the long warm summer evenings, remembering that she felt cradled, and thinking that now she no longer could, or would want to if she could. Papa had no son named for him. Long before Hallie was born, Jonny was shot in the head by a schoolmate with a hunting rifle.

Mama said now, "Jonathan seems a little formal. But you could call him Jonny for short."

"I always thought Jonny was the prettiest name for a boy," Elberta said.

"All right then, Jonny," Papa said, and he closed his eyes and held the baby up toward heaven and said, "I christen thee Jonny," which was a strange thing for Papa to say because Baptists do not christen. Perhaps he did it because Elberta was a Methodist. "Be a good boy, Jonny," he said, and put him back in his basket and sat down to eat his dinner.

Virginia and Hallie hung over the basket on Saturdays and Elberta would stop her work to come and look at Jonny with them, and when they would murmur, "Oh, you sweet little darling baby," she would smile and go back to her dishes. "Go ahead and hold him," she said, as if imparting a privilege, "pick him up and hold him. He sure likes to be rocked."

When Elberta was off cleaning in another part of the house Hallie picked the baby up, undid the blankets and examined him quickly to see if (according to Miss Beulah's predictions) he had a black stripe running down his spine. A little baby as white as this one must show his colored blood in some way. At times his fingernails looked bluer than her own; once just when she had definitely decided that they were, Elberta came back into the kitchen and, passing his basket, touched his fingers, said, "He's cold," and gathered him up. "Look at him, pore little thing, his fingers are blue," and she wrapped him tighter in his blankets and pushed him closer to the range.

When Miss Beulah saw the baby she rolled her eyes, turned her head away in disgust and said to Mama, "What did I tell you?" Long ago before Elberta looked even the least bit pregnant Miss Beulah had predicted that the baby would be white. She had hinted at one time that the father might be Boyce McClure, and Hallie was sure the McClure name meant something to Elberta.

"Mama," Hallie whispered one day when Elberta was out of the kitchen, "do Negro babies usually have blue eyes?"

"No," said Mama, and that was all she said.

The baby lost his redness but did not turn brown or black, rather turned pink and white; the fuzz on his head washed off and in its place grew a new fuzz of light hair, "pink hair" Virginia called it. Jonny kept his blue eyes open longer, and he looked around now and smiled a one-sided smile when Elberta leaned over and tickled him in the stomach.

Elberta blossomed out into a new creature, a proud mother. Oh, she was proud of that baby. But she seemed also to be a laughing, happy girl who sang as she went about her work. " 'When you wake you'll get some cake and all the pretty little horses,' " she sang toward the wash basket. She was not like a girl who had "gotten into trouble" and had an excruciating delivery to pay for her sin; she seemed as silly as Mama was about babies.

One Saturday afternoon in May Hallie saw Elberta downtown. She came by wearing a new dress, a blue dress that Hallie had never seen. Where did she get it? The dress was silk and Elberta looked tall and slender and pretty, a proud princess now. She stepped past the crowd in front of the cotton office, not seeing them at all. They stopped talking as she passed; the men sat on their haunches and stared as she went by. Hallie was sitting in front of the post office waiting for the mail to be sorted and watching Mr. Jess Bailey's store, an old habit not easily shaken. It was as close to him as she dared go these days. Elberta smiled at her as she went by and said, "Hey, Hallie." She did not even glance into the post office (who would write Elberta?), went past the bank and on toward Mr. Jess Bailey's store. Mr. Jess Bailey was standing in front talking to a farmer, and Hallie had been hoping that when he finished he would decide to come pick up his mail. He finished with the farmer and went hurriedly inside. Elberta disappeared around the corner and Hallie was wondering where she could be going so dressed up on a Saturday afternoon when Essie Jones came to the post office and got the store mail. Obviously there was no point in waiting longer and Hallie went home.

17

During March Hallie and Virginia had started new pieces in expression. Miss Corrine had said that both of them should try out in the contest at the end of school. "Start your piece early," she had said to Hallie, "and we'll work hard on it now. I'm going to be extra busy toward the end of school."

At first the significance of this remark did not register on Hallie. But the next Sunday she saw something at church and "extra busy at the end of school" lighted up in her mind. Miss Emmy Belton had held her for a minute in the Sunday School room, asking her some question about a book they had both read. The other girls had gone down with their usual racket when Hallie came down the stairs toward the vestibule. Around the bend in the stairway she saw Miss Corrine and Mr. Jess standing close together at the choir door. Miss Corrine was poised, ready to step up into the choir when Mr. Jess leaned forward and took her by the arm, held her back, leaned forward and touched his lips to her neck, held his lips there, and nibbled her neck under the three brown curls that hung down from her knot. Miss Corrine, her face warming up, turned and looked at him, leaned a little toward him, looked deeply into his eyes as he must be looking into hers, looked as if she longed to turn her lips to him, actually puckered her lips a little as if promising, then gave him a little push as if to say, "This is not the place for that," and turned from him and stepped up into the choir. On the bend of the stair Hallie held herself still for a heartbeat or two. Miss Corrine had been won away from college. She, Hallie, would have given up all—books, learning, seeing the ocean, all—if he had kissed her. Oh, Lord, that would never happen now.

Then she knew why Miss Corrine was going to be busy toward the end of school. It could mean only one thing: Miss Corrine and Mr. Jess were planning to be married.

Naturally Miss Corrine would have a big church wedding. For the girl from Magnolia Hall only the most formal wedding would be appropriate. Hallie planned it all in cryptic notes on M. D. and S. paper. Bride and groom; it was unnecessary to fill in the names of the principals. Bridesmaids? Perhaps some of the teachers from school or friends of Miss Corrine's from GSCW. Flower girl? Mr. Jess Bailey's niece, Carrie, younger sister of Essie Jones, had looks more suitable to a wedding than Essie's. Ring bearer? No Greenwood boy was worthy of the assignment; perhaps Miss Corrine would have to import one from North Carolina. Music? Miss Annie Lee Jones, a member of the family or about to be, might sing "Oh! Promise Me" or "To a Wild Rose." And who would play the wedding march? Hallie had once heard Miss Corrine say that although she could not carry a tune she did know *time* and Miss Toulou Vass' time for hymns was absolutely disgraceful. Of course she smiled when she said this, as if she thought it was just one of those things about Miss Toulou. But the time for the wedding march should be absolutely right. Miss Toulou could not be relied upon; she would rag it up and rush through it if she suddenly felt that way. Miss Corrine would want everything perfect and she would make everyone practice and do it right like a play.

Hallie asked Miss Toulou Vass if she would give her the Wedding March—Mendelssohn's—for her next piece. "Why, honey," said Miss Toulou, "is somebody stepping off and keeping it a secret? Is Virginia quite old enough?" She said this opening wide her amber eyes and looking mock-seriously at Hallie. "I think it's a pretty piece," said Hallie, and she started practicing it every afternoon when she got home from school, stroking firmly down on middle C for the breathtaking beginning.

She could not say to Miss Corrine, "I'm learning the Wedding March and hope that you will consider me a possibility when you come to make your plans . . ." She thought of mentioning it at her expression lesson but she could not quite say it. She would have to let Miss Corrine know in some subtle, roundabout way that she could play the Wedding March and play it well.

Beginning in mid-April, every Sunday after church, while Miss Corrine and Mr. Jess Bailey wended their way down from the choir, stopping to shake hands and talk to people, and then walked around to the front door and toward Miss Corrine's car, Hallie raced ahead across the street, ran into the living room and began to play the "Wedding March." She could not play and watch at the same time—that was impossible—she could not tell if Miss Corrine stopped as she was being gently handed into the car, paused and listened and said, "Where is that music coming from?" and Mr. Jess too stopped and listened, then, being more musical, said, "Oh, darling, do you recognize that piece?" and Miss Corrine's brown eyes looked deep, deep into his blue ones and she blushed and he said, pressing her hand, "Must we wait so long, darling?" and she gave him another look of love and climbed into her car and went home to Sunday dinner at Magnolia Hall with her father. But perhaps the tune, and the expressive way in which it was played, would haunt Miss Corrine. She would begin to wonder whence it had come, and of course once she began thinking she would immediately decide that it came from the Jones' house, the only place that it could come from, and then she would know it was Hallie Jones playing, because that year Virginia had said she wanted to put all her time on expression. And of course after she had decided it was Hallie who played, it would be only a short step to deciding that Hallie must play for her wedding. Hallie worried a little, thinking of "To a Wild Rose" and "Oh! Promise Me." Even the last part of the Wedding March was very hard; the time was tricky. But all that could be faced later.

Hallie tried this plan for several Sundays, after preaching service in the morning and after prayer meeting at night. But here it was already May and Miss Corrine had given no sign that she even suspected Hallie was available to play the Wedding March and Hallie feared she might choose someone else simply because she did not know. Surely Miss Corrine must be making her plans, but she never let on. There was no whisper that she was even getting married.

On this Sunday evening in May as Hallie went out the front door to prayer meeting, Miss Corrine parked her car in front of their house, almost in front of their gate. She called and said, "Hallie, aren't we late?" and they hurried over together. Miss Corrine went into the choir as usual and Hallie joined Mama and Papa and Virginia in their pew. She thought, tonight is the night for Miss Corrine to find out. Her car was so close by that she could not fail to hear if Hallie played the Wedding March at the right moment.

She thought about it all during prayer meeting. It was a dull prayer meeting because so few people came. She hoped to see Mr. Bird Ledbetter; he had attended the morning service, arriving alone in his Pierce Arrow. Brother Jamieson had spoken with more feeling, rising to the occasion of a visit from a distinguished legislator from Atlanta. But Mr. Bird must have gone back to Atlanta in the afternoon. Boyce McClure was there, sitting next to May Belle Ballard; he had finally come to B.Y.P.U. at her invitation and sat next to her in church. May Belle's cheeks were splendid as apples. Shadrack Cartledge was missing; he did not come slinking in after the service started as was his custom. And Benny and the boys who usually crowded into the back pew after the first hymn never came at all, although Papa looked up each time there was a movement outside. Mama seemed to wonder about Benny too; she turned around and looked back when anyone came in behind them as if expecting him to come in a different entrance. And where was Mr. Jess Bailey? Miss Corrine sat next to Mr. Holden in the choir and sang off his book. Mr. Jess had probably driven his mother off somewhere to see one of her daughters.

Mr. Jess' absence changed the picture—he was the really musical one—but even if Miss Corrine was tone deaf she would recognize the *time* of the Wedding March. Her car was so close and she would be able to hear it so well. Anyhow, Hallie felt she must try; Miss Corrine might pick someone else if she did not know. She ducked past Papa quickly after Brother Jamieson had pronounced the benediction, knowing that without Mr. Jess Bailey there Miss Corrine would not linger. She ran across the street and into the house, opened the window on to the front porch, looked out past the fence into the street where Miss Corrine's runabout Ford was parked, saw figures straggling toward the street, then, afraid to wait longer, sat down at the piano, paused a minute, and sat very still to give Miss Corrine time to get across the street. Finally, feeling the moment had come, she began her first sure downstroke on Middle C. By the time she had gotten through the opening, surely, oh surely Miss Corrine would be standing at her car door and could not fail to hear the first solemn crashing chords that anyone could recognize.

In the pause before the chords, like a breathing pause in expression, she heard an unfamiliar low sound, a hollow sound like horses' hoofs, from up the street beyond the church, a half-heard hollow clomp of horses' hoofs muffled in dust. Then she sensed a strange light in the room, a yellow flickering; she played the first chord, played it extra loud, but she could not ignore the dancing reflection on the black wood of the piano. She saw it, wondered, but kept on playing, waiting to hear Miss Corrine's car start up; she must play until then. Then she heard the *clomp-clomp* sound again and now she knew it was horses' hoofs. But no one ever rode a horse at night; no one but Mr. Jess Bailey ever rode a horse, though occasionally a Negro rode a mule. Who rode? She gave up playing and ran to the door and out onto the porch. There, just passing the church and about to pass her house, were white-robed riders on white-robed horses, carrying torches, great chunks of rich lightwood held high and flaring red as the riders and marchers moved forward, filling the street with sight and sound, the same street that Hallie had run across a minute before. What was startling besides the sight and sound was the suddenness of their appearance, as if a grave had opened up and let them out or as if they had lain hidden, yes, they must have lain hidden behind the Methodist Church, which was dark that night, and then jumped forth as she would jump forth from behind a door when she wanted to scare someone. But now she felt like the person jumped-out upon; the skin of her back prickled up into her hair.

The procession passed in front of the church slowly, like a parade before a reviewing stand, and she could see now that the steps were lined with figures silhouetted against the lighted front window of the church. Everyone stood still there, watching. And although it was not a large procession, four men on horses or mules with torches and a few figures on foot, it seemed to take awhile for it to pass, so slowly and solemnly did they walk. As they approached the corner beyond her house, she saw one of the horsemen pause, pull his horse up short and wait for all the figures to come up. Then they turned the corner toward town— and it was only then that she could pause in her looking and say to herself, Ku Klux Klan.

A minute later Mama and Virginia came across the street with Miss Corrine and stood by her car, watching. Other cars started up, and Mama and Virginia came in and went to the window on the orchard side to watch the procession moving toward town. Hallie folded the music on the piano so Virginia would not see what she had been playing. When Papa came in Mama said, "I never knew there was a Ku Klux Klan around here, did you?" said it suspiciously, as if she thought Papa had been keeping something from her.

Papa shook his head. "What are they up to? There's sin, Lord knows there's always sin, but punishment? Who shall cast the first stone?" No one answered and he shook his head.

Mama was the only one who had ever talked about the Ku Klux Klan. When she went up to Macon to get her teeth pulled and a new set made, her dentist, Dr. Youngblood, talked about the Ku Klux Klan. "I declare," she had said, "if I don't sometimes think Dr. Youngblood's mixed up in this Ku Klux Klan. He's always talking about how much good they do, keeping law and order, and how they're in the Southern tradition. Asked me if I didn't think Negroes were more uppity since some of them went away in the army, but then of course he puts his hand in my mouth just when I'm ready to answer him."

Hallie had said, "I thought the Ku Klux Klan was something they had after the War was over. Didn't it keep law and order then?" thinking of *The Clansman* by Thomas Dixon. If it had not been for loyal Southerners and the Klan, what would have happened to the South?

"Maybe it was all right then," Mama said, "but seems to me we've gone past that now. When you come right down to it, I really hate a fellow goes around doing things with his face hidden."

Mama continued to stare through the window as if she might pierce the masks of the riders and expose them to the world. Now Hallie stood near her and said, because the words suddenly rose to her mind from some page, "Mama, what's tarring and feathering?"

Mama shook her head and shivered, "Just what it says, hot tar and chicken feathers." And Hallie had a vision of a chicken with its head cut off dancing its death dance around the back yard.

Virginia said, "Do you reckon they could mean to *lynch* somebody?" She whispered the word *lynch*. Hallie thought, *lynching*, surely not lynching, not in Greenwood; lynching happened far away and long ago, always somewhere else, like the bloody ballads. And like the ballads an aura of passion and honor and loyalty and courage hung over the word, making it acceptable. But now with the riders on their way, she suddenly saw a body collapsed on the end of a rope.

"Who could they be after?" she murmured.

Mama turned the ring on her finger and looked out the window. She did not answer Hallie's question. "Where's Benny?" she asked, looking at them as if they could tell her.

"I kept wondering why he didn't come to church," said Virginia, "but then none of the boys did."

"You're sure he's not back in his room reading?" Papa always hoped the answer would be simple.

"I'll go see," said Hallie and went down the hall to Benny's room. She said, "Benny?" and opened the door. A rolled-up form was on the bed and she said, "Benny?" again and felt for the light cord. But the form was only the blanket and bedspread rolled up. The sheets had been jerked from under them.

She turned out the light and returned to the living room. "He's not there," she said.

"I can't understand why they came by just when church was letting out," said Papa. "Seems sacrilegious."

183

"Maybe they were just showing off," Mama said hopefully. "Once they get themselves all fixed up they just got to show off to somebody. If I hear that Benny's fooling around with that crowd . . ."

Virginia sat on the piano stool and kept whirling around on it. "Mr. Jess Bailey wasn't there, Mr. Shadrack Cartledge wasn't there . . ."

Not Mr. Jess Bailey with his open, pure face. She was not sure how she felt about the Ku Klux Klan; but she knew (knew it from her dreams where she knew him well) that Mr. Jess would never need to cover his face.

Papa said, "Why, I couldn't believe a thing like that of Mr. Jess Bailey. His mother wasn't there either. Maybe she was sick or something, or maybe he was driving her over to see one of her daughters lives off somewhere. There's a hundred reasons why a feller might not come to church." Benny had never found a reason that suited Papa; he never could see why Benny should not be in church every Sunday.

"It'd be just like Mr. Shadrack Cartledge," said Virginia. "Honestly, I think he's one of the meanest-looking men I've ever seen. He has a real mean look out of his eyes."

Mama said to Papa, "Maybe you ought to have a talk with Benny. He's too old to whip. Besides, we didn't start soon enough." Mama was just talking; Hallie knew she would never let Papa whip Benny even if Papa thought it a good idea.

Papa looked unhappy at the thought of talking to Benny. "Well, let's wait and see. Can't tell yet. He may just have gone down in the country with some of the boys; may be attending church down there in the country," he said hopefully.

"Do you think they were just parading around, or were really out to . . . to scare somebody?" Hallie asked, seeing the dancing chicken and the body on the rope.

"Lord, let's hope they're just dressing up and showing off. Maybe it's kind of like when the Masons meet," said Mama. "Your father had a hat with a white plume on it over in Clover."

They sat on in the living room; Papa still held his Bible on his knee and Mama still wore her jacket. Virginia swung round and round on the piano stool; Hallie hoped that she would not notice the music of the Wedding March. Virginia had thought it was the biggest joke in the world when she first heard Hallie practice it. She had told May Belle Ballard about it in front of Hallie, and May Belle had said, "Why, Virginia, you haven't been keeping things from me, have you? Boyce been taking you out?" which left Virginia speechless because though Boyce now came to B.Y.P.U. it was because May Belle had asked him. When he came he sat by May Belle.

Mama broke the silence. Twisting her ring, she said, "I wish Benny would come home."

Papa laid down his Bible and closed the window. "Guess we might's well go to bed. Nothing we can do until he gets home, anyhow."

18

I wonder if I'm going to be like Mama, thought Hallie, as she heard Benny coming in. Though she and Virginia had the room farthest back, she had been awakened by something, a car starting up or a creaking from the front of the house, a door being opened and closed almost without sound, more felt than heard. Mama always heard everything. It was a family joke that Mama slept with both eyes open and one foot on the floor. She always heard the slightest disturbance in the chicken house; she would jump to her feet and run out slamming the screen door, waking up everyone and hollering, "Go away. Leave those chickens alone. Shoo!" This last in case the marauder were a fox.

Later, she thought much later, Hallie woke up again, to feel a trembling in the mattress, to hear the last inflections of a voice though she had not heard words. Mama must have had both feet on the floor, for there was a quiet as if she were listening; then Hallie heard a voice, the sound from her dream, whispering from the back porch near her room. "Mrs. Jones?" She sat up now and when she heard Mama walking across her room and opening the screen door she tiptoed out to the porch too. A figure leaned against a post, holding on to it as if for support. It was Elberta. Mama went to her in her long white nightgown. Elberta's voice shook when she said, "Mrs. Jones, can I talk to you a minute?"

Mama peered at her in the darkness. "Elberta. Is it you, Elberta? Come on in, child. Come in." She took her by the arm and guided her into the back hall and then into the kitchen. Hallie followed. Mama did not turn on a light until she was in the kitchen. Elberta stood there like the girl who had come to them months ago—dejected, beat down, wearing Aunt Relly's sweater and the same faded dress. Mama took her by both arms and pushed her into a chair. "You're trembling, Elberta. Hallie, get a quilt. Now don't wake everybody up," she said softly but sternly.

Hallie tiptoed through the back hall and into her own room, where Virginia breathed evenly. She found a quilt lying on the trunk and tiptoed back with it, carefully, carefully, closing the doors behind her. Surely Papa would wake up with all this opening and closing. The spring on the screen door whined, no matter how gently she closed it.

Mama had stirred up the fire and put some milk in a pan, and she took the quilt from Hallie and wrapped it around Elberta's shoulders. Then she seemed to see Hallie for the first time, standing there in her nightgown. "What are you doing up, Hallie? You just go right on back to bed."

Hallie did not move. Elberta did not look at her; she rested her forehead on one hand and held the quilt around her with the other. But she had stopped trembling.

"Hallie, did you hear me? Go to bed," said Mama, as if she really meant it.

"Yes'm," said Hallie, and walked from the room, through the dark hall, opened the screen door and shut it with a slight bang, then tiptoed back in the darkness and sat down under the summer table pushed against the wall next the kitchen door.

"Mrs. Jones, Mrs. Jones," Elberta sobbed, "I got to go away."

"Why, Elberta?" and, "Where, Elberta?" Mama asked. "Here, drink this hot milk."

"Mrs. Jones," cried Elberta, "Mrs. Jones, them men said I got to leave town."

"Elberta, stop crying," said Mama firmly. "Stop crying now and tell me."

"Them men come by tonight. Oh, Mrs. Jones, I was so scared."

"You mean the Ku Klux Klan?" asked Mama.

"Yes'm, them men all dressed up in white sheets. Them were the ones."

"Elberta, what did they do to you? Did they harm you, Elberta?"

"No'm, no'm, I'm all *right*, but I got to go away. They said so."

"What did they do, Elberta?" asked Mama sharply. "Did they touch you?"

"No'm, they didn't touch me." But she sobbed aloud once more.

"Elberta, you have to tell me," said Mama.

"Yes'm, I will." And there was a silence. Then, "I was sleepin. I done fed Jonny, and Aunt Relly had come from prayer meetin; that woke me up a little. She was settin by the fire and I was about to go to sleep again when I heard somethin and I opened my eyes and I seen this light outside and heard men's voices talkin, and then I heard someone bangin on the steps. I sat up and Aunt Relly she looked up and then stood up in front of the fireplace watchin the door. Then there was this bangin again, someone bangin with a stick, and Aunt Relly looked toward me. I could just see her eyes there in the firelight. We hadn lit no lamp. And she went toward the door and opened hit a crack and says, 'What you want?'

" 'We don't want you, Aunt Relly,' somebody called. Then they said, 'Where's that gal?' " Elberta stopped here, as if to get her breath, as if she could not bear to go on.

"Yes?" said Mama.

"Then Aunt Relly, she calls out, 'What you want with her?' and didn move, just stood there at the door, but I was scared. Oh, I was scared. I slid down under the covers until I was at the foot of the bed, and I lay there shakin. Then I jumped out of bed and went over and picked up Jonny and helt him. I don't know why." She began to cry again, and Mama said, "Drink a little more of the milk, Elberta." Then, "Did you go to the door?"

"They kep on sayin, 'Where's your niece, Aunt Relly? Send her out here,' and Aunt Relly says again, 'What you want with her?' and then someone said, 'We ain't goin to hurt her if she comes out nice.'

"So Aunt Relly come and took the baby away from me and says, 'Wrop a quilt around you and go out.' And I wropped a quilt around me and stepped to the door. And then one of 'em says, 'Step on out here, gal, we got somethin for you,' and helt somethin out toward me. I seen hit were a letter, and I reached forward my hand and taken hit."

"What did it say?" asked Mama.

"Here it is," said Elberta. "Hit says I got to leave."

Mama was silent for a minute. She must be studying the letter. "Who gave it to you?" she asked.

"I couldn tell who give hit to me," said Elberta. "They were all covered up and they weren't a good light. Besides, I was shakin so I couldn really see. I just seen them lights dancin in the air and the horses with the white sheets and the men. All covered up too."

"Didn't you recognize any voices or see anything that would give you a clue to who they were?" asked Mama, her voice trembling now as it had before when she wondered if Benny could be with them. "Think, Elberta."

There was silence for a minute and then Elberta, her voice trembling too, said, "Well'm, when I reached forward my hand to git the letter one of the horses whinnied. He was standin back kind of in the dark, back behind the men, and when I looked there, someone swung one of them lights around and I seen the horse had white on hit's legs." Elberta began to cry again.

Mama said, "A horse with white legs?" in a disappointed voice. But Hallie's insides seemed to jump and she leaned forward.

"Like little white stockins on hit's legs," sobbed Elberta.

"Do you know the horse?" asked Mama. "Had you ever seen it before?"

"Yes'm, I seen hit before," and Elberta cried harder than ever.

"Elberta, you've got to tell me whose horse it is. Stop crying now."

"Hit were . . . were . . ." But apparently Elberta could not say. Hallie wanted to crawl out from under the table and say for her, Lady. Mr. Jess Bailey's horse. Everybody knows Mr. Jess Bailey's horse.

"Elberta, would the owner of the horse have anything against you? Would he have any reason for wanting you to leave town?"

First Elberta said, "No'm," tearfully, then, "I don't know'm."

"There were several men missing from church tonight," said Mama. "Mr. Shadrack Cartledge, Mr. Jess Bailey . . ." She paused here and Elberta gave a sob, but Mama paid no attention and said, "And Benny."

Elberta sobbed again and said, "Mr. Jess Bailey were missin?"

And Mama said, "Yes, we wondered where he was . . . wondered if he . . ."

Elberta said, "Then hit were Mr. Jess Bailey," and cried, "Hit were Lady."

"The horse with the white legs belongs to Mr. Jess Bailey?" said Mama. "Of course somebody could have borrowed his horse."

But Elberta said, "Oh, I feared hit were him. Hit were Mr. Jess." And she cried and cried.

"But why, Elberta, why? Would he have a reason?" and Hallie knew at once what the reason was, knew at last that Jonny's blue eyes did not come from Boyce McClure, as Miss Beulah had once suggested.

"Elberta," said Mama, "was Mr. Jess Bailey the man?"

Elberta made no sound, but she must have nodded her head because Mama went on as if her question were answered.

"Oh, Elberta, Elberta," Mama said sadly, sadly. Then after a minute she said, "How did you know him, Elberta, way down there in the country?"

"He come down there in the country, come down there ridin on his horse, that pretty brown horse with the white legs he calls Lady. He was huntin round down in there lookin for kaolin."

"Yes?"

"He rid up to the door one day and ast for a drink of water."

"Where was your mother?" asked Mama. "Wasn't she there, or your father?"

"They were all away. Hit were cotton-pickin time. They were all out cotton-pickin right down to Clyde, the littlest."

"Why didn't you go, too?" asked Mama, as if she could undo the whole thing simply by having Elberta go out cotton-picking.

"Mama didn't like for me to go out cotton-pickin; she said it was too hard for me. She says I ought to stay home and do the i'nin. I was there i'nin in the front door when he rid up. He ast for a drink and I give him one from the bucket and I told him he could get a cool one over in the woods at the spring."

"And he went away then?" said Mama.

"Yes'm. He come back two or three days later. He brought me a box of Fig Newtons. Said he wanted to thank me for the drink of water."

"And that was all?"

"No'm. He come by two or three times. Sometimes he had a sack of candy. One time he said I ought to go down to the woods and show him where the spring is. I told him I was too busy with the i'nin or whatever I was doin."

"Your family were still out cotton-picking?" said Mama.

"Yes'm, and one day he come by and brought me a dress. Oh, hit were the prettiest dress, the prettiest dress I ever had. Hit were blue."

"Did you show it to your mother?" asked Mama.

"I hid it for a while. I knew I shouldn a taken hit, though Mr. Jess said he just wanted to give me a present for givin him the water. I hid it, and when cotton-pickin time were over and one Sunday we were goin to church I put hit on. Mama ast me where I got hit and I told her. She said I better not tell Pa, and when he ast me where I got hit I didn tell the truth. I said Aunt Relly give hit to me."

There was silence again in the kitchen, and Hallie had time to think of Mr. Jess Bailey handing the blue dress to Elberta, smiling his beautiful smile with the dimples showing briefly, perhaps standing on the top step of her little cabin out there in the cotton fields, or sitting on his horse looking handsome, holding the package out to her from the horse.

Mama said, "That wasn't last summer. After all, you were already here at cotton-pickin time or soon after."

"Yes'm; he didn come around again until May. Everybody was out choppin cotton. Pa wanted me to go, said he needed me, but Mama said I should stay home and do the work. She says I was too weak to chop cotton, and Pa and she had a fuss about hit. I could've gone. I was as strong as the rest of 'em."

"And he came back?"

"Yes'm, came back on Lady, ridin through the fields, sayin he was out lookin for kaolin again. Said he was sho going to get me to show him that spring."

"And you did, I suppose, finally."

"Yes'm. He come two or three times, jus stood around and talked. One time when I seen him comin I put on the blue dress, and when he seen me in it he said now's the time for me to show him the spring. And he taken me up in front of him on his saddle and I rid with him to the spring."

Hallie wanted to call out, no, no, no—that was *my* dream. Crouching under the summer table, her insides moved with pain as she remembered her own dream of riding in front of Mr. Jess Bailey on his horse, her own dream that he would lean forward and kiss the back of her neck and murmur, "My dearest, most precious little angel girl." But after she had seen it really happen to Miss Corrine, had seen him kiss Miss Corrine on the back of the neck as she was about to step into the choir, had seen the look that Miss Corrine gave him in return, she had tried harder to give him up, thinking her dream even more improper than it had been before.

"Elberta, has he ever said anything to you since . . ."

"No'm, he's never *said* anything. 'Course all that time before I had the baby I never went anywheres but here and to church with Aunt Relly. I seen him sometimes pass in a car, or far off ridin on his horse, but I was never real close to him till . . ."

"Yes," said Mama.

"Well, hit were just day before yestiddy. Sat'd'y. I declare, Mrs. Jones, I don't know what come over me. I was feelin so good I put on that blue dress. I told Aunt Relly I needed some condensed milk for Jonny. And I walked right down in front of the stores in my blue dress. What come over me? I walked past his store and he were standin there talkin with a man and he seen me. He looked so scared, I declare, I felt real sorry for him. And he just turned right quick and went back inside. Oh, Mrs. Jones, what you reckon made me do that?"

"Oh, Elberta," Mama said, but sadly, not in an angry way.

It was quiet for a long time in the kitchen. Finally Mama said, "Does anyone else know? I suppose you told your mother?"

"No'm, I never told nobody. I never told Pa even when he got real mad and said I had to leave home less'n I told him. But I guess Mama knew because she knew about the dress. But she never told neither."

"Do you think you could go back to them now, back down there in the country with Jonny?" asked Mama.

"Oh, no'm, I couldn," and Elberta began to cry again. "I got no real place to go."

"Don't you have any relatives who would take you in?"

"Maybe I could go up to Macon and bode with somebody," said Elberta. "They's lots of folks from down here gone up to Macon, or maybe I could find out about somebody up in New York or Chicago."

"Macon's so close," said Mama, as if talking to herself. Then after another pause she said, "If you went to New York you'd have to find some colored folks to stay with."

Elberta took a while to answer. "I don't know nobody. All I could do would be to try to find somebody who'd let me bode with them and then get some kind of work . . ."

"Elberta," said Mama, "you know what I think you ought to do?"

"No'm."

"I think you ought to give up being a colored girl and become a white girl."

Elberta said, "But Mrs. Jones . . ."

Mama said, "I think you'll get along better if you're a white girl, and Jonny, too. He should become a white boy as soon as possible."

"Yes'm," said Elberta, "hit's true he don't look one bit colored. Tell you the truth, Mrs. Jones, he's goin to look just like Mr. Jess."

Hallie thought, but he's still colored just the same. Elberta is part Negro and so is he. You can't just change like a snake shedding its skin. She felt pushed and pulled inside, but Mama was going on now in that excited voice that she always had when she began planning something.

"Elberta, there's no reason in the world why you can't pass, but you've got to learn to speak better. You already talk better than you did but you've got to improve even more. And your name. I think you ought to be called *A*lberta, instead of *E*lberta. *E*lberta sounds like a Negro name. Did you ever hear of a white person called Elberta?"

"No'm, I never hear of anybody with the name, only a peach." Then Elberta said, her voice shaking and sounding as if she would cry again, "But I cain't do hit all by tomorrow, Mrs. Jones, and the letter said I had to go right away."

"I've been thinking," said Mama. "I'll get Mr. Jones to fix you up a ticket to Clover. There's a school over there for colored folks called the Clover Institute, and when I lived there I got to know the people who run it, Mr. and Mrs. Braddock. You can go and stay at the Institute for a while until you learn to talk better. You can help Mrs. Braddock around the house or something while you're learning. And then, when you can talk better and get used to your new name, I have an idea where you can go."

"Yes'm?" said Elberta.

"When we were over in Clover, a good many years ago this was," Mama said, "we took in a girl, a white girl, some relation of Mr. Jones from down on the Saluda River, helped her out a little and finally got her up to a hospital in Philadelphia where she learned to be a nurse. She married up there—married real well, a doctor. I'll write to her and tell her about a girl who needs help."

"You goin to write her about a colored girl who needs help?" asked Elberta.

"No," said Mama, "I'll just write her about a girl. And you go up there and work and some day you'll find a good man and you'll get married too." Mama did not say, "And you'll live happily ever after, Elberta," but Hallie could tell by her tone of voice that she saw it happening, that she was planning it all that way. And for just a moment, carried away by Mama's enthusiasm, the plan seemed right for Elberta and Jonny.

But suddenly she did not feel happy. The ending of the fairy tale held some flaw. All of Miss Beulah's stories came back to her. Elberta would go North and marry some poor white man and then she would have a black baby. The horror of it shook her so that she got up from under the table and walked toward the lighted kitchen and stood in the door, stood there ready to say to Mama that she could not, should not.

The words did not come; she only stood in the door. Mama was leaning against the range as if for warmth. She had put on an old coat that hung behind the kitchen door. Elberta sat in the chair with the quilt around her, her face tear-stained, but she was not crying or trembling any more.

"Hallie," said Mama, "why are you up again?" Then, as if she saw something in Hallie's face, she said, "Hallie, have you been listening?"

Hallie nodded her head.

"I declare you ought to get a good whipping," said Mama. "If I thought it would do any good . . . I'm ashamed of you, listening when you're not supposed to." But she said it mildly, as if she might have done the same. It always killed Mama not to know everything.

"Now that you're up," said Mama, "you and I are going to walk Alberta home. She's got a little boy there may be wondering where she's gone."

Elberta stood up and folded the quilt. "Yes'm," she said happily, as if the idea pleased her.

"Get a coat and put it on over your nightgown," said Mama to Hallie.

They went out the kitchen door to the side yard and on into the street. It was a dark starry night. This is the latest I've ever been up, thought Hallie, the very middle of the night. I must be getting grown up to be up so late.

"Alberta, you come to the depot early in the morning well before train time," said Mama. "Aunt Relly can stay home just this once. She can carry your suitcase, and you carry the baby. Mr. Jones will have your ticket ready and I'll be there to see you off."

Hallie could not say the thought that had brought her from under the table into the doorway, the thought of the Negro baby born to Elberta when she married a white man. Now, walking down the sandy path in the darkness, Mama in the middle holding an arm of each of them, she said, as if she would creep up on the subject, "What's Elberta going to say when they see she's got such black hair?"

"If they say, 'What black hair you have, Alberta,' she should just say, 'Thank you, ma'am,' as if it's a compliment. Up there where she's going there's lots of people with dark hair, Greeks, Jews, Italians, Spaniards. Who was that fellow, that Spanish fellow, who kept looking for a fountain?"

"You mean Ponce de Leon?" said Hallie.

"Who can tell but what he came up in here. He came to Florida and that's not too far away. Just say, 'Ponce de Leon was one of my ancestors.' "

Elberta shivered a little. "I never could say that, Mrs. Jones. Do I have to?"

"No," said Mama, "I was just teasing Hallie. She always wants people to have such noble ancestors. Let's hope people up North don't talk about their ancestors as much as we do."

Now they were in front of Elberta's cabin, and Mama said as she let her arm go, "Get a good sleep, now, and tomorrow you're going to wake up and be Alberta."

"Oh, Mrs. Jones," said Elberta, taking Mama's hand in both of hers and pulling it toward her, clinging to it.

"Run on in, Alberta," said Mama. "Aunt Relly must wonder what's happened to you. I'll see you in the morning."

"Mama," said Hallie, as they turned to walk back under the

water oaks, the sand scrunching under their feet, "Is it right? Elberta *is* colored."

"Not nearly as much colored as she is white," said Mama. "She'll have an easier time if she's white."

"But it isn't right, is it? If she's Negro, even if just a little bit, people ought to know it, oughtn't they? Isn't it kind of like the Ku Klux Klan not to let people know what you really are?"

"I can't see what difference it makes," said Mama, "and it's going to be better for her soul's salvation to be white. Down here a colored girl who looks white has more temptations than either a real black girl or a white one. It just seems to work that way."

Mama's talking about Elberta's soul's salvation made her sound like Papa; he was the one interested in souls and Mama was interested in everything else about them.

"But what if she marries and has a coal-black baby?"

"Why coal black?" said Mama. "Honestly, Hallie, I declare, I wonder sometimes where you get your ideas. I suppose I should just never let you hear Miss Beulah open her mouth. You sound just like her."

But Hallie persisted; she loved Jonny and had grown to like Elberta, but if it were right for Elberta to pass, hiding her little bit of colored blood, then what about all the other Negroes? Would Mama send Elberta north if she were darker and not say that she was colored? If not, then color did make a difference.

"Would you do it, Mama, if Elberta were as black as, say, Adam Lincoln?"

Mama would not say. She shook herself as if she were shaking away an idea she did not like. "Hallie," she said, "I wish you'd stop *pushing* me." But she did not answer the question; she went on to something else.

"Why, when I think you might actually have believed everything Miss Beulah said . . . Why, I imagine you might even think it's a terrible thing to have a baby, listening to her."

"Yes'm," said Hallie, thinking of the watermelon and the keyhole.

"Why, Hallie, having a baby is like all the Christmases and

birthdays and graduations and Valentine days and Halloweens, maybe even wedding days, all rolled up into one. It's the most exciting day there is, and don't let Miss Beulah give you the idea it isn't." She walked on slowly. "I suppose that every time Miss Beulah comes around I ought to make you leave the room."

Hallie said, "When I hear her I know she's silly, but what she says keeps coming back anyhow, just popping back into my head."

They walked on silently. Finally Mama said, "We can't look on the dark side. We'll just have to have faith. Alberta's a nice girl and a smart girl. We're all human beings, black or white, though sometimes the white ones don't act like it."

When they came back into the kitchen and stood in the light Mama put her hands on her shoulders and said sternly, "Hallie, you're not to breathe a word of this, not to Virginia, not to Margaret Craig, not to Benny." She stopped and winced and turned away as if she had a twinge of neuralgia. "I'm afraid to ask Benny," she said.

Mama had not said Miss Corrine's name. She had not said, "Not Miss Corrine," she had not mentioned the most important person. Her insides moved with pain again at the thought of Miss Corrine. "But what about Miss Corrine?" she said, "and Mr. Barksdale? And Magnolia Hall? Is everything going to be the same? Just the way it was before? Is it right? Shouldn't you . . ."

"No," said Mama. "No, I shouldn't and you shouldn't. He never would marry Elberta, not in a hundred years. All right. He has his conscience and what he tells Miss Corrine is up to him. He'll have his worries. Don't think he'll escape worrying. Right now I imagine he's tossing in his bed. He wouldn't've gotten so desperate if he weren't mighty worried. Now go to bed," and Mama kissed her and gave her a push toward the hall door.

I wouldn't play the Wedding March for them if they asked me on their bended knees, thought Hallie. I'll just ask Miss Toulou Vass for a new piece; I'll tell her I'm sick and tired of the Wedding March. At that moment the very thought of the tune sickened her. Mama had seemed to know just what to do tonight, but was she right in saying that Miss Corrine should not be told? And she thought of Mr. Jess's unfaithfulness—to Miss Corrine, to Elberta, to her (Hallie) in her dreams, to Magnolia Hall, oh, most of all, to Magnolia Hall.

19

Hallie wakened the next morning as usual to the rise and fall of Papa's supplications, heard Mama shaking out the ashes in the range, remembered suddenly that Elberta would not come this morning, remembered the black perfidy of Mr. Jess Bailey, a man who would mask his Galahad face and shout "boo" to frighten a weak girl. Her thoughts seemed a horror that the night had brought; surely they would vanish with the light. She tried to turn over and go back to sleep; there was time for another nap before she needed to get up. But there was a vague ache in her legs; they would not be comfortable in any position. Was this what Mama meant by the "jimjams"? Finally, her legs twitching, she got out of bed and started dressing, but though she started well before Virginia, she had to sit down so often to yawn and stretch that Virginia was ready before her.

"What's the matter with you?" Virginia asked.

She could not tell Virginia that she would never rest easy again, that she would never again feel right knowing what she knew. She looked ahead at all the years, each one an endless segment of future, her legs uncertain with the jimjams, her mind uncertain from dancing between Miss Corrine and Elberta. A wrong had been done to Elberta, but should it also be done to Miss Corrine? Oh, Lord, was all she could moan, as she lay back on the bed half dressed.

Mama had disappeared to do the milking when she and Virginia went in for breakfast. Benny sat over his coffee looking sour, and when Virginia said to him, "Where were you last night?" he snarled, "Wouldn't you like to know?" Oh, Lord, oh, Lord. She felt as full of sighs and "oh, Lords" as Aunt Relly.

Margaret Craig met her at the corner with the news of the Ku Klux Klan. Margaret had not been at church last night; she had stayed at home to mind her younger brothers and sisters so her mother could go. She had seen the lights of the marchers out the jail window, seen them stopping in front of Elberta's house, actually seen a figure come to the porch but could not tell if it was Elberta or Aunt Relly. But she figured it must be Elberta.

"And do you know where else they went, Hallie?" giggled Margaret. "Guess."

"Did they come see somebody in jail?" asked Hallie, trying to rise to the occasion, her mind a blank.

"Good Lord, no," said Margaret. "What would they come to jail for? There's nobody there now but some old nigger cut up another one in a razor fight last Saturday night."

"What did your father do?" asked Hallie.

"What did he do about what?"

"About the Ku Klux Klan," said Hallie. "Shouldn't he ask them what they're doing, where they're going? Seems to me the sheriff . . ."

Until last night if she had thought about the Ku Klux Klan she would probably have thought of it as a kind of Southern tradition. This morning all was different. She could still feel the shiver of surprise at the sight of the white-robed figures; the sickening visions of the dancing chicken and the dangling figure slid in and out of her mind. The fear that made Elberta burrow like an animal in the covers had struck Hallie too.

"Well, Papa wasn't around, for one thing," said Margaret. "He was out in the country looking for a dangerous criminal. When he came in he told Mama about Miss Ada Pratt."

They walked slowly along in the warm spring air. The yards were full of the big meaningless faces of hydrangeas, some blue, some pink. Across the street in Miss Lizzie Wallace's private cemetery, tiger lilies bloomed near the graves. Overhead the sky seemed innocent and open. The day was beautiful, but Hallie did not feel in keeping with it. Her eyes felt too big for their sockets, and a headache brooded off there like a circling buzzard, flapping its wings to remind her of its presence. Every once in a while she thought she might be sick.

As they passed Miss Ada Pratt's house they could hear Old Man Pratt yodeling. "Listen to him," said Margaret. "You ever hear the way that old man can yodel? He ought to be hired for the stage." They paused awhile and listened to the yodels, coming high and clear from the back of the house. Hallie had never seen Old Man Pratt, but she imagined him with staring, blind eyes, a man with a long white beard that blew with the force of his yodels.

"I really wonder what Miss Ada Pratt's note said," said Margaret.

"What note?"

"Her note from the Ku Klux Klan. What's the matter with you, Hallie? I just told you, didn't even make you guess."

"Oh," said Hallie, "she got a note." And she thought of Elberta receiving her note last night, coming out trembling to the porch of the little cabin, standing there before the torches and the white-robed men; oh, she had been able to see it all as Elberta told it, and she could remember Elberta's voice shaking in the telling.

And Miss Ada Pratt? Did she open the screen door, hesitate there before it whined back into place, then advance onto the porch with its rockers, its swing, its ferns in jardinieres behind the banisters, stand there big and tall, her hair piled high, glinting red in the torchlight (in her wrapper or fully dressed? Corsets on or body gone limp and soft?). Even uncorseted, Miss Ada would stand there impassive; she would not tremble like Elberta.

"Why," she asked, "why?"

Margaret Craig was trying to yodel and did not answer. She threw her head back and tossed her voice into the sky until her red curls shook with the vibration. The sound hurt Hallie's ears. They were away from the houses now and the sidewalk ran alongside fields; the newly turned earth dark with moisture stood up in slick sharp furrows, bearing the imprint of the plow. Water stood in the ditches and puddles in the street. There must have been a shower before morning. The standing water was alive with spring frogs.

"Look at them," said Margaret Craig, "just look at them. You know what they're doing, don't you, Hallie?"

The frogs kept calling to each other; most of them had paired off and were locked in an embrace. On other days Hallie would have watched with the same interest and speculation that she turned on a rooster straddling a hen, a bull mounting a nervous cow, wondering. But today she felt distaste and a breath of sickness at the whole subject of pairing off.

"This is going to be a mighty good season for tadpoles," said Margaret, poking one of the pairs with her toes. The frogs remained fixed.

The vague feeling of unease in Hallie's stomach grew. At last the road rose toward the school, and the frogs with their monstrous, urgent cries, their slimy embracings, were left behind. As they turned into the driveway to school Miss Corrine passed in her roadster, drove into the parking lot and jumped out. She was wearing her GSCW sweater and carried a book and a big bunch of pink roses, largess of Magnolia Hall, which she would arrange in her studio and share with other teachers.

"You know your piece yet?" asked Margaret. Seeing Miss Corrine must have reminded Margaret of the Expression Contest. Hallie had felt a little sorry for Margaret having to take expression from her cousin, Miss Bootsie Craig, though she professed great loyalty to her and her teaching methods.

"Pretty near," said Hallie. "Do you?"

"Oh, I've known it for weeks now," said Margaret. "Cousin Bootsie and I are working on the finishing touches." She dropped her voice to a deep dramatic register. " 'Stick to the engine and stand by your mother, Jack,' " she said, in what was obviously intended to be a dying voice, although her head was shaking and her eyes were rolling so that she did not look the least bit as if she were dying—rather as if she were yodeling. " 'The hand on the boy's head grew cold, and when they lifted it and laid it back upon the dead man's breast Jack turned to his mother. "Here I am, Mother," he said.' "

Miss Bootsie Craig always chose sad, dramatic pieces. Miss Corrine believed in being more restrained. It was the difference between elocution and expression, although Miss Bootsie Craig claimed to teach expression. Miss Corrine did not believe in big gestures; she believed in being more natural. Margaret Craig's curls, her compact body, her hands and head all seemed to ripple and writhe with the force of her emotion and her voice. What power! Hallie had to admire it although she knew that Miss Corrine would have a fit if one of her pupils carried on like that.

Laura Fitzgerald turned around when Hallie was in her seat and wanted to know all about the Ku Klux Klan. She had been at church and had seen the parade go past, then had to go on home without hearing more.

Hallie told her about Miss Ada Pratt. She could not bear to mention Elberta.

"Who all do you think was in it?" whispered Laura, even though Mr. Holden had begun the algebra class.

"Don't know," said Hallie, pretending an interest in algebra that she did not feel.

Laura was not to be diverted. "Say, where was Benny last

night?" she asked. "I kept watching and watching for him and he never did come."

"Don't know," said Hallie, not looking at her but at the board as if the identity of X was the most fascinating information in the world.

The morning stretched like eternity ahead of her. And after the lunch hour would come her expression lesson with Miss Corrine, a time that had become almost a sacred part of the week, transforming the whole day (from the first moment of awakening when she thought this is Monday, Expression Day, the hours shimmering up to an apex at 1:30 in anticipation, and sliding down again after 2:15 in a glow of having been, and then repeating itself on Thursday). Now the thought of 1:30 and Miss Corrine made her feel queer again. How could she go in as usual and sit in the chair near Miss Corrine's desk, graced by the roses from Magnolia Hall—the pink blouse and the faint perfume (attar of roses?) that Miss Corrine used combining to make her like a rosebud herself. Miss Corrine always waited for her as if she too had been living for this moment (those other dull pupils were to be endured, but Hallie!). Miss Corrine always looked at her in a *special* way, and Hallie would sit for a minute basking in that special attention before she would stand and begin her lesson. " 'The Sacrifice of Sydney Carton,' " she said now to herself, stretching her legs out under Laura Fitz-gerald's desk to try to relieve their cramping, " 'The Sacrifice of Sydney Carton,' by Charles Dickens. 'In the black prison of the Conciergerie, the doomed of the day awaited . . .' " and then the lines faded off and Mr. Holden was suddenly asking for her problems. All through the rest of algebra, and then English, she tried to remember her piece. And once during a study period, just before lunch, while trying to say her piece all the way through, she had a little dream; instead of Miss Corrine in her pink blouse looking and smelling like a rose, she saw Elberta in her blue dress sitting in Miss Corrine's chair, princess pale and princess proud, acting like Miss Corrine. By this time, she thought as she came out of her dream, Elberta should be safely away on the up train.

When the lunch bell rang she decided to walk home because she could not bear to listen to Margaret Craig and Laura Fitzgerald gabbling. If she walked home she would only have a few minutes before having to turn around and come back, but it would be long enough to find out if Elberta got away all right and if Mama had told Papa that the man was Mr. Jess. Mama had named the people whom Hallie was not supposed to tell, but she had not said a word about Papa. Mama would not like it if Papa failed to tell her something important; undoubtedly she had told him, whispering it while he was eating his breakfast, or mumbling it in a quick aside at the depot when she was seeing Elberta off. She would have to explain to Papa why Elberta was leaving. Perhaps Papa would be able to do something to stop Miss Corrine from marrying Mr. Jess. He could speak to Mr. Barksdale as man to man. But Papa was bashful man to man; he held back, became humble. But on Sundays in church . . . She was nearing the corner where Schoolhouse Street ran into the street to the depot and as she glanced in that direction there was Papa coming home for dinner too. She felt a twinge of disappointment. Conversation was harder with Papa around, and she wanted to ask Mama if she had told him and just what Papa had said.

"You coming home for dinner too?" said Papa as she waited for him at the corner. He did not pause to talk but kept on at a steady pace. "Freight's late," he said. "I'll have to hurry to eat and get back for it." There was no way of telling whether he knew about Elberta or not; he simply walked on quickly like a man with something on his mind.

Mama was taking the biscuits out of the oven as they walked into the kitchen. "Well," she said, looking hard at Hallie, "I suppose you get tired of those dry sandwiches."

When she and Hallie were alone together at dinner Mama murmured a quick little grace. But Papa never took grace lightly; Benny claimed that his stomach had time to grow to his backbone while Papa said grace, and today he took grace even more seriously than usual. He blessed the food and then went on, "Lord, Lord, soften the hearts of those who sit in the seats of the powerful" (could he mean Mr. Jess? Not until he lived at Magnolia Hall) "be with the poor and downtrodden" (this might refer to Elberta) "shed Thy grace on those men, forgive them Lord, those whited sepulchres" (Mr. Jess, yes, Mr. Jess) "who under the cover of darkness, hiding behind masks, take advantage of the helpless and the weak. Help us, Lord, help us to know which path to take. Amen."

Mama must have told him. But now Mama looked tremulous. Her voice shook; she must be thinking of Benny again. Mama said, "Then you found out who was in the Ku Klux Klan, darling? The whole town knows?"

"Nobody *knows*," said Papa, "nobody *knows* for sure. But it's easy to guess. Coming down in here thinking he can get everything his way."

Papa wasn't talking about Mr. Jess. He was already here. Benny?

"Who are you talking about, darling?" asked Mama, sounding as mixed up as Hallie felt. Her stomach felt queer again; the fried liver looked greasy. It would have a very livery taste. She did not feel like eating and her eyes were full of crumbs.

"I mean Mr. Bird Ledbetter," said Papa, biting off the *Bird* and *-better* with his thin, nervous mouth, sounding angry for Papa. "If he wasn't with those night riders then he stirred them up to do his work. God will hold him responsible."

"What work?" asked Mama, wanting to know, her eyes bright and eager.

"Leaving a note on Adam," said Papa, "threatening him."

"On Adam?" Mama leaned back and put down her fork. Her nose grew red. "Not on Adam. He wouldn't harm a fly. He's a good man. Why would they do that?" And when Papa did not answer her at once she said, "Who told you?"

"Adam told me," said Papa. "At least he mentioned it in his prayers this morning."

Adam must communicate with people on earth through God just the way Papa did. Suddenly she saw God sitting high in the sky, His golden throne a sounding board; prayers vapored up and struck the golden throne, then glanced like slanting sunrays to the proper heart below. Adam must be just as roundabout in his prayers as Papa was in his, speaking in a code that only God and Papa could understand.

"He prayed long and hard this morning," said Papa, "mentioned the travail of the night, begged God to change the hearts of those who wished to do him evil, begged Him to forgive his enemies . . . like that . . . *you* know."

Yes, they knew; they had heard the same prayers from Papa.

"I asked him after we were all through if he was in some kind of trouble. I remembered him praying about Lucius that time, saying 'the sick in our midst,' and so I said, 'Adam, is there some special thing troubling you?'"

Papa paused, but not to eat. No one was interested in Mama's hot biscuits. He simply paused to swallow, to take a breath.

"He finally said, 'Yessir, Mr. Jones, I reckon I ought to tell you.' Then he told me that he'd just gotten home last night, he'd been leading prayer meeting down at Bethsaida Chapel; he'd just come in and taken off his shoes and was washing his feet before he went to bed when he heard a racket down the road; he saw the lights through the door but he had his feet in the washbasin and he didn't get up right away, and then he heard someone call his name, 'Adam.' He started drying off his feet, and then he took a minute to put on his shoes and whoever it was called, called his name again, two or three of them, different voices, and someone rapped on the porch and said, 'You better get on out here, nigger.' He said he took his time then, he don't like to be talked to like that, but he finally got his shoes on and stepped out on the porch and he could see the lighted torches and the horses dressed up in sheets, and the men. And he said, 'Who called Adam?' And someone stepped forward and said, in a put-on, high voice, 'Adam, here's a note for you, nigger. Take heed.' "

"What did it say?" asked Mama.

"Like the rest. Get out of town or . . ."

"But why would they want Adam to leave town? He's a good worker, knows his place, minds his own business."

"Adam says it's because Mr. Bird Ledbetter wants his old home place back."

Hallie's brains felt as addled as the time she had been swung too hard on the flying jenny; she blinked her eyes two or three times to try to make her thoughts clearer. Of course she had planned for Mr. Bird Ledbetter to take Montpelier back—this was *her* plan—but not this way; she had not planned this.

"Adam doesn't want the Ledbetter Old Home Place, does he?" She concentrated so as not to say Montpelier. "Won't he sell to Mr. Bird?"

"Well," Papa went on, "Adam said that's the way he *used* to feel. Says when he got the land he didn't care too much about the house because he knew he never would live in it. But now he says he's not going to let Mr. Bird come down in here and get it for nothing. Mr. Bird came to him and said he'd pay him for the whole place just what he paid when he bought it five years ago at the Sheriff's Sale. Adam said, 'No, sir, I think maybe I ought to have more now because Mr. Barksdale has come with the planing mill and it's worth lots more.' "

"Couldn't he just sell Mr. Bird the house?" asked Hallie. "Mr. Bird could fix it up and live in it and get the Duckets out . . ."

"Adam's funny," said Papa. (Stubborn, bull-headed, is what Lucius had said.) "He said he *thought* he would sell the house, just the house, if Mr. Bird wanted it. But the more Mr. Bird talked to him the more he thinks he won't sell him anything."

"Did Mr. Bird speak mean to him?" asked Mama.

"Adam didn't say, didn't say any more what he said. Just said he didn't like the way Mr. Bird talked. Said Mr. Bird had gone back on his raising. He said Mr. Bird's mother and father would be ashamed to have a son grow up and act like him."

"What's Adam getting at?" said Mama, mystified. "They say Mr. Bird is doing right well up in Atlanta. He's planning to run for something now, I hear. He must've talked mean to Adam."

"Suppose Adam won't sell. He'll have to go, won't he?" said Hallie. She remembered Elberta's fear and her own feeling when the Ku Klux Klan passed by, and a quivering started in some region of her chest. What would happen to Adam if he kept on being stubborn?

"He says he ain't going and he ain't selling." (Stubborn, said Lucius.) "Says he's going to sit tight, mind his own business, and pray for his enemies."

Mama took away Papa's cold, uneaten fried liver and brought him a dish of canned peaches. "What are you going to do, darling?" she asked.

"I don't know," Papa said. "I'm praying for guidance."

"What about Brother Jamieson?" said Mama, evidently unwilling to wait for God. "After all, the preacher ought to be able to help you."

Hallie waited for Papa to speak, to reassure them that Brother Jamieson would not hold it against Adam for disagreeing with him about where Lucius would spend eternity.

"What about the Board of Deacons?" said Mama. "It's meeting tonight, isn't it? Why couldn't you just bring the matter up to them, ask them what they think of it? They know Adam, know he shouldn't be hurt. Why don't you . . ."

But Papa did not raise his eyes from his plate. "I feel a little backward about stirring things up," he said, "just new in town and all, new on the Board of Deacons, the newest one, I guess. They might think I'm just coming down in here trying to stir up trouble."

"Well, talk to brother Jamieson alone," said Mama, "then maybe he'll take it up."

"Maybe I ought to do that," said Papa, looking at his watch, wiping his mouth and standing up. "The freight's due through in fifteen minutes. I have to get back. I'll pray about it," he said.

"Hallie," said Mama, "you're going to be late getting back to school."

But Hallie sat there, unable to move, unable to think. "Why don't you go back and take a nap?" Mama said. "You can miss school for once. I'll say you had a headache or something."

Hallie sleepwalked to the bedroom and threw herself on the bed. She could not remember pulling the quilt up over her but later when she waked up the quilt was there and Mama was calling to her through the screen door, "Hallie, you won't sleep tonight."

She stretched under the quilt. Her eyes felt better and her legs felt right again. But she had not asked the question she came home to ask. "Mama, did Elberta get off all right?"

"Oh, yes, she got away all right." Mama folded the quilt and spread it over the foot of the bed.

"Did you hear about Miss Ada Pratt?"

"Naturally," said Mama, and smiled. "The neighborhood newspaper never fails. Miss Beulah came by even before I went down to the station to see Alberta off. She told me about them stopping at Alberta's and at Miss Ada Pratt's. Miss Lizzie Wallace had called her up and told her about Miss Ada first thing this morning. Miss Lizzie had just gotten home from church when the Ku Klux Klan came down their street and stopped at Miss Ada Pratt's. Miss Beulah hasn't had as much fun since Shadrack Cartledge shot the highway man. She looked around real quick to see if Alberta were here, kept saying, 'What about Elberta, wonder what she's going to do,' and things like that. But she didn't linger; I guess she was afraid she'd miss something down in Miss Lizzie's neighborhood. She'll probably be back." Mama straightened the quilt now and said, "Child, you didn't eat any dinner. I saved you something in the oven."

Hallie was in the kitchen eating biscuits and jelly when Miss Beulah returned.

"Well, for goodness sake," she said, looking at Hallie. "What're you home for? Got the fantods?"

Hallie opened her mouth to say "No'm," when Mama said, "Hallie's been having these headaches lately. I think she reads too much."

"You better get her some glasses," said Miss Beulah. "Well, Ada Pratt didn't go away. I was down at Lizzie Wallace's and we happened to be sittin near a window in the front room and Ada went by just the way she always does, a little while before the train went up. But she didn have a suitcase or anything, and she wasn't in any hurry as if she might be tryin to ketch the train. She just looked the way she does every mornin, though if it had happened to me I'd be ashamed to show my face . . ."

"Seems to me those fellows were ashamed to show their faces, too," said Mama.

"What fellows you talking about, Mrs. Jones?" asked Miss Beulah.

"Those Kluxers," said Mama.

Miss Beulah looked amazed. "Why, Mrs. Jones, I declare, you sound as if you didn't approve of the Ku Klux Klan. You can't just let things go on and on. Somebody's got to take a hand. As Bubber says, you just can't have a community gettin a reputation for sin and lawlessness."

"Does he belong?" asked Mama.

"Who?" asked Miss Beulah, as if she did not hear right or did not understand.

"Mr. Willy. Does he belong to the Ku Klux Klan?" Mama asked it in a mild voice as if she were saying, "Do you know a good recipe for chocolate cake?"

"Why, Mrs. Jones, I'm surprised to hear you don't know the Ku Klux Klan is a secret society. Bubber's said time after time this town's just got to put its foot down. What's going to happen to our young people with examples like Elberta and Miss Ada?" She paused and no one answered. "But as for tellin whether Bubber belongs—even if I knew I couldn tell. It's a secret."

211

"Oh," said Mama, and rubbed a coffee stain on the tablecloth as if she thought it might come out by her rubbing.

"I really would like to know where that Elberta went to," said Miss Beulah. "Where'd Mr. Jones sell her a ticket to?"

"That's a professional secret," said Mama. "Mr. Jones isn't supposed to tell where people buy tickets to. Lawyers have their secrets, and doctors. And the Ku Klux Klan. And so does Mr. Jones."

Miss Beulah's pock-marked face turned red. She seemed to seethe inside, like a stove with the draft left open.

"But the train just runs from here to Macon," Mama went on. " 'Course there's Verdery, Wheaton, Ripple Creek and Smith-ville between here and Macon. Oh, yes, and the kaolin mill, High Point, that's a flag stop. She could've gotten off at any one. But I imagine she went on up to Macon."

"I'd think you would've asked her, seein as you were down there," said Miss Beulah. She stood up, her head thrust forward, her jaw set; she would be mad at Mama for quite a while. "Well," she said, pushing back her chair, "good riddance to bad rubbish, I say. Bad enough having that baby, but having one with blue eyes and straight hair! I declare, every time I saw it I got right sick at my stomach."

"Then it's a good thing Elberta has left town so your stomach can settle down," said Mama, standing up too. She seemed a little sick herself.

Miss Beulah leaned back, the same stance she took when she was singing alto in the choir, reared back on her heels. "Bubber and I never could see how you could afford havin that girl around here, what with your young girls growin up and gettin ideas."

"The ideas they got from Elberta are not the ones I worry about," Mama said. She looked at Hallie, sitting with a biscuit poised half way to her mouth. "Hallie, what did I tell you?"

"Yes'm," said Hallie, and left the room. Only a few hours had passed since Mama said she was worried about the ideas she might get from Miss Beulah, and in that time she had come around to Mama's side. Oh, she was on Mama's side now. Mama had done the right thing about Elberta; she was sure of that. That was about the only thing she was sure of. She was mixed up about colored blood and what difference it made.

What would become of Adam? Lucius had said he was stubborn, bull-headed, and he was already proving that Lucius spoke the truth. They could not pack *him* off on the up train. And the quiver of fear started up in her chest again, making her forget that deeper despair, the black infamy of the one she had once loved, the infamy of Mr. Jess Bailey.

20

Tuesday was the day for Hallie's music lesson with Miss Toulou Vass. She hurried home after school to ask Mama what Brother Jamieson had said to Papa about Adam the night before. Papa had been late getting home from the Deacons' Meeting and Mama had made her go to bed. And this morning, although she had hurried to get to the kitchen before he left, for some reason Virginia rose just as early and arrived in the kitchen at the same time. Mama had not said she should not tell Virginia about Adam, and Hallie almost asked Papa right out. But his face was forbidding; his eyes glazed with some heavenly preoccupation. He poured his coffee into his saucer to cool, drank it down absentmindedly, rose from the table without looking at any of them, gave Mama a hasty kiss, and hurried out as if he heard the freight whistling in the distance.

Miss Toulou came early for the lesson, or right on time, because when Hallie reached home, her car was parked in front of the house and she was inside talking to Mama. And she could not tell a thing by looking at Mama's face. She tried to read it, but Mama did not look at her in any special way, did not look at her at all.

Hallie returned the Wedding March when she and Miss Toulou moved into the living room to the piano. "It's too hard, I reckon," she said.

"Why, honey, that's a shame. You were doing right well on it, I thought." Miss Toulou spread the music out on the piano and struck the opening notes.

"I don't think it's very pretty after all."

"Too bad you didn't get a chance to play it. Too bad you couldn't have played it this morning." And Miss Toulou giggled, striking the opening C and then the C and E.

"Was there a wedding this morning?" Oh, surely not Miss Corrine and Mr. Jess . . . not yet.

"Yep, I was in a wedding myself. I reckon you'd say I was in one."

"Who got married?" Hallie turned on the stool waiting to hear.

"Miss Ada Pratt and Shadrack Cartledge. They've gone to Macon on their honeymoon."

"But I thought Miss Ada got a letter . . ." said Hallie.

"I guess that's what finally made up her mind." Miss Toulou laughed, her thin elegant hands on the piano, the slender fingers picking out the first chord of the Wedding March. "Guess she just wouldn't've taken the plunge if she hadn't had a little help. Guess she even preferred old Shadrack to leaving town."

"But would Mr. Shadrack like that?" asked Hallie. "Would he like it for her to marry him because the Ku Klux Klan told her to?"

"Honey, I don't doubt but what old Shadrack himself had a

hand in the whole thing," said Miss Toulou, "him and that old rapscallion, Willy Featherstone. They cooked up something, I imagine. He never could've gotten her any other way. In some ways she's down on men."

"You'd think she'd rather leave town than be made to marry when she doesn't want to."

"Sometimes people just can't make up their minds. Or maybe they want something and don't know how to get it," said Miss Toulou. "Anyhow, Miss Ada had her old father to look after. She couldn't just up and leave town. I don't know what those fellows were thinking of."

"But her father went off and left *her* a long time ago," said Hallie quoting Miss Beulah, "and when he came back, sick and old, she didn't even know who he was."

"Somebody's got to look after him," said Miss Toulou.

Hallie turned a little on the stool, thinking, swung a half circle and then turned back. "He must love her very much," she said.

"Who? Shadrack?" Miss Toulou shook her head and laughed again, throwing her head back so that the long golden hair spread further over her hump. "I don't know. There's some as says old Shadrack don't love nothing or nobody . . . not even himself."

"I don't see why he would go to all that trouble then if . . ."

"Well, he wanted to get married," said Miss Toulou. "He was just pure-T embarrassed not being able to get any woman, not even Ada Pratt, to marry him. Oh, he felt mighty bad when Mary Emily left him." And Miss Toulou made delicate arpeggios from the wedding chords.

"That must have hurt his feelings," said Hallie, "if he loved her and took her to live in that beautiful old house, the Cartledge Old Home Place . . ."

"Uh huh," said Mss Toulou, "that's right. But it is a fact that Shadrack Cartledge is the meanest white man in Georgia. Mary Emily said it was like he got up on the wrong side of the bed every morning or like he'd sucked nothing but sour milk from his Mama. She said he was just naturally the sourest man she ever did see, and she just had to leave him—she didn't much care who with. That's why she went away with the highway man. And now that's turned out real well. Frank's made a real nice husband, though they have to live in kind of a small house up in Atlanta. They got a nice little baby and another on the way."

"Oh," said Hallie. "Will Miss Ada move out to the Cartledge Old Home Place?"

"Uh huh, and take along Old Man Pratt too, him and his yodels. Won't that be something? The old place is going to be lively again." Miss Toulou made a little yodel high up in the treble on the piano. "You sure you don't want to play the Wedding March through one more time, honey, just for me to see how you were doing?"

"I don't really like it any more," said Hallie. "I'd rather play something else." How pleasant just to sit and look at Miss Toulou, even with her hunchback. She was almost as pretty as Miss Corrine; they were the two prettiest women she knew. It hurt her to look at Miss Corrine now. All day at school she had avoided her. She sent word by Virginia that she had been sick yesterday and could not come to her lesson. Miss Toulou, with her Rapunzel hair down her back (or was it more like a Danderine ad?), the fine golden hairs on her face, her amber eyes, and her long nervous fingers playing a chord, or a trill or a yodel on the piano . . . how lovely to sit and look at her, rest eyes on her, forget Adam, forget Mr. Jess Bailey. Miss Toulou's little feet in their one-strap patent leather slippers swung like a child's a few inches from the floor; the smallest feet on a grown woman she had ever seen. Like Mama's they could be described as " 'bout as big as two little ears of popcorn."

She would rather keep Miss Toulou talking than play. Knowing that Miss Toulou was about to ask for the Poet and Peasant Overture, she said quickly, "If Mr. Shadrack is as mean as everybody says he is, isn't he hard to work for? I mean, I've seen you down there at the cotton warehouse working for him since the first day I came to Greenwood."

216

"I was just sorry for him," said Miss Toulou Vass. "Just down-right sorry for him. It's true he's low-down mean but it's like he can't help himself. You should've seen him standin up there in the ordinary's office gettin married, him and Miss Ada. He had on his good blue suit and a white shirt, and his hair was slicked down, and he looked like butter wouldn't melt in his mouth. But I bet him and Ada have a fight before they get to Macon and like as not she'll come home alone on the train. And that won't be the way old Shadrack wants it. He just can't keep from pickin on somebody, or wantin them to do somethin a different way, or tryin to show that he knows better than they do. After a while it really kind of makes you laugh." And she did laugh, turning toward Hallie and blinking her long golden lashes over her amber eyes.

Suddenly Hallie remembered one of her first dreams about Miss Toulou, thought of a happier, simpler time and turned to it hopefully now that she believed that Mr. Jess Bailey would desecrate Magnolia Hall. Earlier she had thought there might be a romance between Mr. Willy Featherstone and Miss Toulou (after all, she had knit a blue sleeveless sweater for him). Watching Miss Toulou now and admiring her, Hallie thought again of how suitable it would be, even though Miss Toulou was a hunchback and even though she spoke of Mr. F. as an old rap-scallion . . . still how much better for him to be master of Mag-nolia Hall than that whited sepulchre, Mr. Jess Bailey. Miss Toulou was trying a little piece in the treble, absent-mindedly playing some little tune, and Hallie—a little breathlessly, because at that very moment Miss Toulou leaned forward and turned the music—plunged.

"I wonder why Mr. Featherstone never got married?"

"That old rascal?" said Miss Toulou, widening her amber eyes at Hallie. "Couldn get anybody to have him, I imagine."

"But what about that sweater? You know the blue sweater you knitted for him?" Hallie said, shaken inside to think that she had misinterpreted this signal too.

Miss Toulou paused a minute before she answered. "Well, honey, I like to knit. And I was always right sorry for old Willy. He just didn seem to have much of anybody—Miss Beulah don't pay him any mind. But it's the last sweater I'll knit for him, I can tell you that."

"Why?" said Hallie.

"I sit down there listenin to those men talk, though sometimes I can't listen, of course." Her face turned pink. "Sometimes when I hear them I could just knock their heads together. Take Willy Featherstone—he don't amount to anything. He hasn't done a lick of work in his whole life. Nobody ever pays any attention to him, mainly because he just goes on sayin the same things over and over. Until one day when it suits them—then they decide to listen to him."

"I don't see . . ." said Hallie.

Little beads of perspiration sprung out around Miss Toulou's nose. "He can go on shakin his head and mutterin about a girl like Elberta, saying she ought to be run out of town. Nobody pays the slightest bit of attention to him until one day someone decides *he* wants to run Elberta out of town. *Then* Willy Featherstone is the wise man; *he's* the one we should've listened to all along, *he's* . . ." She was too angry to finish, just shook her head.

As if to shake the whole subject away, Miss Toulou turned purposefully to the piano, played a trill in the treble and said, "Hallie, I do hope your Mama isn't listenin to this lesson. She'd sure figure you weren't gettin your money's worth. Maybe I can make it up to you before I go."

"Go?"

"Now we got old Shadrack married off, I guess I'll take off too in a week or so. I've just about finished my course up in Macon in guitar and uke, and my teacher says I'm a natural for the radio. One thing about the radio is you can be heard and not seen." Miss Toulou smiled. "And I *sound* real good. With guitar and uke, playin the piano and singin a little, he's sure I can get on one of these programs. Anyways, you can be right sure I'm not going to set 'round here the rest of my life suckin my thumb. Lord, there's nothin happened here since before the War."

She paused and in the silence they heard the afternoon train whistle. Then Miss Toulou sat forward in a businesslike way. "Hallie, it's time for your lesson to be over and we haven't even started."

So Hallie played the C scale slow and then fast (messing it up when it was fast), then blundered through the Poet and Peasant with many stops and starts, Miss Toulou for some reason deciding to be very particular about time. Hallie's mind was not on the music. The Ku Klux Klan had called on three people and two of them had feared it enough to carry out its directions immediately. Miss Ada must have feared the Klan or she would not have married so hastily. Adam was the only one left. Thinking of him made Hallie want to finish the lesson and find Mama to ask what Brother Jamieson had said to Papa.

But Mama had disappeared when the lesson was over. Hallie felt angry that Mama had not waited to talk to her, or given some sign before the lesson. Not knowing made the quivering start inside and grow into a kind of panic. Was Adam all right now? She called for Mama out the front door. If she were at the McGhees' she would hear her, or even at Miss Beulah's. But there was no answer and she started toward the depot, running to the corner and slowing down, telling herself that nothing could have happened. Nothing could happen yet; it was too soon.

When she walked into the depot office Mama was standing there talking to Papa.

"Adam?" said Hallie, panting from her run.

"He's out in the warehouse," said Papa, as if Hallie were simply making an inquiry.

And since her question had been taken that way, she walked on out the other door of the office to the warehouse. Adam had been sweeping and he was held in an amber cloud of dust catching the light from one of the big warehouse doors opening toward the tracks and the afternoon sun. He leaned on his big push broom and when he saw Hallie he moved again, gave one push to the broom and released the sparrows overhead to move and twitter. Then he came toward her, big, black, hitching up an overall strap.

"Hey, Hallie," he said, "I was in hopes you'd come by." He wanted to see her too. "I was just leanin there thinkin, now if Hallie would come by I could ask her to do me a little favor."

The trembling started in her chest again; Adam was asking that some step be taken, some decision be made of life and death —some desperate, last minute errand which only she could run, and for which she was not prepared. Adam was in trouble and he was asking her help.

She murmured, "Yes, oh yes," hoping she could do it, whatever the feat that should be required of her.

Adam went to a dim corner near the entrance door and picked up a tomato can full of roses. "My roses just started bloomin around the shanty," he said, "and when I saw 'em I thought I'd pick a handful for Lucius' grave. Thought I'd get a minute to walk up to the cemetery myself, but the freight's kept me busy. Then I thought, if Hallie would come I could just ask her to drop them off on her way home." He shook the water off the stems. "There's a vase up there, I reckon?"

"Yes," said Hallie, weak, relieved, "I can find one."

"Then I'll just put a piece of newspaper around these so they won't stick you on the way."

He wrapped the roses carefully and as he handed them to her she remembered the time he took the flowers from her in the room where Lucius lay dying. Now, as then, she stood looking at him, trying to transfer her thoughts to him, transferring her thoughts of quivering, trembling fear for him, sending him her clenched wishes coming up from her insides with every muscle held taut to wish them.

Adam didn't seem to receive any significant message from her. He acted the same way he did every day. "I got to get on with this sweepin. Mr. Jones gonta wonder if I spend my time out here sweepin or talkin." He laughed. "I appreciate you helpin me out, Hallie," he said and picked up the broom again.

"I waited for you," said Mama as she came back into the office. Papa was busy at the telegraph table, seemingly interested in some vital message rattling through, though it was a slow time of day now. But he was busy and Mama obviously thought they should go; she stood now in the door, waiting.

"Mama, is Brother Jamieson going to help?" Hallie asked as soon as they were outside.

Mama was carrying a paper bag of groceries; she seemed to be occupied in adjusting it for the walk home.

"Brother Jamieson *will* help, won't he, Mama?"

"Well, Hallie, when it came right down to it your father just didn't get a chance to ask him."

"Didn't even *ask* him?"

"Now, Hallie," said Mama, "it's not all as simple and easy as you might think and I don't want you to go thinking things about your father. He was *going* to ask Brother Jamieson but in the end it turned out it just didn't seem best to ask him."

"Oh."

"Your father was going to ask him, went to the Deacons' Meeting with that in mind, but then things turned out different from what he had expected and he ended up by not asking him."

"But what will happen to Adam?" She could feel the trembling in her chest again, and in her voice.

"Now, Hallie," said Mama almost roughly, "Hallie, will you stop worrying. Your father says he thinks Adam will be all right; anyhow he'll be all right until next Sunday. Mr. Bird never comes down except on Sundays and Adam's sure he'll hear from Mr. Bird again before anything happens."

"Oh," said Hallie again, telling the trembling to cease.

"Now about your father and Brother Jamieson," said Mama. "He left home all set to ask him. You remember he left for the Deacons' Meeting right after supper. It was held over at the

Pastorium and he went early thinking he would get there and have a little talk with Brother Jamieson before anybody else came. But he was thrown off because Brother Jamieson had company. Mr. Jess Bailey." (Mr. Jess again!) "Brother Jamieson had asked him to come early and he said right off to your father that he had asked Mr. Jess to stay for the Deacons' Meeting. Well, that surprised your father; he couldn't figure out why Brother Jamieson would do that; they don't usually have anyone there but deacons. Then Brother Jamieson went on to say that long before your father had come Mr. Jess had been considered for a deacon and that he had spoken to two or three other deacons he'd chanced to run into and they said why not, why not go ahead and make him a deacon. Well, your father . . ."

"Did you tell him, Mama, about Mr. Jess and Elberta?"

"Hallie, I should have. Each time I thought I would though, I couldn't. I just couldn't. He was so upset already about Adam. I couldn't add . . ."

"Can they make Mr. Jess a deacon just like that?"

"Well," said Mama, shifting her sack to the other arm, "when the other deacons got there the preacher immediately brought up Mr. Jess and said he hoped they'd vote him in that night, and in the same breath he went on to say that he had good news for the church, that Mr. Bird Ledbetter, even though he's a member of the Peachtree Square Baptist Church up in Atlanta, still he had come down to Greenwood and very generously offered to give a stained-glass window for the front of the church in memory of his father and mother."

"But they wouldn't want that," said Hallie.

"What? Who? But they're dead," said Mama. As if not understanding, she went on, "Then your father realized, though he couldn't tell why, that there was some connection between Mr. Jess and the stained-glass window and Mr. Bird Ledbetter. You know they're both after land. Mr. Jess has been going around buying up kaolin land cheap, and Mr. Bird wants to buy back his old home place. Your father thought then if it's true Mr. Bird's going to run for something maybe he wanted Mr. Jess to kind of manage things for him down here. Maybe they're somehow in cahoots."

"But, Mama, I don't see . . ." Hallie squeezed the bouquet of roses and the thorns pierced the paper and reminded her of what she was carrying and that the cemetery was across the street. "Papa could still have *asked* Brother Jamieson . . ."

"After that, your father said he began to feel uncertain. All the deacons were praising Mr. Bird, saying how wonderful it was he was giving a stained glass for that front window; they'd wanted one ever since the church was built. When Mr. Barksdale gave his stained-glass window they tried to get him to give the front one but he said he preferred the one over the choir, and he wouldn't be swerved. Then they went on to say maybe Brother Bird might do something for the mortgage . . ."

"I still . . ."

"Now, Hallie," Mama spoke sharply. "You can't understand everything." Then she said more softly, "Don't take on so. I had an idea. I told your father he ought to talk to Mr. Craig. The sheriff is really the one to talk to. It's a legal matter, it ought to be handled by the authorities . . ."

"But Mr. Craig might not . . . he was away when the Ku Klux Klan came. Margaret told me so. I think Papa should at least have spoken to Brother Jamieson."

Mama seemed edgy again. "Now, Hallie," she said, "I want you to remember your father's doing the best he can. He's just come here, he's a newcomer you might say, and he doesn't want people to think he's come down in here stirring up trouble." She looked away from Hallie; she seemed to be looking into the past. "You remember he was without a job for a long time, almost a year before we left Clover. That was a bad time for him, for us all. Then when he got this job over here, even though it was a little town, he was mighty glad to get it because he knew it would be his last job . . . He'd lost his seniority in Clover, his age was against him . . ."

Hallie teetered on a tree root, ready to step into the street. The headless chicken flapped at the edge of her mind; she saw the body, heavy, inert, dangling at the end of the rope. The quivering in her chest increased; it shuddered into a great sob that came from somewhere, suddenly and surprisingly, and caught her in the throat and shook her.

"Mama," she cried, and this time it was a cry with tears in her eyes and in her voice, "Mama, what's going to happen to Adam?" And not waiting for an answer she sobbed, "It's wrong, it's wrong."

"Hallie, stop it, stop it this minute." Mama laid the sack against the tree and took her by the shoulders with both hands. "You must stop it now." They were standing in front of the Wither-spoons' and Mama spoke in a forceful whisper. "Hallie, you must stop it. Your father is going to try. He said he would pray about it. He'll pray . . ."

She pulled away from Mama and ran across the street to the cemetery, ran down a lane of graves, her chest still racked with sobs, skirted the rusty iron fence of the Fitzgerald plot and came to the plot marked McGhee, where, just to one side as in life, Lucius had been laid to rest. She stood by the grave and wept, her eyes unseeing from tears; then as her eyes focused she could see that other forces had been at work on the mound of red dirt already rounded and worn by rain. It looked like a children's sand pile. The dirt was pushed up, molded, patted and shaped; runnels had been made for water, a row of mud pies were drying in the sun. And straight above Lucius' heart grew a hollyhock, torn from its place by the fence in the McGhee yard and planted here in the molded clay. Now she remembered having seen the McGhee children parading to the cemetery, Baby trailing behind with the hollyhock. She thought of Baby, holding the hollyhock above her head like a banner, singing something out of tune.

Hallie took the faded daisies and rusty water out of the tin can, added fresh water at the faucet, and arranged Adam's roses. She had promised Lucius a magnolia; soon she would have to steal one from the tree in Mr. F.'s and Miss Beulah's yard. She would do it some day soon when he was on his way to town and Miss Beulah was off to see Miss Lizzie.

If Lucius could say, he would probably say he would rather lie here where the McGhee children could come and play than down in the Tranquil churchyard near his folks. Here Adam could come occasionally too . . . if Adam—here the sobs threatened her again—and soon she would come with the magnolia. Yes, Lucius would prefer it this way. Lucius sitting up there on his footstool in front of the golden throne would giggle and say hit made no difference where he lay. But what would he say about a stained-glass window for his father and mother in a church they did not care for, given by a son who misquoted and misunderstood everything they said? What would that little mountain girl who wanted to see the ocean say about Bird who had seen it?

21

As Hallie dressed for the Expression Contest on Friday night she had a comforting thought. Perhaps Miss Corrine was *not* going to marry Mr. Jess Bailey. They were going together, everyone knew that, but perhaps that was all; no announcement had appeared in the Sunday *Telegraph* and not a soul had ever really said for sure they were going to be married. She turned so Virginia could fasten her in the back, thinking, hoping, maybe I made the whole thing up. Miss Corrine may go off to school next year, and it won't happen after all.

"I've a good mind just to wear my old pink organdy," said Virginia, looking at herself in the mirror. She was still upset about her dress. Mama had bought the yellow crepe de Chine and the pale-blue taffeta at a remnant sale in Macon and Miss Vashti McDougal had come to the house to make the dresses. Virginia had chosen the yellow of her own free will and accord, Hallie kept reminding her, but as Miss Vashti progressed it was obvious that the yellow was not right for her, and when Virginia wanted Hallie to change she would not.

As they came in to supper Virginia must have still been feeling some irritation about the dress because she hardly sat down before saying, "Oh, oh, Benny's cradle-snatching again."

Benny narrowed his eyes and said softly, too softly, "Will you please shut up?"

There were some words that made Mama really angry. "You can't say shut up at this table," she said.

"All right," said Benny in a frightening soft voice, "hush, be quiet."

Benny had been grouchier since last Sunday. It probably made him mad for Mama to look at him sadly and worriedly, he might even wish she would say something and get it out of her system, but Hallie knew Mama was afraid to ask. She was afraid of the answer.

Virginia must have felt encouraged by having Mama's support, or else she did not see how angry Benny was. "Hear you're going to take Laura Fitzgerald home tonight," she said.

"Shut up," roared Benny, jumping up and glowering at her.

Papa looked at Benny fiercely, but Benny carefully looked only at Virginia.

"Benny, leave the table at once," Papa said.

Benny slammed his chair back, and the look of fury faded from Papa's face and he seemed tortured and undecided and sad.

"Make Virginia stop," roared Benny, "make her leave."

"Cradle snatcher," whispered Virginia, and ducked her head down. Virginia must think she had the upper hand and could say anything.

Benny picked up the plate of hominy and milk gravy and for a second Hallie thought he was going to throw it at Virginia. "I'll fix you," he said. "Don't you worry, Miss Virginia, just you wait. You don't know when to shut up, I'll teach you," he muttered through clenched teeth as he went into the kitchen.

Hallie swallowed a mouthful of hominy. When Benny said he would fix *her*, she worried and watched and made herself small. And usually Virginia was on his side; she would ride in to tease when he had started.

It *was* hard to believe that Benny really would pay any attention to Laura Fitzgerald. He had always said she was "boy crazy" and "stuck-up." Of course Laura Fitzgerald had surprised Hallie lately by suddenly seeming older. The lipstick she wore on Sundays gave her face focus, her long nose seemed to have been made to balance her long neck and her hair had changed from mousy to blond. Her carriage, hitherto gangling and awkward, now seemed frail and exotic. She often rode by on Sunday afternoons with a boy, Carlton Seaburn, and he drove with one arm lying along the back of the seat. Laura said he had given her a box of Nunnally's chocolates, and she would sigh, "What am I going to *do* about Carlton?" Her look had became more knowing; she had an abstracted air when talking to Hallie, as if to say there were things she could tell her if Hallie wasn't a child. But Benny? Benny was practically a man, at least in looks. Taller than Papa, a boy who had worked at the Western Union and made enough money to pay board for a while—surely he could not be interested in Laura Fitzgerald.

"Hallie, we've got to hurry," said Virginia, jumping up from the table. "May Belle will be by any minute."

Miss Corrine had asked all her students who were going to be in the contest to come early and meet her in the studio. Virginia, Hallie, May Belle Ballard, Laura Fitzgerald, Mary Beth Dozier from the tenth grade and Lois Adams from the eleventh had been chosen to give a reading in the contest. Margaret Craig was in the contest, too, but since she did not take from Miss Corrine she would not be expected to gather with the group in Miss Corrine's studio.

Miss Corrine wore blue chiffon, the skirt full and floating, the waist tight, and high-heeled shoes dyed pink. Hallie could hardly bear to look at her. Ever since last Sunday, in between worrying about Adam she had thought of telling Miss Corrine about Mr. Jess Bailey. She had rehearsed different ways of doing it. "Miss Corrine?" she would say, pretending she was entering the door of the studio. "Why, Hallie, here you are at last. Does something bother you? Is something on your mind?" Miss Corrine might say. "Yes'm, there is something on my mind." "Well, tell me about it, darling" (here Miss Corrine might even put her arms around her in her loving way). "Well, Miss Corrine, it's about . . ." and then Hallie would imagine the light flicking out of those happy, trusting brown eyes which looked warmly into hers. The eyes would die in the pale face. As she tossed in her bed at night she tried to think how to tell Miss Corrine. She must be told. She would write her a note, signed "An Anonymous Friend and Well-Wisher." Or perhaps a note to Mr. Barksdale. "Dear Mr. Barksdale, I think you should know that your daughter, Miss Corrine Barksdale, is about to make a great mistake. She is about to marry a man who is the father of Elberta Smith's child, Jonny. Signed, a Friend of the Family."

But she had done none of these things because once the words were spoken or the notes read the light would go out in Miss Corrine's eyes. And thinking of her as she would look if she knew what Hallie knew, she began to see Miss Corrine as a person with an incurable sickness, a cancer gnawing at her vitals, while she, Hallie, was caught in the position of a doctor who knows the dreadful truth about his patient and must decide whether or not he should divulge it.

Yet on the outside Miss Corrine looked happier and prettier

each day. This evening after the girls had gathered in the studio, carefully arranging their recital dresses on the folding chairs, she said, "Girls, I've something very special to tell you. I've been saving it for tonight, though perhaps some of you can guess what I'm going to say." She smiled and looked at them questioningly and May Belle Ballard said in a simpering voice, "I don't believe we need three guesses, Miss Corrine." And Miss Corrine said, "Well, you *have* probably guessed it. That I'm going to be married to Mr. Jess Bailey." She paused as they expelled their held breaths with little ecstatic screams. "I wanted to wait until near the end of school to tell you, so the younger children wouldn't get too excited."

"Oh, Miss Corrine," breathed Virginia, "I think it's just wonderful. Mr. Jess is so handsome, and you . . . well, you're going to make the most wonderful couple."

May Belle jumped up and ran and hugged Miss Corrine and all the other girls followed her; all clustered around Miss Corrine, all except Hallie. She stood up because she felt funny with all the chairs empty, but she did not run and kiss Miss Corrine. But in the excitement it was hardly noticed, she was sure.

"Are you going to have a big church wedding?" asked Laura Fitzgerald.

"Oh, Miss Corrine, I hope so," said Virginia.

"Oh, Miss Corrine, please tell us all about the wedding," said Mary Beth Dozier. She had a whiny Flatwoods accent, and Hallie suspected that Miss Corrine had only put her in the contest tonight in the hope that she would show her relatives down in the Flatwoods how much her speech had improved.

"Well," Miss Corrine said, "it *is* going to be a big wedding. Mr. Jess, like all men, I reckon, said he'd just as soon we'd go up to the ordinary and get it over and he didn't care what I wore. But Father wants a nice wedding and since it's the only wedding I plan to be the bride in"—she smiled at her little joke—"I decided we might as well do it right. It's going to be all white; the men are going to wear white suits—even down to Brother

Jamieson. The bridesmaids are going to wear white organdy, and the maid of honor and matron of honor are going to wear white chiffon. And of course I'm going to wear white satin."

"How many bridesmaids?" asked May Belle hopefully. Could she possibly think Miss Corrine would ask her to be in the wedding?

"Six bridesmaids," said Miss Corrine. "Miss Johnson and Miss Hightower from here at school and the rest classmates of mine from GSCW or relatives from up in North Carolina."

"Is Miss Toulou going to play?" asked Laura.

"I thought I'd have one of my friends from up in North Carolina play," said Miss Corrine. "She's accustomed to playing with the violin and cello."

"You're going to have more than the piano," said Virginia. "How wonderful." Suddenly Hallie felt very hot and red at the thought of how silly she had been to think . . .

"Mr. Jess's little niece is going to be flower girl," said Miss Corrine; "you know little Carrie Jones."

"A ring bearer too?' moaned May Belle in ecstasy.

Miss Corrine smiled at her. "Of course. Once you've decided on a flower girl you just about have to have a ring bearer. Danny Hinton. He's the son of a friend of mine, a darling little boy with yellow curls. His mother is making long white satin trousers for him."

The girls said, "Oh-h-h-h," in unison.

Then Miss Corrine said, "I've been wondering if you would help me," and the room became quiet while each girl held her breath.

"You know we're going to have the reception at Magnolia Hall, and I was wondering if I could count on you, my most advanced pupils, to help me out."

"Oh, Miss Corrine," they all cried, everyone except Hallie, "Oh, Miss Corrine, of course." "You know anything you'd ask . . ." "We'd love to . . ." There was a sudden movement of chairs again as if they were all going to run up and kiss Miss Corrine once more.

But she waved them back. "For example, I'll need someone to keep the guest book."

May Belle waved her hand. "Oh, Miss Corrine, may Virginia and I do that together?"

"All right," said Miss Corrine, "and then there's passing mints, and handing out pieces of wedding cake in little white boxes . . ."

"Let me, let me," screamed the other girls—small ecstatic screams, of course.

Miss Corrine gave them each a job. "What do you want to do, Hallie?" she asked and turned her warm brown eyes on Hallie. A rosy color burned along Miss Corrine's cheekbones but Hallie did not see it as the color of health, of excitement or of joy. She knew that it must be a fever, a fever that betokened a sickness of which only she was aware. She pressed her hands against her mouth, fearing that the truthful physician in her would speak out and Miss Corrine would fade like a rose before her eyes and the girls would turn on her as if she had committed murder.

"What do you want to do, Hallie?" Miss Corrine asked again, gently, as if she felt that something was wrong.

"Well," Hallie said, testing out her throat which had been thickening with a large cry-bubble that had oozed up from her stomach, lodged in her throat, and almost suffocated her, "well, I think maybe I won't be here." She had tried to prepare herself for this, but her voice did not sound as she had planned.

"Won't be here?" said Virginia. "Where do you think you're going?"

She could kill Virginia. If someone else had asked the question she could answer, but Virginia asking it, and asking it in such a tone of doubt, made her seem like a child. She answered in a funny strangled voice, "I've been thinking I'd make a little trip over to Clover when school's out."

"Huh," Virginia said. "Bet Mama won't let you."

231

"Well, Hallie," said Miss Corrine, "I hope you'll change your mind. You know, I don't believe the marriage would be legal without you there." She came over to Hallie and lightly put her hands on her shoulders, shook her gently, affectionately, silently spoke words of love. Then she turned to the others. "Now, it's time for us to go in and I haven't said a word about the contest." She pulled herself up straight, as if she were teaching about breath control. "Now remember: breathe deeply, speak slowly, and speak to me." She dropped her straight position and became relaxed again. "I don't think it's important which one of you wins tonight. What is important is that you do the best you can and show everyone how much you've improved during the year, you darling girls." As they marched out she stood at the door and gave them each a little pat.

Benny and some of his friends pushed into the auditorium just ahead of them and sat down in the back row. Mama had tried to get Benny to try out in the Declamation Contest, and Hallie had urged him too, thinking that his deep voice would float out into the auditorium with as much power as Brother Jamieson's. But Benny refused; it was sissy, he said, and probably he was right because the boys who were taking their places on the stage were eighth and ninth graders still in knee pants.

Miss Corrine left the line of girls about two-thirds of the way back and sat down next to the aisle. They marched on up to the front where Margaret Craig was already seated by Cousin Bootsie Craig, a frowsy old woman fierce with paint and powder. Hallie had once remarked on Cousin Bootsie's makeup to Margaret and Margaret had said, "But she's a retired actress, you know," as if that explained everything.

As they took their places Hallie tried whispering to herself to see if any air was coming up through her throat which still felt thick and tight, too tight to make a voice. What she would like to do was to rush off somewhere in the dark and cry. Laura Fitzgerald, who sat next to her, cupped her hands around Hallie's ear and said, "Are you . . ." and then began giggling so much that the rest of her words were lost. Ever since last fall Laura Fitzgerald had been taking the attitude that Hallie was a child. Even when she asked about Benny—"Is Benny coming tonight?" or "What did Benny say?"—she did it as if she were asking a child, not a girl almost her own age. But all this had nothing to do with her tonight; she did not care about that. Miss Corrine, poor sick Miss Corrine. She did not even harbor the thought that one of her pupils might not win the contest tonight. Six of her pupils to one of Miss Bootsie Craig's and she would expect one of her pupils to win—Hallie probably, who did her piece so well, or, if she slipped in some way, Virginia. But Hallie did not feel certain she could win. Her throat was still too thick. " 'In the black prison of the Conciergerie, the doomed of the day awaited their fate,' " she whispered.

Mr. Holden announced the boys' Declamation Contest and the first boy stood and began to speak. His voice rose and fell, came to a climax and dropped to a whisper, but he said nothing that Hallie could understand. Another speaker went through the same routine, followed by a rattle of applause.

Finally the boys filed down and the girls took their places; six of Miss Corrine's pupils and Margaret Craig. Margaret had been placed in the middle. Mary Beth Dozier was first. She began slowly, her voice pitched low, making her O's nice and round. She tried; you could see she tried. Oh, Miss Corrine had worked on her. She had made her say, "An Austrian army awfully arrayed, boldly by battle besieged Belgrade," for days on end. Her piece was a funny one about a family catching a train, but as she approached the climax her voice rose higher and higher, grew more and more nasal, more and more like a girl from the Flatwoods.

Laura Fitzgerald had a long piece that she said in a flat monotone—an absent-minded voice as if she were somewhere else, not there on the platform at all. Tonight her eyes looked big and expressive; she had made question marks of her eyebrows and painted her lips and cheeks so red that her delicate face exclaimed.

She forgot about speaking to Miss Corrine. Hallie could see Mr. Vernon Stribling, one of the judges who sat as far back as Miss Corrine on the other side, leaning forward and cupping his hand around his ear to hear.

Virginia was next. The yellow crepe de Chine was not right for her; she was the same color all over. Suddenly Hallie longed for Virginia to have the blue dress, have everything that would make her look her best, say her piece well and win for Miss Corrine. She had never before thought of Virginia winning, had only thought of herself, but now she longed for Virginia to win. She might have a chance. She had been learning a new piece for the contest, had worked on it for weeks. But as she explained, she could not put her heart in it, and she had begged Miss Corrine to let her recite "The Highwayman" by Alfred Noyes for the contest. And Miss Corrine reluctantly agreed since no one else had a poem.

Virginia could do the piece beautifully. Her voice sank deep when she said, " 'One kiss, my bonny sweetheart; I'm after a prize tonight,' " and when the landlord's daughter let down her hair in the casement, a " 'black cascade of perfume,' " and he kissed its waves in the moonlight, the audience became quiet and the faces turned up toward Virginia watched her with expectancy. Hallie took heart and thought, if my throat is so tight I can't win for Miss Corrine then maybe Virginia will. But all the time her own throat was loosening. She could almost swallow normally now and she tested it by announcing to herself " 'The Sacrifice of Sydney Carton,' by Charles Dickens."

Now the landlord's daughter was watching for the Highwayman to come to her by moonlight. She had been tied up by King George's men with a musket at her breast and she waited with the soldiers for her lover in the moonlight. " 'Tlot-tlot, tlot-tlot! Had they heard it? The horse hoofs ringing clear; Tlot-tlot, tlot-tlot, in the distance! Were they deaf that they did not hear?' " Virginia asked the question and paused—a long pause. Hallie had once questioned this pause. "Isn't that pause too long, Virginia?" she had said. "They'll think you've *forgotten.*" But Virginia had answered, "It's a listening pause. Miss Corrine says to make it good and long." Suddenly in the listening silence, like a shot from the back row of seats, came a long high horse whinny, not loud, but a high-pitched whinny that resounded in the silence of the hall and seemed to strike Virginia like a physical blow. She was standing poised, listening, and the whinny made her sway. There was a tittering in the audience and a rustling as the high-school pupils turned to see who had made the whinny. Virginia pulled herself up again, tried taking a deep breath, struck out, and said loudly, too loudly, " 'Down the ribbon of moonlight, over the brow of the hill, The highwayman came riding, Riding, riding.' " But something had been lost. The audience was restless; in the next verse when Virginia came to the *"tlot-tlots"* she faltered and said them timidly rather than sharply. She did not make them ring out in the echoing night, did not pause after them as she was accustomed to do, but raced on to the climax, " 'Shattered her breast in the moonlight and warned him' " (pause) " 'with her death.' "

After that she slowed down, recovered, and said her piece as she had practiced it. But the high-school children continued to be restless and there was an undercurrent of twisting feet, elbows jabbing into ribs and suppressed giggles. Mr. Holden moved back and sat down at the end of the row of seats where Benny and his friends were sitting. Mama would get after Benny for sitting back there with those rowdies. Which one of them could have done this to Virginia? And suddenly it swept over Hallie it was Benny. It was Benny who had made the whinny, paying Virginia back; he had made the whinny and ruined his own sister's chance of winning the contest. Benny had heard her practicing her piece day after day in front of the hall mirror. No one else could have known about that pause. When Virginia had finished Hallie tried to look into her eyes to show her sympathy, but Virginia came back to her place with her head lowered and her face red.

Now it will have to be me, thought Hallie; it will just have to be me. I'm the only one who can win for Miss Corrine. May Belle Ballard was reciting now but she did not expect much of May Belle. She was too silly and she twittered. She could not win.

Margaret Craig was next. She had been quiet and composed listening to the others, and yet far away and above it all; only occasionally she flung back her red curls with the air of a horse shaking its mane eager to be off.

As May Belle sat down and the audience gave its formal applause, Margaret Craig drew herself up a little, gave her curls a last shake, then stood and walked to the front of the stage. She wore a sea-green watered taffeta the color of her eyes. She had remarked that her mother was making her a new dress, and Hallie had expected some drab garment that looked like Mrs. Craig or like the jail. The jail was dark and ugly and a stale smell of unwashed humanity crept through the iron bars of the upstairs cells and sifted down into the rooms where Margaret lived with her family. But the dress was a beautiful creation, with sides that stuck out—panniers, Margaret said. It shimmered in the light and suddenly Hallie thought that Margaret might be what she always pretended to be—a budding actress, a girl awaiting a glorious future, one with Theda Bara, Mae Murray, or even Mary Pickford.

Margaret Craig announced her piece in a calm, subdued voice: " 'Engineer Connor's Son' by Will Allen Dromgoole," she said, her voice low, almost as low as Brother Jamieson's when he began a sermon, Brother Jamieson beginning back in the Old Testament and building up waters behind the dam. The first climax came soon. Engineer Connor was brought home in a caboose, both legs mashed and an arm gone. Every man had jumped from the engine but him; he had stuck with his train and reached home with only enough life left to gasp out, "I leave your mother to you. Take care of her, my little man." Hallie's throat curdled with sadness, though she told herself that Miss Corrine would not approve. She would never give one of them a piece like that. Margaret Craig was speaking quietly again—Little Jack's mother had gone away, had fallen under the train and died—then her voice became charged with emotion as little Jack died too. A long slow freight went through with its mournful whistle as he greeted his mother in Heaven.

Hallie swallowed hard. The audience was still for a moment, and she could see Mr. Vernon Stribling wiping his eyes. Then there was loud applause and as it died away sounds of throats being cleared. Margaret Craig sat down. Now it was Hallie's turn. She laid her handkerchief in her seat and walked to the front. Her piece was sad too, even sadder really with its story of a man laying down his life for his friend and ending with the beautiful words, "It is a far, far better thing that I do . . ." Her throat felt better, as if the emotion she had felt during Margaret Craig's piece had chased her other sadness away.

"Look at me," Miss Corrine had always said, and "speak to me," and Hallie looked at Miss Corrine as she said, " 'The Sacrifice of Sydney Carton' by Charles Dickens." But as she finished the last word and prepared to step forward Mr. Jess Bailey came down the aisle, tiptoeing and hunched, making himself small as if he knew it was not the right time to come in. Miss Corrine turned and saw him; she moved into the second seat and he sat quickly down beside her and laid his arm along the back of the seat. They gazed into each other's eyes. " 'The Sacrifice of Sydney Carton,' by Charles Dickens," Hallie said again, because suddenly the first line of her piece had gone skittering off into the bushes like a snake. She could see the shape of it on the page, but she could not think of one of the words that she had said a hundred times. She felt herself getting hot all over, a prickle of sweat ran down her spine; but though she felt hot and wet, her mouth was so dry that she thought if a word were spoken it would fall like a brown leaf dry and sere from the tree. Again she opened her mouth and the words, " 'The Sacrifice of Sydney Carton' by Charles Dickens" rustled out between her teeth. Now Miss Corrine turned from Mr. Jess Bailey and sat forward, staring at her, forming words with exaggerated gestures of the lips. She tried to read the words, thought she would have to give up, then heard them being whispered from behind her. Virginia was whispering, " 'In the black prison of the Conciergerie, the doomed of the day . . .' " and Hallie grabbed the words as a dog would a bone and set off with them.

After she had started, it was all right. She went through the whole piece, holding the pauses, rounding her O's, raising her voice, lowering her voice, doing everything that Miss Corrine had told her to do, everything. But she knew there was no hope, knew that she had lost all, knew that Margaret Craig would win the prize, knew that sick as she was, Miss Corrine would not receive this one thing her pupils could offer her. All, all was lost, she thought as she went back to her seat not looking at anyone, shaking off Margaret Craig's glance of sympathy and Virginia's look of surprise and sorrow, sitting up straight as if it did not matter, trying to keep her mouth from twitching into a cry.

Lois Adams was the last speaker, and she did not count one way or another. She had never had a chance. Miss Corrine had only put her on the program because she was a senior. Benny said she was dumb (Low-ass Adams, he sometimes called her, and Hallie had giggled because actually it was not a bad description. Lois had heavy, low-slung hips far out of proportion to the rest of her body.) "All the girls in our class are dumb," said Benny.

Miss Naomi Featherstone announced that one of her pupils would play a selection on the piano while the judges made their decision. The audience moved and stretched and a hum of conversation began while the girls on the stage sat staring out at the turning heads. When the piano piece was finished Miss Naomi announced a second one and during it the judges came in and handed a piece of paper to Mr. Holden. The music finished in a crash of chords and he walked out on to the platform.

"Now," said Mr. Holden, "for the boys' Declamation Contest:

238

second place, Teddy McGhee for his excellent piece 'Give Me Liberty or Give Me Death' by Patrick Henry . . ." Applause . . . "First place to Henry Featherstone for his inspiring delivery of 'A Message to Garcia' by Elbert Hubbard. Henry, if you keep on like this we'll see you in Congress before you're very old."

Henry Featherstone walked up and down the steps and Hallie tried to think what the message was that had been sent to Garcia. But she had not received it.

"Now," said Mr. Holden, looking at the paper again, then straightening up, "now I know the judges had a hard time deciding the winner of this contest. I'm glad I wasn't a judge; I just don't know how I could have made up my mind. I think I would just give all you girls first prize." He paused and mopped his face with his handkerchief. "However, they had a job to do, therefore I take great pleasure in announcing . . ." He held the paper up to his eyes as if he were near-sighted, ". . . pleasure in announcing, second place to Miss Virginia Jones, for her excellent poem, 'The Highwayman.'" There was applause and in the middle of it a whinny, and somebody said, "Whoa, there."

Mr. Holden went on hurriedly, looking hard at the back row of seats, "Now for the first-prize winner, I am very pleased to announce that Miss Margaret Craig wins the medal for her touching rendition of 'Engineer Connor's Son.'" The audience clapped and cheered, and Mr. Holden turned toward the girls and gestured Margaret Craig forward. He handed her the box and said, "The sheriff may have an actress on his hands if you keep on the way you've started, young lady." Miss Bootsie Craig's frowsy head shook with pleasure. But Hallie could not look at Miss Corrine; she could not bear to see her face.

The girls stood, and Hallie pushed past Lois Adams to the exit on her side. In back of the stage a door opened to the outside and she felt her way to it in the semidarkness and stepped out into the night. All the others would walk down the steps to the audience to stand in the light with smiling, laughing friends and relations. Miss Corrine would come up and tell them how well they had done and how proud she was of them; she might even give them a hug in her wonderful loving way. She would congratulate Margaret Craig and shake hands with Miss Bootsie Craig. But Hallie could not bear any of it. She started for home. Under the dark trees and close to the shrubs near the sidewalk she would not be seen by anyone. She would run and get there ahead of them.

Two Fords filled with laughter and loud talk passed her and she slunk over toward the hedge. Were they laughing at her? "That poor little Jones child, couldn't you have just died?" someone was probably saying. "Honestly, I just wanted to go through the floor, it was so awful." And Mr. Holden might say, "She always seemed so smart. Wonder what made her forget like that?" and Mr. Jess Bailey, smiling his dimpled smile at Miss Corrine might say, "I would come in just when that child was swallowing her tongue," or something like that. *That child*, she thought in pain. Another car passed with a familiar churning of the motor—Benny in his stripped-down Ford with Laura Fitzgerald beside him. Laura was laughing and probably asking him if he were the one who had made that whinny, and he would say, of course not, how could you think I'd be that mean.

Miss Corrine would not pass her; she would have turned and driven toward Magnolia Hall. Perhaps Mr. Jess drove in her car or perhaps they left her car at school and drove in his. Miss Corrine still did not know his perfidy. Would no one have the courage to tell her? They would ride close together down the dark road, down through the sweet-smelling tunnel between the trees, over the rattling bridge where bay trees lined the branch, and up the hill to turn under the dark magnolias in front of Magnolia Hall. They were in bloom now and the air would be heavy with their perfume. The pigeons in their dovecote would move and flap their wings and call out to ask who cometh, and the throb of the pigeon notes would be one more embellishment for the two lovers sitting in the car close together—just an accompaniment to Mr. Jess kissing Miss Corrine softly on the back of the neck, as *she* had once dreamed of him kissing *her*, as he *had* kissed Elberta. He would be saying, "But who *cares* who won that old Expression Contest? It doesn't matter as long as we have each other, does it?" and Miss Corrine would answer, "Nothing matters." But like the doctor who knows the worst, Hallie knew that it did matter, that Miss Corrine was sick and that only the truth could cure her.

22

Early on Sunday morning Papa wrestled with God. Hallie heard him every morning; the mumbling of his prayers was a part of the beginning day like chickens clucking, roosters crowing, birds chattering. But his prayers were always louder on Sundays and this Sunday louder than usual. He would be kneeling by the side of his bed, clean from his bath behind the kitchen stove the night before, dressed already in his blue Sunday suit, his head thrown back toward the ceiling, his eyes tight shut. She listened, thinking that this morning she might be able to distinguish the words, but she could hear only the rhythm of prayer, only the rise and fall of his voice, pleading.

She lay in bed thinking of Clover and how peaceful it used to be, peaceful and holy on Sunday mornings. She thought of Sundays in Clover, of her black patent leather slippers neatly shined waiting for her white-socked feet, of the starched dress in the closet, of her Sunday School paper and Bible on the hat rack in the hall. Everything had been orderly in Clover. She remembered the slow carriage ride to church, the turning wheels in the unpaved road outside of town (the indrawn suck-sound of wheels in mud, the outblown sigh-sound of wheels in dust), and—crowning it all, the supreme moment of the drive—passing Montpelier, the big white Southern mansion. She looked back at Clover and all those long happy years she had lived there. How she longed for it again! She would not ask for the Old South; all she asked for was to return to the years in Clover, the sweet, simple, uncomplicated, orderly holiness of the years in Clover.

Papa finished his prayers and the screen door banged as he entered the kitchen. Oh, let Papa's prayers be answered, she prayed, and then prayed one of her own: Lord, Lord, save Adam!

Papa had taken Mama's advice and talked to Mr. Craig about Adam. Mama had told her about it yesterday. He had waited for two days to see Mr. Craig because he was off on sheriff's business in another part of the county. He had been away on business when the Ku Klux Klan rode and that was a disadvantage too. Mr. Craig said so himself; he said right away to Papa he was sorry he had not been in town, then he would have some *evidence*. When Papa asked him, "Isn't there anything we can do to protect Adam?" Mr. Craig said, well, he couldn't do anything unless he could *see* a law being broken. As far as he could tell at the moment Adam was all right. Then Papa said what about the letter for evidence, the one that was left on Adam? Mr. Craig said, "What does the letter say?" and Papa answered, "Get out of town or . . ." and then pictures of skulls and crossbones. Mr. Craig said he didn't see what he could do about that; he'd have to know the handwriting of every man, woman and child in Plum Branch County—maybe even in Macon. Best to keep quiet about the whole thing, he said.

Hallie had stayed near home all day Saturday, too drained and ashamed to show her face in public after the Expression Contest. But this news about Mr. Craig made her forget her own shame.

"Tomorrow's Sunday," she said to Mama as they talked in the kitchen.

"I know, Hallie, I know. Honey, don't take it so hard. The worst won't happen. We'll think of something. Your father says maybe he ought to persuade Adam . . ."

"To go?"

"Well, yes," Mama said, putting another piece of wood in the stove. She was warming up the water in the reservoir for Papa's bath. "Your father would hate to see him go. But maybe it would be better in the long run."

"But he's stubborn, Mama. You know how stubborn he is." (Bull-headed, said Lucius.) "Maybe he won't go."

"I know," said Mama, "but when it comes right down to it he may just have to go if there's nothing else. And maybe it would be the best thing for Adam. He could go up to Detroit and stay with his boys. He and Mary could be together during the week . . . He might even get a better-paying job. I'm sure your father can make him see it."

Sunday. She had waited with fear and trembling for Sunday. And now it was Sunday and she lay in bed, stopped thinking about Clover, and when she stopped thinking about it the fear and trembling returned. Would Mr. Bird Ledbetter come back today and, finding Adam still here, finding him stubborn, minding his own business, would he call the men to mask again and ride to Adam's shanty and . . . She refused to think further. What would happen? She wished she had no imagination, tried to forget the tar and feathers, the headless chicken hopping about the yard, the figure slumped at the end of a rope. Panic rising, she dressed, not caring what she wore.

When she went up to the Sunday School room off the balcony Miss Emmy Belton greeted her in a voice more syrupy than usual, sympathizing with her for forgetting her piece in the Expression Contest. Laura Fitzgerald leaned toward her as she went in; she spoke to her in a different way, almost sisterly. Could she think she was going to *marry* Benny just because he drove her home from the Expression Contest? Margaret Craig came in and sat down next to her. She wore her new gold medal, a round disk fastened to a bar, and on it Spencerian engraving saying, "First Prize, Expression Contest, 1921. Plum Branch County Consolidated School."

Miss Emmy Belton ran on about the difference between Elijah and Elisha, something more complex than spelling, though Hallie could not guess what and did not care. Margaret Craig held her Sunday School paper toward her. "What are you going to do this summer?" was written on it. Hallie wrote back, "Don't know." Then Margaret wrote, "Let's build a theater in your barn." Margaret was offering to be her best friend. Earlier this news would have made her happy, but now, aware of them all, aware of their smiles, their frowns, aware of them but not caring, she could think of only one thing. And when the class was over she hung back, not wanting them to speak to her, not even wanting Margaret Craig to speak to her. She hung back when the bell rang for preaching service and Miss Toulou Vass started playing her marching music. She pretended to hunt under her seat for her Sunday School paper while the others went ahead.

When she came down to the vestibule she wondered if she could bear it. She went to the outside door and stood there, wanting to run away, to escape. But where? Papa was standing in the cemetery, his face raised to heaven, his eyes closed, his mouth moving. As she watched him he opened his eyes and looked toward her, looked at his watch, and came hurrying in. He spit his wad of tobacco under the tobacco bush, cleared his throat one last time and wiped his mouth, then entered the church and swept her before him into their pew where Mama was already sitting.

Miss Toulou finished her march and meandered into a wandering little piece to pass the time away. Miss Corrine already sat in the choir next to Mr. Jess. By now this was customary, but today was different. They were an engaged couple now; they had the right to turn loving eyes toward each other. He had the right now to lean toward her and whisper something, actually brushing some stray curls aside with his nose to speak more closely. He had the right now since Miss Corrine had announced their engagement to her expression class Friday night and the news would undoubtedly be printed in the Macon *Telegraph* today. (Virginia had already claimed the clipping in advance for her memory book.) Yesterday after May Belle had delivered the eggs she and Virginia had spent the whole afternoon trying on dresses and talking about the wedding. They had nothing suitable in their own wardrobes, they said, and they decided they would have to make identical white organdy dresses to do honor to the sacred duty of handling the guest book and to be in keeping with the wedding. Mama kept saying that Virginia should wear the yellow recital dress Miss Vashti had made for her but Virginia said she hated it, hated it; she didn't want ever to be reminded of that old Expression Contest again. Finally Mama agreed that if Virginia would sew the dress herself she would buy the material.

Today Virginia and May Belle sat next to each other in the back row of the church; their joint project of the guest book at the wedding was more important than family. May Belle had forsaken her loud-singing mother and Virginia her family, though Papa looked askance at her. They had plans to spend the afternoon together at May Belle's house; Mama had said immediately that they must not begin to sew on Sunday. Virginia couldn't begin anyhow because Mama would have to go to Macon to buy the material. Hallie knew that May Belle and Virginia would spend the afternoon together leafing through copies of *McCall's* and the *Ladies' Home Journal* looking for a pattern for their organdy dresses, trying on makeup and doing their hair different ways. All for the hateful wedding. She had listened to them enviously, for that moment distracted from Adam. Now she could feel nothing but pain when she heard the word wedding.

But the more immediate pain, the fear and trembling, chased

that other pain away. She watched the front entrance for Mr. Bird. Sunday was his day to come to Greenwood; if he came today . . .

Miss Toulou was weaving a little melody out of the C scale. A wave of excitement ran through the congregation and Miss Toulou added a touch of syncopation when Mr. Shadrack Cartledge came into the church with his bride, Miss Ada Pratt. Miss Ada led the way, a lavender hat with pink flowers riding high on top of her edifice of hair, her face stiff with makeup. Who had brought whom? Miss Ada, leading the way, went to a pew, not the one customarily occupied by Mr. Shadrack. But he did not change her course; he sloped in right behind her. Oh, the power of the Ku Klux Klan; Miss Ada marrying after all these years, and coming to church now like an answer to Brother Jamieson's prayer.

Miss Toulou played a little louder as Brother Jamieson came out from behind the pulpit and took his place in the carved chair. It was almost time to begin. Perhaps Mr. Bird would not come. Oh, Lord, let Mr. Bird not come. Let him stay in Atlanta. Let his Pierce Arrow be broken down so he cannot leave Macon. Now there was someone at the door hurrying in. Mr. Barksdale. Only Mr. Barksdale in a white linen suit, hurrying to get into his pew before the Doxology.

Miss Toulou rambled her little piece around to a point where she could crash into the Doxology and Brother Jamieson walked forward to the pulpit and raised his arms for the congregation to stand. " 'Praise God from whom all blessings flow . . .' " they sang, " 'Praise God . . .' " There was a movement at the door again; Mr. Bird Ledbetter stepped inside apologetically and slid into a pew, the first one handy, next to May Belle and Virginia. May Belle passed him a hymn book—as if anyone would need it for the Doxology.

So Mr. Bird was here. The fear and trembling started up again, a panicky feeling that she should slip past Mama and Papa, run, fly to Adam's shanty, tell him to leave—run, Adam, run. She gripped her Sunday School paper and Bible; there was no use running. Adam would be off preaching somewhere, not in his shanty. No use running, and settling down to stay she resolved that she would never plan again. Somehow she had influenced the course of events; *she* had thought up the plan that Mr. Bird was now carrying out; *she* had planned that he should come back and rescue Montpelier from the Duckets; *she* had planned that he should turn them out and restore Montpelier to its former glory. She had planned it all, but not that it should happen this way. Not this way. ("Me and Adam would have to take turns toting him when he pestered us," Lucius had said, speaking of Bird.) But Bird must have been so small he did not remember who carried him. Or Atlanta had strangely changed him.

Perhaps there was still something of Bird left underneath. Perhaps he could be appealed to. That is what Papa should do; he should appeal to Mr. Bird.

" 'The Lord is my shepherd,' " intoned Brother Jamieson, beginning his Bible-reading in the Psalms, " 'I shall not want.' " Papa should talk to Mr. Bird, appeal to him, recall the days of his childhood when he rode on Adam's back to visit the waterfall.

" '. . . lie down in green pastures,' " " 'leadeth me beside the still waters . . .' " It was a description of the country Lucius' mother loved. Of course she had liked running water better, little branches that meandered through the woods, but she would have liked still waters too. She wished that all these thoughts from the past, what Lucius had said, what River had told about his father and mother, would not come rolling back into her mind with the power of a poem, a poem that had found the day, the hour, the moment to strike.

Brother Jamieson finished the Psalm softly, softly, " 'And I will dwell in the house of the Lord for ever,' " and announced a hymn. They stood and sang "Love Divine, All Love Excelling." Oh, surely Mr. Bird could be appealed to. Papa must try.

Miss Toulou Vass began the music for the offertory and Papa

went forward to help take the collection. When only three deacons presented themselves at the altar Brother Jamieson gestured to Mr. Jess Bailey in the choir and he came down and stood with the others, joining with Papa to pass the plate on their side. After Brother Jamieson gave thanks for the gifts received he announced that at the last meeting of the Board of Deacons a new deacon had been chosen, Brother Jess Bailey, and that he would be ordained after regular preaching service next Sunday. Hallie could not look at Miss Corrine, fearing she blushed with pride.

Then after a suitable pause Brother Jamieson stepped forward to one side of the pulpit and said intimately, "I have a happy surprise for the congregation this morning, I won't say an answer to prayer exactly, but in a way I guess it is too." He smiled and the congregation smiled back as if expecting dinner on the grounds. "You know how long we have wanted to complete our tabernacle, to make it a fitting meeting place, one we can be proud of. And now I take great pleasure in announcing that Brother Bird Ledbetter, though a member of our sister church, the Peachtree Square Baptist Church in Atlanta, the biggest church in the Southern Baptist Convention, in his generosity has offered to give us a stained-glass window for the front of the church as a memorial to his dear father and mother who lived some years ago in this county. His father was a veteran of the War Between the States. Just what kind of a window it will be we cannot as yet announce but Brother Ledbetter informs me he is partial toward a window in the Peachtree Square Church of Jesus as Shepherd, Jesus with a shepherd's crook in one hand, cradling a white lamb in the other arm and underneath it these words . . ." Brother Jamieson paused, stepped back behind the pulpit and intoned, " 'I am the good shepherd, and know my sheep, and am known of mine.' "

Everyone turned to look at Mr. Bird as Brother Jamieson finished. His face was broad and handsome, his brown eyes (not bloodshot brown) fine under the dark brows. It was a younger, healthier, more successful face than Lucius', but like him, very like him. Mr. Bird nodded his head slightly as Brother Jamieson finished, in agreement and humbly, not in a way to call attention to himself. Oh, butter would not melt in his mouth, Hallie thought, her stomach feeling a little sick, her throat tight again. She despaired. It would do no good for Papa to speak to Mr. Bird, a man who had no more feeling for his father and mother than to give a stained-glass window in their memory to a church his father would not set foot in, a man who would mask himself and frighten a Negro who had carried him on his back as a small boy. Oh, he was a sepulchre as whited as Mr. Jess Bailey. From now on he would be Byrd, not Bird.

Brother Jamieson stood quietly while the congregation rustled back to attention. Then he stepped back, wiped his face and said, "John, ten: fourteen: 'I am the good shepherd, and know my sheep, and am known of mine.' I have chosen this verse as the text for the day. It was suggested by our good brother's generous gift. Let us sing number two eighteen."

Number two eighteen referred obliquely to sheep and a shepherd. " 'Whit-er than snow, yes, whit-er than snow, Wash me and I shall be whit-er than snow.' " ("Pa told Old Adam, this Adam's pa, he ought to get hisself a graven image from Africa or make hisself one out of corn shucks, stid a goin up to the Baptist Church and singin, 'Wash me and I shall be whiter than snow.' " The words of Lucius flooded back. She wished she did not remember, wished she had not heard.) She could not sing; she held the book, looked at it unseeing, and sat down at the end, despairing.

Brother Jamieson chose other verses to read. St. Luke—she listened hard to run away from her thoughts—Chapter 15, St. Luke, verses 3 to 8 (here Jesus carried the lamb, the lamb lost and now found, on his shoulders rather than in his arms). Brother Jamieson took the verses, intoned them, began kneading them into shape, fitting them into the sermon rhythm, beginning small and quiet . . .

No, there was no use talking to Mr. Byrd. Then who, who could save Adam? Who were the ones in town with power? The Featherstones? They were the biggest family; there were more Featherstones in houses, the biggest houses if not the grandest, and more in the cemetery than any other name; they had power enough to place the Confederate statue where they could see it rather than on the Courthouse grounds where it logically belonged. What about Mr. Willy Featherstone? At the end of last summer when she first discovered him and Magnolia Hall she would have thought he was the one to turn to, a true Southern gentleman born in a mansion and carrying within himself the traditions of chivalry and honor and justice from the Old South.

What had happened to Mr. Willy Featherstone? He could not help her; she knew he could not help her. Could not or would not? One and the same. He was weak—or worse; not only weak, but wicked, evil, with his mindless sayings, his whinny of laughter.

" 'Ninety and nine,' " roared Brother Jamieson. He had reached the dam-bursting stage. " 'Ninety and nine,' " he bellowed again and the windows shook, the stained-glass window over the choir and the plain glass one in front. This was the peak, the crisis, for after that he spoke softly about the one lamb left out of the fold, the one that caused the rejoicing. His voice sank to a whisper at the end, and his head fell forward on his bosom and the congregation sat very still, awed by the awe with which Brother Jamieson was moved by his own sermon. He stepped back, and said, "Is there anyone here present who would like to add his testimony to mine, who would like to testify to the love of the Shepherd for his sheep? Look into your hearts and speak." He did not look directly at Papa but this was his usual Sunday morning announcement and usually Papa responded. Heads turned in Papa's direction. But Papa sat studying the floor, not hearing. He did not stand now to testify as he was wont to do; he sat still, his eyes cast down, and Mama gazed ahead, her hands quiet in her lap. Papa had prayed out there by the gravestones. Could he have been praying for strength to speak, to stand like a Hebrew Prophet, to use that outthrust arm for pointing out the sinner, for exposing the sin? A wave of heat passed over Hallie in the pause, thinking of her embarrassment if he should. Yet at the same time she was hopeful— dreading it, yet waiting for him to stand and point his finger and denounce the giver of stained-glass windows like a wrathful Prophet of old. Brother Jamieson's face turned even redder in the pause. No one spoke. He said, "Will Brother Jones lead us in prayer?"

Papa slid to his knees, never looking at Brother Jamieson, his face and mind fixed somewhere else, too far away to respond until his name was called. He slid to his knees as he did only on special occasions, raised his face to the ceiling, closed his eyes tight and addressed God. Hallie felt the embarrassment as usual. Then suddenly it was gone. Papa might do some good with his prayer. Adam had told him of his trouble in a prayer; now Papa could send a message up to the golden sounding board of God. It might come back and strike someone's heart.

Like Mama, who could not wait for God but always ran ahead to decide for Him, she asked herself, "Whose?" as Papa prayed, "Lord, Lord, look into the hearts of those who have come to worship Thee . . . Let each one here look into his heart and ask 'Am I innocent? Have I clean hands?' Oh, Lord, thou hast said 'Verily, I say unto you, Inasmuch as ye did it not unto the least of these, ye did it not to me.' Look upon those who are in places of power. Let us not be like the Levite who goes by on the other side of the road, but like the Good Samaritan who had compassion, who lifted his brother, who cared for him in need. Help us . . ."

Papa prayed in riddles. He could not say, even to God, "Help Adam," or, "Help me," when he prayed in public. But surely he

251

had pleaded openly in his prayer alone among the gravestones or by his bed in the morning. She and Mama knew his real prayer, but would anyone else within the sound of his voice know that the cry was "Help Adam, help Adam"?

She opened her eyes and looked up as Papa prayed on, looked at the stained-glass window beyond the choir where a beam of light shot through the amber pane in the Good Samaritan's sleeve and struck gold from the hair of Miss Toulou Vass. "Friend to the Friendless," she read, "In Loving Memory of Adelaide Wingate Barksdale." Mrs. Barksdale had restored the dovecote, had loved to see the white birds fly up . . . Right now on the other side of the church Mr. Byrd sat planning his next step. Panic and desperation surged in her chest. They must find someone—if not Mr. Willy Featherstone, who was born in Magnolia Hall, what about Mr. Barksdale who lived there now? He was a giver of stained-glass windows; he could be matched with Mr. Byrd Ledbetter; he had picked the Good Samaritan in memory of his wife. True, he was a crude interloper, a business-man from North Carolina. On the other hand Miss Corrine said he loved to watch the white birds flying. She must find someone.

And simply because she was desperate and because she could hear in the rhythm of Papa's prayer that he was drawing to a close—the service would soon be over, the congregation would disperse—in uncertainty and a confusion of panic and inconsistency she pulled out her pencil used as a marker in her Bible and wrote on her Sunday School paper, "Could Mr. Barksdale help? Ask Papa."

"Help us find the way, Lord," Papa prayed. "Let us go *foward* in Thy name—for thine is the power and the glory, forever. Amen." Brother Jamieson echoed "Amen" and Papa rose from his knees and slid into his seat. He sat with his head bowed, weak or still caught up in his prayer. As Brother Jamieson announced a hymn Hallie showed the Sunday School paper to Mama. She read the words and touched Papa on the arm with the paper. He looked at it, not seeing for a minute; then, his eyes focusing, he took in the message, his face changed, and his lips twisted into something like a smile. He nodded toward Hallie, and he formed "yes" with his thin lips.

23

Papa said God had spoken through her. He came back from the depot on Sunday afternoon, and Hallie, watching, still trembling inside came down from the tree to meet him. "Daughter," he said solemnly, putting his hand awkwardly on her shoulder, "God spoke through you." And an aura of holiness descended on Hallie; for the moment unsayable holiness rested on her shoulders like white doves. She did not have to say to Papa "Adam?" or "Mr. Barksdale?"; the answer, the release and the holiness all descended at once to sit on her shoulders like doves light-heartedly cooing.

When they walked into the kitchen where Mama was laying out cold chicken and biscuits for supper, Papa insisting he still must go to B.Y.P.U., the three of them were enveloped in this sweet, tender relationship of one wish and the answer to it. Papa became almost garrulous; he who had never before been garrulous with anyone but God now ran on so that she and Mama hardly had a chance to talk.

When Papa said grace he thanked God for those who had heard his voice and spoke, and Hallie had time to consider the voice of God and the way of His speaking. She had expected it to come in some dramatic display of light, like Halley's Comet, or like the streaked lightning over the cemetery cedars, or . . . like the beam of light through the stained-glass window? She considered the beam of light. It had shone through the amber pane of the Good Samaritan's sleeve and had rested on the golden hair of Miss Toulou Vass. But if God's finger were a beam of light pointing, then Miss Toulou Vass should have been the answer. Yet she had never once thought Miss Toulou Vass could help her in this. A few minutes later she had thought of Mr. Barksdale, but there had been no great display of light. She had simply stumbled on him; running helter-skelter down lanes like a scared rabbit, she had stumbled on Mr. Barksdale. First she had thought of Mr. Featherstone, rejected him, then thought of Mr. Barksdale. She had thought of him in uncertainty and desperation. Nevertheless the holiness and light-heartedness remained. Papa drew his prayer to a close, raising his hand over the table, letting his voice fall to the Amen.

It lasted, this new found ease and light-heartedness with Papa and Mama that was better than holiness, it lasted all the time Papa told about his talk with Mr. Barksdale and Mr. Barksdale's later report to him. Immediately after church Papa had approached Mr. Barksdale and drawn him aside. They walked toward the cemetery and stood next to the iron fence of the Featherstone lot so that no one might hear but sleeping Featherstones. When Papa said he had a serious matter to take up, not knowing how to begin, feeling anew his timidity and his desire not to cause trouble, Mr. Barksdale said, "Brother Jones, I felt your spirit in travail today. I was touched by your reference to the Levite passing by on the other side of the road. I wondered if you had been moved by the memorial window to my wife. I thought, it happens often we pass by because we do not see the man who has been attacked by thieves, we don't hear his cries."

Then Papa found the courage to speak to him about Adam and his trouble. First looking stern, pursing his lips and clucking his tongue in disgust, Mr. Barksdale said he had always had great respect for Adam; he kept his place, was honest, God-fearing, and businesslike in his relations. Mr. Barksdale had dealt with him when he rented the house for the Duckets and when he bought the timber rights on the Ledbetter Old Home Place. Papa said Mr. Barksdale really laughed when he told him about Mr. Byrd Ledbetter offering Adam the same price for his old home place that he had paid at the sheriff's sale; Mr. Barksdale said that he would gladly triple that offer any day and consider it cheap.

Then Mr. Barksdale asked if Papa knew for certain that Mr. Byrd Ledbetter had been with the Ku Klux Klan on Sunday night, and Papa said that he was not sure and neither was Adam. Mr. Barksdale stood thinking for a minute and then—and this Papa repeated with an apologetic blushing of pride—Mr. Barksdale said, "It takes someone like you, Brother Jones, to point out the man fallen upon by thieves." Then he shook hands with Papa and hurried away.

Mr. Barksdale drove out to the Fitzgeralds' even before he returned to Magnolia Hall for his Sunday dinner. By the time he arrived Mr. Byrd and the others were gathered around the table. Hallie could imagine that table, even more groaning on Sunday with its weight of fried chicken and ham and sweet potatoes and rice and turnip greens and ambrosia, with the fruit-cake smell hovering over all. Mr. Fitzgerald urged Mr. Barksdale to sit down and join in with them, called on Miss Martha Nelle to get a chair and bring hot biscuits; there was always room for one more. Mr. Barksdale said he was mighty sorry to disturb them at their Sunday dinner but he was passing by and would like to speak a few words privately with Mr. Byrd Ledbetter.

Mr. Byrd, gracious and obliging, came out to the porch and he and Mr. Barksdale sat together on the steps and Mr. Barksdale talked softly, not wanting his words to carry down the hall and into the dining room.

Later at the depot when he was reporting all this to Papa, Mr. Barksdale said you would have thought that all this was news to Mr. Byrd. When Mr. Barksdale told Mr. Byrd that some rough element in the county had gone around leaving notes on people and had threatened Adam, Mr. Byrd was surprised and shocked. Then Mr. Barksdale said that there was a rumor that Mr. Byrd was trying to buy his old home place back. Mr. Byrd said he had been thinking about it, thought he might come down weekends for the fishing; he had a lot of friends up in Atlanta who liked to go fishing. Said he thought he might come down for a month or so in the watermelon season too; he would send River out there to live again. Then Mr. Barksdale said, was he to understand that Adam was willing to sell? Mr. Byrd said, well, he had had a little talk with Adam; actually it was the only time he had seen him since his brother's funeral. He said he and Adam had been having a little discussion about the price.

Then Mr. Barksdale said he did not know who the rowdies could have been who had gone around threatening an old Negro, particularly one who had the good reputation Adam had, a preacher, decent, minding his own business, knowing his place.

Mr. Byrd said he was shocked and horrified to think of anyone threatening Adam. He said, of course the whole state was suffering from uppity niggers these days, that was a fact, and maybe there were people in the community who for some reason had gotten the notion Adam was uppity. Then Mr. Barksdale said he was greatly relieved to hear from Mr. Byrd's own lips—though of course he had never suspected it—that there was no relationship between the offer to buy back the Ledbetter Old Home Place from Adam and the visit of the Ku Klux Klan. "Seems to me that for a fellow running for office a suspicion like that would be a bad thing," Mr. Barksdale had said, "since it is very well known in Greenwood that your own brother Lucius was taken in by Adam when he was sick unto death. Folks might say that was a funny way to pay him back."

Then Mr. Byrd got very red in the face and said he would like to meet the scoundrels who were trying to deal him this blow below the belt. Why, it was a vile insinuation; his relationships with the colored race had always been the very best, and furthermore he and Adam had been raised together. "Why," he said, "I remember being toted all over Tranquil Woods on Adam's back."

Then Mr. Barksdale changed the subject and they talked about the election. Mr. Barksdale laughed and told Mr. Byrd about the Duckets, said that four years ago when he moved down from North Carolina to start the planing mill he had brought along a few families from up in there to run the saw-mills oh, maybe four or five families to begin with. But they had liked it down in here, and sent back for their uncles and cousins, all poor mountaineers who were trying to wring a living from the rocky hillsides. Well, in five years the woods down in here had just gotten full of Duckets. "I imagine," said Mr. Barksdale, "the Duckets by now are a force that must be reckoned with in an election."

Mr. Byrd said he was much obliged to Mr. Barksdale for his advice and that he would have to take time off and get around the backwoods one of these days and meet the Duckets. Mr. Barksdale said he thought it was a good idea, that he always thought it looked bad when a fellow could not carry his home county, and though Mr. Byrd might feel he had been away so long Atlanta was his home, still, he said, to the folks in Green-wood he was just a boy from Plum Branch County.

Hallie listened to all this, smiling when Papa smiled, laughing when Mama laughed, the light-heartedness persisting despite her wondering if this was the way God worked—by cajolery, threats, and indirection? If it were for Adam let God work as He saw fit; she did not care. But the voice calling from the housetops, the angel with the fiery sword, the Old Testament Prophet with his stern face, casting out evil . . . ? Never mind, she said to herself, never mind. If Mr. Barksdale knew the way . . .

Papa paused and took a swig of buttermilk. His throat must be dry from talking.

"It will be all right for Adam then?" asked Hallie. "Adam will be all right?"

"You don't need to worry about Adam now, honey. Brother Barksdale said he was sure it would come out all right." Papa said it in a tone of blessed assurance that God would look after his own. Then Papa said, looking prouder than ever, "He said I should call him *Brother* Barksdale."

Mama said, "He's a fine man."

"Brother Barksdale really took it upon his heart," Papa went on. "He went on back to his dinner down at Magnolia Hall, but on the way back he says he got to thinking he ought to talk to someone else just to find out for sure that no one else held anything against Adam. Then he thought of Jess Bailey, going to be his son-in-law. Decided it would be a good idea to talk it over with him; thought he's a young man, knows the young fellows around town, might have heard some whispering about who was in the Ku Klux Klan that night. When he got down to his place he found Mr. Jess was there for dinner, and after dinner he made a point of taking a walk with him. Said it worked out real naturally for them to go out together; during dinner Mr. Jess had talked about keeping horses down at Magnolia Hall and Miss Corrine had said they would have to be *white* horses if he did, to match the Hall and the pigeons and the white on the cows. After dinner Mr. Barksdale suggested that he and Mr. Jess walk out to the pasture and take a look. While they were standing there by the fence and looking off at the pasture Mr. Barksdale told him about the whole thing and asked if he thought there were any strong feeling in town toward Adam. He said Mr. Jess shook his head and said he thought probably some of the boys were just pranking around with Adam; he imagined the whole thing would blow over."

Hallie sat very still, her good cheer evaporating. The story should have ended before they came to Mr. Jess. Though the thought of him lay there always in her mind, a sore place, tender to the touch, she had almost forgotten him in her concern and relief over Adam.

"Brother Barksdale says he thinks he's going to be proud of his new son-in-law, just made a deacon," Papa went on. "I reckon I misjudged Mr. Jess that night at the Deacons' Meeting." Hallie tried to look into Mama's eyes, to say to her now is the time, Mama, now is the time to tell Papa. But Mama gazed only at Papa, her lower lip sticking out; as Hallie stared at her she drew it into a kind of smile, as if she were trying to imitate the pleasure of the minutes before. She would not look at Hallie.

Hallie remembered now that Papa said she had been touched by God and that he had thanked her and thanked God for her having spoken out. Now she felt moved to speak again but she held it back, examining it, holding it, then surprised, heard her voice suddenly loud saying, "But what about Mr. Jess and Miss Corrine? What about Magnolia Hall?" And she knew that this was the cry that had been in her heart since Elberta had told them; this was the cry that had tightened her throat for the Expression Contest, the cry that must be cried and now was the time to cry it.

"Oh, Hallie," said Mama, and shut her eyes.

Then Hallie wished she had not said it, and hung her head over her plate, the light-heartedness with Mama and Papa vanishing, the cooing white doves taking flight, flying off to the four corners of the earth and leaving her standing, despairing, alone.

Looking from one to the other, Papa said, "What's she talking about?" For once he was as suspicious as Mama at being left out.

"I would've spared you," said Mama. "I did spare you during the trouble with Adam, and I would keep on sparing you if I might."

Papa's harassed face became as sad and tormented as the face of Jesus. He said, "I can drink from the cup if I must . . ."

"Well, Elberta told me the night she came to tell about the Ku Klux Klan leaving the note . . . she told me who the man was . . ."

Papa wiped his mouth and pushed back his chair and sat there without moving. "Hallie knows too?" he asked, as if deciding whether he would ask the next question.

"She knows," Mama said; "she was up too and heard." She did not say, she listened when I told her not to.

Papa's glance roved the four corners of the room, looking for help from the ceiling and from under the table and behind the stove. Finally he said, "It has something to do with Magnolia Hall, with Brother Barksdale?" Again as if Brother Barksdale were the important one.

"Yes," said Mama.

Papa stood up and pushed in his chair. "Jonny's father," he said, and looked at the place where he had christened Jonny that day and named him. "I won't ask any more," he said.

"What can we do?" asked Mama, and when no one answered she went on, "There's nothing we can do. I told Hallie. I told her all along. There's nothing we can do."

They stared at Hallie now and she did not know whether they stared because they hated her for asking the question or because they thought that God might speak through her again and tell them what to do. She waited for the light to come. None did.

Papa said, "There's nothing we can do except never tell." He picked up his B.Y.P.U. paper and his Bible. "Never tell anyone," he said. "It would break too many hearts."

"That's what I said," Mama said.

But now that she had gone so far and had spoiled everything with Mama and Papa, she could not stop. "But it's wrong," she cried, and the tightness in her throat came back, the tightness that could be dispelled only by shouting so the world could hear that it was wrong, wrong, wrong.

24

School lasted for another week. Hallie endured it, she even endured her expression lesson for another Monday and Thursday. At the first one Miss Corrine put her arms round her (all attar of roses) and said, "Hallie, I should have helped you more. You know, there are things you can do to overcome stage fright, and I should have told you about them. You're usually so confident that I just never thought . . ." She listened to the words and tried to think what in the world Miss Corrine was talking about. Miss Corrine stepped back, tender solicitude in her eyes; she seemed to be waiting for Hallie to explain something, to offer some excuse, perhaps to burst out crying, but she could do none of these things. Her throat was tight, so she said nothing. She no longer felt anything about the contest, so she stood there, said nothing and did nothing. Watching her closely, Miss Corrine gave a little shake of her head as if to say, Hallie, you're a mystery to me; then, becoming businesslike, she said, "I suppose I just forgot how strange faces can be when you're looking down on them and they're looking up at you." After that she gave a few suggestions for overcoming stage fright and they went on as if it were any Monday.

School ended and there was a week to live through before Miss Corrine's wedding. Again Margaret Craig mentioned the project of making a theater in their barn, and she half-heartedly swept the dusty loft, helped Margaret assemble benches and seats, and contributed a pair of hoop earrings from the ten-cent store and a red scarf from a bureau drawer for costumes. They discussed plays and Margaret very generously offered to take turns on the leading parts. But Hallie was feeling a lassitude like the summer before; her legs felt better stretched out; she spent a great deal of time lying on her back in the tree house, thinking of nothing; she was enveloped in a green-tinged mist filled with small bird sounds. She felt flattened out, her stomach caved in and her hip bones high as she surveyed herself lying in the tree house.

One morning after school was out, Mama said, "Hallie, I think you might like to learn to milk." Virginia was right there, but she did not suggest that Virginia learn. "Come with me this morning."

But when they were in the barn she did not begin to teach Hallie; she only dumped hulls in the manger, sprinkled in the cottonseed meal, and then squatted down and began to milk. Hallie sat on the opened sack of hulls and watched the milk squirt into the quart cup, watched Mama's hands, knowing and strong. When Mama had emptied the first quart cup she stood up and looked at her.

"Hallie honey, are you all right?"

Hallie could have cried then. She was being offered the chance to cry by Mama's look, and if she cried Mama might even suggest that she go over to Clover on a visit for a while. Mama had once murmured something to her about "a change of scene," but had not said where.

But she did not cry. She said, "I'm all right."

"I know how you feel," Mama said, holding the quart cup in her hand, ready to stoop to the milking any minute because the cow was finishing the hulls and meal. "I think you're doing awfully well. It's wrong, of course it's wrong—we know that. But saying it's wrong won't help. You just don't know how much trouble and sadness we'd cause"—Mama closed her eyes just thinking about it—"if we breathed a word of this. How much better for everyone if only you and I and your father know."

"Elberta knows," said Hallie, "and Jonny."

"Jonny is someone we have no control over," said Mama, "and we won't help Alberta to tell." She stooped to the cow again. "It won't help, I tell you, Hallie, it won't help anyone."

"But Miss Corrine? And Magnolia Hall?"

"It won't help, Hallie. You must believe me. It won't help."

Hallie said nothing more, her throat thick with the injustice. There seemed to be nothing to say. Mama slapped the cow on the leg, and she moved, and Mama returned to the milking. The milk went *ping* as it hit the empty cup, *ping*, a fresh start, and a muffled *pin—g*, and then a quickly reached conclusion as the stream hit the froth and Mama poured the milk into the bucket.

She found her voice again as Mama finished the milking. "Do I have to go to the wedding?" she asked.

Mama picked up the bucket and reflected for a moment. "Go if you can, Hallie. You don't have to, but go if you can."

On Friday and Saturday there was a great bustle of preparations at the church. Cars came and went, Miss Corrine's friends ran in and out, Barksdale trucks driven by Duckets carrying loads of smilax stopped in front of the church. The Duckets must have ripped every tendril of smilax off fences and roadsides for miles around. Virginia and May Belle went over to watch and became involved; Virginia came back breathlessly and importantly: "We need another hammer," she said, and later with May Belle, "They want to borrow our stepladder. They need another one."

Hallie ran to the depot to escape the wedding preparations and went out to the warehouse to have a look at Adam. Adam, safe, went about his business just as he had when he was unsafe. There was no change in him, no sign of having lived through an ordeal. He stood tall and black and in the best of health. He had saved a squashed box of Zu-Zu crackers on the dusty framework of the warehouse and he offered them to her. She took one and chewed it and he took one too. They did not talk, only ate

Zu-Zu crackers. What was Adam's place? He was calm and untroubled; he must know his place; he seemed to have some blessed assurance. But she did not know what his place was now. Adam, she thought of asking, what is your place? But Adam had swallowed his cracker by that time and gone about his business.

Back in the depot office telegrams of congratulation were coming over the wire. Papa took them, thin-lipped, not saying a word. He hunted out the special blank for wedding congratulations and typed them out neatly on the typewriter. Mr. Barksdale came in and ordered a flatcar and said as he was leaving, "Brother Jones, I expect to see you and your family down at Magnolia hall tonight," and Hallie, watchful, waiting, even now hopeful that the Old Testament Prophet in Papa would rise, heard him say, "Thank you, Brother Barksdale, thank you, sir. Yessir-ree, we'll certainly be there. It's a happy time, a happy time."

Until the moment came to get dressed for the wedding Hallie was uncertain whether she could go or not. Virginia and May Belle dressed in the back room—dressed there, it seemed, all afternoon. They came in to early supper in kimonos, their heads tied in handkerchiefs, their faces looking skinned. Seeing her sitting at the table in her everyday clothes May Belle said, "Hallie, when you going to dress? You're going to be late."

She opened her mouth to say she was not going, but that required explanations she was not prepared to give. She wished she had broken out in some fearful rash, some obviously debilitating illness, one that would have reddened her face and laid her low in bed so there would be no question of her going.

She followed May Belle and Virginia back to the untidy room and dived into the closet for her blue taffeta. May Belle threw off her kimono and stood in her petticoat, studying her bouncing buxom shape in the mirror and moaning. Then she tightened her brassière until she could scarcely breathe. Hallie had pulled the blue taffeta over her head and was straining to fasten it in back. "Look at Hallie. Look at what a stylish, flat figure she has," May Belle said.

As if she were saying a memory verse in church Virginia intoned, "We have a little sister and she has no breasts. What shall we do for our sister in the day when she shall be spoken for?"

May Belle said, "She's positively *bean*-breasted." They threw themselves on the beds whooping with laughter and Hallie slunk from the room.

May Belle and Virginia set off for church in their identical white organdies, and Hallie followed with Mama and Papa. No one had prepared her for the splendor of the church lighted by tall white candles instead of bare bulbs, or for the hushed music played by the trio. She felt at once that she should not have come, but Mama and Papa sat between her and the end of the pew, and there was a commotion at the doors and a feeling of expectancy in the music. Even if she managed to get past Mama and Papa she might run right into the wedding party. People still streamed into the church; dozens of Duckets, the children pale-eyed, stringy-haired, and all suffering from colds even though it was June. Straggling into the pew in front of her were Mr. and Mrs. Ray Ducket (Mrs. Ray poked out, though this time not poked out with a baby) and behind them Darleen, Junior, Delta, Paul and Woodruff, who settled down good as gold. Darleen looked as if she had just gotten a letter in her play post office. Who stayed home with the baby? Probably some pipe-smoking old grandmother from up in North Carolina.

Then the pianist started the stroking on middle C for the Wedding March, to be joined in a joyful chording by the violin and cello. She lived through the Wedding March because the violin and cello made it something new, something besides the hateful piece she had practiced. She lived, trembling again inside, while Miss Corrine walked down the aisle on Mr. Barksdale's arm, her chin tucked inside a calla-lily cup, lived—that is lived outside, died inside—when Mr. Jess Bailey, tall, golden and pure-looking, came in with his best man. She lived through it all, suffered through it all, until the bride and groom stood together in front of Brother Jamieson, Brother Jamieson speaking the service in a resounding, deeply significant voice. Then, looking around at the congregation, his glance rested on Hallie, stopped there, pierced her to the quick (was this glance a slanting sunray from the sounding board of God?), he said, "If any man can show just cause why they may not be joined together in holy matrimony, let him speak now or else hereafter forever hold his peace . . ." And Hallie, pierced to the heart by the question, wondered if God were speaking to her now, were telling her to speak now, felt faint at the thought that henceforward and forever the hand of God would be upon her to speak. (She could not bear that, oh, take it away.) Did Mr. Jess Bailey's neck redden above his white suit, did his shoulders shift restlessly as if the suit were too tight, or was it only the shifting shadows thrown by the high candelabra? For one last wild moment she thought God had spoken, that she must stand and say yes, cry out yes, there was a reason, the thought forming into words in her throat, thought of it as she had thought of telling Miss Corrine before the Expression Contest . . . But if she spoke now Miss Corrine would turn to see who spoke, her face breaking into fragments; Mr. Jess Bailey would stand with caught breath, would look tormentedly toward the door for escape; Mr. Barksdale would gaze in sudden recognition; Papa, though knowing the truth, would look angrily at her and his face would turn into an Old Testament Prophet face toward her; Mama would put out her hand to pull her down. She felt it all instantaneously as if she had done it, and her skin burst into a storm of prickles under her blue taffeta. Then Brother Jamieson took a breath, then a step forward; the moment was passing and now she knew she would not do it, could not do it, and she settled back into the seat, torn with regret. She had deliberately shaken off the hand of God, and yet she was relieved that her voice had not had a strange will of its own. Making a period, Brother Jamieson said, "And now, dearly beloved, what God hath joined together let no man put asunder."

After that, how quickly it was over. Mr. Jess turned to face

266

Miss Corrine and she raised herself on tiptoe and looked lovingly into his face and he into hers, as if all their lives had been gathered into this here and now when they kissed. Then the piano, cello and violin burst into "Here Comes the Bride," and those who had been crying—Mrs. Ray Ducket had snuffled and put her handkerchief to her eyes and May Belle had swallowed a sob so noisily she might as well have sobbed it—put their handkerchiefs away and smiled, the triumphal music ending the solemnity and quiet. Miss Corrine turned and smiled at the church full of people, a dazzling smile, as if there were tears in her eyes at the same time, and Mr. Jess helped her to arrange her train, and they marched out together keeping good time to the music, the musicians keeping good time to the very end.

When the crowd streamed out into the dusk it was not like a Sunday crowd at all. The presence of Duckets, all Methodists, made it seem more like a protracted-meeting crowd, an excited crowd that had heard some good shouting in the church and now looked forward with appetite to dinner and frolicking on the grounds. Did they already feel the gaiety of the Chinese lanterns at Magnolia Hall? Everyone who had a party dress was wearing it, and in the yellow, orange, red, green and pink crepe de Chines and organdies and taffetas the girls seemed to glow like Chinese lanterns in the dusk. But she felt no glow. She could see the glow in others, but she felt too drained, and she hung back as they moved toward the cars.

Miss Lill called to say, "We're going right along now, Mrs. Jones. You all ready?" Hallie looked at the ground to shut out the glowing crowd. She could not go to Magnolia Hall. Mama put out her hand and took her arm, but she said nothing and Hallie hung back even more. Mama put one arm around her and hugged her, and seeing her edge away, Papa said, "Where're you going, Hallie?" and she said, "Home." "But aren't you going down to Brother Barksdale's?" he said, frowning his Sunday frown, as if always Brother Barksdale were the important one, and she was about to say she knew not what—wondered if she would ever know the time for truth again—when Mama said, "I declare, Hallie has these headaches too often. I think we ought to get her some glasses," and she hugged Hallie again. Papa said, "I didn't know she was sick. Brother Barksdale said to me today he was looking *foward* to seeing us all down there." He said it just as if he had completely forgotten about Mr. Jess being a whited sepulchre, and Mama said, "Well, home's the best place for her if she's sick, I think." Then, perhaps seeing Mama hug her and remembering the time years ago when he had rocked her on the porch in Clover and she felt the veins in his hands, or perhaps thinking of last Sunday when God had spoken through her, Papa leaned over and patted her awkwardly and said, "Well, child, look after yourself."

It was then, standing in the middle of the wedding crowd in the dusk, with cars starting up and glad calls all around them, that she trembled on the brink of conversion. "Accept, accept," they said to her; the bright dresses, the starting cars, the glad voices, the vision of the Chinese lanterns at Magnolia Hall, all said, "Accept," as if she heard the hymn, "Oh, love that will not let me go, I rest my weary soul in thee." But she could not rest her weary soul though she felt sorry for Mama and Papa as she had felt sorry for God back in those ancient holy days in Clover when she had gone crying up the aisle in the First Baptist Church begging to be saved. Now she felt sorry for Papa in his awkwardness, felt sorry that he was timid, felt sorry that he was old and dyed his hair, felt sorry that she no longer liked to kiss him. And Mama? Oh, she felt sorry for Mama too, whose breasts hung relaxed inside her corset cover, who once had suckled six children (she must have said, offering the milk-stretched breast, "It wants its titty" as joyfully as Elberta). She felt sorry for Mama who would not have done what she had done for Elberta if Elberta had been blacker; she felt sorry for Papa who could not be a Prophet; and she saw them awkward and uncertain, offering her conversion. She could be saved, could abandon herself, could rest her weary soul—after which she could become solemnly and hugely happy. She saw it and was drawn, wanted, longed to accept; she felt a leaning, a wavering, a thawing, a melting. A good cry, finally a good cry, and she could join the party at the reception.

Mama held out her hand offering her light-heartedness again, but she turned away, knowing at last that she could not accept. She turned from them, rejecting conversion, and walked toward the house with someone calling after her, "You need a ride? We've got room for one more." As she entered the dark hall she glanced at the piano in the living room, blushed to think of herself as she was in those romantic days when she thought she might play the Wedding March. She went on back to the kitchen, turned on the light and ran a dipper of water, stood drinking it and thinking of that other liquid now being served down at Magnolia Hall, pink punch with peaches floating in it around a glacier of ice.

She went back to the untidy bedroom, threw Virginia's clothes off the bed, took off her shoes and lay down, still in her blue taffeta. "Bean-breasted," May Belle had said. Hallie ran her hand over the slippery dress, feeling her beginning breasts. Now there was a softness where before there had only been a hardness, a roundness where there had only been a sharpness. Sometimes they hurt; they were growing and they hurt. She would have breasts; she was sure of that now. But for what, for whom?

She thought of Miss Corrine standing in her white satin wedding dress in the reception line at Magnolia Hall. Someone would be sure to say, some Ducket probably, "May all your troubles be little ones," and laugh the loud Ducket laughter, and other Duckets would nudge each other and roll their eyes. Miss Corrine would blush and Mr. Jess would look at her as if he could swallow her whole. (Would the thought cross his mind that he already had a little one?) Laura Fitzgerald, who had already grown breasts and therefore felt superior, would stand near the punch bowl in her polka-dotted dress. She had gone to Macon to buy it and when her mother saw it she said it had too low a neck. Laura said she would wear a scarf, but by now she would have removed the scarf and would stand with her bosom exposed serving punch. Couples would stroll out under the Chinese lanterns and under the trees and the musicians would play something soft and beautiful that would float out through the tall windows into the night.

She tried to stop thinking of the hateful reception. She thought of the evening, of the rest of it and how she would get through it; thought of tomorrow and how she would get through it; thought of the summer made up entirely of dog days, stretching out, stretching out, Oh, Lord, how long ahead. Would her whole future be a succession of dog days? She feared she would always be filled with this vague unease; filled, yet empty, except for a hard gristle of guilt undissolvable by simple offerings of flowers and rusk. Oh, she should have cried, she should have railed. But when? Where and to whom? Resisting conversion and staying away from the reception were hard; yet even harder things would be asked of her in the future. She closed her eyes at the thought and tried to turn to a happier time.

Clover was as serene as ever, looking back—even those first days in Greenwood when she had her dream of mansions. Then she remembered the M. D. and S. paper with her notes. She got up off the bed and dug under the mattress. She had not touched the sheaf of paper in a long time and it bore egg-shaped imprints from the springs. On the top sheet was written, MAGNOLIA HALL. And under it down the page, "Doves and Dovecote." Did anyone else get the same lifting of heart at the sight of the white birds flying up? She leaned back on her pillow thinking of the doves and the white horses. How she had loved this fairy-tale country with its white birds, white horses, white mansions filled with aristocratic people sensitive to the beauty around them. And entering this dream world, deliberately entering it now to escape the vision of the days ahead, entering it perhaps for the last time, because she knew now it was a dream country, she saw the pigeons spread their tails and teeter on the roof of the dovecote; she closed her eyes to see them take off together, a moving, wheeling cloud of birds; saw the white horses dancing in the green pasture, dancing on their shiny black hooves, their pink nostrils flaring. The six columns shone behind the magnolias and the magnolias were in bloom, the air awash with their perfume. The moon hung as round and yellow as Margaret Craig's medal from the Expression Contest; and Here Comes the Bride, Miss Hallie Jones, in her white satin robes, her chin nestled in a calla-lily cup, marching to the anthem on the arm of her bridegroom, a golden Southern gentleman whose name she dared not say. Her two bridesmaids, May Belle and Virginia, twins in white organdy, eaten up with jealousy at her beautiful bosom and her handsome bridgroom, ran ahead and opened the double doors for them. Now she entered the hall, her hall, and she could see that the rosewood piano was being played by Miss Toulou Vass. Her bridegroom leaned toward her and after giving her a long look as if he would swallow her, said, *"Ego amo te."* Mama was there wearing little red slippers on her tiny, tiny feet; she was hardly speaking to anyone because she was the mother of the bride who lived in Magnolia Hall. Papa was not chewing tobacco; he bowed from the waist and greeted the guests like a Virginia planter. When absolutely overcome with the desire to chew he went out to the porch and lit a big cigar and blew smoke rings off at the magnolias. White-turbaned servants moved in the background or came forward curtsying to the bride and groom, saying, "Welcome, Massa, welcome, little Missus, welcome, welcome." Laura Fitzgerald passed punch, the pinkest punch, and in the center of the bowl, instead of ice, a white magnolia floated. She, Hallie, gave a speech with Latin quotations—that is, she said several times, with expression and the proper pauses, *"Ubique Reminisci Patriam."* When she finished the bridegroom stepped forward and kissed her under the curls on the back of her neck, and she could feel herself glowing, glowing and trembling like the Chinese lanterns swaying in the breeze. She glowed with happiness as the lanterns swayed and glowed . . . Then a car door banged somewhere far away, voices called, a screen door opened and shut in some other house, the voices came nearer.

The reception was over. It was time now to get up, time now to say good-by to that sweet dream.

ABOUT THE AUTHOR

"Before I was a writer I was a member of that greatly maligned and misunderstood genus, the suburban housewife, sub-class, Winnetka, Illinois. I think it is not nearly as important *where* you live as *when*. Robert Lowell says in one of his poems, '. . . only by suffering the rat race in the arena/ can the heart learn to beat.' I think Winnetka can be and will be an arena as well as Macon, Georgia, Washington or Moscow. A writer, or a housewife, must relinquish the idea there is any place to hide; she must be involved in the conflicts of her own time.

"As for being a housewife . . . I say hurrah for housewifery. I know of no other human condition that offers as many possibilities and potentialities. To be a writer and a housewife takes patience. Sometimes the writing part has to be put off until the youngest child no longer comes home for lunch. But after that, who in our society has that great unblemished swatch of time from 8:30 to 3:30?"

Norris Lloyd lived until she was sixteen in South Carolina and Georgia. She graduated from Antioch College and studied writing under Thornton Wilder at the University of Chicago. Her husband is a former newspaperman, now a free-lance writer and editor with Africa as his particular interest. They have lived with their four children in Racine, Wisconsin, Geneva, Switzerland, the Feather River Canyon in California, but mostly in Winnetka, Illinois. About the time when her youngest child no longer came home for lunch, Mrs. Lloyd enrolled in a fiction workshop in the Winnetka Public Library, led by Marjorie Peters. A DREAM OF MANSIONS is her first published novel. She is the author of *Desperate Dragons*, a book for children.